THE DAMNATION OF LEANDER WELLES

OR, THE DEATH & LIFE OF BENNETT REEVE

ASHLYN DREWEK

FOX HOLLOW BOOKS

To my mom,

Thank you for indulging my odd interests over the years. And thank you for not being terribly concerned when I zeroed in on vampires and serial killers. I promise, I'm neither.

CONTENTS

FOREWORD

This book contains references to child abuse, self-harm, substance abuse, and suicide. Reader discretion is advised.

CHAPTER 1

The old man's mustache quivered, his eyes burning with unbridled hatred. "Eres el diablo!"

Giving him a brilliant smile, I took the insult in stride. He wasn't the first person to liken me to the Devil and he wouldn't be the last. Personally, I blamed Faust. For centuries, anyone on the wrong end of a contract could point their finger at the other party and blame the unholy for their misfortune. In truth, they had no one to blame but themselves. After all, how hard was it to actually read what you were signing?

"I never agreed to this," the man continued, in heavily-accented English. "I would never agree to selling my family's restaurant."

I nodded sympathetically. "I understand, Señor Ortiz. But the problem is you did. On page six of your contract, third paragraph, subsection c, if you'd like to look." He kept glaring at me, so I kept talking. "When you asked these fine gentlemen behind me for a loan, you put your beloved restaurant up for collateral. You're three months behind on your payments. So, they've come to collect what is, legally, theirs."

Sliding a glance over my shoulder at the gaggle of cholos behind me, I grimaced and faced forward again. "They wanted to saw your head off and mail it to your daughter. Believe it or not, I'm doing you a favor here."

He replied in a string of Spanish. From what I knew of romance languages, there were plenty of insults about my mother and more about me being the Devil. I was pretty sure at one point he told me I was going to burn in Hell, another proclamation I'd heard more than once.

My brows came together sharply. "That's rude, Mr. Ortiz. *I* didn't make you sign it. So, if you'd like to consult an attorney of your own, we can take it to court and argue about it there for... at least two years and several thousands of dollars in legal fees. *Or*, we can go with Option A." I gestured behind me. "I honestly don't care. I get paid either way."

The old man's eyes were watery. If he started crying, I was charging Hector double. "How do you sleep at night?"

"Silk sheets," I replied with another smile. "Changed my life. Honestly."

Mr. Ortiz was not amused, but the emissaries from the Chicago Calaveras chuckled.

Pulling my pocket watch out of its place in my waistcoat, I flicked it open and made a face at the time. "I hate to cut this meeting short, but I do have another engagement across town. So... tick tock, Señor. Which option would you prefer?"

He drew a ragged breath and looked away. I had my answer.

"That settles it, then. Buenas noches." Sliding out of the booth, I touched two fingers to my forehead in a mock salute to the group of Calaveras. "Caballeros."

"Yo, Bennett. Wait up." Hector, who'd been helping himself to tequila at the bar, followed me outside. The heavy chains around his neck clinked with every step, or it could have been the gun swinging from pants about two seconds away from hitting the ground. He shoved his hands in his pockets and hitched up his pants, leaning over my shoulder. "What about that little problem I told you about?"

"You have a lot of problems, Hector, you're going to have to be more specific." I stopped short on the sidewalk. A group of teenage punks were gathered around my Maserati, their eyes wide and their hands a little too touchy for my liking. I whistled sharply between my fingers, jerking my thumb in the opposite direction. They took the hint and scurried off.

Hector sucked on a tooth, throwing a glance to either side before continuing. "The will, ese. My old lady is bugging me about a copy."

"So give her a copy."

"You know I can't. She's going to see my side piece and our kids."

"Well, Hector, that's what happens when you cheat on your wife and spawn not once but three fucking times."

He rolled his eyes. "You ain't married, man. You don't know what it's like."

I scratched the side of my mouth, trying to think of a polite way to phrase my answer. Not because I wanted to spare his feelings, but because I didn't want to have this particular debate with him when I was already running late. No, I wasn't married, but even I, the man-whore that I was, knew it was an asshole thing to cheat on your spouse. "Have you ever, I don't know, thought about telling her the truth?"

"And say what?"

"Maria, I love you. I made a mistake and had three kids with Veronica. I know I promised Jessica was the last. I'm so sorry. How can I ever make it up to you? Here's this incredibly expensive diamond necklace? Please don't divorce me and take half of my shit? I'm actually going to honor our vows this time?"

He scoffed and looked away. "You don't know my wife, man."

A very vivid image of Señora Hernandez popped into my head. A tight red dress. Matching lipstick. The detailed skull tattoo with crimson roses blooming above her panty line. Her nails were as sharp as knives. I still had the scar to prove it.

I bit my lip, dispelling the memory. "What makes you think she doesn't already know?"

"'Cuz she'd kill me, that's why."

Clucking my sympathies, I patted his chest. "Guess you shouldn't have bought that little love nest. Shit like that is discoverable, you know."

I was three steps away when the lightbulb clicked.

"Wait, what do you mean 'discoverable'?"

Vaulting myself over the side of the roadster, I settled into the driver's seat and started the engine. It roared to life, drowning out Hector's voice. Gesturing between my ear and the car, I feigned deafness.

"Bennett! Is she leaving me?"

With a laugh, I stomped on the gas and sped away.

———

"YOU'RE LATE," Del grumbled when I breezed through the door of the art gallery.

"Then tell your cousin-in-law to keep his dick in his pants." I snagged two glasses of champagne from a passing waitress, offering one to Del despite the tumbler in his hand.

When he shook his head, I shrugged and downed the first flute, depositing it on another tray.

"Ugh. Veronica again?"

"Can't say."

"You didn't put her in the will, did you? Maria will fucking kill him."

I held up a hand in the defensive. "What the client wants, the client gets. And I am not at liberty to discuss that, Angel Delgado, as you well know."

"Sorry, Counselor. Must have slipped my mind."

"Just like I let it slip that she knows about his cabin on the lake."

"But she doesn't."

"She will when he goes home, begging forgiveness."

Del shot me a grin. "Sneaky, Counselor. Very sneaky."

Giving him a sly smirk, I sipped the champagne and turned my attention to the crowd. "Anyone else here we know?"

"Other than the Russians? No."

"Good. You haven't seen Brynn, have you?" I cringed, glancing around for any sign of flaming copper hair.

"The curator you were banging a few months ago?"

"That'd be the one."

"No, not yet anyway."

"Phew." I plucked a pair of tiny skewers off the plate sitting on the ledge behind him. A second after I tore the cubes of steak off with my teeth, I hoped it was his plate and not someone else's.

"If you're hungry, we can leave." Del sounded entirely too hopeful.

"You're not getting out of it that easily."

"I'm not trying to get out of anything! I don't want you keeling over from low blood sugar."

I rolled my eyes in his direction, making sure he saw that I wasn't buying it.

"Oh, shit. Redhead alert," he said quickly.

Raking a hand through my hair, I ducked my face, pivoting away from said redhead as she sashayed past in a little black dress. "Did she see me?"

Del took a small sip of his drink, shaking his head. "No, you're good."

"Thank God."

He snickered. "Bad experience?"

"Let's just say we didn't part on the best of terms." The fact she saw me out in public with someone else may have had something to do with it. In my defense, we weren't exclusive. I was never exclusive with anyone. No matter how explicitly I stated that, some people thought they could somehow change my mind.

Once I was in the clear, I resumed scanning the room, landing on a petite blonde across the way. "Well, hello."

Del followed my gaze, shaking his head. "Bad news, bro. I'm pretty sure that chick's from a narc unit."

"Local or fed?" I gave the blonde another once-over, appreciating her dedication to undercover work. The shimmering silver dress barely covered what it needed to. If she had a gun, I'd love to know where she was keeping it.

Del squinted, lips pursed. "Local, I think. She tried to tie up one of my guys on some coke last year."

"I'd let her tie me up anywhere."

The blonde in question tossed her hair over her shoulder. Her gaze flitted over the people nearby until it landed on us. A pouty smirk crossed her lips before she turned her back, sauntering out of view around an exhibit.

Del's hand slashed out across my chest, halting my forward progression. "Don't do it."

"Do what?"

"You know what."

"Is this about the thing from Julia's wedding?"

"No, but you're still not off the hook for that. We're supposed to be here for Sergei's daughter. Remember? That's what you said."

"I *am* here for Alina. I simply want to walk over there and look at that painting."

"You're an asshole," he said with another shake of his head.

I fished my wallet out and handed over my credit card. "Buy two paintings. My treat." While he was distracted with the card, I surged forward into the crowd, tossing back the second flute of champagne.

The blonde in question hadn't gone very far. Standing by herself at the back of the gallery, she was staring at an abstract painting of alternating, colorful squares.

"I don't get it," she said when I approached, keeping her eyes on the artwork. "It's just boxes."

"It's more than that, actually." The corner of my mouth twitched into a smile. Not an art fan, then. And not someone's arm candy, since she was by herself. That meant Del was right — she was here for work.

"Like what?" She leveled a skeptical look at me.

"It's expression." I glanced at her, raising my brows at her dubious look. "Think of it like music. It's an improvisation of color and texture. When you consider the time period, it's truly unique."

"Are you an artist?" she asked with a half-smile and a head-to-toe assessment.

"No." I gave her my full attention. And I do mean full. Scrutinizing her ears, the neckline of her dress, the curve of her hip, her jewelry, even her clutch. "I just appreciate beautiful things."

Cop or no, she blushed like any other woman and looked away. Time to go in for the kill.

"Unfortunately for us, this is barely a quarter of what they have here. Would you like a private tour?" I held my hand out to her, palm up.

Licking her lips, she shot a glance at the crowd. To her partner, or the team outside the large windows? "I probably shouldn't..."

"I probably shouldn't do a lot of things. That doesn't ever stop me."

"Where would we be going?"

My gaze flicked behind her for a moment. "To the back." Not leaving the premise, thus not breaking the rules her agency no doubt laid down.

Laying her hand on top of mine, she gave me a small smile. "Ok."

"Excellent. It's right through here." I led the way through a doorway in the back of the gallery, down a brightly lit hall, to the cavernous storage room.

If she thought she was being led to the center of Sergei's drug-trafficking ring, she was mistaken. The room really was for storing artwork. The fact some of it had questionable provenance was beyond the scope of whatever investigation she was attempting to pull off and since she didn't seem to know — or care — about art, she wouldn't question anything she saw.

We stopped in front of a display hung with a variety of pieces for photographing and private viewing. There was more of the abstract art she hated, along with classical pieces Sergei was auctioning off later in the week.

"What's the story behind this one?" she asked, indicating a colorful, blocky rendition of a church.

"It's Saint Basil's in Moscow." I stepped up behind her, resting my hands on her hips, fingers splayed. No holster there and none in the small of her back either, which I found out when I pulled her against my chest. She leaned into me, tipping her head back.

"And?"

"Some people say it was designed to look like a bonfire," I murmured against her ear. Shivering, her ass pressed even harder against me as she shied away from the sensation.

"Oh?"

"Other people say it was supposed to replicate the Kingdom of God." My lips skimmed across her bare shoulder, working my way up to her neck, to the skin behind her other ear. Definitely no ear pieces.

"Why is that important?" Each word was breathier than the last. I, for one, was quite interested to see how far she was willing to carry out this little charade. I'm pretty sure getting caught in a compromising position during a surveillance operation was a no-no for any cop but far be it for me to point that out.

"It was unprecedented in Russian architecture." Dragging my tongue over her skin, I slid one hand up between her breasts. Still no gun, which was good news for me. I hooked my fingers over the shimmering fabric, pulling it down over her bra. What she didn't seem to notice was that her necklace — and its tiny camera — came with it.

I tossed the jewelry behind me as she spun in my arms, kissing me hard.

Well, then... That was a new tactic for law enforcement. Maybe they were using a few moves from the CIA playbook. Lucky me.

Gripping her hips, I hoisted her in the air. She wrapped her legs around my waist as we traversed the short distance to the shipping clerk's desk. I swept the stacks of folders out of the way before laying her down. There went Pavel's entire filing system. Sorry, buddy. It was for a worthy cause, though. I'm sure he'd understand.

She unwrapped the thin, black scarf from my neck until there was only one loop, which she used to yank me closer. The part that came next was a simple matter of pulling her to the edge of the desk and unzipping my pants. Given the exigency of the situation, there wasn't time to waste with foreplay. Besides, I was pretty sure she didn't need the warmup.

Shoving her skirt up her thighs, she yanked her thong to the side and out of my way. I sank into her, groaning against her lips before she captured my mouth with hers.

A part of me felt bad about railroading her investigation. And possibly her career. And probably upending any previous cases she worked on due to her clear lack of judgement and conduct unbecoming... But at the same time, she made her choice, even if she didn't have the foresight to know how it was going to turn out. The least I could do was make it worth her while, then. I wasn't *that* much of a bastard.

Although, admittedly, my motives weren't entirely altruistic. Aside from the obvious pleasure of an impromptu encounter, the fact it meant Sergei owed me was an even bigger thrill. With the circles I ran in, a favor was sometimes worth more than any amount of money in the world. And having a Russian kingpin in your back pocket? Absolutely priceless.

CHAPTER 2

he auction house was unusually busy for a Thursday afternoon. It could have had something to do with the small collection of Roman antiquities my mother shipped over from Italy — always a crowd pleaser. There were also a number of artworks up for sale, including those Sergei pawned off on me after my hookup with the blonde beauty.

"Bennett," Stanley smiled at me as he cut across the aisle, his polka dot bowtie looking especially crisp. "How are you?"

"No complaints." I shook the man's hand, nodding toward the people milling about. "Business seems to be going well."

"Yes, yes. You should be quite pleased with the quarterly revenue." He glanced around the room with a polite smile, as did I, seeing two different versions of the same scene: he saw cash cows waiting to be milked for all they were worth — I saw puppets to be played with for my own amusement. In the end, we were both right.

"Always good to hear." Not that my funds were anywhere close to getting low, but it was nice to keep building up the nest egg for the day I inevitably said "Fuck it" and fled to some remote corner of the world.

"How is your mother?"

"Oh, you know Camille." I forced a smile to my face, even if it made my cheeks hurt. No need to tarnish the family image in public if there wasn't a financial benefit to it. "Now that Allegra is out of the house, she's galavanting across the continent once again. I expect she'll announce Husband Number Five sometime soon."

"Well, give her my best." He patted my arm and stepped away, calling out to one of his team members as they hurried by.

I resumed glancing around the room, assessing the other people gathered. Based on the day's catalogue and their various outward appearances, I could almost tell who was going to bid for what item. The joy, or curse, of growing up among the cultured elite for most of my life — I could smell pretension a mile away. Nothing was more pretentious than the sort who flocked to Bancroft's for some one-of-a-kind artifact they could show off to their friends at cocktail parties.

The only one who didn't fit the mold was a young woman seated in the back corner. She was dressed in a black suit, complete with staggering stilettos that came into view now and again when she uncrossed and recrossed her legs in a sure sign of boredom.

Considering her from a distance, I tried to get a read on her. She was too severe looking to be here for the paintings. The only jewelry she wore were diamond studs, so it wasn't any of the baubles. Nor did she look like the type who dropped a couple grand on a broken marble statue so it could collect dust in a luxe apartment on the Gold Coast. So, what in God's name was she here for?

The brunette's gaze swept across the room, landing on

me with an unflinching confidence. Her face remained devoid of expression as she took me in from head to toe and back again, no doubt contrasting my ensemble to the traditional business attire of the people around us. It wasn't every day someone paired a gray suit with a burgundy waistcoat and a navy shirt, left unbuttoned.

Either that, or it was the hair, a disheveled mess of fringe and texture more appropriate on a musician than a lawyer, or the heir of the great Bancroft estate for that matter. I could hear Camille's voice now, chastising my appearance and trying to tell me my father wouldn't approve. Even if he wasn't dead, I was fairly certain he would give zero fucks about the clothes I wore or that my hair wasn't perfectly gelled. Then again, she cared more about his family history than he did. She always had. I mean, that was the reason she married him. Well, that and his money. The fact she always blew it off with a "Bennett, don't be ridiculous," didn't help sell her case.

Shoving my family drama to the back burner, I refocused my attention on the brunette. Before the auction officially kicked off, I sauntered toward the back. Despite all the other empty chairs I could have chosen along the way, I sat in the one right next to her.

There was no mistaking her huff. When I glanced at her, she stared straight ahead. Her jaw was as chiseled as her cheekbones, her glossy lips forming a hard line.

I opened my mouth to introduce myself, but she beat me to the punch.

"Save it," she said, her gaze fixed forward. "I'm not interested."

Ouch. I couldn't remember a time when someone shot me down before I even said anything. "Who said I was offering?"

Her head swiveled toward me, revealing a sharp flick of

black eyeliner as piercing as her eyes. "Couldn't find another seat?"

"I like this one," I replied with a bittersweet smile. Challenge accepted, kitten.

She rolled her eyes and returned her attention to the podium.

"Would you like me to move?" I asked, leaning far closer to her than necessary. She smelled expensive. Something French, if I had to guess. Dark florals and just enough spice to remind you she wasn't a pushover, in case you somehow missed the "Fuck Off" written across her forehead.

She didn't even turn to look at me when she answered through clenched teeth. "Yes."

With a nod, I stood. I took one step to the right and sat again, my vacated seat between us. If she thought being mean would hurt my feelings, she was in for a surprise. I intended to play this trivial game for as long as possible. It was far more exciting than waiting for the auction to end so I could report back to Mommy Dearest how much money she should be expecting in her bank account.

The brunette's head whipped toward me, her sleek ponytail lashing out behind her. She glanced at the seat before giving me another glare. "Very mature."

I tossed my head, shaking pieces of dark hair out of my eyes. "You're one to talk about maturity."

"Excuse me?"

"I simply tried to initiate a friendly conversation and you took my head off."

"Well clearly it didn't work." She tapped her auction number against her crossed leg, refusing to look at me.

"Obviously." I grinned at her, even if she despised my entire being for no apparent reason.

The auctioneer began, trotting out the rare documents and books first. Numbers on little paddles flew up around the room at various intervals as the items went, one by one. With an arm draped on the chair between us, I had a clear view of her in my periphery. The mystery woman didn't stir at all, nor did she look at me again.

"Lot Sixteen," the auctioneer said. "A first edition copy of *The Raven and Other Poems* by Edgar Allan Poe. Published in 1846. This is the London edition, ladies and gentlemen, in near perfect condition. We'll start the bidding at $5,000."

The woman in black raised her card at last.

"I have $5,000," the auctioneer said, pointing at the woman before moving on to the other bidders.

"$5,000 for a book?" She had my entire attention now. I didn't peg her as a bibliophile, but clearly I was mistaken. Guess it didn't matter, since she ignored me anyway. Sadly for her, I was too piqued to leave her alone. "What are you going to do with it?"

"None of your business," she hissed, raising her card.

"You must really want it…"

She ignored me again.

The bidding zipped around the room, climbing to $10,000.

"Why do you want it?" I asked.

"Why do you care?" she spat back.

I shrugged, raising my hand and crooking two fingers at the auctioneer.

"$10,500!" he crowed. "Do I have $11,000?"

She glared at me, raising her number again.

"Tell me," I said, lifting my hand toward the auctioneer. The rest of the bidders fell by the wayside once it reached double-digits.

"You're going to spend over $11,000 just for an answer?" Up went her hand.

"No." I smiled darkly. "I'm going to spend over $12,000."

"You're insane." She lifted her hand, but her gaze was locked on mine.

I chuckled. "You have no idea."

"What are you going to do with a book like that?"

"If I'm being honest, probably use it as a coaster."

"What?!"

I shrugged. "I have no use for it."

"Then why are you bidding?" Her brows came together as sharply as the line of her mouth.

"How else was I going to get you to talk to me?"

Her jaw dropped, but the card went up again.

At $20,000, she practically growled at me. "It's not my money, you asshole."

"Ooo, even better!" I winked at her. Spending other people's money was a talent I inherited from my mother. If the law didn't work out as a career, I always had the option to be some sort of slick-talking salesmen. Not the kind who sold used cars, but the type conducting million-dollar deals over bottles of Dom Perignon.

"You're such a dick."

"You could have stopped this ten grand ago."

"My boss wants it, ok? He's a collector."

"A collector of what? Books?"

"Yes. I mean, no. Poe shit. He's a huge fan."

"Well, why didn't you just say that?" My hand dropped to my lap, remaining still.

She glowered at me. If looks could kill, I was pretty sure I'd be skewered to the chair.

"Sold!" The auctioneer's gavel slammed onto the podium. "To the woman in the back, Number Thirty-Three."

I gave her a broad smile and clapped politely for her win.

Whipping the paddle at me, she stood and strode toward the back of the room to complete her purchase.

Chuckling, I followed her. "Let me take you to dinner."

"After you tripled the price of that book for no reason?" She snorted, digging around in her purse. "Yeah right."

"I told you my reason. I wanted to talk to you."

"Don't you know the meaning of the word 'No'? Surely they must have taught that to you in whatever pompous boarding school you went to."

"Believe it or not, it's not in my vocabulary." I leaned against one of the gilded columns, watching her fill out the requisite paperwork and cut an absurdly expensive check for an unimpressive little book. I'd wasted some money in my day, but never that much on something as trivial as a book.

With the precious antique wrapped carefully and stowed away in her Chanel bag, she whirled on me, nearly coming nose-to-nose with me thanks to the stilettos' added height. "What's your name?"

Now we were getting somewhere. "Bennett Reeve."

"Well, Bennett. It was nice knowing you." She spun with the grace of a dancer, whipping her dark hair in my face.

"That sounds like a threat," I said to her backside with a smirk.

"It was."

"What's *your* name?"

She stopped in the doorway, sliding a glare over her shoulder. "Olivia." And with that she was gone, disappearing into the busy sidewalk traffic.

CHAPTER 3

he day after the auction, I'd nearly forgotten about the mysterious Olivia when my personal cell phone rang. It was an out of town number I didn't recognize, but I answered anyway. Curiosity and all that.

"Mr. Reeve. My name is Leander Welles. I believe you met an acquaintance of mine at Bancroft's yesterday." His voice was smooth and dark. I liked him immediately, even if he was calling to take my head off for wasting his money.

I smiled, shifting my laptop to the side and sitting upright. "Ah. You must be the Poe fan. How's the book?"

"Olivia told me what happened. She was quite adamant in tracking you down."

"Well, you know the saying... Don't believe everything you hear." Although in my case, it was probably all true.

"I never do, which is why I'm calling you directly."

"Is it customary to call your victim before a hit?"

"I'm sure I don't know what you're talking about." I could almost hear a coy smile through the phone.

I tried to picture a face to go with the conversation. He sounded like he was around my age. His word choice and self-assured tone lent a certain elegance to his voice. But was he fair, or dark? Tall, or short? I had no way of knowing.

What I did know was Leander Welles was obviously a man of means. For starters, he had an assistant. Secondly, he could afford to send said assistant out with a blank check, which meant he trusted her. Speaking of trust...

"How did you get this number?" I asked.

"A very chatty man named Gavin. I believe he's your assistant?"

Gritting my teeth, I closed my eyes. Apparently we were going to have to go over the rules about handing out my personal phone number to random people. Again.

Leander continued, unfazed by my lack of response. "You're intriguing, Mr. Reeve. I like intriguing. Would you do me the honor of joining me for dinner tonight?"

I stole a glance at my pocket watch. It was already after seven. "I can probably move some things around."

"Let's meet in an hour. I'll send you the address." He hung up without any further ado, typical of a businessman with too much going on to waste time drawing out a goodbye.

A moment later, the address of a well-known and very public restaurant appeared. If it *was* a hit, at least I'd have a good meal before I died.

———

FOR THIS MEETING, I went with a shimmering dark purple shirt, unbuttoned, of course, beneath a patterned black vest and a black sport coat. If I was going to die, might as well go out in style. Raking my fingers through the front part of my hair, I brushed some to the side while other pieces stuck out in random spots. Rebellious until the end.

The maitre d' led me through the main dining room, past politicians and business tycoons, all the way to the back of the restaurant. Unless we were en route to the kitchen for a nice slaughtering, Russian style, I surmised our destination was one of the wine rooms. Besides being private, they were expensive. I was flattered my mystery host went through all the trouble.

Olivia was seated on the far side of the table when I walked in, next to a man in black whom I could only presume was her boss. The sight of him literally stole my breath. It wasn't everyday I'd call a man beautiful, but no other word would remotely do him justice. Based on the pale perfection of his skin I think I overshot his age, but I was spot-on about the wealth. From his perfect posture to the watch he wore, he exuded old money in a way the nouveau riche never did.

"Leander Welles," he said, rising to his feet and extending a hand. He was tall and thin, with slim hands that didn't know the meaning of hard labor. It wasn't a judgment — my hands were the same. No heavy lifting was required when you came from the kind of money we did. The only part of him that wasn't perfectly refined was the mass of dark, curly hair skimming his shirt collar.

"Bennett Reeve." Thankfully my voice didn't betray the initial awe I felt. If I *was* going to die tonight, at least it would be at the hands of two of the most gorgeous people I'd ever laid eyes on. Somehow, I was ok with that.

"You've met my assistant, Olivia Harlow." Leander gestured to the woman at his side. Like her boss, she was dressed in all-black again. With their dark hair and razor-sharp cheekbones, I wouldn't be surprised to learn they were related somehow.

"Pleasure's all mine," I said, offering her my hand.

She looked at it flatly before taking it in hers. "It certainly is." Her smile may have been sweet, but the way she crushed my rings against my fingers was anything but.

Hiding my wince in a chuckle, I took a seat across from them. I glanced around the room, trying to remember the last time I was here. Possibly when I brokered a deal between Connolly Construction and their local alderman. Or maybe it was when the Albanians were in town. After ten years, the meetings and the parties involved were all starting to blur together.

"I must admit I'm surprised to be here right now," I said, directing my attention to Leander.

"When Olivia wouldn't stop talking about you, I had to see you for myself." Leander glanced at her out of the corner of his eye, a faint smirk on his lips.

"Oh, really?" I shifted my gaze to her as well, a smile pulling at my mouth. "I'm glad to see I made an impression."

"I wouldn't be too flattered. I was begging him to kill you," she said matter-of-factly before taking a sip of her red wine.

The smile turned to a smirk.

"Would you care for any?" Leander gestured to the bottle between them. The fact he didn't refute Olivia's statement or try to minimize it spoke volumes. She did, indeed, beg him to kill me. So either he'd decided he would grant her request, or the answer was "No" and I needn't worry. I was curious to find out which fate this marvelous specimen of a human decided on my behalf.

"No thank you. I brought my own." I slipped a silver flask out of my inner pocket and took a sip of the bourbon inside before offering it to him. "Aged fifteen years."

"Who could say no?" Leander accepted the flask and took a sip, his eyebrows raising appreciatively.

"I know the word isn't in my vocabulary." My gaze slid to Olivia as I spoke. She glared at me in return.

Tucking the flask back in my pocket, I shifted my attention to her boss. "So, Leander. What sort of business brings you to Chicago?"

"Who said I was here for business?"

"Your phone number is from out of town. Your voice, while polished, has the faintest hint of an accent I don't usually hear north of I-80. Besides, if Poe meant that much to you, you would have been there in person. Which leads me to believe you're here on business."

A slow smile spread across his face. "I'm impressed."

"I have that effect."

"So modest," Olivia said, toying with her knife. Was he going to let her stab me during dinner service? Maybe that was her consolation for not being able to kill me outright. I hoped she didn't go for the face. That would seriously cramp my style.

My concern was allayed when the tablecloth on Leander's right side jerked, a soft 'thump' sounding under the table. Olivia turned her glare on the wall and left the knife alone, forcing her hands to her lap.

Leander took a sip of his wine before answering. "Back to your question — I am here for business."

"Where do you normally live?"

"Have you ever heard of a town called Easton?"

A virtual atlas flipped through my brain, but I couldn't place the town he was talking about. I shook my head with a small shrug.

"I'm not surprised. It's easy to overlook. Save for the tourists, we prefer to keep it that way."

"Are you going to make me guess what sort of business you're in?"

His eyes held a mischievous glimmer, meanwhile the small quirk at the corner of his mouth let me know I was being put to the test.

I assessed him again, looking for a telltale sign. His suit

was expensive and impeccably tailored, but not indicative of any particular profession. He traveled *with* an assistant, either to sleep with her away from the missus or because there was paperwork to deal with. As striking as they both were, I didn't get the sense there was any sexual tension. Plus, there was no ring on either of their fingers, which meant there was no reason for a clandestine "work trip."

Finding nothing else to scrutinize, I returned my gaze to his. He didn't look away, nor did I expect him to. Someone who radiated that much intensity was not used to backing down. Whatever empire he ran, it was with an iron fist. "I'm afraid I'm at a loss. Finance, perhaps, but not from a small town. My guess is on real estate."

"Well done." An amused smile played at the edge of his mouth. "My company has *diverse* interests. Real estate, construction, transportation, mostly."

"Mostly." I raised an eyebrow. A lifetime around mobsters meant I knew what "mostly" meant, and where it fell on the spectrum of legality. "How mysterious."

The glint remained in his eyes, suggesting he was more amused than annoyed. "Says the lawyer with no public profile save for what the newspapers have to say about him."

I almost groaned aloud. Of course he had done his research. Just how much remained to be seen. As it was, I hoped he was referring to the handful of front-page legal battles I'd waged over the years for some of Chicago's more colorful characters, instead of the twittering and fawning in the social column. "I don't read the papers, so I couldn't say."

"Would you like to talk about your philanthropic family?" He leaned forward, his voice lowering. "Or your business relations with some rather unsavory people?"

I mirrored his pose and conspiratorial tone. "Like your company, my clients have *diverse* interests. I simply do what I can to help them avoid the pitfalls of corporate law. No one wants to be the next Al Capone."

"It's surprising someone with your intellect didn't pursue criminal law instead. It seems like more of a challenge."

"Criminal law is nothing but smoke and mirrors." I smiled when he squinted slightly, as if he didn't believe what I was saying. If Del was there, he'd be rolling his eyes, spouting off all the reasons criminal law was superior, despite the fact civil lawsuits were far more persnickety. Planting the seed of doubt in a jury's head was child's play. Proving, or *disprov*ing, your client's involvement when the requirements for a verdict were so much lower? *That* took finesse.

Leander's brows lifted again. "Do tell."

"The Devil is in the details and nothing is more detailed than contracts. People will sign anything without reading it. They sign away their houses, businesses, rights and inheritances, everything. And the beauty of it is they have no one to blame but themselves."

"A valid point." Leander's gaze flitted over me once more, like he was seeing me in a new light, giving me phantom tingles wherever his eyes roamed.

"Criminal lawyers are all well and good," I said, leaning back and propping my elbow on the arm of the chair, hoping to shake off the feeling, "but I do everything in my power to make sure my clients don't have to go to court in the first place. It doesn't stop law enforcement from investigating, but if you do things the smart way, they drown in a mountain of paperwork and dead ends. Don't hide your business transactions. Give them a legitimate reason for existing and law enforcement doesn't have a leg to stand on."

Leander was quiet for a moment, his elbows resting on the table with his hands clasped, his chin resting on his knuckles.

I maintained my relaxed pose, waiting for him to break

the silence. Maybe I'd misread him. But with the way his pale eyes sparkled in the dim light, equal parts lethal and bewitching, I knew in my heart of hearts I found someone extraordinary.

Next to him, Olivia gave me a long, considering look. Her countenance was less intrigued and more irritated, even when she stole a glance at her boss. Whatever she saw in his face made her lip curl.

Before any of us spoke again, the waiter appeared with a tray perched on his shoulder. Apparently Leander had pre-ordered the chef's special, which was just as well. I wasn't picky when it came to food. Or alcohol. Or, anything really. After the dishes were distributed, the man bowed out again, closing the door behind him.

"So what is it, exactly, you do for your clients?" Leander asked, slicing into his steak with a methodical precision.

"Contracts, corporate advising, real estate transactions." I shrugged, dragging a mushroom through the thick cabernet sauce.

"Did I read that your father was also a lawyer?"

"He was a defense lawyer. It's because of him that I prefer not to run after my clients, cleaning up like a nanny."

Olivia finally broke her silence. "I'm sure he'd be proud. Do your clients know you look down on them with such disdain?"

"Perhaps if they were smart enough to see what's in front of them." I gave her a languid smile before biting the mushroom off the end of my fork.

"You work for mob bosses and criminals. Even if your family hails from the one percent, I wouldn't be so flippant," Olivia shot back.

Leander chewed his steak silently, glancing between the two of us like a tennis match. I wondered who he was betting on.

I smirked at Olivia. "I can be as flippant as I want. What are they going to do to me?"

"They could kill you, for starters."

"I know you find this hard to believe, but not everyone wants to kill me the minute they lay eyes on me."

Olivia rolled her eyes and stabbed a green bean. "Has anyone ever tried?"

"Yes." I beamed at her disappointed look. "And you can see how well that worked out for them."

"One of your clients?" Leander asked quietly, bringing my attention back to him.

He was too quick, too intelligent to openly lie to, so I answered honestly. "Yes."

"How did you respond?" He watched me with obvious interest.

I met his gaze and held it, letting the question linger for a moment. "Hypothetically speaking?"

"Hypothetically," Leander repeated solemnly.

"There's only one philosophy I subscribe to: 'Men must either be pampered or annihilated.'"

"Machiavelli." He practically lit up, a genuine smile spreading across his face.

I inclined my head. The fact he recognized it as a Machiavelli quote spoke to his intelligence; the fact he *approved* spoke to something else entirely. We exchanged half-smiles and a knowing look.

"One can learn a lot from the Italian Renaissance if you're willing to sacrifice a few modern morals." I shifted forward to the edge of the chair, setting my utensils down.

Leander did likewise, propping one elbow on the table and stroking the underside of his chin in thought. "I found *The Prince* quite inspiring. Especially his analogy of the lion and the fox."

"One of my favorites. His opinion on love and fear is equally astute."

"I concur."

"And you obviously surround yourself with a particular kind of personality." My gaze flicked to Olivia. Leander's coy smile was back, confirming my observation.

She skewered a tomato with her fork, not flattered in the slightest. "Have you put your little philosophy to the test?"

"Hypothetically?"

"Hypothetically," she replied, rolling her eyes.

"Yes." I arched an eyebrow at her, daring her to ask more.

She didn't disappoint. "How did that work out for you?"

"Splendidly."

"So you pampered your way out of a bad situation? Figures."

"No," I replied with a Cheshire Cat grin. "I annihilated it."

The bored expression vanished from her face. Her spine straightened as she turned toward her boss slowly, her eyes wide.

Leander's lips curled into a dark, dazzling smile. He lifted his wine glass, his gaze locked on mine. "To kindred spirits."

———

THE THRUMMING of the city seemed muted as soon as I stepped out the front door of the restaurant. It wasn't just the bourbon and the wine Leander insisted I share. Something was wrong. I could feel it along the back of my neck like a cold wind. For starters, the valet was nowhere to be found. The giant SUV parked near the corner was yet another clue. Like a fox, I smelled wolves in the air and hurried my steps accordingly.

Snatching my keys off the valet board, I was all the more grateful Leander and Olivia had gone out the side door to a waiting car. Whatever was about to come crashing down on my head didn't need to involve them.

A hand clamped on my shoulder before I could step off the sidewalk.

"Bennett Reeve, my least favorite lawyer," a man said to my right. "You weren't about to jaywalk right in front of us, were you?"

I sighed, looping my keys around my finger. "Agent Denning. To what do I owe this distinct pleasure?"

The agent smiled, but didn't remove his hand. "I was out for a drive. Saw your car parked nearby. Thought I'd stop, see how your friends are doing."

"Friends? You must be mistaken. We all know lawyers don't have friends."

"Aw, gee, I wonder why. You're all so likable."

"You're so lickable, too, Agent Denning." I reached for his face, using every bit of self-control I had not to laugh when he darted away from me.

"So you came here to have dinner by yourself?" Agent Diefendorf, Denning's saintly and long-suffering partner, appeared on my left. The wedding band on his finger glinted when he gestured at the restaurant. He looked less than thrilled to be out and about at such a late hour, especially with his buffoon of a companion. How he didn't strangle Denning with his obnoxious magenta tie by the end of every shift was a mystery.

"Absolutely. I am my own best company, after all." I smiled brightly at the pair. "Now, if you'll excuse me, I have somewhere else I need to be." I didn't need any of my clients seeing me chatting up a couple feds outside a restaurant known for hosting extralegal meetings amongst the upper crust. Besides, I had to meet Sergei across town after already pushing our meeting back once. I couldn't afford to dillydally anymore if I wanted to keep all of my body parts intact.

"One more thing," Denning piped up, practically using his partner as a human shield. The fact he thought I might actually lick him gave me an immeasurable amount of joy. His perfect blond feathers were so easy to ruffle. "Have you talked to your buddy Hector?"

"Hector who?" I blinked innocently.

"You know who. Hector Hernandez from the Calaveras."

I gasped, eyes widening in faux delight. "Oh, is that like a band? Is he famous or something?"

Diefendorf smirked. "Let's go, Josh. We're wasting our time here."

Denning didn't make a move to leave. "You want to know the first thing I learned at the bureau, smart ass?"

"STD tests don't screen for herpes?" I ventured.

Diefendorf sighed.

Denning continued, unfazed. "'Follow the money.'"

Nodding solemnly, I wiped all traces of humor from my face. "That is excellent advice, Joshua. I'm going to have to remember that one. Was it included in the official Special Agent handbook? I want to make sure I have my source correct when I pass that little nugget along."

Denning puffed up, but the fact he was still behind Diefendorf's shoulder didn't do much for his bravado. "We're watching you, Reeve."

"I'll leave the curtains open." I winked and strolled away. Spinning my keys around my finger again, I whistled leisurely all the way to my car.

Once I was on the road, away from prying eyes and listening devices, I called Del. "Good news and bad news, amigo. The FBI is looking for Hector."

"I get the bad. How is that good?"

"Because it means they can't find whatever hole he's crawled into. But I think it's time for your cousin to take that trip you were talking about."

"Yeah, right. I'll tell her. Thanks for the heads up."

"Give my love to Maria."

Disconnecting from Del, I dialed Gavin's number next.

He picked up without saying hello. "How was dinner? Tell me all about it! Is he as cute as he sounded on the phone?"

Rolling my eyes, I ignored him. "I need you to get all of the Hernandez files together and forward copies to Angel Delgado."

He scoffed. "Why? Can't his lazy ass secretary come make her own damn copies?"

"Now, now. You can't be mad at Sofia forever."

"Says the king of grudges. And yes, I can. That skank never sent the Kasprak file like she was supposed to!"

"She said she did."

"Are you seriously taking her side?"

"It was three years ago!"

"That is *so* not the point, Bennett."

"Anyway," I said loudly over the top of him. "My besties at the bureau stopped by, which means the next step is to come to the office. So try and get ahead of it, will you?"

He huffed. "I'll get on it first thing in the morning. Are you on your way to Sergei's?"

"As we speak."

"Good. So are you going to tell me about dinner, or not?"

"Not."

"Fine, be that way." He hung up with a huff.

Shaking my head, I tossed the phone on the passenger seat and focused on weaving my way through slow-moving vehicles.

I was nearing my next meeting point when the flow of traffic came to a screeching halt at one of the movable bridges.

Groaning, my head slammed back against the seat. "Come on!"

The warning bells chimed their obnoxious melody and the gates were down, but the bridge hadn't split apart yet. I glanced in the mirror for any sign of a squad car before swerving around the line of cars. Whipping around the gate, I floored it to a cacophony of shouts and honking.

Sorry, folks. Couldn't keep Papa Sergei waiting.

CHAPTER 4

a loud beeping woke me from a dreamless sleep. I buried my face into the pillow, trying to tune it out and buy myself five more minutes. That's when I realized the pillowcase was cotton, not silk, which meant I wasn't in my bed. And if I wasn't in *my* bed, whose bed was I in?

Before I stirred too much and alerted someone I was awake, I tried to piece together the night before. It was a bit of a blur. Ok, a lot of a blur. After dinner with the achingly beautiful out-of-towners and tap-dancing around the FBI's questions, I zipped across the city to meet Sergei about the possibility of expanding his distribution network.

Memories of music and vodka came back relatively easily. I was pretty sure there was some molly, too. But that was the extent of it. No clue who I left with, who I spent the night with, or whose bedroom I was in.

When I pushed myself into a sitting position, I realized there was an arm draped over me. A tan, muscled arm, covered in a sleeve of tattoos. A skull and crossbones stood out on his forearm, surrounded by Cyrillic script.

Well... shit.

Inch by inch, I slipped out from underneath the weight of it, hoping I wouldn't wake my sleeping companion. I'd just cleared his fingers when he spoke, still half-asleep, in accented English. "It's the neighbor's alarm."

"Oh." It's all I dared say since I couldn't remember his name. I think it started with an M. Mikhail? Maxim? Eh, guess it didn't matter. If Sergei found out, we'd both be dead, so it was probably better I didn't know.

"Are you leaving?" The mystery Russian was awake now, rubbing the sleep from his brilliant blue eyes.

"Yeah. I've got work." I slipped into my pants before scanning the floor for the rest of my clothes. Thankfully they seemed to be centrally located in the bedroom and I didn't have to conduct a scavenger hunt through the rest of his apartment. Shirt, vest, blazer, wallet... where were my socks?

M, or whoever, propped himself up on one elbow, watching me with a frown. "Can I make you breakfast?"

Fuck the socks. I could buy new ones. "I'll grab something on the way."

"Coffee?"

"I'm good." Double-checking my phone was in my jacket pocket, I tried to avoid his crestfallen expression.

"Am I going to see you again?"

I refrained from sighing. "Probably best if we didn't."

Nodding, he sank back down into the pillows, staring up at the ceiling. "At least you're honest."

If he only knew. Lying came with the job — literally. I was paid to lie for people who couldn't lie for themselves, but there was no reason to lie to a one-night stand, especially not one who could pick me off with a sniper rifle from a mile away.

Tugging my shirt on, I left it unbuttoned and grabbed the rest of my stuff. I leaned over and kissed him gently, a thank you and an apology all rolled into one. He reached for me, but I pulled away, making a beeline for the door without a backward glance.

Exhibit A of why I tried to disappear under the cover of darkness. Sneaking out was far less awkward than the next morning. The next morning gave people hope. No one should ever hope for anything when it came to me. They were only setting themselves up for disappointment.

I finished dressing in the elevator and took out my cell phone, bracing for the real world. There were a couple missed calls, even more text messages, and a plethora of email to sort through. The most important thing, however, was the SOS text from Gavin.

Swearing under my breath, I called him the second I stepped out onto the sidewalk, trying to figure out where I was. It was Chicago, I knew that. But the exact neighborhood was still fuzzy.

More importantly, where was my car? And my keys, for that matter.

"O.M.G. I have been calling you all morning!" Gavin hissed, the volume of his voice unusually quiet.

Uptown. I was in Uptown. I pivoted and started south-bound. "Yeah, I, um, forgot to set—"

"The feds are here like you said and they're asking all sorts of things about you and your schedule and your clients and I don't have enough Xanax to deal with this right now! Please tell me you're on your way already! They said they're not leaving until they talk to you."

Even though I knew it was coming, I was still surprised. They were moving pretty fast as far as alphabet soup agencies went. Either it was a time-sensitive case or someone higher up was breathing down their necks.

"I'll be there as soon as I can."

I gave up the search for my car and flagged a passing taxi.

By the time I got to my office, my hangover was in full

effect despite the surge of adrenaline I got after Gavin's phone call. Between the pounding headache and the nausea, the last thing I wanted to deal with were agents traipsing around asking me questions I wasn't prepared for.

"Coffee," I said to Gavin as soon as I walked in. "Now."

Any other day he would have snapped at me, but he looked relieved to get away from his desk and the pair of suits hovering over it.

"Well, well. Look what the cat dragged in," one of the agents said at max volume. "Rough night, buddy?"

I groaned out loud when I realized who it was. "Agent Denning."

"Good morning to you too."

Wincing, I held up a hand. "Would you please stop shouting?"

"I'm... not?" Denning glanced at Diefendorf.

"Shhh." Closing the distance between myself and the blond agent, I touched a finger to Denning's lips. "You're prettier when you don't talk."

Diefendorf snorted into his notepad.

Denning swatted my hand away, but I was already stalking forward to grab the coffee from Gavin. Once I was fortified, I faced the agents again, microscopically more sober than a minute ago.

"Now, maybe Agent Diefendorf can fill me in?" I shifted my attention to the quieter of the two. "What do you want?"

"Are you familiar with Carmelita's restaurant?" Diefendorf asked. "In South Deering?"

I made a face and gestured unhelpfully. If I thought about Mexican food too long, I was pretty sure I was going to throw up in the fiddle-leaf fig in the corner. "Maybe?"

"You were there a few nights ago," Denning said.

"Shhh!" I glared at him before turning back to Diefendorf. "Ok. If you say I was there, then I was there. So what? I can't grab a chimi on my way home?" …except South Deering was nowhere near home, I realized a split second too late. Get it together, Reeve.

Diefendorf didn't seem concerned with my geographical slip-up. "Was Juan Ortiz still alive when you left?"

"Who is Juan Ortiz?"

"The former owner of Carmelita's, before he sold it to Hector Hernandez."

The pieces of their logic strung together in my brain, like a row of lightbulbs turning on one by one. They wanted to know where Hector was last night and now they were asking about the little, misty-eyed old man. Fuck.

"I don't know what you're talking about," I said, trying to focus and stay six steps ahead, even though my brain was currently pickled in vodka. Thanks M.

"Six months ago, almost to the day, you wrote up a contract for Hector Hernandez and Juan Ortiz. It was a payment plan since Mr. Ortiz had been turned down by the bank for an extension. We found the contract. If Ortiz defaulted on his repayments, ownership of the restaurant transferred to Hector."

"Sounds like Mr. Ortiz was an idiot then." I crossed my arms over my chest, still waiting for the big reveal.

"Yeah, I'm sure he'd agree." Diefendorf shuffled through the folder in his hands and unearthed a bright, bloody eight-by-ten of Juan Ortiz. Or what was left of him.

The body had been thrown on a pile of trash behind a building, broken and bruised. Tiny little lacerations were clustered over his skin. It took me a minute to realize it was from the rats chewing on him. The most visceral part, however, was the fact he was holding his own head in his hands, a look of pain and terror permanently etched onto his sun-weathered face.

Averting my gaze, I took another gulp of coffee. It was too fucking early to be looking at corpses.

"Something wrong?" Denning asked, obviously pleased by my disgust.

"Joshua, the adults are talking now." Eyes narrowed, I held a finger up to my own lips as I spoke.

"You were there that night," Diefendorf continued over the top of his partner's retort. He made sure to keep the picture front and center while he spoke, so I had no choice but to look at it — or him. "Did Hector do this?"

Hell no Hector didn't do that. I mean, he ordered it. Obviously. But actually severing someone's head? That was a job for an initiate. Some punk probably no older than fourteen or fifteen got the pleasure until his little, stringy muscles couldn't take it anymore and an enforcer had to step in and finish the sawing. A hacksaw, to be exact, instead of the machete their counterparts south of the border tended to rely on.

"You know what?" I snapped and pointed at Diefendorf. "Let me get my lawyer on the phone. I'm sure he'd want to be present for this little chat." I pulled up Del's office number on my cell phone and hit ENTER.

"That's not necessary, Mr. Reeve. We just want to know what you saw. *Who* you saw."

I ignored him. "Sofia, Mamita. Put Angel on the phone. Yeah, I'll wait." I rotated the phone away from my mouth, looking back at Diefendorf. "This will only take a sec."

"We don't want *you*," he said with a huff. "We want Hector. Help us out here."

"Are you kidding me right now? You want me to give up information on a client? Do you even know how the legal system works past the 'hook 'em and book 'em' stage? Even if I don't end up with a fucking bullet in my head, I'll never work again."

"Would you shut up for two seconds and just listen?" Denning snapped. He grabbed my cell phone and hit END before tossing it on Gavin's desk.

"Talk, don't talk. Make up your mind, Josh! You're giving me mixed signals here," I shot back. I wasn't particularly upset about him hanging up on Del. It told me Diefendorf was telling the truth — they *were* desperate for help if Denning felt compelled to trample all over my basic rights.

Diefendorf sighed, probably seeing his career flash before his eyes thanks to his partner's antics. "One last time. Where's Hector?"

"I have no idea."

"How about his wife, Maria? You slip her the old taquito lately?" Denning sniggered like a teen who touched a boob for the first time and now saw himself as the epitome of masculinity.

"Well now I know you're making stuff up. Frankly, I'm more concerned with the fact you're even fantasizing about me in a state of undress, Special Agent Denning. Perhaps I should speak with your supervisor. I'm feeling a little sexually harassed right now. Matter of fact... Gavin, get the Chicago branch on the line. Ask for that agent in charge. What's his name? Amanda? Miranda. Whatever. I'm sure he'd love to hear about this and the giant fucking lawsuit headed his way."

Diefendorf stepped in front of Denning and his outraged reply, talking louder than I'd ever heard the man. "We need to talk to her. It's *important*."

"Noted." I smiled brightly at Diefendorf. So they really wanted Maria, not just her dolt of a husband. Thanks for that little tidbit, boys.

Diefendorf pressed his business card into my hand. For a moment, I considered tossing it back at him, but the look of helpless frustration on his face stopped me. Instead, I pocketed it and gave Denning a brilliant smile and a little wave. "Ciao."

Gavin took that as his cue and hung up the phone. He showed the agents out the door while I strolled into my personal office, finishing the rest of my coffee. I set the empty cup on the coffee table and shrugged out of my blazer.

"That's the same outfit you wore yesterday," Gavin said with a sniff, sizing me up from the doorway.

Making my way to the closet, I swapped out my shirt for a fresh one, tossing the others to Gavin. "Send those out for dry cleaning, would you?"

He caught the clothes, shoving a handful of pink message slips at me in return. "Your mother called."

"Uh huh." I shuffled through the papers, dumping the unnecessary ones — including hers — into the trash.

"And your sister."

"Did they say why?"

"Only that you're not returning their calls and they wanted to make sure you still had a pulse."

"Well, I'm sure you told them I did, so there's no need to call."

"Bennett, call them. They're worried about you."

"Do we have to do this right now? I just got rid of two nags and then here you come."

"You hardly ever talk to them."

"How often do you talk to your family?"

He bristled, his fingers digging into my poor blazer. If I wasn't careful, he'd end up ripping off a sleeve. "That's different. You know my parents don't approve of my..."

"Gayness?"

"Lifestyle," he snipped.

"Well, my family doesn't approve of my *lifestyle*, either." I dropped into the chair behind my desk and turned to the computer, willing him to go away.

"Which part? The drinking and the drugs or the fact you sleep with everyone you meet?"

I clicked through my email, glaring at the computer screen instead of him. It wouldn't do any good to give him withering looks. He'd continue to be a mother hen and I'd continue doing whatever the hell I wanted. "I haven't slept with *you*."

He scoffed, rolling his eyes behind his black-frame glasses. "You don't stand a chance."

I smirked, scanning an email from Stanley about the next board meeting for Bancroft's. "Whatever helps you sleep at night."

"Dick."

"Bitch."

Gavin pulled out his phone, typing quickly. "Oh, and some scary Russians called for you."

My heart rate went up a notch. It wouldn't be Mr. M from this morning. He knew the gig. But that didn't mean Sergei didn't catch wind of what happened. He Americanized pretty quickly in the years he'd been here, except for his Soviet view on queerness.

Gavin stopped typing briefly, glancing up. "They have a delivery for you. I didn't know if you wanted it here or at home, so I told them we'd have to schedule it later."

I vaguely remembered Alina's exhibit. The hot blonde had taken more of a priority, along with the trophy I handed over to Sergei at the end of the night. Needless to say, he was quite pleased to get the tiny surveillance camera, along with information on the woman. Any minuscule amount of guilt I may have had was assuaged by the fact Sergei wouldn't kill her. She was much more useful to him alive than dead.

The paintings took a back burner after that. God only knew what Del picked out or what exorbitant amount he charged to my credit card. Which he still had...

"Great. Find a spot for whatever it is here. I don't need anything else at my apartment," I replied, typing a quick text to Del, demanding its return.

"You don't even know what you bought?" Gavin asked, interrupting my texting.

"I was… preoccupied." I threw my cell phone on the desk and arched an eyebrow at him, waiting for another round of chiding.

Gavin merely rolled his eyes and walked out of my office, muttering under his breath. The only word I heard clearly was "slut."

"Your biphobia is showing again!" I yelled after him. "Might want to tuck that back in!" I may have taken real offense if I wasn't used to it after a lifetime of judgment from both sides of the spectrum. Plus, in my case, it was kind of true.

Glancing at the computer's clock, I sighed, calculating the difference across the time zones. Closing my eyes, I debated if I really wanted to endure yet another lecture while hungover.

Before I even came to a solid decision, I was dialing Allegra's number.

She answered after two rings. "Pronto."

"*You called?*" I asked in Italian. Leaning back, I kicked my feet up on the desk, crossing them at the ankle. If I pulled the shades, I could definitely squeeze in another couple hours of sleep before court in the afternoon.

"Bennett?" Even her irritated huff had an accent. "*Where have you been? I've been calling you for days.*"

"*Busy. What do you need?*"

"*I don't need anything. It's nice to know my big brother is still alive.*"

"*You mean to tell me you're not calling for Camille?*"

The other line went quiet. Church bells rang in the background, along with the murmur of people chattering. She was out and about, not tucked away at home with her boyfriend, Esteban, or whatever his name was. It also meant the scolding would be kept to a minimum in public.

"Yeah, that's what I thought." I pushed against the pressure point along the inside of my eye socket, next to the bridge of my nose. No more molly. A few hours of fun wasn't worth it anymore.

"Are you coming home at all this year?" she asked, her voice quiet. Dare I say, hopeful.

I quickly dashed it for her. *"I am home, Allegra."* America was my home — Europe was hers. That was our family dynamic, as it had been our whole lives, except for the eight years I spent abroad, like a helpless ward in some Victorian novel.

She sighed. *"That's not what I meant..."*

"Ok, well, I have work to do." I swung my legs down, my finger hovering over the release button on the phone.

"Bennett?"

"What?" It paused, a centimeter from the bright orange button.

"Mi manchi."

Talk about a knife to the heart. I winced, swallowing down the rush of guilt. *"I miss you too."*

"Ciao."

I hung up the phone and slumped forward over my desk, burying my face into the crook of my arm. Damn her and her innocent little guilt trips.

Except Allegra didn't do it out of sheer manipulation, unlike most people. She really was a good person, kind and caring and thoughtful. I don't think she had a mean bone anywhere in her body. It must have come from Allegra's dad, given the fact we shared Camille as a mother.

"How's your sister?" Gavin asked, a paper bag rustling as

he reemerged, stopping across from me. Something heavy thunked on the corner of my desk.

I didn't bother looking up. "Fine. I guess."

"How's school?"

"She didn't say."

"You didn't ask?"

"Was I supposed to?"

"Did Sergio propose yet?"

"God, I hope not. She's too young to even think about marriage." Picking my head up, I quirked a brow as he pulled out a sandwich and a cup of soup. "What's that?"

"Your lunch, genius."

"No, the box." A simple black box sat on the corner of my desk, neatly tied with a black ribbon.

He handed over a little white envelope. "I don't know. It was just delivered."

Opening the card, I spied perfect, slanting script inside. To my delighted surprise, it was from Leander. I tried to keep my expression as neutral as possible so I wouldn't have to hear about it from Gavin for the rest of the day.

Bennett,
"They who dream by day are cognizant of many things which escape those who dream only by night." — E. A. Poe
Thank you for an enlightening conversation.
I do hope we speak again.
— Leander

Tugging the ribbon free, I opened the box, blinking at the contents. It was bourbon. But more than that, it was very old, very *expensive* bourbon. I didn't realize I'd made such an impression.

Gavin raised his brows at me. "Wow! Who's it from?"

"No one."

"Then why did you smile?"

Ignoring him, I turned my gaze to the food, staring at it for a beat. "I'm not hungry." My head dropped back down to my arm, conveniently tucking the note under my hand so he couldn't retrieve it.

"You need to eat. And shower. I can smell the alcohol from here."

"I need to find my car."

"Where did you park it?"

"If I knew that, then I would know where to find it."

Sighing, he slid his fingers behind his lenses and pressed them into his eyes. "You are such a mess. Hot, but a mess. Like a hot hot mess."

Angling my head, I glared up at him with one eye. "I get the drift."

"I'm just saying. There's a difference between living your life like there's no tomorrow and putting yourself in an early grave."

Before I could help it, I smirked at him. "Been there, done that. Could literally write the book."

"Yeah, well, next time they might not be able to save your ass." He raised an eyebrow and plopped the sandwich an inch from my nose. Without any more scolding, he turned and sauntered out of the room.

Eying the sandwich, I made a face, even if it was one of my favorites.

Maybe Gavin was right.

Maybe it was time for a change.

CHAPTER 5

"Couldn't we do this at a hotel or something? A restaurant? Anywhere without so much... dust?" I swatted a cobweb off my burgundy jacket and glared at the man on the skywalk above who'd inadvertently kicked it loose. It was my fault for wearing vintage velvet to a meeting with Giovanni Marchese. In my defense, I was summoned at the last minute when Johnny, one of the Marchese goons, showed up and ruined my date.

Giovanni threw an irritated glance in my direction, chewing on the end of a toothpick. "This is the only place in the city I know that isn't bugged."

"It's a warehouse, Gio. There's so much crap in here you wouldn't know if they installed an entire surveillance team let alone a tiny little bug." I slid my laptop out of the bag and set it up on the makeshift table I'd assembled on the top of a fifty-gallon drum. I was definitely invoicing my dry cleaning bill on top of my usual fee.

"Boss, there's a car coming," Enzo said from the second floor. He resumed his place by the window, gun drawn and at the ready.

The rest of the Marchese crew fanned out, assuming various positions throughout the warehouse.

My eyes rolled skyward as I typed. "I thought you wanted to make nice with this guy?"

Giovanni snorted, spreading his hands innocently. "I do."

"Maybe lose the firing squad. People tend to get nervous staring down the barrel of a gun."

He chuckled. Without word from their boss, the Italians stayed right where they were.

"What's this guy's name?" I asked, clicking through the various documents.

Giovanni gave me a blank look before turning to Tony, brows raised. "What was it again?"

The larger man shrugged. "I don't know. Welch, I think?"

"Helpful, as always." I left that part blank and moved into the standard contract Giovanni used in all of his business transactions. It was the one designed to crush an unsuspecting partner for any minor inconvenience the Marchese family suffered. It was so rote at this point, I could type them in my sleep.

A moment later, the car Enzo mentioned pulled through the open doors and stopped. The driver got out and buttoned his black suit jacket, though it didn't hide the tattoos creeping up the side of his neck. He walked to the backdoor and opened it for his passenger — Mister Welch, or whatever.

I glanced over the top of the laptop, inhaling sharply.

It was Leander.

Dressed again in a perfectly tailored all-black suit, he surveyed the Italians scattered around the warehouse with an unimpressed look. Even his driver looked unconcerned with the fact they were outmanned and outgunned. When his gaze landed on me, just behind Marchese, one dark eyebrow lifted.

Brushing my index finger across my lips, I flicked a glance at Giovanni and resumed typing.

"Mr. Marchese," Leander said, stepping forward and extending a hand. "Leander Welles."

"Thank you for taking the time to come up here, Mr. Welles." Giovanni took his hand and reeled him in to kiss both cheeks.

Leander's polite smile bordered on a grimace. "Of course. This type of thing is best done in person."

"I assume Marco filled you in on what we're looking for?"

"Transportation, as I understand it. You need barges going to and from New Orleans."

"That's right. We have the logistics covered for the ground, but water is a new territory for us."

"Lucky for you, my family's been in shipping since the 1800s." Leander smiled. From where I stood, he looked like a cat, moments away from pouncing on its prey.

Giovanni nodded. "Good to hear. Good to know you know what you're doing down there."

Leander didn't look the least bit flattered. "High praise, I'm sure. What are you willing to offer for this service?"

"A flat fee. One hundr—"

Leander exhaled before cutting him off. "Thirty percent."

Giovanni snorted. "What?"

"I expect thirty percent of the inventory cost." Leander clasped one hand around the opposite wrist, settling into a position that screamed he was not in the mood to negotiate. The glint in his eye sent a chill down my spine, the same way it did during dinner when the context of our conversation shifted beyond the obvious.

Giovanni sputtered. "You've got to be fucking kidding me. Tony, get a load of this guy."

Marchese's right-hand man remained stoic, looking at Leander with a mixture of curiosity and admiration. It had been a while since anyone held their ground against the boss.

"And if it's confiscated," Leander continued, clearly bored by Giovanni's clucking, "I'll deny this arrangement ever existed. As far as I know, you snuck your cargo onboard and I am nothing but a victim."

"Do you know who I am?" Giovanni asked, taking a step forward.

I exchanged a look with Tony, shaking my head. I knew enough about Leander to know he wouldn't take a threat well, nor would he submit to Giovanni's blustering.

Leander smiled again but it was far from pleasant. "A man with product to move and no way to move it. I don't think you're in a position to make demands."

"You've got some nerve."

Leander checked his watch, raising his brows. "Ten seconds, Mr. Marchese."

"I don't need ten seconds to tell you to fuck off."

"Gio," I snapped under my breath. He'd been looking for a way to tap into the Mississippi River for months. Was he really going to blow it the first chance he had? Let me think. Hot-headed Italian? Yes. Yes, he would.

Tony stepped forward, touching Giovanni's arm.

Leander looked at his driver and tossed his head toward the car. "We're leaving. Call Mr. Sidorov and tell him we're all set."

The driver nodded and pulled out his cell phone as he walked, opening the back door again.

I appreciated Leander's tenacity, blatantly throwing out the name of Giovanni's rival. For someone from out of town, he had certainly educated himself on who the main players were. Or, at least who the Italians' competition was.

"Wait, wait!" Tony said, putting his hands up. "Just wait a second." When Leander stopped walking, Tony grabbed

Giovanni by the arm and dragged him away a couple feet, hissing in a combination of English and Italian. I perked an ear toward their conversation while meeting Leander's gaze across the warehouse. The corners of his mouth curled in the faintest smile.

The solution to their problem was the usual, according to Tony — use Leander for a while, let him get comfortable with the arrangement, then screw him over like everyone else. Or, there was always Option B, kill him outright and strong-arm his replacement into a more favorable deal. For some inexplicable reason, neither prospect sat well with me. Leander was too majestic to let someone as base as Giovanni destroy, one way or another.

With the matter settled, Giovanni turned and nodded. "Alright. Deal."

"Wise choice," Leander replied.

"Bennett?" Giovanni turned to me expectantly.

"One second." I typed quickly, modifying the part in the contract where it said Giovanni was entitled to Leander's company in the event of a law enforcement seizure. Knowing Gio, he'd call the police himself to make it happen after that little power play. While I was at it, I cleared out a few other provisions in Leander's favor.

Despite my continued warnings over the years, Giovanni didn't read anything he signed. It may have been crazy to put my money on the dark horse, but I was all in. I couldn't think of any other way to explain it except that it felt *right*.

As soon as I finished the modifications, I transferred the document to my tablet and handed it to Giovanni. He scribbled his finger roughly over the screen and shoved it back at me. Without another word, he stomped off to his car. I felt sorry for whatever girlfriend was going to have to soothe his ego tonight.

Turning toward Leander next, I gave him a smile once my

back was to the Italians. "If you'd be so kind," I said, handing the contract over.

"How carefully should I read this?" Leander asked quietly, scrolling through the pages. "I heard the Devil is in the details."

"Lions need not fear the wolves."

"Apparently not when there's a fox around." The corner of his mouth twitched, threatening a smile, as he signed underneath Giovanni's signature with the stylus.

"Speaking of lions… Before you leave town, you should really see some of the sights," I said, loudly enough for anyone else to hear. My fingers moved deftly over the screen, emailing copies to all parties involved. "The Field Museum is one of my favorites, especially the African mammals exhibit." I raised an eyebrow at him.

"I'll look into it. I think I have some free time around noon."

"Pleasure doing business with you." I winked and spun on the ball of my foot, returning to the dirty barrel. Once I tucked away the tablet and laptop in my bag, I stopped next to Tony, watching Leander's car back out and disappear the way it came.

"What do you think?" Tony asked.

I smirked. "You might want to tell your boss he's met his match."

"You know he hates middle men."

"Well, he's going to have to deal with it unless he wants to lose out to the Russians."

"You think this guy really called Sidorov?"

I considered the empty space where Leander stood moments ago. Unlike most people, I got the impression he undertook everything with the utmost seriousness. He wouldn't waste his time entertaining Marchese if there was a better offer. Plus he had no reason to lie when he knew damn well there were other options. "Absolutely."

"Don't you have ties to them?" Tony looked at me, suspicion as clear as day on his face.

"I'm a patron of his daughter, Alina," I said blithely. "No professional connections." That Marchese needed to know about… Exchanging tidbits now and again with the Russians in the name of friendship — or self-preservation — was hardly what I considered a "professional connection."

"What the fuck is a patron?"

I managed to repress an exasperated sigh. "It means I buy her really expensive artwork."

"Why?"

I blinked. "Why support an artist or why support *her*?"

He opened his mouth to answer, but Giovanni rolled down his window and huffed from the passenger side. "Tony, let's go!"

Tony and I exchanged another look before he trudged away. I slung my bag over my shoulder and headed for my own car down the block.

Seeing Leander again, and the question of patronage, sparked an idea. A crazy, fiendish idea. Watching him deftly handle one of Chicago's leading mobsters like it was child's play stirred something infernal inside of me. If there was any doubt it was time for a change, meeting Leander Welles was the serendipitous push I needed.

CHAPTER 6

hankfully, the rainy autumn afternoon and the fact it was too early into a new school year for field trips meant the Field Museum wasn't particularly busy. I navigated my way toward the Rice Gallery, glancing around now and again to make sure none of the rougher denizens of Chicago were lurking on the balconies above.

The gallery was dimmer than the main lobby and much quieter. Various mammals from Africa lined either side of the hall, the smell of formaldehyde wafting in the air. The Lions of Tsavo exhibit, one of the Field's most well-known attractions, took prominence at the far end.

I wasn't the least bit surprised to see Leander was already there. All our talk of lions could have only meant one thing when it came to the Field Museum and he was clever enough to put two and two together.

When I walked up, his back was to me, hands clasped behind him. Still, he seemed to know when I was there without turning. "Mr. Reeve."

"Mr. Welles." I stopped next to him, studying the pair of taxidermy lions in front of us.

The lion on the left stood tall, poised. The other crouched low over the rocks, positioned in a way that looked like he was ready to strike. Their skulls were displayed on the left of the tableaux, along with the large, infected canine tooth that was supposedly the source of all the trouble.

"They're called 'the Ghost' and 'the Darkness,'" I said, tipping my chin toward the duo. "They terrorized railroad workers in Kenya in the 1890s, killing at least thirty-five people, though some say it could have been in the hundreds."

"The Man-eaters of Tsavo," Leander said, reading the sign behind them. "They're marvelous. Though I'll admit I have no idea why we're here." He turned toward me, his head cocked.

"What makes them so remarkable is that they hunted *together*, something unheard of in male lions. The entire region feared them." I turned as well, meeting his gaze head-on. We were nearly eye-to-eye, though I had a slight advantage. "Do you know what your name means?"

He shrugged. "It's from Greek mythology."

"It means 'lion.'" I let the information, and my implied meaning, sink in. Excitement tingled along my skin the moment his green eyes came alive with understanding.

Like the predator he was named for, Leander circled around behind me slowly. I could practically feel his gaze as it raked over me, assessing every angle, until he stopped again on the left side of the display. His gaze was fixed on the skulls, his face unreadable. "What are you proposing?"

"What is it you want?"

"Who says I want anything?"

"It's human nature."

Leander glanced over his shoulder. "Then tell me. What is it *you* want?"

"A kindred spirit." I canted my head to the side, dragging

my teeth across my lower lip. "Someone who thinks like I do. Someone who would make Machiavelli proud."

His gaze dropped to the floor before returning to the lion skulls, his lips twitching in thought.

I stepped closer to the display, staring into the glass eyes of the lion poised to attack. "Together, we would be unstoppable. Like them."

"Despite their prowess, they were still killed."

"Well, we have an evolutionary edge." I flashed him a dark smile.

Glancing out of the corner of his eye, he took me in from head to toe again. "Isn't this a conflict with Marchese?"

"Only if he turns it into one."

"None of your other clients would object?"

"They can object all they want. Until now, I've only ever offered my services on a case-by-case basis. I choose my clients, not the other way around."

"And for some reason I've yet to uncover, you've chosen me."

I leaned sideways toward him, lowering my voice and meeting his gaze. His beautiful, enigmatic gaze... "I see potential."

"Why would I trust someone I just met?" Those mesmerizing eyes were dark, but curious, as they searched my face for the real answer.

I didn't move, nor did I look away, though I was sure that was his intent — a test, of sorts, to see if I could match his fervency or if I'd crumble. "I'm not asking you to trust me. But if it helps, I've already demonstrated I have your best interests at heart."

"How so?"

"The contract. I changed the wording so Giovanni can't snatch your company away from you whenever he feels like it."

Leander's arms folded across his chest, the muscle along his jawline tensing beneath his pale skin. His composed anger was impressive, though I wondered what it would look like if he unleashed it. "Come again?"

"What do you think he and his henchman were discussing? He took the deal knowing he would steal your company later or kill you outright."

"You didn't have to help me." Leander's voice dropped, along with his gaze, fixed on some unknown point on my chest. Either my necklace, or the exposed skin it sat upon.

"I know." I gave him an impish smile when he looked up again. "I wanted to."

"Why?"

I shrugged. "Is it bold to say I find you equally intriguing?"

"You arranged all of this because you find me 'intriguing'?" While still skeptical, at least he was amused.

"I've done far worse with a much weaker motive."

"Are you always so reckless with your business proposals?"

"Believe it or not, this is one of the least reckless decisions I've made in a while. I'd hate to think we squandered an opportunity to build something great."

He nodded as I spoke, contemplative again. "What would this arrangement look like?"

"Whatever you want. Call me your in-house counsel, if you like."

His attention shifted past my shoulder, to the lions. "This is the last thing I expected when I came to Chicago..."

"Do you believe in fate?"

His gaze snapped back to mine. Despite his suspicion, another emotion registered in his eyes, one I couldn't quite pinpoint. I didn't know who he was having a harder time trusting — me, or his own instincts. "You'd really give up everything you have here?"

"I've grown bored with Chicago. I'm always looking for new challenges and you, Mr. Welles, look like you're quite the challenge."

His attention shifted past my shoulder, obviously in thought as he chewed the inside corner of his mouth. I couldn't help but be drawn to it and its just-bitten lushness. It was easy to imagine his lips tasted like blackberries or pomegranate — something deliciously dark, walking a fine line between sweet and tart.

At last, his eyes returned to mine, snapping me out of fantasyland. He unfolded his arms and offered his right hand.

A mischievous grin crossed my face. My hand slid into his perfectly, solidifying a pact the Devil himself couldn't undo.

CHAPTER 7

*S*liding my sunglasses down the bridge of my nose, I stopped the car and stared at the massive house in front of me. A grand Italianate, architecturally speaking, but with a twist on the usual paint scheme. Black trim stood out against the blood-red siding, giving the house a menacing facade.

Pushing my sunglasses up, I continued around the circular drive and parked behind an expensive black car. Just the sort of thing I'd expect a mysterious millionaire to drive.

Luggage in hand, I made my way up the front steps and rang the doorbell.

To my surprise, Olivia was the one who answered the door.

"Oh great, *you're* here." She pushed the door open further and gestured inside with a roll of her eyes.

"I knew you couldn't stay away," I said, stepping past her and glancing around the foyer. Dark wooden panels lined the walls, topped with sumptuous wallpaper in varying jewel tones. Aside from modern utilities, it looked like a majority of the house was its own sort of time capsule. God knew Camille would love to get her mitts on the antiques.

"Please," Olivia scoffed. "I'm only here because Leander is tied up in a meeting. This way." She sauntered into the house on heels so tall we were nearly eye-level.

Leading me up a sweeping staircase and down another hallway, she navigated the house with ease. We stopped again in the threshold of a dark red room. "You can stay here."

"Reminds me of Venice." I stepped inside, shrugging out of my leather jacket. I dropped it, along with my bags, in the center of the old carpeting. If I had to guess, it was original to the house, as was the dark, carved furniture. Everything was crimson, accented with gold, from the damask wallpaper, to the heavy drapery hanging above the bed from a wall teester.

"Make yourself at home."

"I plan to." I returned to the doorway with a smirk. "Do you live here too?"

She made a face, as if it were the most ridiculous idea ever. "Of course not."

Leaning against the doorframe, I gave her a half-smile. "Then where do you live?"

"None of your business."

"You know I can find out."

She rolled her eyes, her jaw shifting. "God, you're annoying. Why are you here again?"

"Because your boss likes me." I smiled angelically at her. Her irritation was fuel for the fire, a fact I thought she learned in Chicago. "If you gave me half a chance, you'd probably like me too."

"Doubtful. Very doubtful." She twirled and strode away, disappearing around the corner and descending the stairs again with an authoritative stomping of her heels.

I followed the echoing, making my way down the stairs,

through a series of hallways until I emerged in a large, black-and-white kitchen. It was outfitted with more professional appliances than some restaurants. "Damn."

"He likes to cook," Olivia said offhandedly, disappearing into the fridge to retrieve a stainless-steel creamer.

I slid up onto a stool at the large, granite island, watching from afar as she made coffee despite the fact it was the middle of the afternoon. "So other than buy Leander rare books and wander around his house like you own the place, what is it, exactly, you do?"

"I'm his personal assistant."

"He said as much. That doesn't really answer the question, though."

"I do whatever he asks." She all but slammed the canister of coffee grounds down, glaring at me like a bug that needed to be squashed.

I cocked an eyebrow, giving her a very pointed once-over. "Anything?"

She leaned across the island, her hazel eyes smoldering and her voice getting husky. "Anything."

"He's a lucky man."

Smirking, she turned away and returned to the coffee pot. "I'm assuming you'll want some of this?"

"Are you talking about the coffee or...?" I waggled my brows at her when she slid a murderous look over her shoulder. And I thought Maria was a wildcat. Olivia put her to shame.

"Why are all men so disgusting?" She thunked a heavy mug of coffee down in front of me and leaned one hip against the island, blowing on her own before taking a tentative sip.

"Do you want me to answer that honestly?"

She shot me a flat look. "No."

"But seriously, do you and the boss have any 'extracurric-ular' activities?"

"Not that it is *any* of your business, but no."

"Is it a family thing? You do have a similar bone structure."

She wrinkled her nose at me. "Wrong again."

"Well, that's a relief."

"What is?"

"That you're not Leander's cousin or some such. I'd hate to have kill him in a duel over your honor."

"Didn't they teach you about sexual harassment in law school?"

I pretended to think, tapping my lips with my index finger. "Might have been covered in the semester I didn't go to class..."

She snorted. "That explains it. You're some two-bit lawyer who barely made it through law school and now you're here to ruin everything Leander has built."

"For your information, Kitten, I graduated summa cum laude."

"By blackmailing your professors?"

"No, but now that you mention it, it would have been a hell of a lot easier than reading all those books." I snapped my fingers in faux frustration. "Damn it! Why didn't I think about sleeping my way through school?"

"Are you ever serious?"

"Are you ever nice?"

Another heated glare served as her answer before she shifted the topic. "If you're going to be staying here, you might as well know some things up front."

Leaning on my elbows, I cupped the mug in both hands, listening attentively.

"Leander is an insomniac. He's also incredibly particular about what he eats and drinks. Don't be offended. Also, his clothes. Do *not* ruin his clothes. Yolanda takes care of the laundry and housekeeping. If you need something dry cleaned, put a note on it. Oh, and he likes things quiet. So you might want to work on shutting your face for half a minute."

"Thanks for the heads-up, but I think I'll be fine." Batting my eyes at her, I blew on my coffee before taking a sip.

She shook her head, touching the space between her eyebrows with the tip of a perfectly polished black nail. "I can't believe he's letting you stay here. This is such a bad idea."

"He's not letting me. He insisted. Something about a dispute with the owner of the only hotel in town and not trusting the people who run the B&Bs."

"Yeah, that sounds like him…"

I decided to shelve my smart-ass attitude and adopt a more serious one for the moment. "I know you've loathed me from the moment you laid eyes on me, but I am actually here to help."

"Help with what?"

"Whatever I can."

"Anything?" She mimicked my tone from earlier and raised an eyebrow.

I replicated hers in return, smoldering and husky and telling the God's honest truth for once. "Anything."

She looked me over again, nodding to some thought or decision she'd made. "You're going to face some pretty stiff competition."

"From?"

"The main players at the Welles Corporation are a tight-knit bunch, to say the least. Besides me, you have Elijah, Cole, and Jake running different parts of the company. And believe me, they are *not* going to be happy to hear he's bringing in an outsider."

I gave an exaggerated exhale, laying both hands flat on the countertop as I pushed off the stool. "Guess I'll have to win them over with my sparkling personality."

She snorted an unimpressed laugh. "Yeah, too bad you don't have one."

CHAPTER 8

*S*ettling into Leander's house was one of the easiest transitions I'd made in my life. Being able to adapt to any surrounding or circumstance was all thanks to my advanced sense of self-preservation. I'd been working on it from the age of ten onward, perfecting the art of not getting attached to people or places. Thus far, it worked marvelously. It made traveling — and moving — an absolute breeze.

The only problem with my usual M.O. was Leander himself. Physical perfection aside, it was safe to say it didn't take long before I grew attached to *him*. His dark intelligence, his predatory grace, how his eyes lit up whenever we were deep in conversation. It all fed into a peculiar sense of knowing him, yet constantly being in awe. The strange protectiveness I felt in Giovanni's warehouse intensified as the days passed.

It was during one of our many midnight conversations over flickering candlelight and drinks — wine for him, bourbon for me, except for when we plied the other with our preferred alcohol — that I first got the feeling something else was afoot. For reasons I couldn't entirely articulate, I found myself drawn to him in a way I'd never been with anyone else.

It wasn't any one thing in particular. It wasn't anything he said, or did. It was a feeling that struck me in the way the light illuminated his face, the way his quiet laugh filled the darkness, despite his efforts to contain it. It only drove me to amuse him more, just so I could hear it, or the half-hearted requests for me to stop my antics.

Meanwhile, my absence in Chicago had not gone unnoticed. Varying members of the Marchese outfit called or texted. I declined the calls and gave vague texts in return. Apparently Giovanni had a new deal he was working on and wanted my opinion, despite the fact I told him I was unavailable. The last voicemail from Tony was a thinly-veiled threat, dressed up a little nicer.

"Don't forget about us, Bennett. You're family and you know we don't turn our back on family..."

Message received, Tony. However, I took issue with the fact he thought I was weak enough to come scurrying back that easily. The Marcheses were *not* my family. I owed them nothing, something I more or less texted Tony after half a bottle of bourbon one night.

"Should you be so antagonistic with them?" Leander asked, leaning against my shoulder, watching me tap out my rankled reply.

"Are you worried?" I bit my lower lip, hitting SEND in the process. When Leander didn't answer, I dropped my head back against the couch and let it loll in his direction.

"Haven't you learned by now? Worrying is my specialty." His face was surprisingly close, his eyes glassy in the dim light.

"I hear sex helps." My internal filter slammed shut a second too late. But since it was out there, all I could do was hold my breath and see what his reaction would be.

The quiet laugh I so loved escaped him as he stood, crossing the parlor to the dry bar and refilling his wine glass. "Easy for you to say. You don't have this... cloud, hanging over you."

"Cloud?"

He returned to the couch, dropping into the corner and angling himself toward me. The position may have been better for conversation, but the physical separation meant the left side of my body was colder without him sitting so close. "The Welles curse." He snorted into his wine as he took a sip.

I swiveled where I sat, settling into the opposite corner so I could see him without craning my neck. "Tell me about your family."

"You don't want to hear all that."

"I do." At any rate, it couldn't have been worse than the bloody history of my own ancestors.

A sad smile pulled the corner of his mouth. "Once upon a time, an entrepreneurial man moved to the muddy nothingness on the edge of the Montbrun River. He set up shop as a trader and each generation thereafter expanded the family holdings with corruption and bloodshed. Practically everyone with the Welles name dies violently, by murder or suicide or sheer tragedy, but they look beautiful while it happens so somehow it's less horrific. And that about sums it up." He toasted me with his glass and took a sip.

"Sounds like my family. I guess Easton isn't all that different than Chicago."

"You're descended from murders and madmen?"

I cracked a smile, swirling the bourbon in my glass.

"Aren't all rich men? The Bancrofts in particular knew their way around labor laws and federal regulations. If things didn't go their way? Well, bodies tended to disappear in the stockyards."

"You certainly don't make any excuses for them." He raked his hand through his hair, stopping halfway through so he could prop his elbow on the back of the couch and hold his head.

"Nope. I also don't pretend *my* hands are clean. I own every nefarious deed I've ever done." It was my turn to toast him, polishing off the rest of my drink.

"You don't just own it. You appear to relish in it." He smirked at me.

"There's freedom in not giving a shit about social mores."

"Do you give a shit about anything other than money?"

"Oh yeah. Totally. Me." I gave him a wicked grin. "And now you."

"Because I can make you more money?"

I pressed a hand to my chest, wincing. "Do you think so lowly of me?"

He laughed, shaking his head. "I don't know what to think about you. You come out of nowhere with this preposterous offer and yet I couldn't help but be persuaded."

"You sound conflicted about that." I watched his pensive expression morph to one of sadness.

"I'm conflicted about everything." With that, he drained the rest of his wine.

————

THE NEXT MORNING, I somehow managed to beat Leander downstairs. He wasn't an early-bird by any means, but his chronic insomnia was evident from Day One.

Instead of waiting for him to make one of his amazing,

gourmet breakfasts, I decided I would cook for him for a change, despite what Olivia said. Given his tastes, I opted for a classic with a twist — croque monsieurs with soft-boiled eggs.

Stacking the ham and cheese sandwiches, I snagged one of the large knives from the wooden block and cut them into strips. Assembling them in a fan around the silver egg cup, I dusted off my hands and returned to the stove for the eggs.

Leander appeared in the kitchen from the narrow stairway that ran along the back of the house, knotting his tie as we went. "Good morning." The question mark on the end of his greeting was as clear as day. I was sure he was searching for some sort of angle, but I was more curious about the fact he was in a suit, when all the other days he'd merely worn sweaters and trousers — all black, of course.

"Coffee?"

"Absolutely." He stopped on the other side of the island, surveying the kitchen. "You cook?"

I laughed, carefully dropping a soft-boiled egg into the cup and pushing the plate toward him. "Not really. I only do a few things, but those things I tend to do well. Bon appetit."

Sliding onto one of the stools at the island, he eyed the egg for a moment. Hesitantly picking up the delicate spoon, he started cracking the shell with quiet little taps.

To complete the Francophile breakfast, I fetched the French press from the other counter and poured us both a cup of coffee. I busied myself assembling a second plate, giving him space to decide if he was going to eat. Cracking the top of the shell off, I dunked a piece of the sandwich into the soft-boiled goo and took a bite.

"Not something you typically see for an American break-fast," he observed, scraping the inside of the egg with his spoon.

"I developed the habit while I was in France." I remained

standing, but leaned forward, propping my elbows on the counter. Taking a sip of my coffee, I tried not to be obvious about watching him, waiting for some sort of reaction.

"Were you there long?"

"A year." Of hell. But that wasn't the question.

He nodded, finally taking a bite of the sandwich. "Well, it paid off."

Chuckling, I took another bite of my own breakfast, pleased he wasn't put off by the food. After all, it was the least I could do since I'd been loafing at his house for the past week while we "worked remotely" aka: read over a few contracts, discussed a few business strategies, and then spent the rest of the time doing anything *but* work.

"What is that? I keep seeing it." He furrowed his brows at me.

"What?" Glancing down at myself, I hoped I didn't spill egg yolk all over the place. Instead, I spied the flash of silver on my chest where my teal shirt wasn't buttoned. "Oh. That. That is my memento mori."

His brows lifted slightly, but he didn't press for more. For some reason, his respectful silence compelled me to explain further.

Circling around the island, I fished it out so he could see it better. The pendant was silver and black, a melted and misshapen lira I fashioned into a necklace so I'd never forget. As if I could. The day was burned into my mind — literally.

Leander turned the coin over carefully, studying it from different angles, his brows still drawn. "What happened?"

"I died." I forced myself to smile, trying not to be too bitter about my stupidity all those years ago. I mean, what were the odds? Actually, one in five-hundred thousand. I knew that now.

Looking up with a blink, Leander searched my face to see

if I was joking. When he realized I wasn't, his lips parted and he lowered his hand slowly. The coin swung back against my skin like a pendulum.

Clearing my throat, I retreated quietly. Once again, I felt compelled to answer him in the wake of his silence. "A storm came out of nowhere. I was caught in the middle of it. And I was, um, struck by lightning."

His eyes widened, but still, he said nothing.

"This was one of the coins that was in my pocket," I continued. "The others were clumped together, but this one made it."

Swallowing visibly, he turned his attention to his coffee.

"So yeah. I was dead, technically, for three whole minutes." I scooped the carton of eggs off the counter and shoved them back in the fridge. Why the hell couldn't I stop talking? He didn't need to know any of this. No one did, which is why I didn't tell anyone. Ever. People tended to look at you differently once they knew. It was right up there with the whole sexuality thing. At this point in life, *I* didn't give a shit, but apparently other people did and they sure liked to let me know about it.

At last, Leander spoke, though his voice had gone quiet. "How old were you?"

"Fourteen."

He nodded, apparently processing the bizarre information while picking the crust off of his sandwich.

"I think I can count on one hand the number of people who know that about me." I shook my head, hoping it would clear the cobwebs.

Leander dunked his crust-free sandwich in the yolk, his lips pursed. "What do you usually tell people?"

I sipped my coffee, taking a moment to rack my memory. The answer was surprising. "No one's ever asked. I guess they assume it's part and parcel of my eccentricity. The rings, the bracelet. The necklace just fits."

"It's interesting... You present yourself as an open book, but you're not," he commented before taking another bite of egg.

"Maybe." A half-smile lifted the side of my face. "You, on the other hand, read like some ancient text in a language few people speak."

"No one speaks it, I'm afraid."

"No one?" I raised my brows at him.

He shook his head, his dark curls falling in his eyes.

"I suppose it's not that surprising," I said, giving him a considering look.

"Why is that?"

"I think it's safe to say you are unparalleled, Leander Welles. The person who finally deciphers you will have to be... I don't even know. Extraordinary?"

He smirked, ducking his head and picking at a melted lump of gruyere. "If you keep talking like that, you're going to fill my head."

"Are you not used to compliments?" He should be. Between his looks and his money, I was surprised he didn't have a harem of women at his feet. Yet, every time I mentioned something the least bit flattering, he demurred or ignored it outright.

He shook his head again. "Not in the slightest. People here are..."

"Judgmental?"

"Reticent."

"Same thing." I sipped my coffee with a smirk.

"I have a feeling you're going to get me into even more trouble than I could manage for myself." He popped the gruyere in his mouth, biting off the bit that stuck to his thumb. It was the first time in my life I was officially envious of a cheese.

"But it'll be fun." I gave him a devilish grin, trying to ignore the stupid tingling in my stomach.

CHAPTER 9

"This is the sixth house we've seen," Olivia said, practically stamping her foot when she crossed her arms. The ring of keys jangled on her wrist, echoing her irritation.

I wandered around the empty living room, nose wrinkled. "It smells."

"You said the last one smelled."

"The last one *did* smell. Like the river."

"It's a river town, genius! It's going to smell. Just like the property on the edge of town is going to smell like manure because of the hog farm down the road."

I moved to the window and looked out into the pitiful backyard. It almost lined up perfectly with the house behind it, meaning zero privacy for either household. "This won't do."

Growling, she stomped outside. I hurried after her, sliding into the passenger seat of her car before she could speed off and leave me.

"Maybe if you told me what you wanted, this whole process would go a lot quicker." She pulled the car out onto the street and sped up the hill, past modern houses to the historic section of town.

"But then we wouldn't have the opportunity to spend so much time together." I clamped a hand on her shoulder and shook her playfully.

She shot me a glare, shrugging off my hand. "You're incredible, you know that?"

"I know."

"It wasn't a compliment."

"You don't mince words, do you?" I still wasn't offended, if that was her intention.

She was less than pleased when Leander asked her to show me rental properties (at my insistence) and even less happier it was taking all day. Not that I didn't adore his house, or his company, but the whole roommate situation was bound to get old for both of us at some point. Before we trashed our partnership over petty bickering, it was time I found my own place.

"I'm sure that's hard for your little pea-brain to understand, but no. And if you're going to work with Leander, you better get used to it."

"I don't think there's been a single instance where he's been as mean to me as you have, completely unprovoked, I might add."

She ignored me and kept going. "He is, without a doubt, the most intelligent person I've ever met. He doesn't tolerate people trying to manipulate him. He values honesty above everything, even if it's bad. If he finds out you lied to him. Well... let's just say it's not pretty."

"Are you worried about me?" I clasped my hands over my heart.

"No. I don't want to see him get hurt." She gave me another side-eye as she turned the corner, her lip curled. "And you reek of trouble."

"Funny, Leander said something similar over breakfast the other day." I extended my arm out the window, letting the wind rush under my hand. The autumn sunlight caught the emerald in one of my rings, glittering and full of secrets.

Her grip tightened on the steering wheel, the leather creaking softly. "Good. Maybe he's starting to see how annoying you are. Here's hoping you'll be gone by Christmas."

Snickering, I made a vow right then and there I'd win her over one day. I didn't know how long it was going to take, nor did I care. It was my new mission. Make Olivia smile — actually smile — or die trying.

"I think you're the first person I've met who truly despises me," I mused out loud.

"I doubt that."

"Fine, the first person I haven't actually given a reason to despise me."

"Really? I can think of about $23,000 reasons to despise you."

"It's not your money. Why do you care?"

She shook her head, her glossy lips forming a thin line. "Must be nice to grow up with so much money its value has no meaning to you anymore."

"Oh, it has value to me. Make no mistake about that." I ignored her disbelieving snort and turned my attention out the window again, watching the historic houses rolling by. "So tell me about Easton."

"What's to tell? It's small and backward and chock full of tourists depending on the season."

"Well, there must be some appeal if you and Leander are still here."

"Us being here has nothing to do with the town itself. It has everything to do with giving the townsfolk a giant middle finger."

"Trouble with the locals?"

"If you're expecting a warm welcome, forget it. This isn't Mayberry. These people are going to hate you even more than they hate us."

"Us?"

"Leander, me — the Welles Corporation in general."

"Why?"

"You're not from here. They don't take kindly to outsiders. Plus you look like that." She gestured at me, her nose wrinkling.

I glanced down at the outfit in question. Compared to some things in my closet, a mustard yellow button-up with black pants and brown leather suspenders was hardly shocking. Raking a hand through my hair, I redirected the majority of it off to one side, out of my eyes, so I could look at her.

"Anyone openly associating with Leander is automatically hated," she said blithely. "Some are openly aggressive about it, others are just scared shitless. But they all hate him. They hate what he's capable of."

"What is he capable of?"

"Going scorched earth on this fucking town and dancing in the flames." The image was provocative in more ways than one. The quiet anger I'd seen in Chicago was just the tip of the iceberg, if Olivia was to be believed, and from what I gathered of her personality, she was.

"How can one man generate so much contempt?"

"You don't know the history here..."

"That's why I'm asking. What sort of history?"

"Despite the money, he hasn't led the charmed life you obviously have."

"See, there's that unnecessary bitchiness again... You realize I had *zero* say about how I grew up, right?"

"Are you going to finish growing up at some point?"

"Ooo. Burn." I rolled my eyes, flicking through my phone

and replying to a few missed texts from Gavin and Del. Del in particular was not happy with the four-hour move south, despite my reassurance it was for greener pastures.

Leaning next to Olivia, I tipped my head against her shoulder and took a selfie. I sent it off to Del before she tried to chuck my phone out the window.

"What are you doing?" Olivia asked, trying to steal a glance at my phone. "What was that?"

"Showing off what a gorgeous creature you are. Angry, but gorgeous."

She groaned and pulled into the driveway of a dark teal cottage with ornate white trim. "This is the last house I'm showing you. If you don't like it, you're shit out of luck."

"Way to sell it."

Surprisingly, the house was renovated on the inside. It was small, but that wasn't my primary concern. I surveilled the outside from each room, checking for exit routes and vulnerable spots. Years of working with sketchy clients left a mark, even if there was virtually no way anyone could track me to Easton.

I was in the midst of touring the master suite when Olivia circled back to our previous conversation.

"They say he murdered his grandmother," she announced from the hallway, as if it was any old topic.

My hand fell away from the curtain and I pivoted slowly. She was leaning against the doorframe, her arms crossed.

That was... interesting. I knew he'd orchestrated someone's death before, either personally or by decree. It was a feeling I had the first time I met him, the way he spoke, the way his eyes flickered in recognition. I never imagined it was his grandmother. If that part was true, I admired his ruthlessness. Murdering family took a special kind of hatred.

"How did she die?" I asked.

"She had her face caved in with a crowbar." There wasn't an ounce of remorse in her voice.

I raised my brows appreciatively. Now *that* was truly unexpected. Leander said people in his family died violently — looking back it was a bit of an understatement. For someone so cultured, using a crowbar to bludgeon an old woman to death was a curious choice. I expected a more refined means of killing. There had to be more to the story.

"Did she deserve it?"

Olivia gave me another side-eye. "That doesn't bother you? That you're working with an alleged murderer?"

"Apparently you forgot my Chicago clientele. If I quit working with people based purely on morals, I'd be out of a job."

"Oh, poor you," she cooed as I retraced my steps to the door. She grabbed my chin and squeezed, her tone a step above baby talk. "I'm sure you'd find a way to make money with that pretty face of yours."

"I am more than my good looks, thank you very much."

She let go of me with a shove. "Arrogant, aren't we?"

"It's called confidence, Kitten."

"Ugh. You have an answer for everything, don't you? And don't call me that!"

"If we're going to have a relationship, *Kitten*," I said with all seriousness, taking her hands in mine and holding her menacing glare. "You're going to have to retract the claws at some point."

"There's a lot of things I'm going to do in this life, Benny Boo," she murmured as she moved closer, dragging her black nails up my arms, over my chest, and around to the back of my neck. Pulling me down toward her mouth, she turned at the last second, her breath hot against my ear. "But being in any sort of relationship with you is *not* one of them."

Spinning away with a laugh, she sauntered down the hallway, a self-satisfied swing to her hips.

"Never say never," I called after her before catching myself against the doorframe with a slow exhale. Damn, girl. That was *not* nice.

———

"How was house hunting?" Leander asked as he meandered through the conservatory, watering plants as he went.

Shrugging, I followed along on the opposite side of the table. "Exhausting."

"Did you find something?"

I stopped in front of a familiar plant, cocking my head at it and answering distractedly. "I went with the teal gingerbread house over on Hyacinth."

"That's across the river." The watering can stilled for a moment.

Snapping back to the present, I looked up, my brows furrowed. "Is that a problem?"

He shook his head, moving on to another plant so quickly I wondered if I read his reaction correctly.

"This one is interesting." I ran my finger along the edge of a velvety purple petal. "Planning on poisoning someone?"

Leander chuckled. "If the occasion calls for it."

Considering him from across the table, I assessed the perfect planes of his face, trying to decide how best to approach the topic that had been rolling around in my head since Olivia told me about his grandmother.

Well, no time like the present. "Has it?"

He paused again, his eyes locked on the hot pink azalea in front of him. I could practically see the wheels turning, his analytical mind filtering through a thousand scenarios in the blink of an eye. When he lifted his gaze to mine, I had my answer before he opened his mouth. "Not yet."

Nodding, I circled around the end of the table, joining him on his side. "There's an art to it, you know. Some say the Italians perfected it, starting in ancient Rome."

Leander held his ground when I came nearer, despite the closeness. The air was thick and warm in the late autumn sun, magnified a dozen times over by the glass walls surrounding us. "You find murder to be artful?"

"You don't?" I raised an eyebrow, a whisper of a smile curving my lips.

A muscle along the sharp angle of his jaw clenched briefly. "I suppose I haven't given it much thought."

I wasn't the least bit convinced. "From what I know of you, you give *everything* thought."

Leander sidestepped, literally and figuratively, watering another plant in silence.

"Is it true?" I asked, moving behind him like a shadow.

"Is what true?"

"Did you murder your grandmother?"

Leander set the watering can down, his shoulders rising and falling with each measured breath. The seconds ticked by until he turned and faced me, his eyes dark and dangerous. In a way, it was more thrilling than Olivia's breathy teasing earlier. "Yes."

"But not with poison..."

"No."

"It's cleaner than a crowbar." My bicep brushed his as I moved past him, picking up the watering can. Resuming his duties at a relaxed pace, I carried on down the line of plants.

He spun slowly, trailing after me. "It sounds like something you know quite a lot about."

"Are we still pretending we don't know what the other

has done?" I shook my hair out of my eyes to cast a glance over my shoulder.

The lines of his body were perfectly straight, his chin tipped up a fraction of an inch.

The corner of my mouth lifted in a small smile. I appreciated the fact he wasn't going to give up his secrets without a fight, but it was unnecessary at this point. "Life's short. Sometimes it's the best way to remove an obstacle."

"For your clients, or yourself?"

Pausing, I turned and leaned closer to him, my voice dropping conspiratorially. "Both."

A thrill shot straight through me when his eyes met mine, looking positively sinful. He smelled amazing, something dark and woody, with a touch of floral to keep it clean. He and Olivia were wreaking havoc on what little self-control I had.

Forcing myself away from him before I got into trouble, I strolled down the aisle. When I reached the end, I set the watering can on the table and surveyed the variety of greenery. "You need an orchid."

"An orchid?" The confusion in his voice was apparent, but I didn't dare turn around until my body settled down.

"Yeah. An orchid." I glanced up at the glass roof and walked to the other side of the room, judging the sun's trajectory before gesturing to an appropriate space in the back corner. "This spot would be perfect. Plenty of indirect sun, but plenty of darkness. Orchids need to rest at night."

"Is that so?" His voice was laced with amusement. Shifting his attention back to the plants, he picked up a pair of pruning shears, clipping them now and again.

"It is. We'll find you something perfect at the orchid show next year."

"Orchid show?"

"In St. Louis. Or Chicago. Whichever. Oh, we should go

to Singapore. Or Copenhagen! Why stay in-country when you can go international?"

The doorbell rang before Leander could respond to my orchid-show idea. "That's the kitchen door," he said.

He took a step forward, but I held up a hand. At the moment, it wouldn't hurt to get a little extra distance from him. "I got it. Finish your pruning."

Navigating the labyrinthine hallways, I wound my way across the ground floor to the kitchen. Through the glass, I glimpsed our unexpected caller on the back porch. It was a young, clean-shaven man with a country-boy charm, save for the fact he was *pissed*.

"Who are you?" he asked in lieu of an introduction, his brows slanted sharply. "And why the fuck is the door locked?"

Well, then. I braced my forearm against the doorframe and leaned into it casually. "And a fabulous afternoon to you too, whoever you are."

"Is Leander here?"

"That depends..." I'd been warned how unfriendly Eastonians were, but experiencing it was something else. And they said Chicagoans had an attitude. "What do you need?"

"I *need* to talk to Leander," he sneered back at me.

"About?" Since we weren't going to be friends anytime soon, I pushed off the doorframe, folding my arms over my chest. It may have been impudent, but I wasn't about to let my newfound partner get his head taken off by this guy, especially since I had no idea what he was so pissed about.

"Oh my God. Are you serious right now? Who the fuck do you think you are?" He took a step forward, throwing his broad shoulder into me.

I rolled with the momentum and spun, coming up behind him. Grabbing his wrist, I shoved his arm upward behind his back, slamming his face into the door.

"Get the fuck off of me!" He thrashed, trying to rip his arm free from the wrist-lock.

"Yeah, that's not happening, kid."

It didn't stop his struggling. "Leander! Get the fuck out here!"

Leander appeared a moment later, looking less than pleased, but I wasn't quite sure with whom. "Jake! What are you doing here? Bennett, let him go for Christ's sake."

I held on a second longer, proving a point, before letting the kid go. Retreating a step back into the kitchen, I assumed a casual lean against the wall at Leander's elbow, spinning the large ring on my index finger idly. Since Leander's scowl was fixed solely on Jake, I felt safe in assuming the irritation was meant for him alone.

"Who the fuck is this?" Jake demanded, flinging a hand toward me. "Why is he giving me the run around? And why the fuck is the door locked?"

"Jake Murray, may I present Bennett Reeve," Leander replied in a clipped tone, gesturing between us. "My new in-house counsel. And apparently my new security guard. The door must have been his doing."

It certainly was, and for good reason. I winked at Leander before giving my new friend Jake a languid smile. He glared daggers at me in return.

"Another lawyer?" Jake spat. "Why do you need another lawyer?"

"That's not really any of your concern," Leander replied sharply. "Is there a reason you're here and not, oh, I don't know... at work?"

"I'm here *because* of work. You're letting Cole oversee the church renovation?"

Leander's face was completely blank, but the muscle in his throat twitched. Whoever Jake was, I had a feeling he was in for an ass-chewing if he kept it up. "What of it?"

"It was my idea to get involved with that project."

"Do you want a pat on the head?" Leander arched an eyebrow at him incredulously. "You secured the lead. Congratulations. Cole is more apt to deal with the construction. If you'd like to learn from him, be my guest. But I'm not losing hundreds of thousands of dollars on inexperience." Leander folded his arms over his chest, as if daring him to keep complaining.

Jake's jaw clenched. He glanced between Leander and I, withholding a rebuttal with what looked like a great amount of effort.

Leander's posture softened, somewhat. "I appreciate your passion for the project, but the decision is final."

"This is bullshit." Jake shook his head and stormed back down the porch steps.

"Nice meeting you!" I called after him.

Leander snorted and closed the door. "Sorry about that. He's..."

"Young?"

"Headstrong."

"Weren't we all at that age?" I sighed. Once I crested thirty, each passing year felt like a century. I dreaded the idea of forty.

"What was all that about, anyway?" Leander glanced at the door again, amusement crinkling the corners of his eyes.

I shrugged, unfolding myself from the wall. "I didn't know who he was when he tried storming the castle."

"And you thought you'd defend it?"

"Defend *you*, yes."

"You are quite the peculiarity." He paused, giving me a long look with an expression I couldn't quite decipher. "I can't wait to see what the future has in store for us."

CHAPTER 10

The morning after my less-than-golden encounter with Jake, Leander announced it was time to introduce me to the rest of the staff so no further dust-ups occurred. After breakfast, he drove us to the office, parking in front of a narrow, two-story building along the river. Flanked by a coffee shop and a clothing store, it was completely unremarkable from the outside.

Like all river towns, this section of Easton was obviously the oldest, evidenced by the architecture and the fact 1857 was carved into most of the stone buildings. You'd never know it housed the headquarters of a multi-million dollar company.

The moment we walked in, a perky brunette jumped out of her seat and darted toward Leander with outstretched arms. "Good morning Mr. Welles!"

"Good morning, Madison." He gave her a polite smile and sidestepped her, gesturing to me quickly like a sacrificial lamb. "This is Bennett, our new corporate attorney."

"A pleasure," I said, kissing her hand with a gentlemanly

bow. If flirting with a cute receptionist was one burden I could alleviate for Leander, I'd gladly do so.

Blushing, her smile grew even brighter. "So nice to meet you."

Leander laid a hand on my shoulder and tossed his head toward the hallway. "This way."

I let go of Madison's fingers slowly in tandem with Leander's grip tightening. "She seems nice," I said when Leander forcibly steered me away and down the hall.

He chuckled, dropping his hand once Madison was safely behind us. "She's a hugger — consider yourself warned."

"Why, Leander Welles!" I threw my arm around his shoulders, crushing him against my side. "Are you telling me you're not?"

He tensed under my arm, but didn't shrug it off. "Not particularly, no."

"We're going to have to remedy that." I squeezed him tighter, looping my other arm across his chest so I could nuzzle his cheek. God, why did I do this to myself?

All forward movement immediately stopped. He turned into a statue, shrinking into himself like a turtle and scrunching his face. "Ok, ok! You've made your point!"

Olivia intercepted us in the hallway with a wrinkled nose. "Does the concept of personal space mean nothing to you?"

I stayed where I was, holding Leander and breathing in the scent of his hair. No, Reeve! No wondering about what kind of shampoo he uses…

"I think she's talking to me," I said in a loud whisper, focusing my attention on Olivia's disapproving gaze.

Leander eased himself out of my arms and ran a hand down the front of his suit, also fixated on his assistant. "Olivia, can you have the others meet us in the conference room in fifteen minutes?"

She nodded, stepping past us and sauntering away on

another pair of stilettos. Gavin would love her, if they didn't battle each other to the death with their bitchiness.

Upstairs, Leander gestured to a closed door before stepping through. "You can set up in here."

I walked in after him, surveying the space. As far as offices went, it wasn't bad. Exposed brick and wooden beams, plenty of natural light, the kind of thing that easily went for half a million in Chicago. It was pre-furnished with a large desk and a wall full of built-in shelves. There was even a small fireplace, reminiscent of the building's origins.

"Perfect." I dropped my laptop bag on the desk and shoved my hands in my pockets. That was about all that was required for me "setting up" anywhere. "Where's your office?"

"This way." He continued down the hall. The next door was his, overlooking the river on the front side of the building. It was similar to mine, except his shelves were crammed with books and ledgers and his desk was covered in neat piles of folders and paperwork.

"Olivia and Cole are downstairs," he said, gesturing over the balcony, "along with the conference room and the kitchen. Elijah is down that way." He pointed across the open space to the other side of the building. "And Jake is back there."

"What was this place? Before?"

"The trading post I told you about, then the family's main shipping office. There was a smaller building on the Mississippi but it flooded a couple decades ago and they never rebuilt. We do maintain a private commercial dock, one of the remaining few. Otherwise, the barges fleet downriver in the lock and dam."

"Is that the majority of your revenue?"

"Yes, although lately we've been making gains in the real estate market."

I gave him the side-eye and nudged his elbow with mine. "Are you sure you're not branching out to form your own little mafia down here?"

He chuckled, scratching the back of his neck. "Quite. I only own one restaurant and zero dry cleaners."

"Don't forget the carwashes."

"None of those either."

"We'll have to remedy that, won't we?"

From our vantage point on the balcony, we watched the others file into the all-glass conference room. Once they were seated, we made our way downstairs. Olivia and Jake, I recognized. Leander's driver was also there, along with a totally unknown man. They were in the midst of a discussion that stopped abruptly when the door opened.

"You must be Bennett," the mystery man said, standing and extending a hand with a polite smile. "I'm Elijah."

I shook his hand, then turned to the driver. "So that makes you Cole."

He smiled as he stood, taking my hand. "That's right. Good to see you again."

"Now that we're acquainted," Leander pulled out a chair for me before assuming his place at the head of the table. I couldn't help but notice it was the chair to his immediate left. Glancing around the room, I wondered who had previously occupied it, or if I was the first.

"Let me explain Bennett's role," Leander continued, his gaze settling on Jake at the end of the table. When Jake looked away, Leander's attention carried on. "Bennett is a corporate attorney. *Our* corporate attorney. From now on, anything legal goes through him. All contracts, lease agreements, billing, lawsuits. Everything and anything that could land me in court. If he doesn't sign off on it, it's not approved. Understood?"

There was a collective nod around the table.

"If he asks for something, give it to him. If he tells you to do something, do it. He is well versed in *all*" — he glanced at me, the corner of his mouth ticked up in a roguish smile — "aspects of our business and I assure you his being here will only benefit us in the long run. Questions?"

Cole leaned forward. "Are you still working for Marchese?"

I shook my head. "Our arrangement was on an as-needed basis. From now on, I'm exclusively Leander's."

"Good. That guy was an ass." Cole leaned back, apparently satisfied. I had a feeling Cole and I were going to get along just fine.

"Do you know anything about accounting?" Elijah asked.

"As much as I need to. Why?"

"Our fiscal year is ending soon and one of the accountants says she has an issue with a source of income."

"What kind of an issue?"

Elijah shrugged. "She wouldn't say. She set up an appointment to talk to Leander next Thursday."

"Do you know what account she's talking about?"

"Yeah."

"Ok. Get me everything you have and I'll see if I can find whatever her issue is." I turned my attention to Leander. "How long have you known this woman?"

His brows dipped briefly. "She's a newer associate. Maybe two years?"

Perfect. Just... perfect. Young meant she still had morals and a sense of self-righteousness the world hadn't been beaten out of her. If there *was* a hiccup in the books, I hoped she was smart enough to look the other way.

"Is that a problem?" Elijah asked.

"I guess we'll find out," I replied with a smile.

TWENTY MINUTES LATER, I was still in the conference room, sorting through a year's worth of income and expense reports for a handful of businesses in town, along with banking information for over a dozen accounts at different banks.

I'd rather not work in a fishbowl, but with the amount of paperwork I had to get through, there wasn't much of an option. My desk, while spacious, would hardly be enough for the amount of room I needed.

Rolling up my sleeves, I dove into the financial history while the others milled around, either watching curiously or outright glaring as I worked. Elijah seemed most interested in the process, though he respectfully stayed out of my way. Olivia and Jake stood near Madison's desk, exchanging glances and clearly making comments. I may have been new, but it was easy to see the dynamics at work and how this hierarchy actually went. My arrival had inadvertently bumped a few people down the totem pole.

Cole popped in around noon, uninvited. "Hey man, you hungry?"

"No thanks." Eyes narrowed, I highlighted another trans-action, comparing receipts with deposits.

"Are you a workaholic too?"

"Oh, no. I have plenty of work-life balance." Somedays more life, than work, truth be told. Another streak of yellow, which meant another deposit slip that didn't correlate with sales.

"Cool. Come on, then."

Cole didn't look like he was taking "No" for an answer, so I relented and capped the highlighter.

Once we were seated at an Italian restaurant down the road, Cole launched into an easy conversation before getting to the heart of his curiosity.

"How did this whole thing come about, anyway?" he

asked. "I mean, one minute you're on the other side of the table and the next you're here?"

I drew lines in the condensation on the side of my water glass. "I saw an opportunity to make a change."

"Some change."

"You don't believe me?" I arched an eyebrow at him. What was I supposed to say? From the minute your boss and I dove into the finer workings of Machiavelli, I was drawn to him like a magnet? That our combined intellect would be enough to conquer anything in our path? Not to mention the fact he was hotter than sin.

"Trading Chicago for this shithole?" Cole gestured around with a grimace. "I mean, more power to you, man."

Ah... so that's what he meant. "I've never lived in a small town. I figured it would be an experiment of sorts."

"Hate to burst your bubble, but Easton blows. If it wasn't for Leander, we'd all probably have left by now."

"Olivia said something about sticking it to the people here?"

He chuckled. "Yeah. That's one way of putting it."

"So what's the story there? You're such an eclectic group, it's hard to imagine how you all came to be connected with Leander." I took a sip of my water, crunching on an ice cube.

"Eclectic? Is that a nice way of saying 'fucked up'?" Cole shot me an easy grin. "We each have our own story, I guess. Simple version is, Elijah's been friends with Leander forever, which is how I met him. Olivia used to work at the coffee shop next to the office. And Jake? Leander picked him up at the library like a flea and we haven't been able to shake him since."

"I don't think he likes me," I said with a smile. "Olivia either."

"Olivia doesn't like anyone, so don't take it personally.

And Jake? Jake is a pain in the ass. But he'd do anything for Leander. So, I guess he's ok."

"Would you do anything for him?"

"Hell yeah I would. We all would." He got quiet for a minute, staring at the salt shaker. "You're going to hear some shit about him around town, but those people don't know what they're talking about. They don't know him — they know Irene's version of him. His fucking grandmother has been dead for seven years and he still has to put up with her shit because of these people."

I sucked on another ice cube, pondering the loyalty Cole and the others exhibited. What had Leander done to win them all over, and so fiercely? I'd seen gangs made up of actual family members that weren't as devoted as this group seemed to be. Then again, I couldn't exactly claim objectivity since I was equally taken with him.

Cole stiffened beside me, a murderous look hardening his face. "Motherfucker."

I followed his line of sight to the front door, assessing the middle-aged man who walked in. The man sneered at Cole with equal contempt before following the hostess to the other side of the restaurant.

"Who's that?" I asked quietly.

"Keith Starkey." He spat each name like venom. "That's the asshole who got me sent to prison." Prison? That explained the crude tattoos peeking out beneath his shirt collar and cuffs.

I glanced across the way, sizing up the older man. Short hair combed just so, cell phone clipped to his belt, facing the door. "Is he a cop?"

"Was. He's retired now. The last I heard he up and moved to Arizona. So what the fuck is he doing here?"

Since it was rhetorical, I didn't bother answering. "You want to get our stuff to go?"

Cole thought about it for a minute before nodding, his teeth clenched. "Yeah. I've got another year left on parole. I wouldn't put it past that cocksucker to start something so I get sent back."

I flagged the waitress down, adding a radiant smile for good measure. "I'm so sorry," I said as she drew nearer. "Can we get it to go? Something at work came up and we need to run."

"Sure thing. I'll be right back." She disappeared into the kitchen, returning a moment later with a brown paper bag.

I dropped a hundred-dollar bill into the check presenter and handed it back to her. When she started to protest, I held up a hand. "I don't need any change. Thanks."

Shoving the bag of food into Cole's hands, I ushered him out the door before he actually went and did something stupid. It seemed I'd turned into a nanny after all, keeping my little ducklings out of trouble. Del would be laughing his ass off.

Back at the office, at the kitchen table, Cole looked up from his chicken parm sheepishly. "You're not going to ask?"

"Oh, yes. I'm sorry." I wiped my mouth with the napkin and gestured to the aluminum container, completely dead-pan. "How's your lunch?"

He snorted, a smile cracking his solemn expression. "Funny..."

"And no," I answered him with a half-smile. "I'm not going to ask. Believe it or not, I don't make a habit of prying."

"It's ok. Everyone else knows. So, you should probably hear the story too."

I twirled a strand of fettuccini around my plastic fork. "It's really not necessary. We all have a past. Some of us just haven't been caught yet."

"Really? Does your past involve murder?" Before I could answer, he plowed on with an exasperated huff. "Oh, wait.

Manslaughter. That's what they called it. Topped off with a side of aggravated battery with a weapon." He stabbed his chicken with a scowl.

"You'd be very surprised what my past consists of, young grasshopper."

"Oh yeah? Like what?"

Instead of telling him, I figured a demonstration was in order. Slipping my hand into the backside of my waistband, I pulled out the ice pick pierced through the fabric. Without warning, I drove it into the center of his chicken breast.

He jerked back, his eyes wide. "What the fuck?!"

I smiled cheerfully and took a bite out of my fettuccini.

————

"I FOUND YOUR PROBLEM," I said to Leander, breezing into his office after lunch. Tossing a stack of reports on his desk, I gestured to the notations I made next to the highlighted marks. "Or, I should say problems."

As he looked it over, his brows furrowed. His lips pressed into a thin line the more he read. "You think she found this?"

"It's the only thing she could have found. I've been over every scrap of paper Elijah had on file. This is it. This one business."

He flung the papers on his desk and rubbed his eyes. "Now what?"

"Have your meeting, as scheduled. Once you know for sure what she knows and what her next step is, you can respond accordingly."

"What do I say about the differences she found?"

"Easy..." I circled around his desk and leaned over, flipping through the pages until I found the deposit slip with the sloppy signature on it. I tapped it as I answered. "You say... Jason is at fault."

Leander glanced up at me. He almost seemed surprised I was so close, but he didn't recoil. I, on the other hand, forgot my entire train of thought until Leander's voice snapped me out of my reverie. "Blame him entirely?"

"Entirely." I smiled darkly and drifted away, settling on the edge of his desk in the hope he hadn't noticed my momentary distraction.

He leaned back in his chair, his long fingers drumming on the leather arms.

"He was supposed to deposit $500," I said, looking at him expectantly. "Right? Filter the dirty money through the bar and make the deposits at random in the different banks?"

He nodded, remaining mute.

"And it would have been fine. But — he's been increasing the deposits incrementally for months without factoring in the bar's actual revenue. Did you tell him to make more deposits?"

Leander's gaze narrowed. "Of course not."

I spread my hands, my point proven. "Not only has he disobeyed, he's also put your finances in the crosshairs. If an entry-level accountant can spot this, what do you think the IRS or the SEC will do?"

Leander exhaled and leaned forward, propping his elbows on his desk and raking his hands through his hair. "This is exactly the sort of thing I wanted to avoid."

"You still can."

"How?"

"Jason was operating without your knowledge or permission. You're a victim of theft, even fraud depending on what documents he used with the banks."

"So what options should I be looking at in terms of a resolution?"

"Option A, you let the accountant do what she's going to do and possibly face questions down the road. Risky but doable. Option B, turn him into the police — which I don't endorse, by the way. Or Option C, root out the problem."

He dropped his hands and looked at me, his face blank. "Just like that?"

"Just like that." I smiled brightly.

"What if the accountant continues to push, regardless of how much weeding I do?" He arched an eyebrow at me.

My hand swept over the pile of papers. "Remember, it's not what you know, it's what you can prove. Here's the proof Jason has been skimming from the bar without your knowledge and padding his own bank account."

Leander leaned back in his chair, glaring at the papers. His hand curled into a fist, inadvertently cracking his knuckles. "I'd say our meeting was rather fortuitous, wouldn't you?"

I tossed my head to the side and ran a hand through my hair, fluffing it dramatically. "If you're saying I'm something of a divine gift, then yes, I agree."

Shaking his head, he laughed quietly. "You're impossible."

CHAPTER 11

When I strolled into the kitchen at work, Leander was at the fridge, filling the water reservoir for the coffee pot. From the scowl on his face, I knew he was lost in some dark thought and I was pretty sure it centered on the upcoming meeting with the accountant.

Sidling up next to him, I opened the other fridge door. The water stopped dispensing while I grabbed a carton of oat milk. Once the door closed, the water resumed.

Two steps away, I spun, returning to the fridge and opening the door again. I shoved the carton back inside and nudged it shut.

I made it three steps away before I circled again, my hand outstretched for the handle.

"Don't even think about it," Leander said, his voice barely above an actual growl.

I took another step closer, fingers brushing against the stainless steel.

"Don't do it," he warned, enunciating each word. The reservoir was almost filled.

I yanked open the fridge door.

Abandoning the water, Leander lunged for me. He caught me in a headlock and tried to wrestle me downward. I wrapped my arms around his waist, pushing as much as he was pulling.

Olivia's stilettos were the first thing I heard, followed by her clearing her throat loudly. "Whenever you two are done playing grab ass, the accountant is here."

Standing up straight and shoving away from each other like two kids caught fighting on the playground, I smoothed my shirt and gave Leander a mock glare. "My God, Leander. We have a meeting to go to. Get it together."

He smacked the back of my head on his way by. Grabbing the reservoir again, he set it in the coffee machine and leaned against the counter, glaring at me with his arms crossed.

Strolling over to him, I leaned against the counter, mirroring his pose and intentionally pressing my arm against his. "What's going on?"

"Waiting for the coffee."

"...And?"

"And what?"

I bumped my shoulder against his. "You're giving yourself worry lines. You shouldn't mar that beautiful face of yours."

He smoothed his brow and turned his gaze to me, once again oblivious to the compliment. "What if this doesn't work?"

"It'll work."

"How can you be so sure?"

I unfolded my arms and took ahold of the back of his neck, gently bonking my forehead to his. "Because I'm that fucking good."

He rolled his eyes, fighting a smile. "Humility really isn't one of your strong suits."

"Nope." I straightened and adjusted his tie, centering the knot from where it had gone askew. "Now, let's go."

Once we were seated in the conference room, Madison served the coffee with a polite smile and left again. It was just the three of us — the accountant, Leander, and myself. Legally speaking, it was better that way.

Dana, the woman of the hour, was young, as I imagined, and full of self-righteousness from the get-go. Between her mousy brown hair and her plain face, there wasn't much to work with in terms of flattery. Even I, slut that I was, had standards.

"As you can see, Mr. Welles," Dana said, using her pen to point to a variety of line items on one of her many, many spreadsheets. "There's a discrepancy between your reported revenue and your expenditures. A pretty significant discrepancy, which is why I flagged your account."

"I'm sure there's an explanation," Leander said, his voice as soft as velvet.

She adjusted her glasses. "I'm sure. But as it stands, I have a legal obligation to report all suspicious activity."

Leaning forward, my hand drifted to Leander's knee, silencing his rebuttal while I interjected. "Did you already write your opinion?"

She looked at me, her face pinched. "No. I wanted to speak with Mr. Welles first. I don't think Mr. Westbrook was being forthcoming with me."

"Are you saying Elijah wasn't cooperating?" Leander asked.

"No, he was cooperating in technical terms. But I have a feeling he is hiding something."

Spinning the large, emerald ring on my forefinger, I nodded along as she spoke. "That is frustrating, I'm sure. Please, accept our apology on his behalf."

Leander leaned back in his chair just enough that I caught

him looking at me in my periphery. After staring at me, he pushed away from the table abruptly and stalked to the edge of the conference room. Hands on his hips, he stared out at the lobby with his back to us.

This woman would not budge. There'd be no convincing her it was all a mistake or a misunderstanding. That left one option.

Sliding forward to the edge of my chair, I refreshed my coffee before holding the silver pot up to our guest. "Would you care for some more?"

"Please." Dana pushed her cup toward me. The moment her gaze turned to the papers on the table, I flicked open the emerald ring's compartment, sprinkling its contents into the coffee as I poured. The white powder dissolved on contact, a magical concoction both odorless and tasteless.

"Sugar?" I clicked the jewel back into place and moved the sugar bowl closer.

She took a lump and dropped it in her coffee, stirring lazily.

Leander turned slowly, his head canted to one side. He glanced between Dana and I several times, but didn't say anything.

When I caught his eye, I gave him a wink before sipping my coffee. Setting it aside, I turned back to the accountant with a brighter countenance. "Was there anything else you wanted to discuss?"

———

THE MOMENT DANA stepped out the front door, Leander shoved the conference room door closed and whirled on me. "What was that? What did you just do?"

I held my hands up, palms open. "I'll admit, that may have been impulsive. But she left me no choice."

He stared at me with wide green eyes, his jaw slack.

"In my defense," I said, lowering my hands to his shoulders, "you hired me to protect your interests. I just protected your interests." If I needed to shake some sense into him, I would.

"By poisoning her?"

"Would you preferred I used a crowbar?"

Scowling, he pulled away from me, pacing back and forth along the glass wall.

"What did you want me to do?" I asked, depositing myself into the closest chair and kicking my feet up on the desk. "Let her walk out of here and sing like a canary to the SEC?"

His hand flew toward the front door, staring incredulously again. "She *did* walk out of here!"

Slipping my pocket watch out, I rocked my other hand in a so-so motion. "She won't make it back to her office. The hope is she crashes out on High Point Road and rolls down the cliff."

Leander let out a slow exhale, rubbing his eyes with his thumb and forefinger, murmuring to himself.

"Relax... They'll never know it was us." Ok, me. I should have said me. But he knew it was Option C, so it only seemed fitting to include him as a co-conspirator.

He dropped his hand from his eyes, arching an unamused eyebrow. "Your confidence is not reassuring right now."

"It should be. I've had plenty of practice."

He blinked, processing what I said before asking his follow-up question. "How much practice?"

"I don't know." I laughed, waving him off. "I don't keep track of those things. It's kind of like sex."

"How can you *not* know? How many have there been that you've lost count?"

I frowned at him for a minute. "Wait... Are we talking about dead people or notches on the old bed post?"

Dropping into the chair next to me, he covered his face with his hands and groaned. "I can't believe we're actually having this conversation."

"Would you prefer I lie?" I lowered my feet to the floor and leaned forward, pulling his hands apart so I could level a flat look at him.

"Of course not."

"That's what I thought."

His hands fell to his lap, mine along with them. I leaned back in my chair, kicking an ankle up across the opposite knee while he worked through whatever was in his head.

After a minute of studying me, he broke his silence. "How are you so casual about the whole thing?"

"You mean murder, right?"

His eyes drifted shut and he shook his head.

Chuckling, I went back to toying with my emerald ring. "I think we should talk about more important things... Like, what are we going to do about your little money leak?"

Shifting forward, he surprised me when he took hold of my right hand and lifted it for closer inspection. His attention was entirely on the large emerald, and mine was entirely on him.

"I think I have an idea," he said quietly. Both the look in his eye and the lilt to his voice made my heart stammer.

A dark smile spread across my face. "Do tell..."

CHAPTER 12

The bar in question was every bit the hole in the wall I imagined in a town like Easton. The variety of neon beer signs and scuffed pool tables reflected its age. I'm sure on the weekends it was a haven for the blue-collar folk and good ol' boys.

We entered in the afternoon, before opening, right after the delivery truck pulled away.

The bartender looked up from his invoice with a scowl. The look vanished, replaced with one of surprise. "Mr. Welles. I didn't know you were stopping by."

"That's because I didn't tell you." Leander glanced around the dimly lit room as he walked, assessing it with a critical eye.

"Uh, ok." The man looked at me next, giving me a confused once-over before Leander's voice pulled his attention away.

"Jason," Leander said quietly, clasping his hands behind his back. "We need to talk."

"Sure." Jason tossed the papers to the side and leaned against the bar. "What's up?"

"It's about your deposit schedule." Leander cut a glare at him from across the room.

I sidled up on a bar stool, pointing at a bottle of bourbon on the top shelf.

Jason's eyes narrowed, but he complied and handed me the bottle and a glass. "What's wrong with the deposits?"

"They're larger than what they should be." Leander's wandering brought him to the bar, his hands resting casually on the worn wood.

Swirling my drink, I gave Jason a pitying look before tossing it back.

"Mr. Welles, I—"

Leander sprung forward like a panther, a flash of sleek, black lines and utter precision. In the blink of an eye, he grabbed Jason by the back of the head and slammed him face-first into the bar top.

A rush of excitement coursed through my veins, hotter than the familiar burn from the bourbon. The unambiguous display of violence, the fact Leander wasn't afraid to carry out the punishment himself — it was like throwing gasoline on a fire.

"Fuck, man!" Jason yelled when he ricocheted back up, blood gushing between his fingers. "You broke my fucking nose!"

Leander's beautiful face darkened. "Get the books before I break something else."

Biting my lower lip, I made a mental note not to stand up anytime soon. Instead, I tried to distract myself by pouring another glass of bourbon. I slid it toward Leander before leaning over the bar, retrieving two more.

As soon as Jason turned his back and shuffled off, I slipped a small vial out of my pocket and tossed it to Leander.

He caught it deftly and shook a few drops into the third glass, pocketing the vial.

"Cheers," he said, tossing back the shot of bourbon.

"Salute."

Jason returned a moment later with a wad of paper towels on his nose and a stack of books. When he tried to hand them to Leander, I snapped and beckoned him my way with two fingers.

Taking the books with a smirk, I gestured to the drink. "You look like you could use one."

Jason's glare shot between the two of us, but he didn't argue. In one gulp, the drink was gone — poison and all.

The effect was immediate. He fell to the floor, twisting and groaning in a heap of denim and flannel. He alternated between clawing at his chest and holding his stomach. Foam bubbled up out of his mouth until he stopped moving with one final twitch.

Leander's attention turned to me, an unreadable expression on his face. "I didn't know you were going to kill him that quickly."

"Technically *you* killed him."

"I think you're splitting hairs." He peered over the bar, the odd look melting to one of curiosity. "Why not use something slower, like last time?"

"I never use the same thing twice in a row. Keeps the coroners guessing, if they even bother with toxicology."

Leander nodded. "Makes sense."

Pouring another two shots, I clinked my tumbler against his. "Congratulations."

"For?"

"Your first clean kill."

"It's so different." He swirled the liquid in his glass, his brow furrowed. "Less... intimate."

"You didn't tell me you wanted intimacy. You told me you wanted him dead." I gestured to the body. "I gave you dead."

"I didn't know I had a choice."

"Next time I'll be more explicit with your options."

"Next time?" He shot me a look, somewhere between exasperation and disbelief.

"*If* there's a next time," I conceded. There was definitely going to be a next time. It was kind of like chips — you couldn't have just one.

"I'll admit, I'm not a fan of poison."

"Why is that?"

"Because I've been on the receiving end." His gaze darted to mine, almost hesitantly.

"Dare I ask?"

"All a part of growing up with the most vile person to ever grace this planet." He looked down at his glass, spinning it in slow circles on the bar top. "I didn't exactly have an easy childhood."

"I know," I said quietly. When he looked up sharply, I gave him a small smile. I wasn't going to ask. I didn't need to. I'd heard enough and seen enough to draw my own conclusions about the kind of environment he grew up in.

He shook his head, scratching idly at a groove in the old wood. "I suppose you're going to tell me you had your own trials and tribulations?"

"No." His suspicious glance was met with a broad smile. "My childhood was great. Lived in the lap of luxury. World-class education. Travel. Except for my dad getting killed, it was golden."

"What happened?"

"He was collateral damage in a mob hit." I waved off the sympathetic look on his face. "Don't worry. Camille did the completely rational thing and packed us up the week after the funeral and moved to Europe."

"Camille?"

"My mother." Ugh, even saying it made my stomach sour.

"I take it you didn't like living in Europe?"

"An American kid growing up alone in foreign countries? What wasn't to like?" I poured another splash of bourbon and drained it immediately.

He furrowed his brow. "You never told me why you... *do* what you do."

"Because I can?" I met his gaze directly so there was no doubt I meant it. He didn't blink. In fact, his green eyes had the same sparkle as the first time I met him, when we discussed Machiavelli. "Does the lion apologize to its prey? No. Neither will I. Neither should you."

He gave me a slow, impish smile before tossing his head toward the corpse. "What do we do with him?"

I considered the position of the body, assessing it from an investigator's standpoint. "Leave him. Looks like a heart attack to me. Or a seizure of some sort."

Nodding, Leander's gaze dropped, landing on the glass in his hands. "Bennett... I need your help with something. Something deeply personal and not at all related to work."

"Anything." I swiveled on the stool to face him, inadvertently bumping my knee against his. He didn't seem to care, if he even noticed.

"I need to plan another murder. Actually, a couple..." His pale eyes flicked up to mine. I swore he saw straight through to my soul, watching the dark delight unfurl within.

"Your wish is my command."

A deviant smile crept across his lips. "I feel I should warn you... it's going to be bloody."

CHAPTER 13

"*W*hat time is that meeting today?" I asked Gavin as he walked into the conference room, carting a stack of color-coded files.

After bitching at me for nearly a year that I *must* be embarrassed by him since I "refused" to introduce him to the people in Easton, Gavin finally made his grand appearance at the Welles Corporation, lime-green pants and all.

As predicted, he and Olivia embraced one another's cattiness immediately, giving poor Madison that side-eyed, lips-pursed look of disapproval when she tried to join their conversation. Cole's welcoming slap on the back nearly sent Gavin sprawling and Jake, like a sulking teenager, refused to leave his office. The only two missing were Leander and Elijah.

"At one. They're coming here." He dropped the files in front of me and leaned against the table, staring out at the lobby with a bored expression.

"Who, again?"

"It's in your calendar."

"I didn't look."

"Oh my God..."

"You can go back to Chicago anytime now."

"Trust me, after I hit that wine and cheese shop tomorrow I'm out."

"Too quiet for your liking?"

He rolled his eyes. "It reminds me of the hick town I grew up in. Are you ok? Like, has anyone started shit with you down here?"

Giving him a small smile, I patted his forearm. "I'm good. Don't worry."

"That's true. You have an easier time passing as straight, even with your style."

"For the sake of avoiding a lawsuit, I'm going to ignore that comment." Shaking my head, I went back to reading through the Bancroft statements.

"Stop being sensitive. I love the way you dress."

I shot him a dirty look. That was not what either one of us were talking about and he damn well knew it.

"You know I'm just—Oh.My.God..."

Closing the file, I exhaled a steadying breath. I knew without turning Leander had walked into the building, fully visible from where we were. Besides the exclamation and the little squeak, Gavin's jaw nearly hit the floor. The only other person who could have garnered that sort of reaction would have been Cole strutting around half-naked. Since he left to oversee a renovation twenty minutes away, I put my stupidly expensive education to work to did a little deductive reasoning.

"Could you please stop eye-fucking the CEO?" I murmured, pulling another folder forward and signing off on the papers inside.

"I can't believe you've been hiding him from me!"

"I haven't been hiding him. He's been right here in Easton."

Gavin wasn't even listening — he was still too busy drooling. "I asked you if he was as hot as he sounded on the phone. Remember that? He is on fire!"

I looked up blankly, refraining from comment. I didn't trust myself to say anything without Gavin reading into it.

"Aren't you glad I gave him your number?" Gavin gave me a smug smile.

"Thrilled. Do you want a raise now?"

"It's not like I'd turn it down. The city is getting so expensive. I might have to move to the suburbs."

I gasped in faux horror. The look faded to a smirk, disappearing altogether when Leander approached. As far as I knew, this was the first encounter he'd ever had with an openly gay man, and a flamboyant one at that. To say I was curious about his reaction was a bit of an understatement.

Leander stuck his head in the doorway, blinking when he saw Gavin. Given his aversion to anything colorful, I'm sure it was the navy and lime-green ensemble that had him reeling internally. I mean, he was used to my wardrobe, but at least my clothes were still relatively dark. "I'm sorry... you are?"

"Gavin Brooks." Gavin rushed forward, extending his hand. "Bennett's executive assistant."

Leander didn't hesitate to take it, which I considered a good sign. Not that I'd ever gotten a phobic vibe, but now I knew he wouldn't run screaming for the hills whenever Gavin came to town. "It's nice to finally meet you." Leander gave him a polite smile before turning his gaze to me. "Are you ready for your first scolding?"

"Looking forward to it."

We exchanged a wry grin before he turned, disappearing down the hall.

Gavin sighed dreamily as soon as he left. "He smells good too."

"You're not going to be allowed back here if you keep it up." I picked up the stack of folders and walked over, giving him a stern look to accompany my verbal warning.

"Ooo, did I strike a nerve? A little possessive, are we?"

Ignoring his attempt to bait me, I dumped the folders into his arms. "Like you said, it's not Chicago. Besides, I hate to break it to you, but you're not his type if you catch my drift." I patted his arm sympathetically.

Staring off in the direction Leander had gone, Gavin sighed again, this time in defeat. "What a waste."

———

IN THE THREE decades I'd been alive, I learned to read people rather quickly and I knew from the minute he laid eyes on me, Richard Scheible despised me. At this rate, I should consider starting a club for all my adoring fans down here.

The esteemed criminal attorney obligingly shook my hand before turning his narrowed gaze to Leander. "I didn't realize you were looking for a new lawyer. I could have recommended someone... local." Another side-eye, another once-over. I hoped he had better control over his expression in court, for God's sake.

"I didn't want local," Leander replied loftily. "I wanted the best."

Richard blatantly gave me another long look, as if he was trying to see what Leander saw. I stopped toying with my necklace and grinned at him. Good luck to him. Even though *I* knew my talents, I never found out why Leander ultimately agreed to my proposal last year.

"What is so urgent?" Leander asked, cocking his head.

"Easton PD called me yesterday." Richard punctuated his sentence with a blink, as if that explained everything.

Leander and I exchanged a glance. From the cloud of

suspicion in his eyes, I knew he was equally at a loss as to what the old man was referring to.

"And...?" Leander prompted, along with a little circular wave of his hand.

"You do know one of your employees died a few months back? Jason Richter?" Richard explained, none-too-patiently. It wasn't condescension, but more of a fatherly tone. I suppose when you defend someone for murder at the age of eighteen, you have some justification for assuming a parental stance.

"What of it?"

Richard's eyes narrowed again. "Another body turns up with a connection to you. Guess what the police think?"

"Oh, Richard, you *do* know how much I love guessing games." Leander's voice took on a silken purr, made all the sexier when his gaze locked on Richard, like a cat waiting to pounce.

The lawyer huffed, oblivious to the danger seated across the table. "They want to know where you were that night, so I hope you have a good alibi."

"Do I have a good alibi, Bennett?" He bent his head toward me, but kept his attention on Richard.

I sucked in a breath through my teeth, pretending to mull it over. "I don't know... What night was that again? I want to make sure I keep all the alibis straight. Hate to have a repeat."

"This isn't a joke," Richard snapped. "You're lucky they didn't press charges before. With the right prosecutor, they could have gone for it. The more bodies that stack up in this town, the more they have to throw at you. I told you! You could be in Bermuda when someone is shot in the middle of downtown Easton and the police would *still* make you their primary suspect!"

"Ooo... Is that the scolding?" I asked in a mock whisper, leaning against Leander's shoulder.

"He's just warming up," he replied with a dark smile, nudging my shoulder ever so slightly.

I slid forward on my elbows, my chin propped on one heavily-ringed hand. "Go on, Dick. I'm positively *dying* to hear the rest of this."

The other lawyer scowled at me, but he was smart enough to keep his mouth shut and turn his attention to his client. "I don't know what you're up to — and I don't *want* to know. But whatever it is, you better watch it. Do you hear me? You know Albrecht has it out for you. He's had it out for you since he was on the streets. And now as chief? He will use anything he can to arrest you."

Leander sighed. "An arrest isn't a conviction, Richard. I don't know what you're fretting about."

"Why can't you just stay on *this* side of the law for a change?" Richard motioned to the left, past some imaginary line of legality. "One of these days you're going to come up against the wrong person and you're not going to like what happens."

"Ouch." I winced and looked at Leander, his expression stony. "Did I hear him correctly? Does he think you're not capable of handling your own affairs?"

Leander's gaze shifted from me to his other lawyer. "Is that what you think, Richard? Do you think I don't know what I'm doing? That you, somehow, see more of the bigger picture than I do?"

Richard bristled, the tips of his ears turning red. "Look, I don't know where the hell you found this guy" — he pointed at me, rudely — "but he does *not* have your best interest at heart. I have been looking out for you since you were eighteen and despite my best efforts you keep putting yourself in the middle of every police investigation in Easton!"

"I think he just insinuated you don't know what you're

doing, either," Leander said to me, the purr back in his voice. "Where did you do your undergrad?"

"Stanford." I smirked when Richard blinked.

"And law school?"

"University of Chicago."

"Now, I did *not* go to college, Richard, but I'm pretty sure both of those universities consistently rank in the top ten every year. Is that impressive enough for you, or should Bennett produce a list of his notable legal wins? I believe a few have made case law." He turned to me again, his brows lifted. "Isn't that right?"

"Quite right. I'm flattered you noticed." I touched a hand to my chest, giving him a sappy smile.

Richard shook his head, scowling between the two of us. "I'm glad to see you're taking this seriously."

The amusement vanished from Leander's face. "I take everything seriously. I would have thought you knew that by now?"

"I'll put the police off as long as I can. In the meantime, I'd shore up that so-called alibi of yours." Grabbing his briefcase, Richard got to his feet with a growl.

"Pleasure to meet you, Dick." I didn't bother standing. Neither did Leander.

Richard rewarded me with an extra-heated glare and stormed out.

I couldn't help but laugh immediately. Leander at least held it in until the door swung shut.

CHAPTER 14

"*I*'ll see you next week," I said, slinging my messenger bag over my shoulder and heading for the door.

"Where are you going?" Leander looked up from his desk, his brows drawn.

"Shareholder meeting at Bancroft, then, you know, Chicago shenanigans."

His lips twitched. Just the once, followed by him twisting his pen between his fingers, lengthwise.

I looked at him flatly, my thumb hooked around my bag strap.

Still, Leander didn't say anything.

"What?" I prompted.

"Marchese." He set his pen down and laced his fingers together before looking at me again.

"What about him?"

"Have you heard from him?"

"Not lately. He knows I'm not in town anymore."

"But you will be in town."

With a soft sigh, I crossed over to his desk and leaned

forward on my knuckles so I was eye-level with him. "I haven't talked to him since last year. Stop worrying."

He didn't look the slightest bit convinced. The tightness in his jaw remained, along with the cant of his head.

"As far as he knows, everything is going along swimmingly," I said with more enthusiasm than I felt. Giovanni hadn't been real happy when I referred him to another lawyer. As I told him then, I gave zero fucks about his personal feelings and past history meant nothing to me. My only loyalty was to the better offer, which Giovanni failed to provide.

Leander merely blinked in response.

"He's had no reason to think there is anything off about your arrangement, thus no reason to care if I'm in town or not." That part was at least true. The shipments had been running like clockwork. As discussed, Leander's company picked up the cargo from the Gulf and brought it up the Mississippi. After everything was unloaded, Marchese's men took possession of their property and everyone went on their merry way. To date, there hadn't been a late delivery or any whiff of law enforcement. Giovanni may have been pouty I didn't want to help him anymore, but he didn't have any reason to suspect I sabotaged the contract between him and Leander.

"That's the thing about a double-cross. You're not supposed to see it coming." Leander leaned back in his chair, his arms folding across his chest in a silent challenge.

I made a face at him. "If you're so worried, why don't you come with me? It would do you good to get out of the office for a while."

"I have too much to do here."

"Exactly my point." I snagged his suit jacket off the back of his chair and hauled him to his feet. With an arm slung over his shoulders, I physically marched him to the door.

"Come on. We can take the plane. Beats the hell out of rush hour traffic."

"Bennett, I'm not going!"

———

LESS THAN TWO HOURS LATER, we landed in Chicago. Why didn't I do this all the time? It was so much faster. Except, I had a sports car I loved driving and weekend jaunts to the city were the only time I really got to drive it anymore.

"When's the meeting?" Leander asked when we were settled in the backseat of a hired car.

"Tomorrow at ten. Are you hungry?" I didn't bother waiting for him to answer. His response was always "No," unless he was the one cooking. Leaning forward, I tapped the driver on the shoulder lightly. "Sorry, change of plans. Make a right up here."

"Shenanigans starting early?" Leander asked.

"I have no idea what you're talking about."

Once we were dropped off at the best hamburger spot in town, I grabbed ahold of Leander like a toddler about to bolt into traffic. Wrapping one arm behind his back to clamp down on the arm furthest away, I secured his closer arm against my side. From the look on Leander's face, I knew I had a fight on my hands.

"It tastes better than it looks," I said, steering him up the uneven, concrete steps to the front door. Getting him inside was like trying to shove a cat in bathwater.

"I'm not hungry."

"Bullshit."

"It's true."

"You haven't eaten all day."

"I'll survive."

"Just open the door."

He grudgingly yanked it open, glaring at the bells that chimed overhead.

A waitress in a blue, retro uniform bustled up. "Well, well. If it isn't my favorite trouble maker. Haven't see you in a while."

"I've been keeping my nose clean," I said with a smile, dropping my hand from Leander's arm.

"Let me guess. Booth?"

"Back corner if it's available."

Deb grinned, chomping on her gum. "Sure thing, hun. This way."

Leander didn't budge.

"Come on." I coaxed him forward, placing my hand in the small of his back and gently nudging him. I thought about hanging on to his jacket in case he tried to make a run for it, but I knew his contempt for anyone manhandling his clothes.

"My shoes are sticking to the floor," he hissed over his shoulder. "How does this place even pass inspection?"

I laughed. "Oh, my sweet country boy."

"Don't patronize me." Jerking away, he slid into the corner booth the waitress presented. "Having a standard of cleanliness is nothing to be mocked."

I slid in on the other side, fighting a smile.

"I'll give you guys a minute." Deb set menus down and walked away, humming along to the Del Vikings song playing overhead.

"No one knows you here, so you don't have to worry about the food thing," I said, not even bothering to look at the menu.

He rolled his shoulders back, smoothing down his tie. "I'm more concerned about salmonella than arsenic."

"Would I do that to you?"

He cocked his head, staring at me a beat too long.

I made a face at him, quickly erasing it when the waitress came back.

"What can I get you two?"

"Two number ones," I replied with a smile. "And a chocolate shake, please."

"Perfect." She scooped up the menus and disappeared.

"What did you just order me?" Leander raised his brows. At first glance, he might have appeared curious. I knew better. It was carefully controlled irritation masked as a polite inquiry.

"Your last meal if you keep it up." I slipped my cell phone out, answering a stream of texts from Del and Gavin. "For this partnership thing to work, you're going to have to trust me. Just a scosche."

"Who says I don't?"

I lowered my phone briefly, shooting him my own irritated look. "I'm not just a pretty face."

"You don't say." He rolled his eyes and looked away, glancing around the red, white, and black interior. 1950s memorabilia covered every available inch of wall space. It was kitschy and probably offensive to every single one of his refined senses.

"Are you saying I'm not pretty?" I clutched my non-existent pearls.

Leander's gaze shot back to me. "Bennett Reeve, you are the prettiest man I've ever seen," he said, completely deadpan.

"Stop, you're making me blush."

Deb returned shortly thereafter, delivering the all-American meal of a cheeseburger and fries, plus my chocolate shake. That, however, she set between the two of us with two straws.

Leander lifted a brow at the straws.

I wasted no time dunking a fry into the shake.

He wrinkled his nose.

"Don't start with me, Welles." I pointed my half-eaten fry at him. "I will not have your snobbery ruining this meal."

"You act like you haven't eaten since you moved."

"It's nostalgia." I popped the rest of my fry into my mouth and turned my attention to my cheeseburger.

Leander's cell phone rang, saving him from the agony of having to endure a meal made for common folk. He frowned at the screen before answering. "What's wrong, Jake?"

I kept my eye-roll to myself. The lad was needier than a fifteen-year-old girl. Over the course of getting to know everyone else in Leander's life, Jake remained the biggest pain in the ass. Even Olivia, with her biting comments and razor-sharp smiles, seemed to accept my presence with a smidge less hostility.

"I'm in Chicago," Leander said. His gaze drifted to me, lingering a moment before he blinked and looked away sharply. "Does it matter? I don't know... Well, next time I'll be sure to clear my schedule with you, Jacob." He hung up abruptly and tossed his phone on the table.

"Problems?"

"No."

"Sounds like there's a problem."

He huffed, staring at the salt shaker with rapt attention.

"He seems very attached to you," I ventured, treading carefully with my speculation. The blatant hatred toward me, the wistful gazes toward Leander when he thought no one else was looking — if I was a betting man, which I was, I'd bet everything I owned on the fact Jake was head over heels in love with Leander.

"Unfortunately our early years were remarkably similar. I feel for him, especially since he didn't have the inheritance I did. He's looked up to me since he was a kid. It doesn't feel right to abandon him now." It was *so* much more than that for Jake, but I wasn't going to point it out to Leander if he didn't want to see it.

"Does he know you're with me?"

"He assumed as much."

I nodded, toying with a French fry. "So, should we set up the duel now or wait until we get home? I'd prefer a Monday, if that's ok, just to get it out of the way. I have meetings scheduled the rest of the week."

His attention darted back to me, the corners of his eyes crinkling. "What are you talking about?"

"Well, it's clear we're going to have to battle to the death for you."

"Hardly." He shook his head, pointedly ignoring the deeper meaning while picking at the silver edge of the table.

When he glanced up, it was my turn to shake my head. "How are you so brilliant and so daft at the same time?"

A curl shifted across his forehead as his head tilted. The corners of his mouth turned downward. "I don't follow."

I waved him off with another fry. "Never mind."

AFTER LUNCH, we decided to walk to my apartment instead of taking a car, enjoying the spring sunshine that came in large swathes through the skyscrapers. I gave a personal architecture tour along the way, pointing out iconic buildings and answering his questions about the city's history.

As with any major metropolis, Chicago was great for people-watching. In addition to looking at buildings, there were plenty of pedestrians out and about to generate more than one conversation about who they were and where they were off to.

One woman in particular caught my eye as we walked. Maybe it was the sense of authority in her steps, or the determined look on her face that made me stop and take notice.

I'd no more than given the blonde an appreciative once-over when her hand lashed across my face.

"You son of a bitch!" she snarled, glaring up at me.

Leander reacted first, since I was too stunned to do anything other than stare at her. He seized my arm, dragging me backward and angling himself between the blonde and I.

"I'm sorry?" I touched the side of my face. The skin was on fire. Jesus. What did this woman do when she walked by a goddamn construction site? I didn't even say anything!

"You set me up!" She jabbed her finger at me, her eyes welling.

"Set you up? Who *are* you?" I shot a look at Leander, but he was just as bewildered.

"Oh, that's fucking great." She shook her head, dashing a few stray tears from her eyes. "Glad to see I made such an impression. Do I even want to know how many girls you've filmed while fucking?"

"Maybe you have me confused with someone else?" I may have been open to a lot of things, but turning into an amateur pornstar was not one of them.

She shouldered past Leander and shoved her hands into my chest. "You almost cost me my job! And now Sidorov has enough to ruin the rest of my life!"

I skipped back a step, racking my brain for a trace of a memory. Oh... There it was. The night in question popped up front and center. Hot blonde, silver dress. Alina's gallery.

She kept coming, swinging wildly for any part of me she could reach.

"That's enough!" Leander grabbed her around the waist and pulled her away. She elbowed him and swore like a hell-cat, but he refused to let go. Once she stopped struggling, he released his hold, lifting both hands as a sign of goodwill. It didn't seem to matter, since she visibly seethed where she stood.

I cringed. "Guess that drug case fell apart, huh?"

"No thanks to you!"

"In my defense, it's not like I was the one who actually filmed it. You should have known there were security cameras. I mean, *you're* the cop." I gestured to her and her very sensible outfit — plain suit, no heels, no makeup. A far cry from the sizzling femme fatale at the gallery.

She took a step forward again, her hands clenched at her sides. "One of these days you're going to get everything you deserve, you piece of shit." She stormed off, ducking into the driver's seat of an unmarked squad. It peeled away from the curb, leaving me staring after her.

"Are you ok?" Leander asked, his fingers touching my chin. He turned my head gently, inspecting my face.

"Yeah. Just... surprised." I laid a hand on my cheek again. It still stung like a bitch.

"Do I even want to know what that was about?"

"No... probably not." Since I'd been around Leander, I'd somehow kept my lascivious side in check. Unless he heard about it from Gavin, there's no way he'd know what my Chicago-self had been like. I kind of wanted to keep it that way.

"I didn't realize you had ties to Sidorov too," Leander said, thankfully glossing right over the blonde thing as we continued on our way.

I squinted at him slightly. "Is there a question in there somewhere?"

"Does our arrangement have any impact on him?"

"No. Should it?"

"I don't know. He was my second choice after Marchese."

"I remember. Quite the power play, I might add."

As usual, he seemed oblivious to the compliment, or

chose to ignore it. "I wouldn't want him to think you screwed him over to give the deal to the Italians."

I waved him off. "Nah. Sergei and I are good. I got him hooked up with another opportunity to keep him happy."

"Bennett Reeve, master manipulator of the Chicago underworld."

"Maybe once upon a time. Now, I serve only you, my prince." I gave him a sweeping bow.

He shoved my arm. "Stop it. People are looking."

"Of course they're looking. They're in awe of your majesty, your grace, your—"

"You are ridiculous." He ducked his head, running a hand through his hair. I was pretty sure I saw a blush.

"Oh, here we are." Fortune saved him once again as we strolled up to the lobby doors of my apartment building.

The doorman inclined his head and opened one quickly.

"Thank you, Harrison," I murmured. A step away, I spun and pointed at him. "How's your brother, by the way?"

"He's doing better. Thanks for asking, Mr. Reeve."

"Good." Nodding, I turned around again, punching the button for the elevator. I caught Leander looking at me out of the corner of my eye. "What? What now?"

"Nothing."

"Why do you keep looking at me like that?"

"It's like you're two different people — the one who lives in Easton, and the one who lives here," he said as the elevator whisked us up and away.

"Public persona." I gestured grandly around the gilded box, then motioned to him. "Private persona."

"It sounds exhausting." It was, truth be told. However, it was a necessary theatric in the game of life.

Before I could say as much, the gleaming doors slid open, depositing us directly into my living room.

"Home sweet home," I said, shrugging out of my jacket

and tossing it over the back of the couch. "Make yourself comfortable."

"You go from this to a Victorian cottage?" Leander asked, cutting across the open space to the wall of windows on the east side, overlooking the lake.

"It's just a place to sleep."

"Mhmm." Once he'd had his fill of the lake, he .pivoted and wandered around the living room, taking in the various pieces of art along the wall, his hands clasped behind his back. "I didn't realize you were such an aficionado."

"Part and parcel of growing up under the shadow of the Bancroft name. You had to like the arts or you were disowned."

The painting at the center of his attention was one of the Cézannes, a murky vanitas featuring a pile of skulls and books. Not surprisingly, it was one of my favorites.

"Another memento mori," I said, walking up next to him and tipping my chin toward the painting.

"An interesting choice, given your personal history."

"I'm hoping if I face it often enough, I'll glean something useful for the afterlife."

"There are books for that," he said with a smirk. It morphed to a frown as he circled the living room again. Dragging his fingers along the glossy, black surface of the piano in the corner, he stopped suddenly and looked at me, perplexed. "There are no books. Where are your books?"

"I don't like books," I said with a chuckle, preparing for the onslaught.

He froze, his hand resting on the edge of the piano. He had the same look on his face as if I drop-kicked a puppy right in front of him.

"Are *you* going to disown me now?" I asked, crossing the room leisurely.

"How can you be so well read and not like books?"

"They give me a headache. Reading in general gives me a headache. I can't really make it past thirty minutes these days."

"But you're a lawyer. Reading is what you do."

I chuckled again and slid onto the piano bench, cracking my knuckles before I started playing softly. "Only when it's necessary. And I prefer to do other things with my spare time."

"Yes, like collaborating with Russian drug runners." He smirked at me.

"I'm going to ignore that jab." I hit the keys a little louder to emphasize my point.

He strolled back to the window, gazing down at the bustling city while I played. Music filled the silence, a dark and brooding lament I knew he'd appreciate.

"God, what I wouldn't give for a little anonymity in a city like this," he said as the song neared its conclusion.

"So move." I switched to a slower, softer melody so as not to drown out his voice.

He laughed quietly, still facing out the window. "Yeah, right."

"No, I'm serious. Move. Or, better yet, clear out the bank account and disappear."

His sad green eyes met mine across the expanse of the piano. "It's not that simple."

"It *is* that simple."

"Sounds like you've given it some thought."

"I have, as a matter of fact."

He looked over at me again, the sadness replaced with curiosity. "Where would you go?"

"Wherever we want."

"We?" A dark brow lifted, along with the corner of his mouth in a bemused smirk.

"Hell yeah. I can't go anywhere without my partner-in-crime. I'd be *so* bored." My attention dropped to the keys as I played the final bridge.

"Whatever did you do before me then?"

"I plead the fifth." I bit my lips in mock silence and picked up the tempo, transitioning to a different song.

CHAPTER 15

"*H*ave you heard from Fontenot Shipping yet?" Leander looked up at Olivia, shifting a folder out of his way on the conference room desk.

She flipped through her planner, clucking her tongue until she found what she was looking for. "We're all set for the twentieth. I cleared your schedule for the day."

I slid the appropriate classification folder toward him. "That's what we're proposing. You know they'll counter with half, so you can go from there."

Leander flipped through the offer, glancing at me over the top. "Aren't you coming with me?"

"I hadn't planned on it, but you know me. I never say no." I gave Olivia a wolfish smile.

On cue, she snorted, scribbling something in the corner of her agenda.

Jake scoffed as well, shaking his head and muttering to himself on the other end of the table.

Leander looked up again, his pen hovering over the papers. "Is there a problem?"

"I mean..." Jake glanced at Olivia. If he was looking for

help, he didn't get any. She steadfastly ignored him, her thumbs moving at warp speed on her phone. "Do we really need to take four people?"

Leander set his pen down and laced his fingers together, his jaw set.

Sitting up in my chair, I suddenly wished I had popcorn. Watching Jake hang himself with his ego was the highlight of the day thus far.

"It's just... I thought I was going to start taking on more responsibilities?" Jake practically squeaked the question. "I've done all the research and the comparables. I have info on their main competitors and I—"

"And who is going to go to Missouri?" Leander asked, watching Jake with the intensity of a hawk tracking a field mouse.

"Elijah can go."

Elijah grunted in the negative. "Not happening. I have a meeting with investors that week in Springfield."

"Then Cole," Jake offered. Big of him, since Cole wasn't even there to speak up for himself.

"Cole has other priorities. That leaves you." Leander still hadn't blinked, or looked away, or done anything to minimize Jake's discomfort.

Finally, Jake got the hint and shut his mouth.

"Good." Leander stared at him a beat longer before turning his gaze to Olivia. "My office." Sweeping his padfolio off the desk, he strode out without a backward glance.

Olivia swatted Jake with her planner as she stood. "Learn to quit while you're ahead."

Elijah shook his head and followed her out, leaving Jake and I alone in the conference room.

"Better luck next time, sport." I pushed away from the table with a wink.

He was on his feet in a flash, rounding on me. "I am so sick of you!"

Humoring him, I stopped and turned, arching a brow. "Do tell."

"You think I don't know what's going on?" He came toe-to-toe with me. It was adorable, considering our first introduction. "I don't know how you got your hooks into Leander, but I see you for what you are."

"Ooo, this ought to be good. What am I?"

"You're a liar."

I actually laughed. "If you think *that* is the worst thing about me, you clearly don't know anything."

"I know Leander doesn't tolerate liars."

"Well, he keeps you around." I gave him a pointed once-over.

He jerked back as if I'd hit him. "What are you talking about?"

I leaned in closer, lowering my voice. "*I* know, even if Leander doesn't."

"Know what?" He sneered back at me, trying to recover some of his machismo.

"That you're in love with him."

With a sudden fury, Jake seized the front of my shirt and slammed me against the wall.

I laughed again, despite the thumping in the back of my skull. I wouldn't be surprised if there was a dent in the drywall.

"Shut the fuck up!"

"Methinks thou doth protest too much, Jacob."

He shoved me again with one hand, rearing back for a punch with the other.

Cole ran into the room, barreling into Jake. The two crashed into the table and chairs in a tangle of limbs. Cole was on his feet first, hauling Jake up by a fistful of cloth. "What the fuck is wrong with you?"

I smoothed the front of my own shirt, smirking at Jake. Guess that officially confirmed *that* speculation.

"Why don't you ask him? He started it," Jake spat.

"Grow the fuck up, Jake."

"Fuck you, Cole."

Cole punched him in the jaw, sending him sprawling.

Before he could punch him again, I grabbed Cole and hauled him back a safe distance. "It's not worth it."

"You asshole!" Jake scrambled to his feet, fists clenched for Round Two.

"Keep it up, you little shit, and see what happens!" Cole took a step forward, but I yanked him back.

Jake glared at the two of us and stomped off, holding his jaw.

Once he was out of the room, I let go of Cole. "Thanks. But in his defense, I did provoke him."

Cole either didn't hear me over his adrenaline rush or he didn't care. "You ok?"

"I'm fine." Somewhere in the building a door slammed. "Apparently I struck a nerve."

"Fuck him." Cole balled his hand into a fist again, rubbing the reddened knuckles.

"You don't think much of him, do you?"

"He's like the kid brother I never wanted."

"Have I told you how much I like you?" I chuckled.

He gave me a lopsided grin, but the mirth didn't quite reach his eyes. "You're one of the few."

"Form was a little off." I gestured to his hand. "Let's get you some ice before it swells."

He nodded, falling into step next to me. "Gotta admit, I've been wanting to do that for years."

I laughed, clapping a hand on his shoulder.

CHAPTER 16

The flight to New Orleans was relatively short, but incredibly bumpy. I self-medicated with a tiny bottle of whiskey. Or two. Fine, four. If we were going to any other city, I might not have hit it as hard, but I had a feeling it would be forgiven in the Big Easy.

"Are you up for this, Benny Boo?" Olivia asked, grabbing my chin and narrowing her eyes at mine. "You look like you're ready to hurl."

"Right as rain, Kitten." I tossed a couple mints in my mouth and climbed into the waiting car. She was lucky I didn't kiss the ground when we landed.

Olivia gave me a disapproving look from the seat across from me, but she didn't say anything. Instead, she handed a tablet to Leander. "The latest numbers on Fontenot."

"They went down." Leander flicked through the screens, his smile broadening. "Perfect."

"All over it, boss." I saluted him, closing my eyes and resting my head against the side of the car. We were already in the better bargaining position and knowing their company was still struggling made my job that much easier. I mentally slashed our numbers by a quarter to accommodate the latest news.

The president of Fontenot Shipping was waiting for us in the lobby when we walked in. He smiled warmly and held his hand out to Leander. "Mr. Welles. It's nice to finally see you in person."

"Likewise." Leander gave him a polite smile. "Olivia Harlow, my assistant. And Bennett Reeve, my corporate counsel."

"This is Brandon Hebert," the president said, gesturing to the smart-dressed lawyer at his side. "He can help you with whatever you need."

"It would be my pleasure," Brandon added, giving me an admiring glance even a blind man couldn't miss.

"Well, then." I cocked an eyebrow at him, the flattery fueling my predatory side. Between a thirsty young lawyer and favorable numbers, this was going to be a fucking cakewalk. "Let's go someplace a little more private, shall we?"

Leander watched the exchange with a blank expression, meanwhile Olivia looked like she was a step up from her usual state of annoyance.

Brandon led the way to another room, leaving Leander and his boss to exchange pleasantries while we haggled over the paperwork.

"Is this your first time in New Orleans?" Brandon asked as we settled into leather chairs kitty-corner from each other.

"Oh, no. I've had the fortune to visit several times."

"Shoot. And here I was hoping I could show you around when this is all said and done. Maybe grab a drink or something."

Ok, Brandon... I'll play. "Who says you can't?"

He gave me a coy smile and a lingering glance before

turning to the paperwork at hand. "If these terms are acceptable, we can close within the hour."

I took the contract, grazing his fingers in the process. Skimming through it quietly, I made sure my expression read as mildly bored. He was cute, but I wasn't an idiot. I wouldn't have agreed to this contract as a ten year old, let alone an actual lawyer.

After I made a few modifications, I handed it back with a half-smile. "That should about do it."

Brandon scanned through the amendments, his eyebrow rising higher with each passing line. "There's no way."

"No?" I turned my pen over and slid my fingers down the barrel, only to flip it and do it again on the opposite side, an entirely innocent gesture to anyone not paying attention. And I definitely had Brandon's attention.

He licked his lips before answering. "Peter's only comfortable with a two-year contract."

I cocked my head to the side, meeting his gaze despite the hair shifting across my eyes. "We want five."

His gaze dropped and flicked up again. "Two and a half."

Both of my brows came together. "A half? Really?"

"Fine, three," he huffed.

"Five," I reiterated, mimicking the purr Leander used when he wanted his way.

"That's not how negotiating works," he replied with a teasing tone.

I leaned forward, propping one elbow on the arm of the chair. Pretending to strategize, I dragged my finger across my lower lip before my chin settled in my hand. "What do you want for five?"

He gave me a long, thoughtful look. Actually, he gave my *mouth* a long, thoughtful look, which was just as well. "Quarterly bonuses."

"Yearly."

"At ten percent?"

"Done."

We shook on it and made the necessary amendments to our clients' paperwork. I bit the bullet and stood first, strolling toward the door with the heat of his gaze following me back to our respective CEOs.

"It was a pleasure, Mr. Reeve," Brandon murmured as he walked by, slipping his business card into my pocket. My pants pocket, brazen boy.

"Pleasure's all mine."

The corners of Leander's mouth turned down a fraction when we emerged from our private chat. Maybe Peter Fontenot was more annoying than I first thought. Either way, the look was gone by the time I stopped at Leander's elbow.

"We're all set," I said with a smile.

"Wonderful," Leander replied smoothly. I couldn't help but notice the underlying edge in his voice, or the way he subtly shifted away from me.

"I've taken the liberty of ordering lunch," Peter said, laying a hand on Leander's shoulder and guiding him down the hallway. "You must try the crawfish etouffee."

"Our plane," Olivia said, tapping her watch.

"We'll get you out of here in time. Promise." Peter smiled brightly.

———

LIKE ALL BUSINESSMEN, Peter lied. We didn't make it back to the tarmac for our flight by a long shot. While we waited for the pilot to clear a new flight plan with the tower, the autumn storm that had been lurking in the atmosphere came down with a vengeance.

"Looks like we're spending the night," I said, watching the

rain lash the car windows. Or at least *I* was. There was no way anyone was getting my ass in an airplane in a storm like that.

The only problem with deciding to spend the night instead of risking it was every other traveler in New Orleans facing the same problem. Thanks to quick thinking, Olivia secured a hotel reservation, hoping to negotiate for a second room when we arrived.

The hotel lobby was packed by the time our car dropped us off, but it didn't stop Olivia from shouldering through the crowd of sopping tourists to make her way to the front desk.

"I'm sorry, ma'am, we only have the one room available," the clerk said, frowning at the computer screen.

Olivia groaned, meanwhile the muscle in Leander's jaw twitched.

"It's one of our largest suites," the woman said helpfully.

"We'll take it," I said, darting between the two of them and plunking down my company credit card.

She smiled. After a few more clicks in the computer, she handed us the room information. "You're all set."

Keycards in hand, we stepped into the elevator, smushed into one corner while a family from Texas took up the the majority of the space with their brood of children. As soon as they exited, Leander darted to the opposite corner, exhaling and raking a hand through his damp hair.

"Could today get any worse? We don't have any clothes. Any toiletries. Anything." Olivia crossed her arms, glaring at the polished doors, three floors from the top.

"Yes, I'm sure New Orleans is completely without a pharmacy or a fucking gas station," I muttered. Or a liquor store. I needed more bourbon STAT. Somehow today had turned into one of those days I just wanted to forget.

"Don't be an asshole."

Leander, curiously, remained silent. He'd settled into his corner, staring at the dark carpeting the rest of the way.

When the elevator opened, Olivia stomped out first and took off down the hallway. She shoved the keycard in the door so hard I thought she was going to break it, which would have been the icing on the cake. "Oh, that's just fucking perfect."

As soon as I turned the corner, I saw what had her all riled this time — there was only one bed. A king-size, but still, just the one.

"It's fine," Leander said quietly. "You can have the bed."

Olivia crossed her arms over her chest, her jaw shifted to one side irritably. "And where are you two going to sleep?"

"The couch. The chair. Not at all?" Leander rubbed his hands over his face. "I'm going out. I'll pick up some stuff for you."

"I'm coming with you," I said, hurrying after him. Once upon a time I would have loved to be alone with Olivia in a hotel room. Now? Fuck that. I didn't want to be anywhere near her when she was in a mood. Besides, it was New Orleans. There were always high jinks to be had and Leander looked like he needed to lighten up even more than I did.

———

ONCE THE RAIN TAPERED OFF, Leander and I wandered around the French Quarter instead of darting from store to store. After a quick stop at Cafe du Monde, we carried our beignets and cafe au lait to Jackson Square, settling ourselves on a bench that wasn't entirely soaked.

"You're going to regret wearing black after this," I said, watching Leander try to navigate the problem presented by the mountain of powdered sugar on his beignet.

"Can you look somewhere else?"

"Not a chance."

He shook his head and I'm sure a string of silent curses ran through his mind. He was about to take a bite when the breeze shifted over the levee, dusting him in the powdered sugar he was desperately trying to avoid.

I bit my lips, trying not to laugh.

Closing his eyes, he muttered to himself.

I couldn't contain the laughter anymore, nearly spilling coffee on myself when I doubled over.

"Shut up," Leander said, trying not to laugh.

With great effort, I stopped, blinking at him innocently. A second later, I busted out laughing again.

Without warning, he threw his beignet at me. It bounced off my arm with a puff of sugar and fell to the ground.

I dusted off my sleeve and handed him a wad of napkins, still snickering.

"You *are* an ass," Leander said, trying to glare at me despite a smile that kept surfacing.

"But you love me," I countered with a grin.

Smirking, he dabbed the napkin in rainwater and wiped his jacket, removing most of the powdered sugar.

"I didn't hear you refute it," I said, sipping my coffee.

"It doesn't need refuting." He was still tending to his suit, his gaze downcast. "I am as incapable of love as you are."

"I wouldn't say I'm incapable..." I reclined with a sigh, stretching my legs out and tipping my head back on the bench. Since the rain stopped, everything was brighter, clearer. The moon illuminated the city and a few resilient stars appeared through the wisps of clouds.

"Then what would you say?"

"I don't know. You're the expert."

He scoffed, rotating his coffee cup between his hands idly. "I'm far from an expert."

"You're an expert on Poe. Same thing."

"Do you know much about Poe's love life?"

"No. But I know he's the one who wrote 'We loved with a love that was more than love.' Pretty romantic, if you ask me."

When Leander didn't give me a lengthy answer right away, I rolled my head to the side to see what he was doing. He, too, was looking at the sky.

"Most people think the idea of romantic love is the highest goal in life. The only goal," he said quietly, his face upturned. "But it's not enough. Not really."

"What else is there?"

"A soul mate." His gaze lowered to mine, his features soft in the light. Soft and sad. "Someone who truly understands you. Not only understands, accepts you. Unreservedly."

"Do you think that's even possible? I mean, can anyone ever truly know someone else?"

"For some people, sure. Not us." He shifted his focus to the statue in the center of the square. "We're cursed to be alone, set apart from the rest of the world by the very traits that make us unique. Or, you have to subject yourself to living a lie."

"Well, they say it's lonely at the top." I took a sip of my coffee. Even though I tried to sound breezy, I was anything but. He wasn't wrong. He and I were not like other people, that much was clear. And if we weren't like other people, what did that mean for us? What did "normal" things, like happiness and love, look like for the abnormal? Did we sacrifice those things for power along the way?

"Are you?" Leander's voice broke through my thoughts.

"What?"

"Lonely."

I scoffed. "No." Stealing a glance at him out of the corner of my eye, I recoiled slightly. No surprise, he was looking at me with an arched brow. "Are you?"

"'Satan had his companions, fellow-devils, to admire and encourage him; but I am solitary and abhorred,'" Leander murmured.

"Ok, Frankenstein. That's not really an answer." The fact he didn't immediately correct my misattribution was alarming. I sat up, angling myself so I could face him directly. Over the past year, I'd seen dark and I'd seen moody. This version of Leander was something I hadn't encountered before and I didn't know what the right course of action was.

"I've spent my whole life alone," Leander stated simply. "I don't know how to be anything else."

"Being alone isn't the same as being lonely." I tried to get him to look at me, but he was staring at his hands. "Besides, you're not alone anymore. Your fellow devil is sitting right beside you."

He cracked a wistful smile, shaking his head. "Sometimes I think you are the Devil."

"I'll take that as a compliment." I grinned at him.

"Only you would be pleased to be likened to the Lord of Hell."

"Of course I'm pleased. They say Lucifer was the most handsome angel."

"Wasn't it the most beautiful angel?"

I shrugged. "I'm good either way."

"Yeah, I noticed," he muttered into his coffee cup.

"Ouch." I couldn't tell if he was kidding or not, but something in his tone told me he wasn't. Even if he was, it stung more than I wanted to admit. Of all the things Leander knew about me, the fact he took issue with *that* was surprising.

"Sorry." He bit his lips and looked away. "I didn't mean it like that."

I remained silent, trying to remind myself of our different upbringings. We may have shared a similar world view overall, but it was colored through vastly different lenses. Plus, he wasn't entirely to blame. I never really revealed that part of myself to him. There was never a need.

"I was surprised, is all," Leander said after a while, his voice low.

Even though he wouldn't meet my gaze, I refused to look away. If this was suddenly going to be an issue, it was best to get it out in the open now. Too many of my relationships had been trashed by shit like this. I needed to know where I stood now that he knew. "Surprised by *what?*"

"That you're…" He shook his head, cutting himself off.

God, he couldn't even say it, could he? For some reason that was even more infuriating. Was he as repulsed by the word as he was the concept?

"What?" I snapped. "Bi? Perhaps the word you're looking for is 'bisexual'?"

Rising to his feet swiftly, he tossed his cup into a trash can, still avoiding direct eye contact. From the way it sounded, the cup was practically full. "We should get back."

"Yeah. Right behind you." I swirled my coffee before taking another sip.

He ran his tongue along his teeth, nodding. Without another word, he stalked off. It was probably better that way.

Once I was alone, I exhaled slowly. Despite my murderous disposition, confrontation wasn't my favorite thing in the world. I had enough of it in childhood and I certainly got enough of it through work. Not to mention, I didn't want to lose Leander and everything we'd been steadily building over a stupid difference of opinion. I'm sure it *was* shocking to someone like him, from a place like Easton. It shocked a lot of people, even though we were in the twenty-first goddamn century and it didn't fucking matter, except when it did.

In time, one of two things would happen. Either he'd get

over it, or he wouldn't. I couldn't make that decision for him, so I'd cross that bridge if it ever came.

Still, I was in no hurry to face his judgment again.

Rather than go back to the hotel, I fished Brandon's business card out of my pocket. He answered after a few rings, jazz music blaring in the background.

"It's Bennett," I said. "How about that drink?"

———

THE NEXT MORNING I regretted every bit of rum in the many, many Hurricanes I drank. Or maybe it was all the citric acid. Regardless, I had killer heartburn and I was thirstier than hell, which only made the heartburn worse.

"What the fuck happened to you?" Olivia asked when I flopped into my seat on the plane.

Ignoring her, I balled my jacket up and wedged it against the closed window shutter.

She walked over and kicked the side of my boot — hard.

"Ow! What?" I glared up at her.

"Where were you?"

"What do you care?"

"We've been calling you all goddamn night. Your phone is going straight to voicemail. I spent the morning calling hospitals and police stations looking for your sorry ass!"

"My phone died." I closed my eyes and nestled into my jacket.

She slugged me in the shoulder.

I jerked upright again with a wince and rubbed my arm. "Jesus! What?"

"Why didn't you come back to the hotel?"

"I made other arrangements. Is that ok with you, warden?"

She seethed through her teeth, her thumbs moving at

warp speed over her cell phone. "I hope you have a better story when Leander gets here."

"I don't think he'll really give a shit."

"Aw, what happened, Benny Boo? Did you two have a lovers' tiff?"

I flipped her off and readjusted my balled-up jacket.

I was almost asleep when Leander appeared. I knew he was there because the temperature in the aircraft dropped by about twenty degrees.

"Let's go," Leander snapped at the pilot before he strode down the aisle, sitting in the far back of the plane.

"That's it?" Olivia asked.

I cracked an eye and looked at her. I couldn't see Leander from where I was, so I had to gauge Leander's mood from Olivia's. She did *not* look pleased.

"You spent the night thinking he was laying in a fucking gutter somewhere and you're not going to say anything to him?" Olivia gaped at the back of the plane, as if I was entirely too drunk or hungover to realize I was the subject matter.

"What would you like me to say?" Leander asked. His voice was soft and controlled, but even in my fuzzy state I could hear the bitterness in it.

"Fuck it." Her head whipped toward me, a black lacquered nail about a millimeter from my face. "You're a selfish asshole. He won't tell you because he's too fucking proud, but you literally made Leander throw up last night with your bullshit."

"Olivia!"

She ignored him. "You didn't have the decency to call, text, anything! Just so we're clear, I don't give a flying fuck what happens to you, but he does for whatever goddamn reason. He thought you were dead somewhere, you fucking prick!"

"I'm not that easy to kill," I muttered, closing my eyes again. The fact Leander was that worried erased some of last night's unexpected anger. But a stranger emotion crept into the pit of my stomach. If I had to name it, I think it was something along the lines of guilt.

"If you pull a stunt like this again, I'll find a way." She huffed and stomped to the back of the plane, presumably to sit with Leander. A moment later, I heard their voices but the plane's engines were too loud to make out what they were discussing. Probably me and what an asshole I was. At that point, I didn't really care. I'd been awake for over twenty-four hours and drunk for a good portion of it. All I wanted to do was sleep.

Less than two hours later, I jolted awake when the plane landed. Even in my exhaustion, I patted myself on the back for being smart and driving my own car to the airport the day before. It meant I wouldn't have to listen to any more nagging from Olivia or endure the icy silence from Leander.

Olivia was the first one off the plane, slamming her expensive satchel into the back of my shoulder so hard I was pretty sure one of those ornate metal corners left a divot to go along with the bruise she gave me.

Leander was next. I grabbed his wrist as he strode by, pulling him to a halt. He spun to face me with a narrowed gaze and a set jaw.

"Is it true?" I asked. I maintained a hold on his wrist, to keep from swaying as much as to keep him from bolting.

"That Olivia will kill you? Yes, it's true."

I shook my head. "No. That you were worried?"

"I don't have time for this." He went to pull away, but I hung on, even though he dragged me with him a step.

"Make time."

He closed the minimal distance, nearly nose-to-nose with

me, his glare as sharp as his tongue. "You don't dictate what I do or don't do."

"Well it sounds like I do if you spent the night searching New Orleans for me."

"You disappeared, Bennett! You said you were coming and then you didn't. I had no way to get ahold of you. No idea where you were. What was I supposed to think?"

"Par for the course, isn't it? You just don't know *what* to think when it comes to me."

He opened his mouth and snapped it shut just as quickly, expelling a sharp breath. "Is that what this is about?"

"You tell me."

"I don't care who you sleep with."

"Sure seems like you do."

"I don't want your... proclivities... to interfere with work."

"My proclivities?" I raised my brows at him, mindful to keep my voice as even as I could, even though it felt like a sucker punch right to the gut. "For your information, my *proclivities* got you everything you wanted — and more. You wanted a three year contract? I got you five. You hate quarterly bonuses? I got you yearly ones, at a measly ten percent, I might add. So the next time you want to judge my *proclivities*, you better fucking think twice."

I didn't wait for a response. Shouldering past him, my anger was sobering enough to get me off the plane without falling and into my car. I sped away from the airport without a backward glance.

The next morning I woke to a knock on the door. By the time I got there, the front step was empty, save for a bouquet laying on the mat. Purple orchids and black lilies, no card. Not that I needed one.

"I'm sorry, too," I said aloud.

CHAPTER 17

The Walker House hotel was bustling with tourists coming and going from all of the charming activities Easton offered in the spring. Antiquing, flowers, and wine, of course. Thankfully, we were set apart from it all in one of the conference rooms off of the main lobby.

"Would you care for something to drink?" I asked. Since our relic of a host didn't bother offering, I crossed the room to the coffee cart and helped myself.

The old man practically growled before answering. "About time you asked. Black, no sugar."

What was it about old people that made them so goddamn rude? Was it the fact they knew they were on death's door? Even still, a little graciousness went a long way.

I looked at Leander, blatantly gaping at him behind the old man's back and gesturing impatiently. When he didn't acknowledge me, I wiggled my right index finger at him, the one with my emerald poison ring. "Leander? Would *you* care for any?"

His brows dipped ever so slightly. "*No*, thank you."

I poured the coffee with a frown. That's what I got for

asking for permission. In my experience, it was always better to ask forgiveness. Like with the accountant.

"I might be old but I'm sure I still move faster than you," Mr. Walker barked, turning partly in his chair to glare at me with blood-shot eyes. He looked like a fucking basset hound.

My jaw shifted irritably. Arching an eyebrow at Leander, I pinched my fingers together a minuscule amount. I wouldn't kill the old coot, just make him miserable for a week with the worst diarrhea and vomiting known to man. If he happened to die from dehydration along the way, all the better.

Leander gave a barely perceptible shake of his head and pushed the offer closer to the crippled asshole. "As you can see, you'd retain the majority share of the hotel."

"I own all of it now. Why would I give up any of it to the likes of you?" Mr. Walker's contorted hand gripped the handle of his cane.

"You can't carry the weight of this hotel forever," Leander said in that dark, silken voice of his. The one reserved for people he was going to destroy. "The plumbing needs to be replaced, the roof completely torn off and redone. My electrician was appalled by the wiring. How many other mechanicals are failing? How many other structural issues would the building inspector find?"

"You're not going to buy me out that easily."

"Think of this as more of an investment than a buyout."

The asshole 'hmphed' and stomped the cane on the floor. "You think just because I'm old that I don't know what you're doing? You forget, *boy*, that I knew your grandfather. I know what you people do. I'd rather burn my hotel to the ground than get in bed with a Welles."

Leander's perfect smile never faltered. "I won't ask again."

"Is that supposed to frighten me, pup?"

"If you weren't senile, it would."

My eyes lit up as they shot to Leander, my thumb hovering next to the green jewel. Leander cocked his head, his lips pursed. Not the signal I was hoping for.

"Your coffee, sir." Rolling my eyes, I rounded the old man's chair, purposely kicking the ornate clawfoot. Coffee sloshed over the side of the delicate cup and splashed all over his lap.

Mr. Walker jolted like a cat thrown in water. For an old man twisted with arthritis, he moved surprisingly quickly when two-hundred degree liquid was tossed all over his man bits.

"Oh my!" I gasped, looking at Leander, who was quietly retrieving the offer and swiping coffee droplets off it. "I'm so sorry, sir! I guess I was in a hurry." I offered the old man a cloth napkin and a pitying smile.

He swatted my hand away with a glare. "Don't touch me!" He opened his mouth to say something else, but ended up clicking his dentures shut and tromping out of the room.

"Should have let me do it," I said when he was gone.

Leander ran a hand over his face with a groan. "And what would that accomplish? His son is set to inherit everything and we'd be back at square one."

"One less asshole in the world?"

He fought a smile, shaking his head. "You can't kill everyone in Easton."

I gestured to myself, feigning innocence. "Me? You're the one with a hit list. I was merely pointing out that heart problems run in families. Perhaps the Walkers should watch their cholesterol."

Leander shot me a look and handed me the coffee-speckled papers. "We don't want any other bodies in town, now do we?"

"They say death comes in threes."

"I'll be sure to tell Richard that the next time he calls, screaming about murder charges and alibis."

"Does he really think you murdered that cop last week?"

Good ol' Keith Starkey, the man who made Cole and Leander miserable as children, was found beaten to death in his house by the mail lady. While they were processing the scene, the police also discovered that someone — ahem, Keith, ahem — stole all of the evidence from Irene Welles' murder, including the crowbar used to bash her brains in. The same crowbar was put to use again on Keith and the stacks of cash used to bribe him were quietly returned to their owner, who promptly stuffed them back in their hidey hole in the ginormous mansion on the hill.

Leander sighed. "He knows better than to come right out and say it."

"So the police dropped the investigation into the bartender? Jason, whatever?"

"Someone getting bludgeoned to death tends to take priority over what appeared to be a natural death, especially when that someone used to work for the investigating agency."

"All the more reason they should have referred the case to the sheriff's office. Do they have any idea what a competent defense attorney will say about the inherent conflict and biases?"

"No matter. When it goes to trial, we can always use that as a fallback plan to get it dismissed." He checked his watch, rising to his feet smoothly. "Time to get dinner started. The others are coming at seven."

"Need help?"

"No." He ran a hand down the front of his suit jacket, throwing a smirk over his shoulder. "But I wouldn't mind the company."

———

ALLEGRA CALLED while I was idly plunking out a song on Leander's piano, waiting for dinner to finish cooking.

"*Is this a bad time?*" she asked.

"No. Why? What's wrong?"

"*Nothing is wrong. I know I need to nail down plans now if I ever hope to see you.*"

"*See me for what?*"

"*Christmas.*"

"Christmas in Barcelona?" Sold.

"*No, Venice.*"

I laughed and shook my head, even if she couldn't see it. "Yeah, no. Not happening."

"*Bennett, please. I haven't seen you in over a year and this is the only time I know we'll have together. Between my exams and your work, we never have time anymore.*"

"Is this about Santos? I don't need to meet him to know I don't like him."

"*It's Sergio, and no. It's not about him. It's about me not wanting to spend the holidays alone.*"

I held in a groan. "Where's Camille going to be? Off in Rome with her latest conquest?"

"*It's not the same without you. You make Christmas fun! Ice skating, the opera. Come on!*" That did not answer my question, which meant Camille was going to be in Venice as well. So, my answer was not only "No," but "Hell no."

"Allegra..."

"*For me? Please? Just think about it?*" Fuck... Here it comes. "*I miss you.*"

"Yeah, yeah. Mi manchi." I hung up with a sigh. Leander was watching me when I looked up, a faint smile on his lips. "What?"

"Nothing." He returned to sketching in a flash, as if

someone pushed PLAY on a recording. "It's fascinating to hear you going back and forth between English and Italian. Is that conscious after all this time, or no?"

"I don't even know anymore." Resuming where I left off, my fingers drifted over the keys to the slow, melodic song. "But I know some things are better said in Italian."

He blew on the paper and squinted at it, making minor adjustments with the pencil. "Such as?"

"Mi manchi," I repeated, throwing him a smirk. "It means 'you're missing from me.' It has so much more feeling than a basic 'I miss you,' at least according to Allegra. She gets mad when I say it in English. She says I don't care."

"She sounds sweet."

"She is. I'd do anything for her."

"Except visit." Dick.

I shot him a glare before turning my attention to the piano in earnest, tuning him out with a darker song.

When the timer on the stove went off, Leander tossed the sketchpad to the side and headed for the kitchen.

I stood to follow, but his drawings caught my eye and I diverted to the couch. To my surprise, he was sketching me. And he was good. Really good. The study of my hands was so detailed it could have been a photograph. Nosy bastard I was, I flipped through the previous pages. There were sketches of flowers from his private island in the middle of the river, statues from the garden, a combination of landscapes and still lifes. Strangely, I was the only human subject.

Before he caught me looking, I set the sketchpad down and headed for the kitchen. Circling the island, I did my best to stay out of his way as he darted back and forth. "Need help?"

"If you're comfortable with a knife, you can slice the tenderloin when it's done resting." He nodded to the platter on the counter.

"If?" I quirked a brow at him and slipped a long, thin knife out of the block, balancing it in my hand. Once I had the weight of it, I flipped it in the air and caught it again on its way down. "I'd say I'm comfortable."

He rolled his eyes with a smirk and turned back to the sauce pot on the stove. "I should have known you were into knives."

"Why's that?"

"Poison. Knives. It's so..." He stopped stirring for a minute and looked up, staring at the tiled backsplash in search of the right word. "Italian."

"Cute. But that's not why I like knives."

"Mhmm."

As soon as his back was turned, I slipped up behind him, tossing the knife into my other hand. My right arm snaked around his torso and I pressed the blade against the backside of his ribcage with my left. With the right angle, the right amount of force, it'd go straight through his lung.

Sucking in a breath, he froze in place. From the way my hand was splayed across his chest, I could feel the initial increase in his heartbeat.

"This is why I like knives," I whispered into his hair, trying to focus on proving a point instead of the fact we were nearly the same height. On a basic level, I knew we were, but being this close, in this position, well... it reminded me of things I shouldn't be thinking about. "They're fast. And silent."

"You are a terrifying person sometimes. You know that right?" He angled a glance over his shoulder. For someone who claimed I was terrifying, he didn't look fearful. He seemed more at ease with a knife in his back than he did exchanging pleasantries in a boardroom.

Chuckling, I released my hold and backed away to use the

knife for its intended purpose. "Says the man who has an entire town under his heel."

"It's more the name than the actual man."

"You're selling yourself short."

He turned around with the sauce pot and a smirk. "You're just flattering me."

"Is it working?" I leered at him over the tenderloin, wagging my brows for effect.

He laughed, drizzling the slices as I plated them. "No," he replied loftily.

"Damn. I'm going to have to try harder."

"I shudder to think what that entails," he murmured, licking a drop of sauce off his finger in an entirely ordinary, everyday manner that left me gaping like a moron.

"What what entails?" I managed to spit out before he noticed my distracted silence.

"Being courted by the Devil." He gave me one of his looks, smoldering and cryptic. In the blink of an eye, the look was gone, as was he, headed for the dining room as casually as could be with the platter.

Dumbfounded, I stood there like an idiot, trying to figure out if that was some sort of challenge to try harder. Shaking my head, I gave myself a mental slap. Of course it wasn't. It was banter. That was it. Our usual back and forth. Just like Del and I. Except, Del never looked at me with that *look* before, and I never wanted to sleep with him. Ever. Even on spring break in Cancun after one too many shots of tequila.

"*Get a grip,*" I muttered under my breath, grabbing the stack of plates and silverware. Exhaling quickly, I set off for the dining room.

CHAPTER 18

"**F**riends of yours, I presume?" Leander asked, turning away from the front window in his office.

My pulse stuttered for a minute. Tony, and then Giovanni himself, had been calling with increasing frequency, despite the fact their calls were continuously ignored. Maybe they finally put two and two together and figured out where I was?

I slid along the wall to Leander's side, peering over his shoulder. I nearly breathed a sigh of relief.

Not the Italians, just my Bureau besties.

They were so cliche it was borderline painful. Big, black SUV. Tinted windows. Government plates. It's almost as if they wanted me to know they were there. What kind of surveillance tactic was that? Guess I'd better go find out.

I patted Leander's shoulder. "I've got this."

Slipping out the back door, I followed the alley to the end of the street and cut over to their side of the road. I could have waited them out. I could have followed them wherever they went — out of town or back to their hotel. There was no point in being coy. As much as I disliked them, they weren't stupid. This was the biggest white flag I ever saw.

Rapping my knuckles against the driver's side window, I stifled a snicker when Josh jumped.

The window slid down with a hiss. Both occupants greeted me with a scowl.

"What in God's name are you two doing down here? Doesn't this thing have navigation?" I asked, patting the side of their SUV.

"It took us a while, but we found you, smart ass," Denning said.

"Wow. Josh, you look so tan." I skimmed my fingers over his bicep, right beneath the sleeve of his dark blue polo. "Still playing volleyball, I take it? Or more vacations in that speedo of yours?"

He opened his mouth and clamped his teeth shut, turning to Diefendorf for help. Some things never got old.

"What's with the move?" Diefendorf asked, ignoring his partner's plight.

"Oh, you know." I gestured vaguely before bracing my forearms against the door. "Taxes in Chicago are outrageous. You get much more value for your money down here."

"Yeah, I can see. Your new boss has quite the real estate portfolio."

My smile may have been flawless, but my heart skipped a beat. They knew about Leander. Of course they did. They were the FBI. But they pulled his property records, which meant they probably pulled the rest of his financials too. Two agents with an axe to grind and plenty of time was not something I wanted to deal with in the midst of everything else we had going on.

"Nothing wrong with investing in community develop-ment," I replied lightly. "Speaking of communities... did you two transfer to another field office just for me?" I pressed a hand to my chest and inhaled deeply. "I am *so* flattered. You gave up everything back home to chase after little ol' me?"

"How about Maria? Did she give up everything back home for you, too?" Denning asked.

"Maria?" I pursed my lips, brows furrowed. The confusion may have been exaggerated, but I *was* confused. First they brought up Leander, but now we were back to Maria. What in the hell were they after?

He rolled his eyes. "Maria Hernandez."

Straightening, I gestured widely to the historic buildings behind me. "Do you think someone like Maria Hernandez is going to fit in here? I can name three Mexicans in town. The editor of the *Sentinel,* a house keeper, and a third-grade teacher. Even the gardeners are white. So why the hell would Maria Hernandez come here?"

"Maybe for that flauta you keep giving her?"

Inwardly, I groaned. It was one time. Jesus. Ok, two times. Two times does not equal any sort of clandestine relationship with a gang leader's wife.

Outwardly, I leaned into the window and ran my fingertip over the ridiculous pen clipped in Josh's sleeve, circling it in slow, suggestive strokes. It was literally a round head with a smiley face, topped with a mop of blue microfiber cloth. What a grown-ass man was doing with a pen like that was yet another reason I felt sorry for his poor supervisor.

"You sound jealous, Joshua... Would you like a crash course in Mexican food so you can see what keeps someone like Maria Hernandez happy? The hotel is one block that way."

Denning jerked his arm away, leaning as close as possible to his partner. "Get the fuck off of me!"

I laughed so hard I nearly snorted. "You are so uptight!"

"I am going to ki—" Josh lunged for the car door, but Craig grabbed his shoulder.

"Knock it off! He's yanking your chain and you keep falling for it." Diefendorf shook his head. Once his partner somewhat settled down, Craig directed his irritation at me. "We're not going away, Bennett, and we're tired of asking nicely."

"I have answered every question you've asked me today. What more do you want from me?"

"Where is Maria Hernandez?" Diefendorf practically shouted it, surprising all three of us.

I blinked, forgetting momentarily how to be a smart ass. "How the fuck am I supposed to know?"

"You're her husband's lawyer! You've slept with her I don't know how many times! And you're her cousin's best friend! Don't act like you don't know where she is!"

"I swear on Josh's life I don't know where she is!"

"Would you swear on Leander's?"

Biting my lower lip, I shook my head and took a step backward. "Have a safe drive, boys. The roads out here are so tricky, especially at night."

Diefendorf's gaze hardened even more at the dismissal. "You have two weeks to find out where she is and call me, or I'm coming back here with SWAT and a search warrant."

"Do it and I'll hit you with a civil rights violation so fucking hard neither of you will ever work in law enforcement again." My molars ground together, keeping any further threats tucked away safely.

Denning started the engine while Diefendorf and I engaged in a heated staring competition. Without waiting for a signal or any formal goodbye, Josh pulled away from the curb.

I stayed on the sidewalk, waiting until the SUV crossed the bridge and turned northbound, out of town. The summer sun beating down on me was nothing compared to the white-hot rage blistering inside. They'd gone from being mildly annoying, but dedicated agents just trying to do their job, to the Number One and Two thorns in my side. I'd never taken out law enforcement before, but there was a first time for everything.

———

I DIDN'T TELL LEANDER what Diefendorf said. He asked, of course, but I stayed mum. I didn't tell anyone — not Gavin, not Hector, and certainly not Maria. I did, however, text Del immediately and secure dinner plans in Chicago. He tried to wheedle more information out of me, so I ignored him altogether.

By the time Friday night rolled around, he'd texted and called a dozen times, all without answer. The only time I picked up was when I was twenty minutes outside the city.

"Dude, what the fuck? Where have you been?" he snapped.

"Are you already there?"

"Yeah, I'm here."

"Great. See you soon, hot stuff." I tossed the phone on the passenger seat and coasted into Chicago.

The paranoia I'd been trying to ignore for the better part of a week doubled the minute I took my exit. Keeping an eye out for cops, feds, and Italians, I took twice as long to get to the diner.

Parking several blocks over, I hunched my shoulders and shoved my hands into my pockets as I made my way through the crowd.

Del was in our usual spot — the back corner booth — angrily chewing on a cheeseburger. He stabbed a fry into his ketchup and watched me sit with dark eyes.

Shrugging out of my leather jacket, I tossed it into the booth before sliding in after it.

"Ok, I'm here," he said, setting his burger down and wiping his hands on a paper napkin. "Now, what the fuck?"

I threw a glance over my shoulder before answering. "Maria."

He made a face at me, some odd mix of surprise, confusion, and annoyance. "This is about Maria?"

"Tell me she's out of the country."

"She was, but now she's—"

"Ah, ah, ah! I don't want to know."

"Then why are you asking?"

"What about her dumb-ass husband? They together?"

"No. Things went south between them over, uh, business. And Veronica."

"Figures." I raked a hand through my hair, pushing it out of my eyes. How Hector could have a woman like Maria and still step out on her was a mystery I'd never be able to solve. "Remember the agents working Hector's crew?"

"Yeah…"

"They went from hounding me about Hector to outright threatening me over Maria. They're desperate to find her."

Del stared at the chocolate shake in front of him, his brain probably whirring a million miles a minute along with mine. "But why?"

"I don't know and I don't care. You're her cousin. You figure it out."

"What else did they say?"

I stole one of his French fries before answering. "Just that they want to know where she is."

"Not Hector?"

I shook my head. "No. They didn't even ask about him last time. It was *all* about her. They thought she was with me down south."

"Seriously? Ugh, I'll try and talk to her. Find out what's going on."

"Just be careful. They're still in Easton, watching me and now Leander. Plus, they know about this little bromance of ours," I said, gesturing between the two of us. "Which is why I didn't answer you."

He nodded. "Yeah, no, I get it. Interception and shit."

"She's not the shot-caller, Del. I've been around the Calaveras long enough to know that." I raised my brows at him, hinting at the truth without saying it outright.

He made another face, like I was some idiot intern. "They can't use her in Illinois *or* Federal court. Their communication is all privileged. You know that."

"Unless they want to force her testimony to prove or disprove other aspects of the case."

He shook his head, sitting back in the booth. "They know better. They know wives don't say shit even under compulsion. *Especially* once they have kids! Maria would never put her kids at risk like that."

Stealing another fry, I leaned back as well, trying to think like a good guy for a change. The realization hit me about as hard as the lightning did.

Del sat up straighter. "What? What's wrong?"

Casting another quick glance behind us, I lowered my voice all the same. "What if she turned?"

"Hello? What did I just say?"

I shook my head slowly. "Think about it. You said they're not together. If she cut a deal and then disappeared, *that* explains why the feds are losing their minds."

"She wouldn't. She wouldn't! That's crazy."

I leaned forward, hissing over the table. "She's fucking pissed, Del! She knows about Veronica and Jessica and everyone else Hector has slept with along the way. What are her options? Shank the asshole while he sleeps and get chopped up into little pieces by his gang or turn him into the feds so a rival cartel can take him out in prison? She gets a fresh start with the kids, no strings attached."

He exhaled slowly, holding his head in his hands. "Madre de Dios."

I knew it was crazy, but it was the best theory I had to explain Diefendorf's behavior. The quiet, intense insistence he needed to find her last year, practically pleading for help from a scumbag lawyer like me. The outrage and the threats when I refused to cooperate. He was worried about her. Genuinely worried about her, because he knew what happened to people who talked. He was a family man, after all, with a driving sense of good, given the profession he chose.

"What am I going to do?" Del asked. "What do I even tell her?"

"I have no idea... But you better think fast. If they take Leander down over this bullshit, I personally guarantee it's not going to be pretty for anyone."

CHAPTER 19

*F*ollowing my conversation with Del, I did my best to limit the amount of time I was seen publicly with Leander. The FBI may have already been scoping him out, but I didn't need to add fuel to their fire. Cole, in particular, was happy to be my new social companion, as was Elijah on the rare occasion when he wasn't herding the others like a mother duck.

It was well after midnight and the warmth of the summer day faded, replaced by a chill in the air that signaled the coming autumn. After Cole and I closed down the bar, I declined a ride home, opting to walk the relatively short distance to my house.

Two blocks from the bar, I picked up a tail. As something of an apex predator, it wasn't often I felt a sense of unease in dark places. So when that odd, prickly feeling crept up the back of my neck, I listened.

All the signs were there — the gut feeling; the faint fall of footsteps stopping and starting when mine did; the uncanny sensation of being watched.

At the corner, I stopped and whirled around, coming

face-to-face with one of the last people I ever expected to see in Easton.

"Johnny?" I took in the Italian from head-to-toe. His hands were at least empty, but I knew better. He didn't go anywhere without at least two guns. "What are you doing here?"

"Bennett. Pal." Johnny smiled. It may have been pleasant, if it weren't for the fact he was one of Gio's go-to collectors. "We've missed you up north."

"Aw, shucks, Johnny." I glanced up and down the street, seeing just how many people were about to witness my abduction. The answer was zero. We were completely alone. "You came all this way to tell me that?"

"Actually, I came because you've been ducking Mr. Marchese's calls."

"I haven't been ducking anything. I have no reason to pick up."

He chuckled darkly. "When Mr. Marchese calls, you answer. You know that."

Feigning a wince, I rocked back on my heels. "Unfortunately, I've never been very receptive to people telling me what to do."

"You've always been a pain the ass, even for a lawyer."

"I'm touched, Johnny."

Taking out his cell phone, he tapped the password into the screen, shaking his head.

"Any chance you'll pretend you couldn't find me? I'll make it worth your while." I slipped my hand along the backside of my right hip, shifting my weight to that foot to disguise the movement.

"Not on your life." He hit the button for his contacts and started scrolling.

"I figured you'd say that." I sighed, extending my left hand. "No hard feelings, then?"

He glanced at my hand before gripping it with a resigned expression.

Taking a step forward, I yanked him in close and drove the ice pick into the side of his ribcage. For good measure, I also stabbed him in the kidney and the side of his neck. One way or another, he'd be dead in minutes.

He gasped in surprise. The gasps turned to gurgles. His cell phone clattered to the sidewalk, Giovanni's name lit up on the little screen.

Keeping ahold of him in what could be mistaken for a parting hug, I lowered Johnny down gently onto the steps of the antique store as he wheezed his last breath.

"Should have taken the money," I whispered, prying his fingers off my shirt.

Once I got him slumped over on his left side, the blood more or less hidden beneath him, I splashed a bit of bourbon on him for effect. I crushed his phone underfoot before slipping it into my pocket. Tucking the ice pick inside my waistband, I wiped the blood off my hand with a handkerchief and strolled away, whistling calmly into the quiet night.

Tossing Johnny's phone into the river as I walked, I cut through the alley and slid into the driver's seat of my car.

As soon as I was out of Easton, heading northbound, I called Gavin.

"Do you have any idea what time it is?" He yawned mid-grumble.

"Did you tell Marchese where I was?"

"No. Why?"

"I mean it, Gavin! Did you tell *anyone* where I was?"

"No! God, why? What happened?"

"Get me an apartment in St. Louis. A sublet, or buy the whole fucking building with money from the trust. I don't care. Use the Singapore account. Whatever it is, I want a key in my hand by noon."

"Um, ok. Yeah. I'll take a flight first thing."

"From now on, if anyone asks where I am, tell them Philadelphia. Point of fact, book me a hotel room there for at least three weeks. A car too."

"Bennett, what's going on? You're making me really nervous."

"Oh, you know me. Making friends everywhere I go."

"Are you ok?"

"Call me when you have the apartment. Do *not* text it." I hung up and sped through the winding, country roads. Rolling down the window, I flung the ice pick out as far as I could. With any luck, it would bounce its way down a bluff and get completely covered when all the leaves fell. Either way, it was far enough away from town that no one would search the area for it.

As if he knew something was wrong, even miles away, Leander's name lit up my cell phone. I bit my lip, weighing the pros and cons of answering. The biggest pro? Easy. Him. Plus, I wanted to see what he was calling about. The biggest con? The fucking feds being able to pinpoint my location thanks to the stupid cell tower and thus blowing any alibi I had when a dead mafia enforcer inevitably showed up on their radar.

Before I decided, the screen went dark.

Swearing under my breath, I stomped on the accelerator. The Maserati surged forward until the landscape was a blur of blue and black nothingness, fireflies winking in and out in the distance.

I had no idea how they found me. The FBI was a little easier to understand, but Marchese? No clue.

When Johnny didn't call or return home, they would know something was wrong. They'd send even more people next time and I couldn't have them tramping through downtown Easton on a warpath. Nor could I have them targeting Leander for something that was entirely my doing.

So, time to go home and tie up loose ends.

———

THE THING no one ever tells you about stalking is how much time it actually takes. How much patience. And how many leg cramps you'll get crouched in one position for hours on end.

I was rubbing another knot out of my leg when my phone vibrated in my pocket. It was Leander. Again. I really didn't want to answer, but I'd been ignoring all forms of communication for the past three days, so I figured I owed him. Plus I was bored to tears.

"What's up?" I asked casually, as if I hadn't up and disappeared with zero explanation.

"Why... are you whispering?"

I cleared my throat, trying to sound completely normal despite my surroundings. "I'm not. You ok? It's kind of late. Or early, depending on your perspective. Trouble sleeping?"

"Yeah... Something like that. Where have you been? You missed a conference call with the auditors on Monday."

Slamming my palm against my forehead, I cringed inwardly. "Oh, shit. I forgot. Um, something came up. Unexpectedly. It was unexpected."

"That's generally what 'unexpectedly' means." He exhaled slowly while I tore into myself for being such a goddamn idiot. "Does this 'unexpected' business have anything to do with the body the police found downtown the other day?"

I blew out a breath. I didn't want to lie to him, but I didn't want him to worry, either. Rock, meet hard place.

"Bennett...?"

"Hmm?"

"Who was he?"

"Umm…"

There was a soft 'thump' outside and the jingling of keys. I shifted my position, hiding any light the phone might be giving off.

"I gotta go." I disconnected and shoved the phone back in my pocket. Grabbing the knife from the floor, I adjusted my gloved-grip on the crosshatched handle, curling into a crouch behind the driver's seat.

The car door opened and closed, the Suburban rocking slightly with the movement. Before the key made it into the ignition, I lunged forward. Yanking the seatbelt taut across Diefendorf's chest and left arm, I pressed his own tactical knife to his throat.

"What the fuck?!" He tried to throw off the restraint with his left hand, while his right dove for his hip.

"Go for your gun and I'll open your artery. Understood?"

"Bennett?"

I jerked the seatbelt harder when he tried to crane his neck to look at me. "Answer the question. Do you understand me?"

"Yes."

"Good. Did you tell Marchese where I was?"

"Why the fuck would I tell Marchese where you are? *I* didn't even know where you were until a month ago."

"It's a simple 'yes' or 'no' question."

"No!"

"Did they follow you?"

"I don't know!"

"How did *you* find me?"

"I'm not—" I pushed harder with the blade. "Ok, ok! We put a tracker on your car the last time you were in town."

I swore under my breath. Note to self, buy a new car. "So you've been watching me for a month?"

"More or less."

"All because of Maria Hernandez?"

"Look, Bennett, I—fuck! Stop!" He hissed and pressed himself as hard as he could into his seat, trying to get away from the bite of the blade. "It started out that way, yeah. But then we got a tip about the Welles Corporation and once we saw you were connected to the CEO, it spiraled from there."

"What kind of tip?"

"Just that they're into some shady shit. You know how it goes."

I kept my growl to myself. Fucking Marchese. Instead of tipping off PoDunk PD, they went straight to the feds. I guess I underestimated how pissed he would be when I ghosted him. Some guys were *so* unpredictable when it came to a breakup.

"Who's the tip from?" Even if I already knew, I wanted to see how much he'd tell me.

Diefendorf scoffed. "Come on, you know I don't know. Some rookie answers the phone and forwards the information up the chain. The information can be days or weeks old by the time it hits my desk."

"What about the Calaveras?"

"What about them?"

"Are you telling me that now you don't care about Maria?"

"Of course I care about Maria!" he snapped, trying to look over his shoulder again. "But we can't look away from all the shit we've seen in Easton."

I pulled back on the blade ever so slightly, my teeth on edge. "Well you better fucking look away, Craig, or I will make you regret the very moment you heard the name Leander Welles."

"It's not up to me anymore. Ok? I take my orders from the top." He was getting bolder. Louder. His muscles flexed under the restraint, even with the indentation of the blade in his neck. If I didn't wrap it up soon, he was going to do something heroic aka: stupid.

"I'm warning you. Find a way to make the SAC lose interest."

"Oh, *you're* warning me? How do you know I'm not going to have you arrested for this little stunt? Huh? Yeah, you're connected, but you're not invincible! No one is!" He turned his head as much as he dared, the fight plain as day on his face. Time to make him think twice about being valiant.

I rested my chin on his shoulder and held the knife up so he could see it. "Well, I'll tell you, since you asked so nicely. See, I'm going to take this knife with me, and if I have to, I'll frame you for murder with it. Then, once you're locked up, unable to do a damn thing, I'll come back here and fucking annihilate your little family while they sleep. Got it?"

"How do I know you won't do that anyway?"

"Wanna make a deal?"

He snorted. "With you?"

"No, with the fucking Devil. Of course me."

He clenched his teeth, swearing for a minute. "What?"

"If you leave Leander Welles and his company alone, I promise not to gut your wife in bed and strangle her with her own entrails. And as far as your boys go, I think I'll—"

"You're lying! You don't have it in you."

"Don't I?" I tipped his chin up with the point of the knife, lowering my mouth to his ear so he wouldn't miss a single syllable. "Do you want me to describe the first time I did it, so you can get a clear picture? You want to know about that hot, salty smell; the way the intestines pulsate in your hands while you're ripping them out? Or how about the way the blood positively gushes from the abdominal cavity?"

"You're a fucking monster." The condemnation came in a horrified whisper.

"Born and bred. Do we have a deal or not?"

"I told you," he snarled through gritted teeth. "It's out of my hands!"

"Then I guess you're going to have to get creative with your sabotage. After all, what's more important? Your job? Or your family?"

"Fuck you."

"You have five seconds to decide. Five. Four—"

"You're never going to get away with it."

"Three…" Canting my head to the side, I nudged him with the blade.

"Deal! Deal!"

"Wonderful. No matter what you think about me, a deal *is* a deal. As long as you hold up your side of the bargain, your adorable little family is safe. At least from me."

"Does that mean you're going to have someone else do your dirty work?"

"Nope. I am my own judge, jury, and executioner. Hiring a hitman is something lazy mob bosses do. And you can tell Marchese I said that." I released my grip on the seat belt, but kept the knife in place to make sure he wasn't going to be reckless.

"I swear to God, I don't have anything to do with Marchese!"

"Mhmm. Have a good day at work, sweetie." I kissed his cheek quickly and ducked out of the car.

CHAPTER 20

*A*s far as my besties were concerned, Diefendorf kept his word. In the weeks that followed, I saw neither hide nor hair of him or Denning in Easton. I didn't see them lingering outside of my new St. Louis apartment, either.

Splitting my time between St. Louis and Easton, I alternated the days I was in each city and the length of time I stayed. I'd throw in Chicago every once in a while for good measure, like a giant shell game for anyone trying to find me.

Even with Diefendorf and Denning's notable absence, it didn't mean the FBI cleared out of Easton altogether. There were plenty of brand new SUVs cruising around, along with a gaggle of clean-cut guys shopping for hurricane glass and artisan wine. Unless Easton somehow turned into the new Boys Town, there was no way they were tourists.

Still, I considered Diefendorf's part of the deal upheld. I knew he couldn't stop his bosses from sending others to sniff around, but I also felt confident he would misplace, misfile, or otherwise mismanage any information that crossed his desk. I painted a pretty enough picture of what would happen if he didn't and he wasn't the type to risk his family. Heroes never were.

Regardless, it didn't stop Leander from worrying when I finally clued him in on what was going on. The move to St. Louis was a giant red flag something was up and I had a hard time justifying it to him. When he caught sight of one of the "tourists" on the edge of the mansion property, snapping away with a telephoto lens, I had no choice but to come clean about the FBI.

Needless to say, he was *not* pleased. Thankfully, the subject didn't come up often, unless he caught wind of another surveillance team in town.

Today, was one of those days.

We were the only two left after Leander's regular Friday night dinner. Still nursing our drinks at the dining room table, I mulled over the predicament presented by both the FBI and a pouty mafia don. It was hard to help Leander carry out a revenge plot and world domination with the fuzz watching your every move.

"You're quiet," I said, one arm draped over the back of my chair.

"I'm tired." As if the exhaustion wasn't clear to see, he closed his eyes and held the side of his neck with a grimace.

"Migraine starting?"

He ignored me, his fingers digging into the base of his skull.

I got to my feet and circled around behind him, swatting his hand out of the way. I'd barely touched the other side of his neck when he grabbed my wrist.

"What are you doing?"

"What do you think I'm going to do? Just relax already." Shaking his hand off, I proceeded to massage the back of his neck and upper shoulders in ever-widening circles, working methodically. "Oh my God..." I'd felt corpses with softer muscles than him.

"What?"

"Take off your jacket."

Surprisingly he didn't protest. I helped him shrug out of it and draped it over the back of another chair. Once I had a better feel of what I was working with, I pressed the heel of my hand into a giant hard spot in his shoulder. I was rewarded with a faint crunching noise and a groan.

"What was that?" Leander asked, arching his back.

"A calcium deposit." With one hand clamped on his shoulder, I worked the area with the other to make sure it was sufficiently broken up. "Have you ever heard of a thing called stress management?"

"I don't have the time." Little by little, he started to relax under my hands.

"You need to find some. If I have to drag you to a spa myself, I'll do it." I dug into the beginning of another deposit, holding him firmly when he tried to squirm away. "It isn't healthy for a person to have this much built up in their muscles."

"Says the one who lives on takeout and bourbon. Ow!" He flinched to one side, sucking in a breath through his teeth.

"Oh, I'm so sorry, did that hurt?" I cooed, easing up on the pressure. "Here... Let's try this." Smirking, I rubbed my thumbs in small circles over his scapula, moving over the tender spot more carefully once I made my point.

He chuckled quietly, letting his body loosen again. "Where did you learn how to do this, anyway?"

"Picked up a few things from a girl in Thailand." I switched to his other shoulder, kneading the knots of his poor muscles. The phrase "wound tight" didn't even come close to what I felt. His perfect posture hid what must have been daily agony. Or, he'd grown so used to it over the years, he didn't notice anymore.

"You know this would be a lot easier if we went upstairs and you laid down," I said, making sure to keep my voice as neutral as possible. For once, I wasn't trying to be a perv. I was genuinely trying to help before he ossified right in front of me.

"That is *not* happening."

"At least take your shirt off?"

If the look he meant to give was exasperation, it failed. Or I was projecting, thanks to the groans and soft sighs.

Clearing my throat, I bowed my head and went back to work, which forced him to face forward again. "Suit yourself."

The sighing resumed now and again, especially when I shifted to his neck and up the back of his skull. His hair was like silk. God, did it smell good. *He* smelled good. No! Bad Bennett!

"I envy you," Leander murmured, interrupting the dangerous path my thoughts were barreling down.

I couldn't help but laugh at his proclamation. "Dear God, why?"

"The life you've had. You've been all over the world. You're not beholden to anything or anyone. You don't worry about anything except what you want."

"If you want to go, go. It's not like you have to ask for permission."

"I keep telling you it's not that simple."

"And I keep telling you it's not that complicated. Just go! Who is going to stop you?"

"It's easier said than done. Besides, there's too much to do around here."

A sudden thought struck me. Why the fuck didn't I think of it sooner? I stopped kneading abruptly, my hands on his shoulders. "Why don't you come with me to Venice for the holidays?"

He swiveled in his chair, looking up at me with a furrowed brow. "What? No."

"Come with me to Venice," I repeated, meeting his incredulous look with an emphatic nod. "Two weeks. No work. No worrying. You can actually relax."

"I can't. You know I can't."

"When's the last time you had an actual vacation?" I arched an eyebrow at him. I didn't know if he was refusing to relax, or travel. Either way, I wasn't accepting any answer except "Yes."

His gaze fell as he shook his head. "It's imposing."

"Bullshit. You're going." Spinning away from him, I hurried away in search of my jacket. I found it laying on the chaise in the music room, my phone tucked inside the inner pocket.

"Bennett!" His chair scraped the floor. I was able to track his movement down the hallway by the long strides, which only made me type faster.

"I can't hear you," I replied in a sing-song voice, clicking through the airline's app as fast as the screens would load.

He appeared in the doorway right as his flight was confirmed.

Grinning, I waved my phone at him. "And... done."

Biting his lips, he rolled his eyes and folded his arms over his chest. At least he knew it was pointless to argue.

CHAPTER 21

Somewhere over the Atlantic, I fell asleep without even trying. I woke up when the plane landed in Italy, my head on Leander's shoulder and a crick in my neck.

"Good morning, sunshine," Leander said when I sat upright, rubbing the back of my neck.

"Sorry. I guess the Xanax hit a little harder than I thought."

"I didn't know you were on medication." It sounded more like a question than a condemnation.

"Just for this trip," I replied, standing and arching my back with a groan and a series of crackles. "Shall we?"

Grabbing our bags, we headed off the plane. Outside the airport, we hopped into a water taxi and I gave the driver the address of our ultimate destination.

"This is different," Leander said, settling into the boat.

"Welcome to Venice."

I thought I'd escaped the whole conversation about the Xanax since Leander seemed preoccupied with the architecture as we cruised along through the canals. Wrong.

"You don't talk about your mother very much," he said quietly.

"That's because I don't like her very much."

"Is that why you're drugging yourself?"

Winking, I clicked the side of my cheek, pointing a finger-gun at him. Spot on the nose, as usual.

"Maybe we should stay at a hotel?"

I sighed wistfully. "Allegra insisted."

He patted my knee gently before whirling toward the window. "Is that the—"

"Bridge of Sighs, yes."

"Incredible." His breath fogged the glass as he stared up in wonder.

"Yes, it is." I realized a second too late I was looking at him, not the Doge's palace or the bridge where hundreds of people crossed to their deaths. Clearing my throat, I angled myself away from him and looked out the other window at the city.

Venice was draped in sparkling lights and illumination, doubly reflected in the shining black water. Christmas lights of every color, massive glittering balls, and huge blinking stars covered nearly every shop and alleyway. I remembered the first time I saw it, how magical I thought the city was. Now I knew better.

Even though the boat dropped us off as close as it could, we still had a bit of a walk to the palazzo.

By the time we reached the heavy, iron gate at the base of the soaring Venetian Gothic building, the dampness of the night air had seeped in the collar of my coat and up my sleeves. I'd take it over a sub-zero Chicago winter any day, but it was an adjustment after so many years *not* holidaying in Italy.

The sound of our shoes echoed across the tile as we made our way to the wide staircase winding its way from the ground-floor to the residences on the upper levels.

"The gardens are out that way," I murmured, tossing my head toward a heavy door. "And we're this apartment here."

Leander spun in a small circle on the second floor, marveling at the historic frescos and ornate plaster from the baroque renovations. "Does your mother own all of this?"

"Surprisingly, no. Although I wouldn't put it past her to marry Signore Pavan just to inherit it."

Knocking on the apartment door, I sighed, resigning myself to the fact two very different worlds were about to collide. I'd been trying to make peace with it all day but neither the Xanax nor the bourbon were doing their job. On the one hand, Allegra meeting Leander was perfectly fine. And then there was Camille...

"I'm going to apologize now for anything she says or does," I said in the last few moments before the door opened. "If you want some Xanax, I've got more than enough. Or, say the word and we're gone. I mean it. I made hotel reservations for every day we're here. We do *not* have to stay."

He blinked at me with wide eyes. "Um, ok..."

The tap-tapping of kitten heels on centuries' old tile sounded before the carved door swung inward. Camille appeared with a cloud of perfume and a perfect French twist.

"Bennett!" She threw her arms around my neck and kissed my cheeks. "And you must be Leander." Without warning, she whirled on him and repeated the process.

The smile he gave her was fleeting, meanwhile, his wide eyes found mine. I mouthed "Sorry" over the top of her head and marched inside, the moisture from her kisses drying in itchy patches on my skin. "Where's Allegra?"

"Sleeping. She took an early flight." Camille closed and locked the door, muttering to herself. "*Penny-pincher, like her father.*"

"Isn't that why you married him? More money for you in the end?" I made sure to ask it with a smile, so Leander didn't know I was fighting dirty in the three seconds we'd been here.

She opened her mouth, but must have thought better of it since she turned on her mega-watt smile and looped her arm through Leander's. "How was your flight?"

"Fine, thank you." He glanced at me, a cry for help in his eyes. Forced affection and closeness with complete strangers was the perfect way to get him settled in... Not.

"Why don't you go to bed?" I stopped in front of the two of them and spun, trying my best to actually mean my smile. "We can save the chit chat for the morning."

"Alright, sweetheart. Let me know if you need anything."

When she leaned in to kiss my cheek again, the smile twisted to a grimace. "English, Camille," I hissed in her ear.

She gave me a polite, thin-lipped smile before turning to Leander. "Goodnight, boys."

I suppressed a groan and headed straight for the stairs. Leander was right behind me. If I made it through this trip without murdering her, it would be a miracle.

"She seems... nice," he said once we crested the stairs.

"Don't be fooled. She's a viper." I stopped at the juncture of the main hallway with the one that ran to the western wing. "I'm this way, guest room is down the hall on the left, second door."

"See you in the morning."

Leander disappeared in the direction I nodded, while I peeled off the other way. I'd just dropped the bags at the foot of the bed when Leander called for me.

Brow furrowed, I retraced my steps down the hallway. "What's the matter?"

He bit his lips and glanced around the room. There wasn't

a bed in sight. Instead, easels and canvases in various stages of completion ringed the room.

Gritting my teeth, I spun on my heel and strode down the stairs again. "Camille!"

"Yes, angel?" She appeared with a smile that made me want to puke. She must not have realized I was alone.

"What happened to the guest room?"

"Oh, I turned it into my art studio. The light is so much better in there than where it used to be."

I stared at her, pissed she was a) still speaking Italian and b)... "Why didn't you tell me there wasn't enough room?"

"Enough room? What are you talking about? The apartment is four hundred and eighty square meters, Bennett. We have plenty of room."

"Right. Well, I guess we're going to the hotel, then, so we both have a place to actually sleep tonight."

"What are you talking about? Did you two get into a fight?"

For once, I was happy she wasn't speaking English. Even still, I threw a cautious glance toward the stairwell before answering her. *"What? No. Why is that even a question?"*

She flung her hands in the air. *"I don't know. You finally bring someone home and now you're the one making a big deal out of bedrooms and sleeping arrangements."*

"Bring someone..." I closed my eyes, inhaling a slow breath and exhaling it even slower. I knew I was tired, but I was certain I didn't refer to Leander as anyone other than my friend in the one phone call we had discussing this disaster of a vacation. Once again she was drawing her own conclusions. Exhibit A of why I didn't visit.

"You know what? Forget it. Forget I said anything." I shook my head and tromped back upstairs.

Leander was in my room when I came back, staring out the window overlooking the canal. Moonlight glimmered on the water, the black silhouette of the city a touch darker than the sky behind it. "This view is marvelous."

"It's all yours if you want. I'm going to the hotel." If I could only remember which one it was for the first night... Metropole? Londra? Didn't matter. I'd figure it out on the way.

Leander pivoted away from the window, his mouth downturned. "I'm not kicking you out of your room. I can go sleep on the couch."

"You flew all this way. You're not sleeping on a couch."

"You took the same flight and you shouldn't be forced to go to a hotel over something as trivial as a bed." He held my gaze. I broke away first. Shaking my head, I considered the bed that laid between us.

"Let's just get some sleep," he continued. "We'll figure out what we're going to do for the rest of the trip tomorrow."

Conceding to his logic with a sigh, I dropped my luggage again. "You know, it's a good thing I packed pajamas, 'cuz I usually sleep naked."

He tossed a glance over his shoulder, unzipping his own suitcase. "Don't make it weird."

Laughing, I grabbed said pajamas — in reality, a tank top and a pair of pajama pants — and my bag of toiletries and headed into the bathroom.

When I reemerged, Leander was also in sleep clothes, except his were proper pajamas. Black silk, of course. He grabbed his dopp kit and brushed past me on the way to the bathroom.

I climbed into bed first, assessing how much space there actually was. It wasn't terrible. I knew two people could lay comfortably on this mattress. But usually those people wouldn't object if I happened to roll over on them in the middle of the night.

Stuffing a pillow under the covers as a makeshift barrier,

I stretched out safely on my side, staring up at the ceiling. It was fine. It was going to be fine. Del and I passed out in how many hotel beds together? Not to mention the frat parties. No big deal. Even the whole bi thing wasn't an issue. It hadn't been an issue for over a year. It was out there and it changed nothing. So why should this?

Leander came out a minute later and slid underneath the covers.

My heartbeat kicked up a notch. I was sure he'd hear it any moment with the darkness pressing around us. I told myself it was a lingering surge of adrenaline from seeing Camille. That was all.

"When was the last time you were here?" Leander asked, his voice low, as if he, too, was afraid to disrupt the quiet.

"It's been a while."

"Why?"

"It's… complicated."

He rolled onto his side, folding one arm under his head. Even in the dark, the disbelieving look was unmistakable.

My fingers tightened on the top sheet for half a second before I turned over, facing away from him. "Goodnight."

———

I DON'T KNOW which woke me up first, the boom of thunder or the flash of lightning. Whatever it was made me shoot up in bed, gasping for a breath that suddenly dissipated from my lungs.

Instinctively looking at the window, I swallowed forcefully, hoping it would dislodge the tightness in my chest. It didn't. My heart continued to pound a mile a minute, beads of sweat drying on the nape of my neck in the frigid air.

Leander jerked awake as well, eyes wide. "What's wrong?"

"Nothing." I ran a hand over my face, trying to remember

how to breathe like a normal human being. It was hard when my throat felt like it was stuffed with cotton.

He slid a glance over his shoulder as another streak of lightning tore across the sky. "The storm?"

Exhaling slowly, I slipped out of bed and dropped to the ground next to my suitcase. Groping along one of the pockets, I located the prescription bottle and shook a couple pills out into my hand, swallowing them dry.

Thirty minutes. That's all I needed. Thirty minutes and I'd start to feel that warm haze of not giving a shit, followed by blissful, dreamless sleep.

I crawled back onto the edge of the bed and sat, bracing my hands on my knees, willing the time to fly by.

"Can I do anything?" Leander asked.

"No."

"When my grandmother locked me in the cellar, I'd be down there so long I'd lose count of the days. The only way I staved off the panic attacks was with literature. I'd recite poems, stories. Anything that gave me an escape. It might work for you, too."

"No wonder you fucking killed her." Forcing myself to lay down again, I kicked the covers off in case I had to make a break for it. Plus it was hotter than hell in here.

Leander fluffed his pillow and laid down, facing me. "Do you want to talk about it?"

About what an idiot I was? About the fact I was worse than a five-year-old who gets scared during storms? I squeezed my eyes shut, trying to block out the bursts of white light. "No."

As if God himself was punctuating my response, thunder clapped so hard the walls shook. The wind shifted, driving rain against the glass in a deafening staccato. Fucker.

"I would kill for a drink right now," I muttered.

"You just took medication."

"Your point?"

"I'm certainly not a doctor, but I don't think it's advisable to mix the two."

I chuckled, toying with the lira around my neck. "Good thing you weren't around in college."

"I can only imagine the amount of reckless things you've done in your life."

"The reckless things are what make it fun."

The storm was getting closer, evidenced by another flash of lightning, followed by a rumble of thunder. Once again, I jumped like an idiot, swearing under my breath. It'd been over two decades already. When the fuck was I going to get over it?

Leander cleared his throat softly. "'In visions of the dark night/I have dreamed of joy departed—'"

I turned my face toward him with a half-smile. "Are you really reciting Poe for me?"

He wrinkled his nose, trying not to smile. "Would you prefer Byron?"

"No, I like Poe." In truth, he could have read the phone book and I would have preferred it to my own whirlwind of thoughts.

"Shall I continue?"

Nodding, I nestled into the pillow again. I closed my eyes and concentrated on the timbre of his voice, as soothing as the cadence of the poem itself.

After finishing *A Dream*, he moved on to *Annabel Lee*. He was only a few lines into *To One in Paradise* when I slipped off to sleep.

CHAPTER 22

*D*espite the night's disruption, I woke with a sense of calm, blinking against the morning light. It was then I realized my fingers were curled around Leander's, resting atop the pillow meant to separate us, like a couple of otters adrift in the sea.

I cursed silently. The last thing I needed was for him to wake up and see that. Sharing a bed out of convenience was one thing. Holding his hand? He would *not* be ok with that.

Moving a millimeter at a time, I pressed my own hand deeper into the pillow to slide it out. I listened for any change to his breathing and kept an eye on the angles of his face. His beautiful face. I gave myself a mental slap and focused on disentangling us as slowly as possible instead of daydreaming about what it would be like to kiss him.

As soon as my fingers cleared his, I rolled away and dropped off the side of the bed like a ninja. Years of stealthy escapes finally paid off. But I had a bigger problem now than an awkward morning-after conversation.

Padding to the bathroom as quietly as I could, I darted

inside and closed the door. Slumping against it, I let out the shaky breath I'd been holding.

What was wrong with me?! There was a clear divide between friendship and... other. Leander was on the *friend* side of things, from Day One. Despite what my dick apparently wanted, my brain didn't want to ruin that. Not to mention the slight problem that I was *not* his type, nor was I about to be a predatory douche. At least when it came to him.

It was just pent-up sexual frustration. That's it. I hadn't been laid since... Fuck me. New Orleans? That was over a year ago. No wonder I was losing my goddamn mind.

As soon as I turned the shower on, I shed my pajamas and stepped in, gasping aloud. It was a terrible, yet necessary, decision that needed to be made if I was going to make it through the rest of the day without any other form of release.

With cold water spraying over me, I turned my lawyer-logic on, examining the facts as I knew them. Leander and I had been friends for over two years. I never made a move on him; he certainly never made a move on me. Was he gorgeous? Absolutely. Did I want him in all the ways one shouldn't want their friend/employer/partner-in-crime? Absolutely. Was I going to fuck all that up because I couldn't keep my hands to myself? Dear God, I hoped not.

There was one odd aspect of the previous night I wasn't able to work out, though. Who initiated the midnight hand-holding? I'd never noticed any otter behavior on my part before. Then again, I usually never stayed the whole night. Maybe Leander was the otter, a secret snuggler who would vehemently deny it if he were ever questioned.

I finished showering and toweled off, feeling marginally better. Peeking out the bathroom door, I eyed the distance between it and my suitcase. In my mad dash to the bathroom, I didn't even think about grabbing clothes.

Leander was awake, his nose stuck in a book. "Good morning," he murmured without looking up.

"Morning." Running a hand through my wet hair, I walked to my suitcase as casually as I could in nothing but a towel. I scooped out an armful of clothes, hoped it would turn into a decent outfit, and ducked back into the bathroom. Once I was properly dressed, I walked out again. "Bathroom is all yours."

He dog-earred his page and set it aside. Pausing in front of me, his brows dipped slightly. "Are you alright?"

"Yep. Why? Do I not look alright?"

"I don't know…"

I finger-combed my hair in the other direction. "Better?"

He squinted slightly, his lips pursed. Apparently he decided to drop it, since he grabbed an outfit and proceeded into the bathroom without another word.

I reprimanded myself silently to get it together. I couldn't fool him anymore than he could fool me. If I didn't get a hold of myself, this was going to be an excruciating vacation. Well, more excruciating than it already was.

Wandering downstairs, I followed the sound of voices into the dining room.

Camille spared no expense in covering the massive mahogany table with a spread that could have fed an army. She and Allegra sat at the far end of the table, chatting away until Allegra spied me.

"Bennett!" With a girlish shriek, she darted out of her chair and flew into my arms, squeezing my neck. *"I've missed you so much! I'm so happy you came!"* She shoved away from me, her dark brows furrowed as she looked past me. *"Where's Leander?"*

"He'll be down in a minute. Which reminds me, Mother—" I

gave her a dour look to go along with M-word I choked out for Allegra's benefit. *"Can you keep it together while we're here? He's not used to crazy family dynamics and the last thing I need is for you to freak him out."*

Camille huffed, setting her juice glass down with more force than necessary. *"Do you have to pick a fight on the first day you're home? I haven't done anything except be happy the two of you are here."*

"Well, be a little <u>less</u> happy."

Allegra elbowed me a second before she faced our mother with a bright smile. *"I'll go get the brioche."*

I watched her float out of the room before turning my bittersweet smile to Camille. *"I'm here for two reasons and you're not either of them. So drop the act."*

She lifted a perfect brow and ran her knife through a slice of melon in one, smooth motion. Skewering the severed chunk, she bit it off the tines with a vicious smile.

"Careful with that knife, Camille. Wouldn't want you to cut yourself."

"You'd know all about that, wouldn't you?" Bitch.

I wiped all trace of hatred off my face and spun to take the platter of brioche from Allegra. *"Here, let me."*

Leander walked in next, smoothing his tie down. "I'm sorry I'm late."

"You're not," I said quickly. "We're going out for breakfast."

"Bennett," Camille said sharply.

It was mostly obscured by Allegra springing out of her chair again with an ear-to-ear smile, her hand stuck out toward Leander. "I'm Allegra. It's so nice to finally meet you! Thank you for giving up your holidays to spend them with us."

"I wouldn't have missed it for the world," Leander replied,

slipping his hand into hers and kissing her knuckles. "Thank you for having me."

"Why don't you both sit down?" Although it was technically a question, coming from Camille it was nothing short of a command.

I bristled immediately and wrapped my fingers around Leander's bicep. "We'll see you later." Spinning him toward the door, I stayed a step behind him so I could meet Camille's furious gaze as I rounded the corner.

"Is everything alright?" Leander asked as we pulled on our coats.

"Perfect. Why wouldn't it be?" I wrapped a scarf loosely around my throat and headed out, stuffing my hands into my pockets.

He made a disbelieving noise, pulling the door shut behind us. "'Truth in a masquerade.'"

I smirked at him when I hit the landing. "How apropos, Byron."

"We are in Venice, after all."

"Then it should please you to know we're going to Cafe Florian."

A slow smile spread across his face. "Are you serious?"

"'We are all selfish and I no more trust myself than others with a good motive.'" I held open the door on the ground floor, leaning against it as he walked through.

"Are you really quoting Byron to me right now?" His smile turned to a mischievous smirk, mirroring our conversation from last night.

"'Here's a sigh to those who love me, and a smile to those who hate.'" I gestured widely to the city before us.

"Ok, show off." Leander bumped his shoulder against mine as we walked.

AFTER THE USUAL MUST-SEE SIGHTS, I took Leander's elbow and pulled him down one of the narrow side streets. "Alright. Enough touristy shit."

"What did you have in mind?"

God, I wished he would stop phrasing things like that — or using that tone. That conspiratorial, mischievous tone that made me stupidly giddy, since it meant we were bound to do something illegal or dangerous — or both. After this morning, Little Bennett didn't need any more encouragement.

Ducking into a shop, I held the door open, watching his face transition from mild curiosity to pure ecstasy.

Towering stacks of books were crammed along every wall, in teetering piles on random chairs, and old, sagging bookcases. At one point there might have been a means of organizing it all, but over the decades it became a haphazard treasure trove for book worms.

"Figured we'd take a little break," I said, trailing after him. "Have some espresso and chill for a while."

Like a kid in a candy store, Leander was gone, disappearing to the furthest reaches of the store. I let him go, watching from a distance as he ran his hands over spines, pulling down the occasional book only to put it back and move on to something else.

"This is what you should be doing," I said, leaning against a shelf next to him once he stopped, flipping through a collection of Byron's works. Naturally.

His gaze flicked over the top of the page. "What?"

"This." I gestured around the musty building. Venice, watery grave that it was, lent a certain smell to the place, combined with the books' own natural process of disintegration. "Move to Europe. Buy a bookstore. Do something you love."

"Like you love the law?" His lips twitched into a smirk as he turned the page, giving it his utmost attention.

"I love fucking with people."

"All I heard was 'fucking' and 'people.'"

"Smart ass."

He shelved the book and mirrored my pose against the shelf, giving me an incredulous look. "You hated growing up here. And now I should suddenly walk away from everything and move to Europe?"

"As an adult, I see the appeal."

"Oh really? So if you up and left, where would you go?"

"Malta. Or Spain."

The corners of his eyes crinkled. "Not that you've given it much thought."

"Me? No. Not at all." If only he knew about the palazzo I'd been renovating in Valletta ever since he stood in my Chicago apartment and wished out loud for anonymity. On the surface, it was a good investment for tax purposes. But even back then I knew I was lying to myself as I pored over a catalogue of professional-grade kitchen appliances.

"Will you at least give me fair warning before you disappear into the sunset?"

"I would never disappear on you." Ignoring his disbelieving look, I pulled a book off the shelf. As I thumbed through it, my nose wrinkled involuntarily. "Oh yeah. This was the one with the shitty translation." Shoving it back on the shelf, I grabbed another.

Leander took the discarded book and scanned it with a lifted brow. "You know how much I love reading, but even I can barely recall the various editions and their slight modifications."

I tapped my temple. "Photographic memory."

"Mhmm."

"You don't believe me?"

"I don't think I believe half of what you say." His tone was haughty, at odds with the smile he was trying to hide as he stepped sideways.

"That's an entirely separate issue we'll address later." I tossed my head toward the shelf. "I'm pretty sure I've read all of these at one point. So, pick a book. Test me right now."

Leander's lips curled fully into a smile. "Alright then." He wandered down the aisle, scanning the shelves until at last he stopped. Stretching up on his toes, he snagged a volume from the top shelf and spun it around with an arched eyebrow. It was *The Prince*. "1903 edition," he said smugly.

"Bring it." I cleared my throat and clasped my hands together, settling into a comfortable stance.

"Page nine, third paragraph."

I closed my eyes, scanning through the library in my head. "'For the Romans did in this case what all wise princes should do, who look not only at present dangers but also at future ones and diligently guard against them.'"

"Lucky guess." He flipped forward again. "Page seventy-nine. First sentence."

I cocked my head at him. "Really?"

A serene smile replaced the smug one as he blinked at me, oh-so-innocently. "What? Can't remember?"

I licked my lips, shaking my head. "'Whoever examines in detail the actions of Severus, will find him to have been a very ferocious lion and an extremely astute fox.'"

Leander closed the book, but he didn't put it back. His gaze settled on mine in a way that made my heartbeat quicken. "You never cease to amaze, Bennett Reeve."

"And yet, you doubted me." I sidestepped him, murmuring over his right shoulder. "Page seventy-one, middle of the page. 'Everybody sees what you appear to be, few experience what you are.'"

As I moved left, he shifted, meeting my gaze over his

shoulder. His lips parted slightly and his pulse was visible on the side of his throat.

It took every shred of self-control I had not to throw him against the bookshelf and kiss him until neither of us could breathe. My logic from the shower was completely gone, erased by the fervid look in his eye.

Or maybe it was the dim lighting of the bookstore. Nothing more than wishful thinking on my part.

To be sure, I stole a backward glance. As usual, whatever look may have been there was gone. His face was obscured by his dark hair as he perused the book in his hands. The only thing I could see clearly was his mouth — his perfect mouth — as he chewed his lower lip.

———

WHEN IT CAME time for bed again, there was no discussion about making alternate arrangements. We had all day for either one of us to bring it up, yet it never happened. I tried not to read too much into it as we quietly assumed our spots.

"Do you ever take that off?" he asked randomly, reaching over to flick the wide, silver cuff on my left wrist.

"Not really. Why?"

"Just wondering. I don't think I've ever seen you without it."

"I don't like when it's off." I glanced at him out of the corner of my eye when he didn't say anything else. "What?"

He raised both brows at me, waiting. There was no need for a verbal question. His look said it all.

Sighing, I wriggled it off and held my left wrist out to him. The mottled, white mark normally hidden was visible thanks to the moonlight streaming in the window.

"Is that from the lightning?"

"That's where it went in. It came out on my hip."

"Incredible."

"Want me to show you that one too?" I asked, slipping the cuff back on. "It's even bigger."

He gave me a sidelong look before answering. "I don't think you have the balls."

I gaped at him. Did he not know who he was dealing with? "Oh really?"

He smirked.

"Fine." He asked for it. It wasn't crossing a line if he's the one who started it. Right? I hooked my thumb around my waistband and yanked it down over my hip.

"No! I believe you!" He held up a hand and turned his face away, laughing.

"Are you sure? It's right here it you want to look."

"No. I'm good. I believe you."

Shaking my head, I let go of the elastic and settled back into position.

"Why do you keep it covered?" he asked. "It's only one scar."

"It's annoying. I used to let people make up their own reason for it, but that shit got old. Telling the story behind it gets old. So… cuff it is. It's easier if no one sees it."

"That it is." He blew a curl out of his eye. His voice lost its teasing tone, shifting to something more somber.

"What are you talking about?"

"Nothing. Goodnight." He rolled over onto his side, away from me.

I rolled him right back over by the shoulder. "If you're telling me you have some hideous scar somewhere, I'm calling you a liar. You're perfect. I've never seen anyone with better skin."

He frowned at me, his brows furrowed. "You haven't seen all of it."

"Ooo, is that an offer?" I bit my lip and elbowed him lightly.

Instead of chuckling, he exhaled, his gaze fixed on the ceiling.

It was my turn to look at him with consternation. There was more to it than a simple scar. Way more. "Show me?"

He shook his head, refusing to look at me.

"Hey." I propped myself up on an elbow, trying to get a better read on him. "Whatever it is, I bet it's not as bad as you think."

By the way his lips twitched, I knew he was biting the inner corner of his mouth. If he kept it up, he was going to give himself a canker sore, which would make eating all the briny seafood dinners an absolute bitch. But I wasn't going to push. I'd wait him out, the same way he used pointed silence to get information out of me.

After another moment, I was rewarded for my patience. He pushed his sleeve out of the way and held his left arm out to me.

"Shit…" It didn't take a genius to see what he was talking about. White hatch marks covered his entire arm, from just below his cuff, all the way to the elbow. The scars ran every which way, up, down, across; some thinner, some thicker — a history of pain and suffering he'd only hinted at.

I traced my fingertips down the vein in his wrist, where the thickest lines were concentrated. Our conversation on loneliness took on an entirely new meaning in light of his revelation.

Swallowing thickly, he rolled away from me again, taking his arm with him. He tucked it underneath himself and let out a shaky breath.

I shifted the barrier pillow out of the way and slid closer, trying to figure out the appropriate response. At a loss, I wrapped my arm around him tentatively. When he didn't throw it off, I pulled him backward, against my chest. He didn't resist that, either, so I held him as tightly as I dared, turning myself into the human equivalent of a weighted blanket.

How he kept this to himself for so long was baffling. Given everything else we knew about one another, every other horror and misdeed, it was the last thing I expected. But, looking back, it made sense. The torment that was his childhood, the fact he always wore long sleeves. Even the color black — because it didn't show blood as easily.

He expelled a breath and sniffed. He might have been able to cry in relative silence, but he couldn't disguise his uneven breathing. With every tremble, I imagined he was bottling his memories back up one by one, enduring everything alone, as he always had.

"Per aspera ad astra," I said softly. For some reason it was the only thing I could think of to say. It's what the priest told me at my father's funeral when he was trying to give me a "be strong" speech. I responded by throwing a Bible at him and storming out. Pretty sure that was my ticket to Hell, never mind all the stuff that came later. But it must have stuck if I was dredging it up now.

Near-silent laughter shook Leander's body. "I don't speak Latin. What are you saying about stars?"

"It means 'Through hardship to the stars.'"

"Ah... I should be in another galaxy then."

"Can I come?"

He chuckled out loud. "Why would you want to?"

"You know me. I never turn down an adventure."

"Yeah, well, you're going to have an adventure to the hospital if you don't get off of me." He rolled into me even further, sliding a pointed glance over his shoulder.

A glutton for punishment, or a secret masochist, I squeezed him tighter, nuzzling the side of his face. If he was back to bantering, it was clearly my duty to do likewise. "Oh come on. You don't want to snuggle? It gets so cold in here at night."

"Do I strike you as the type of person who snuggles?" He started squirming, trying to roll away, but I grabbed ahold of his waist and held onto him.

"Shh... don't fight it."

He gave up with a huff and shook his head, doing his best to suppress a chuckle.

"You're so hot," I said, like a moron. Squeezing my eyes shut, I kicked myself for not thinking that one through. I didn't even mean it like *that*. It was truly a statement about body temperature.

His gaze darted over his shoulder again.

I cleared my throat, pushing away from him. "You're like a furnace." Retreating to my side of the bed, I rolled over to face the wall and berate myself for the next half hour.

"Try not to wake me up tonight," he said, adjusting his pillow.

"No promises."

CHAPTER 23

*D*ay One was the PC touristy shit. Day Two was the dark, creepy touristy shit. After all, there was a brand new torture museum Leander insisted we see. I wasn't going to argue, but I didn't want to weird him out after last night's discovery. He wasn't fazed in the slightest, and I know I found it all *very* educational.

Afterward, the history lesson continued as we wandered the city. I pointed out the remaining Lion's Mouths and other lurid tidbits of Venetian history.

"I guess you could say I've always had a thing for lions," I said as Leander stared up at the giant, winged-lion atop the column in Piazza San Marco. When his gaze dropped to mine, I winked and spun away. "Come on. Time for gelato."

"Gelato? In December?"

"Uh, yeah. Gelato anytime."

With our frozen goodness in hand, we headed back into the sunshine. Since Venetians didn't believe in any form of public seating, we continued on aimlessly, watching people bustle around for their last minute Christmas shopping.

"Are you ever going to tell me why you hate your mother?" Leander asked, licking the pale green gelato off the flat side of his spoon.

"Wow. Just diving right into it, aren't we?"

"It's only fair. You know the whole wretched story of my upbringing."

I stalled, taking a bite of my gelato. "I wouldn't even know where to start."

"Why did your mother come to Europe after your father was killed?"

Exhaling, I turned my attention to the buildings and the dramatic arches ringing the piazza. "On the surface, it's because she wanted to be an 'artist' and Europe is where 'artists' go."

"Beneath the surface?"

"She's a gold-digging, murdering whore?" My laugh was short and bitter. "She was an appraiser at Bancroft's when she met my father. It was a whirlwind affair resulting in yours truly, followed by an unhappy marriage. He worked, she whored around, spending his money. Then he died and she was free. Except, she didn't get the money she was expecting. I did. My grandmother saw to that. So, off to Europe we went to blow whatever money she got for selling everything we owned.

"She hopped from guy to guy. Then she met Massimo, Allegra's father. And wouldn't you know? Another whirlwind romance, followed by Allegra. Once Massimo was out of the picture, she moved on to Filippo." I spat the last name.

"Who is he?"

I gave him a grim smile even as the milk curdled in my stomach. "The first person I ever killed."

Leander was quiet for a moment, the muscle along his cheek twitching.

Shaking my head, my gaze dropped to the flat stones beneath our feet.

"How old were you?" he asked half a block later.

"Nineteen. Allegra was three. I came back for the summer. Apparently Camille didn't tell him, since I walked in and found him with my sister." I closed my eyes, trying to keep every nauseating minute from resurfacing. "I didn't even think. I just grabbed a letter opener from his desk and stabbed him. Twenty-seven times."

Leander's hand encircled the back of my neck, the touch and the warmth equally surprising. "I'm sorry..."

"Oh, don't be." I waved him off, straightening my shoulders, which inadvertently signaled him to drop his hand. "Once the first one's out of the way, it's all downhill after that. I mean, you know."

He ignored my teasing, his face still drawn. "What about your mother?"

I huffed a laugh. "Yeah, well, she was already at least two bodies up on me so she couldn't exactly turn me in. She helped me stage an awesome break-in, though. Even sacrificed a Roman vase for me. I guess that's love when you're a psychopath."

"Who did she...?"

"After the will reading was over, she smothered my grandmother with a pillow, which I also walked in on. You'd think I would have learned to knock at that point... Anyway, for years she had me convinced she didn't kill her, that I didn't know what I saw, that my grandmother died from a 'broken heart.' When Massimo died, it unleashed a floodgate of memories she couldn't argue with."

Leander's brow furrowed. "Why would she kill Allegra's father?"

"Couldn't say. Maybe he caught her sleeping with someone else. Maybe she was tired of him. Hell, maybe Allegra isn't even his. I never asked. They were yelling right before I heard him fall. When I got there, she was standing over him, smiling, as he bled out on the marble floor. I just kept my mouth shut when the police arrived. Little did I know I was paying it forward."

He nodded, processing everything in that quiet way of his. I was dying to know what he really thought of the whole fucked up family dynamic, but I was terrified to ask.

"Well this was fun," I said cheerily. Leaning over, I snagged a scoop of his pistachio gelato. "We should talk about our horrible families more often."

"Get off," he said, nudging me with his elbow when I came in for another scoop. "You have your own."

"Stracciatella isn't the same as pistachio." I swiped for his dish again, leaning into him and stretching outward. "Besides, you're not even eating it."

He held it further away, trying not to laugh. "You're incorrigible."

My face was so close to his, I forgot to breathe for a minute. I gave him a fleeting smile and shoved off of him, hoping he didn't notice. "You know it."

Wedging his spoon in the pistachio, he handed it to me and took my stracciatella with a smirk.

"Thief," I said, watching him with his stolen gelato.

The corner of his mouth lifted in a sly smile.

———

IF LEANDER WAS at all disturbed by my psychotic mother's past, he hid it well. Over dinner, they exchanged pleasantries as if they'd been friends for decades, discussing art and literature and steering clear of anything too personal. I had to hand it to them — they were both gifted actors.

I, on the other hand, focused the majority of my attention on Allegra, save for the few glances I threw in Leander's direction to make sure everything was status quo.

"Are you coming to midnight Mass?" Allegra asked between bites of fish. Ah, shit.

"I, um… Leander?" My head swiveled toward the epitome of an American WASP at my side. He was cultured enough to appreciate a Catholic Mass, but religion, and God in particular, was one of those topics we'd only ever discussed in the vaguest of hypotheticals and usually with a lot of alcohol. "Midnight Mass?"

He froze for half a heartbeat before blinking once, as if snapping himself awake. I'm sure the idea of me attending Mass was as bizarre to him as it was to me. "Is that what you do on Christmas Eve?"

"Of course," Camille interjected. "You should come. St. Mark's is beautiful, especially this time of year."

"Or we can stay here," I added quickly, hoping he chose the latter. "It's so crowded."

"*I thought you came to see your family?*" Camille's gaze narrowed as she spoke, but her lips remained twisted into something of a smile.

"And I have," I replied through gritted teeth.

"*Your sister wants you to go.*"

Allegra spoke up, though her voice was still soft considering she was trying to play the referee. "I never said that, Mama."

Leander laid his napkin on the table and pushed his chair out quietly. "If you'll all excuse me, I think I'm actually going to turn in early. It was a very long day."

"Goodnight!" Allegra chirped.

"*See what you've done?*" I snapped at Camille as I got to my feet, throwing my napkin on my chair.

"*Me?! You're the one who made a big deal out of going to Mass for no reason!*"

"No reason?" I gaped at her. "*You're not even Catholic!*"

"*Stop it, both of you!*" Allegra gave us each a glare.

I kissed the top of Allegra's head on my way by. *"I'm sorry. Goodnight."*

Cursing Camille the entire way up the stairs, I switched to formulating some sort of an apology on my walk to the bedroom. Knocking gently, I waited for Leander's permission before stepping in.

"Why are you knocking? It's your room." He was sitting in bed, a book in his hands. Marking his place, he set it aside and turned his full attention to me.

"Are you ok?" He looked ok, but I knew how exhausting Camille was. If she triggered one his migraines with her bullshit, I was going to... do something painful. I don't know. I'd improvise.

"I'm perfectly fine. Are you ok?"

"Why wouldn't I be?"

He cocked his head, as unconvinced as ever.

"I'm fine," I said, holding up my hands. "Promise."

"You looked like you were going to shove that sea bass down her throat."

"Tempting. Very tempting..."

"Are you going to make it through tomorrow without killing her? From my understanding, everything will be closed. You'll be trapped here."

I waved him off, wandering over to my suitcase. Blocking his view, I rummaged through the pockets before carefully removing the thing I was after. "I've got half a bottle of pills and an entire fridge of wine. We're good."

"I did see a chess board in the library..."

Item in hand, I stood, making sure to keep it behind my back. "Are you challenging me, my prince?"

He slid off the bed and stood, spreading his hands oh-so-innocently. "I'm simply saying, some games can take all day if the players are up to it."

There was a joke in there somewhere about my stamina, but I let it go. "Not just days, years."

"Awfully confident." He gave me a lazy once-over, a smirk on his face. I'm sure the look was meant as nothing more than jest, but I couldn't help when goosebumps spread over my skin.

"The fact you doubt me after all this time wounds me." I laid a hand over my heart, feigning a wince.

His smirk widened as he crossed his arms. "Oh, I'm not doubting your ability to play, only your ability to win."

"You will live to regret that," I said with as serious of a tone as I could while fighting a smile.

"Mhmm."

"Anyway… I know we said no gifts, but I got you something regardless. You might want it for tomorrow." I withdrew his present from behind my back and held it up with a cheesy grin so he didn't kill me outright.

As predicted, his face morphed into a look of displeasure and he made no move to take it.

"Just open it," I sighed. "If you don't like it, I'll throw it in the canal and I'll never buy you anything else ever again. Promise."

Grudgingly, he took the black, damask rectangle and unwrapped it carefully. As soon as he saw the title of the book, he shot me a curious glance.

I smiled, a bit smugly, and made a show of peering at the book.

Lifting the cover, his jaw dropped. "It's a first edition. Where did you…?" The first few pages fell out of the way, revealing a pair of train tickets to Geneva.

"And for your birthday, we're going to the place where *Frankenstein* was written." Boom. Mic drop.

"Bennett, I—" He alternated between glancing at me and looking at the book, apparently speechless.

I held my hand out. "If you don't like it, I can always just..."

He snatched the book away, clutching it to his chest. "Don't even think about it." Like a dragon with a new piece of treasure, he drifted away, throwing cautious glances over his shoulder every few steps to make sure I wasn't following him.

"I guess it's a good thing I picked this up, then," he said, reappearing sans book. A little black, velvet box sat in the center of his hand.

It was my turn to make a face. "You said no gifts."

"And look how well you listened." He had a point. He said no gifts last year, which I also blatantly ignored. After spending the better part of four months tracking down a beautifully embroidered waistcoat owned by Poe himself, I was not *not* giving it to him.

I lifted the box off his palm and studied it for a minute. It was an antique ring box tied with a black ribbon. I had no idea what he could have possibly found that fit in a box so small other the box's original intent, which was an intriguing prospect all the same.

A bright smile swept across my face as soon as I cracked open the box. "You didn't!"

Inside lay an exquisite silver and onyx ring. From the design alone, I knew it was a poison ring, which made me doubly in-love with it, given how Leander felt about poison. I slipped the emerald one off my index finger and replaced it with the onyx. I admired it for a split second before seizing him in a hug. "It's perfect. Thank you."

He squeezed me in return. "Thank you for another memorable Christmas."

CHAPTER 24

I was in the bathroom shaving when the door swung open.

"Oh, sorry, I didn't realize you were in here," Leander said, taking a step back out.

"It's ok. I'm almost done." I swished the straight razor in the water and dragged it across my chin carefully.

"Something else you picked up in some exotic place, no doubt." Wetting his toothbrush in the other sink, he smirked at me in the mirror.

"No." I made another pass, scrutinizing my reflection. "This one I got from my dad."

Leander didn't say anything, preoccupied as he was with brushing his teeth. I may have been bitter about losing my dad relatively young, but at least I had a few good memories. It was more than Leander could say for either of his parents.

Finished, I wiped the remaining shaving cream off with a towel. "Want to give it a go?"

He shook his head, spitting out a mouthful of toothpaste. "Look at me. A five o'clock shadow is one of those things I never really have to worry about. Besides, I'd end up cutting myself."

"The perks of a baby face." I ran my hands through my hair, mussing it up even more than it already was. The crazier the better for Mommy Dearest.

"Says the one who looks ten years younger than he actually is."

"Don't be jealous. Besides, with a straight razor you'll have to shave even less than you do now. Sit." Without waiting for an answer, I pushed him onto the edge of the tub.

I wet another towel with warm water and pressed it along his jaw before buffing the shaving cream into his skin with a brush. Tossing a dry towel over my shoulder, I picked up the straight razor and tilted his head back, arching a teasing brow at him. "Do you trust me?"

"Probably more than I should." He rolled his eyes with the admission.

Chuckling, I swept the blade over his skin. "I promise I won't pull a Sweeney Todd on you."

"How comforting." He closed his eyes and sighed. I'm sure he was visualizing arterial sprays every time I moved the blade down his throat. Thankfully, he was as still as a statue, which made the work that much easier.

When I was done, he smoothed a hand over his jaw. "Wow."

"You're welcome." I flashed him a smile as I tossed the towel in his face. Spritzing on cologne, I vacated the bathroom, leaving him to it.

"Can I borrow your conditioner?" he yelled over the top of running water. "I ran out in Cologny."

"What's mine is yours."

While he showered, I pieced together an outfit and headed downstairs for a much-needed espresso. Our whirlwind trip to Switzerland was amazing, including an impromptu stop in Verona on the way back, which meant we didn't get in until the wee hours.

Allegra was in the kitchen when I strolled in, picking at a fruit salad and texting on her phone. *"Where's Leander?"*

"In the shower." I set the pod in the espresso machine and hit START before leaning against the counter and crossing my arms comfortably.

"How was Cologny? Was the villa as beautiful as the pictures?" She dropped her phone and looked up expectantly.

"Even more so. Leander loved it, which is all that matters."

"I really like him. He's so nice." Yeah, sure. As long as you didn't cross him. *"For an American,"* she added with an impish grin.

"Mhmm. Glad you approve." I turned back to the espresso machine and retrieved my cup.

"Well, I didn't know what to expect. We've never met one of your, um... Partners, before."

I almost dropped my cup. Somehow I managed to hold on and give her a blank stare at the same time. *"You still haven't."*

"You two aren't together?" She frowned, blinking her big brown eyes.

"No." Thank God the conversation was in Italian... Much like the unconscious hand-holding incident, which had happened a few more times, although the identity of the otter was still unknown, *this* was something else I did not need Leander finding out about.

"Are you sure?"

"Pretty damn." What the hell kind of a question was that? Of course I was sure. Despite what conversion therapists preached, you couldn't change someone's sexuality. If you could, I might have been inclined to turn into a predatory douche after all.

Taking another sip of espresso, I sidled up next to Allegra

and picked a strawberry out of her bowl. *"What's Diego doing for the holidays?"*

"Sergio," she huffed, rolling her eyes. *"And he stayed in Barcelona. He's working on a really big project and wanted to use the time to get ahead."*

"How industrious of him."

"Not everyone has a photographic memory to fall back on."

"Well if Stefano wants to fry his brain with three-hundred million volts, I can show him the perfect spot." I gave her a mock smile as I snagged another strawberry.

She smacked my hand, withholding a comment when our mother sashayed into the room, wagging a finger at me.

"You're lucky," Camille said with a hint of a glare before turning her attention to Allegra, dropping the finger and the attitude. *"It's the only thing that saved him in law school, since he never went to class. I was so worried he would flunk out."*

"Yeah, right. I'm sure you tossed and turned over it." Who was she kidding? She wasn't even the one who paid for it.

"I don't know how you managed to make it as far as you have in life, but I thank God everyday that you have." Camille actually dredged up a tear, her voice going all breathy with restrained emotions. *"You were always getting into trouble as a child, running with the wrong sorts of people. Just like your father."*

"And there it is… I'm going to head out now." I downed the rest of my espresso, ignoring the fact I pretty much scalded my esophagus in the process. Exhibit B why I didn't come home and Exhibit C of why I knew I would regret agreeing for Allegra's sake.

"Bennett, stay." Camille's hand landed on my shoulder.

"I'm not a fucking dog." I shrugged her off as roughly as I could. The fact the command came in English was even more grating, as if I'd listen to my American mother more than the Italian one she tried to be.

"Bye," I said to Allegra, kissing her cheek quickly and

ducking out before Camille started in with the crocodile tears in earnest.

Leander was coming down the stairs as I strode past the landing, his brow furrowed. "Is everything alright?"

"Peachy." Yanking open the armoire, I ripped my coat off the hanger and pulled it on. "I'm going for a walk."

"Do you want company?"

"I don't care." I *did* care, but I also knew I was in a shitty mood and I didn't want to ruin the rest of Leander's day. Without waiting for an answer, I flipped the collar up on my coat and stormed out.

When I reached the ground floor and stepped out into the foggy morning, I knew I was on my own. Shoving my hands in my pockets, I hunched further into my coat and headed toward the piazza.

———

STARING AT THE MASSIVE, tortured body of Christ before me, I felt nothing.

The painting was dark and foreboding, set in a funerary chapel with as much symbolism of Christian mortality crammed in to it as possible. It didn't generate a stirring passion within me, or even a cautionary tragedy. Once upon a time it inspired pity, to think someone would sacrifice themselves for the greater good. But now? I felt nothing. Maybe a dash of contempt for humanity. But that was it.

Footsteps echoed around me in the quiet hall, drawing nearer.

I knew without turning — before his cologne enveloped me, before his voice broke the stillness — that he found me.

"I had a feeling you'd be here," Leander murmured, stopping at my side. His presence alone was as comforting as the heat radiating off of him in the chill gallery.

"Do you think if Christ could do it all over again, he would?" I asked, cocking my head and squinting, as if I'd be able to spot something new, or divine some deeper meaning I somehow missed all the times before.

"I have no idea... Probably. That is his role, after all."

"Yes, the sacrificial lamb. He knew he was going to die and he didn't do anything to stop it." I shook my head, inadvertently shifting strands of hair across my eyes. "What an idiot."

Leander chuckled softly. "He's the son of God. It's not very Christ-like to rebel. Unlike you."

"It's not rebellion." I shifted my weight to the other foot, keeping my gaze on the painting.

"No? Then what is it?"

"It's wanting to get the most out of life. There's nothing on the other side. No bright light. No pearly gates. Just an empty blackness. The worst part is, I know it's inevitable." I exhaled, trying to shake off the coldness creeping down the back of my neck. It was at odds with the memory of the lightning tearing through my body, the burning heat followed by complete numbness.

Leander laid a hand on my shoulder. The weight of it brought me back to the present.

A short, bitter laugh escaped me. "Ironic, isn't it? A murderer fearing their own death. Ironic or just pathetic?" I didn't wait for a reply. I didn't want one.

Spinning away from him, I cut across the room as fast as my legs would carry me.

Venice held so many conflicting memories, it was hard to keep them straight. I loved my adopted city and hated it. It was the place I died, and the place where I was brought back from death. The place I made my first kill. And now Leander was here, creating new memories and muddying the waters even more.

Leander caught up to me in a few strides. "Where are you going now?"

"I need a drink."

"Bennett." He hooked my elbow, pulling me to a stop. The planes of his face were as sharp as the look in his eyes.

"What?" I shouldn't have snapped at him, but I did.

"Stop running," he snapped in return.

I turned to leave again, but he held fast to my arm.

"'The great art of life is sensation, to feel that we exist, even in pain,'" Leander said quietly, his eyes softening.

"Existing isn't the same as living, Byron."

"Running isn't living, either."

Since he hadn't let go, I leaned in closer, eyes narrowed. "I'm not running."

He held his ground, tipping his chin up while the challenge flashed in his eyes. "Prove it."

My irritation gave way to suspicion, causing me to linger a moment longer.

"Prove it. Stay." He let go of my arm and gestured widely, calling my bluff.

The urge to flee was overwhelming. My muscles twitched, ready and waiting, but the knowing look in Leander's eyes kept me rooted in place. Goddamn him.

After an eternity of basking in his surety, he stepped around me, his shoulder brushing mine. "Tell me about this one."

I inhaled and subsequently exhaled a slow breath before pivoting on my heel. A series of art history texts flashed through my brain. "Titian's 'Sacred and Profane Love.' Scholars can't agree on the meaning. He painted it, but it's generally thought someone else came up with the allegory."

"What do you think?"

"I tend to agree with those who see the Twin Venuses — one a figure of beauty and carnal love, whereas the other represents a higher, spiritual love." I tilted my head to the side, assessing the details. It had been so long since I'd seen it in person. Usually it hung in a gallery in Rome, but it ventured north for a special exhibit on its master painter.

"Sacred and profane... As in Durkheim's dichotomy? Or vice versa, as the case may be."

"Yes. The profane was the earthly, common aspects of religion. The sacred, however" — I couldn't help it when my gaze slid to him — "was everything that was forbidden."

Thankfully, he was fixated on the painting, oblivious to the silent agony raging inside of me. The museum lights cast a soft glow on his profile, a living, breathing work of art in his own right. I'd never wanted anything, or anyone, more than I wanted him. Knowing he would always be just out of reach gutted me.

As Leander turned to face me, I cleared my throat and walked away quickly. "There's a sketch by Da Vinci over this way."

I was *so* screwed.

CHAPTER 25

I knew something was wrong by the way Camille's voice lost its carefully cultivated trill. She spat out questions rapidly into the phone, giving me enough context clues to figure out the other half of the conversation. By the time she came back to the dinner table, I'd narrowed it down to one conclusion: someone croaked.

"Who died?" I asked, sipping my wine.

She ignored me and looked at Allegra, laying a hand over hers. *"It's Uncle Antonio."*

Leander leaned closer, nudging me with his elbow, the corners of his mouth pulling ever so slightly in question.

I gave a slight shake of my head, rolling my eyes at the same time, before returning to my squid-ink risotto. It made no never mind to me, but cue the theatrics from Camille in three... two... one...

Allegra touched her fingers to her quivering lips, tears falling down her cheeks silently. She sniffed and excused herself from the table.

"I saw that," Camille hissed at me as soon as Allegra

cleared the doorway. "Your sister is already upset without you making things worse for her!"

"Saw what? I'm eating."

"That *look*."

"What look?"

"Oh, Bennett, please. I'm tired of fighting with you." She huffed into her wineglass before taking a sip. Or a chug.

"My condolences," Leander murmured, earning him a sappy smile. Kiss ass.

"It's so nice you and Allegra are both going to be there for Aunt Isabella," Camille said with a sigh.

I nearly spit out a mouthful of black rice. "Come again?"

"The funeral is on Friday." She said it like that was that, end of discussion. I was eleven all over again, being stuffed away at a boarding school in France despite the fact I spoke zero French and knew zero people. Once Queen Camille made a royal decree, no one could dispute it.

I set my fork down and laced my fingers together to keep from lunging across the table to strangle her outright. "That's the day before we leave."

Camille narrowed her eyes, switching over to Italian for a proper ass-chewing while still trying to appear polite. *"So what's the problem?"*

Even though it was rude as hell, I joined her in our adopted language to shield Leander from as much of the fight as I could. Except for the fact he had ears and, regardless of the language, his rapt attention wouldn't miss a single expression or gesture.

"The problem is we're here on vacation*, and now you expect me to drop everything and go to the funeral of a guy I've met, like, three times in my life?"*

"He's your great uncle."

"He's Allegra's *great uncle. And he was almost a hundred. This shouldn't be a great shock to everyone. Not like Grandma. Broken*

heart, my ass!" I glared at her pointedly. The last time I reminded her there was no statute of limitations on murder in Illinois, she slapped me. I always hoped she'd try again — I'd break her fucking wrist.

Her eyes widened before narrowing in a heartbeat. *"When Massimo and I married, they accepted you as one of their own. And now you're going to disrespect them like this?"*

"Spare me your family loyalty speech. Your priority has always been you*, Camille."*

"Are you ever going to stop holding that over my head?"

"Which part? The part where you turned my entire life upside down on a fucking whim? Or—"

"Oh, that's right, because living in Europe was the worst parenting decision I ever made."

My exasperated laugh turned into something more akin to a snarl. *"You really want to talk about your fucking track record right now? Need I remind you what that fucking animal did to my sister?"*

"How dare you bring that up right now!"

"How dare you play the victim when you know what he did! And then to sit there and make comments about my *life like you're a goddamn saint?!"*

She switched to English abruptly, hoisting the bread basket into view and smiling at Leander as if he hadn't just sat through the entire exchange. "Would you like some more, dear?"

He demurred and promptly dove into his wine.

Allegra reappeared, resuming her seat and unknowingly bringing about a cease-fire. *"I just got a text from Lucia. Iacopo is going to be there."* Her dark gaze lifted to mine, full of apprehension. *"I didn't know he was in town."*

Swearing under my breath, I bit my lower lip to keep the rest of it at bay. If there was one Italian prick I should have killed, it was Iacopo Bonato. Maybe this time I'd get my chance.

Leander leaned across me to refill my wine to the brim, murmuring in my ear along the way. "Sounds like we're going to a funeral."

CHAPTER 26

I rifled through my suitcase again, as if new clothes would suddenly appear. When they didn't, I huffed and turned to Leander's, sifting through his assortment of black. Shrugging out of the emerald green shirt I was wearing — and deemed inappropriate by Allegra — I slipped into one of his button-ups.

"You need a tie." Leander pointed at the suitcase from where he was reclined in bed, engrossed in *Frankenstein.* Again.

"I'm not wearing a tie."

"You're a lawyer. You have to wear ties."

"Have you ever seen me in a tie?"

He 'hmphed' at me and turned the page.

To preserve some sense of my own identity, I pulled on a navy vest. Unless it was in direct lighting, you could hardly tell the difference. Not that I cared what the Faveros thought, anyway. Well, except Allegra.

"Cuff links," Leander chimed in, gesturing vaguely toward his suitcase again.

"I'll just roll them."

The book dropped suddenly. He held my gaze, his jaw set and a brow lifted slightly, until I trudged back to the suitcase and retrieved a set of cuff links.

While I was in the bathroom dicking around with my hair for the tenth time, he appeared behind me, a length of black silk in his hands.

"What a lovely garrote." I smiled at him in the mirror, gleaming teeth and all.

He returned the lethal smile. "Turn around."

Sighing like a four year old, I spun to face him. He smirked and finished buttoning my shirt before he slipped the tie around the back of my neck. His fingers couldn't help but graze my skin in the process. I shifted my footing to disguise my inadvertent reaction to the tingling.

"Stand still," he said, apparently none the wiser. "I'll keep it loose." I tried to obey while he expertly tucked and wove the material over itself, but my fingers tapped out a concerto on my thigh as an attempt at distraction. He was so close, I could have kissed him. God, I wanted to kiss him.

Finally, he took a step back, admiring his work, or my sullen expression. "You should wear ties more often."

I grimaced and pulled at the knot. "It's strangling me."

"You're fine." He patted my bicep and stepped out of the bathroom.

———

THE WAKE for good old Uncle Antonio was being hosted in the home of some relative whose name I couldn't remember. It didn't matter. It looked like the entire district was there, making the sprawling palazzo feel like a shoebox.

I watched over Allegra like a hawk, waiting for any of the Bonato assholes to make an appearance. Unfortunately Camille spotted Iacopo before I did. She seized my arm, her nails digging into me despite the several layers of cloth. Her mouth pressed into a thin, red line when I went to pull away. "Don't even think about it."

"Or what?" I succeeded in yanking away from her a second time, drifting to another corner of the room where I could keep an eye on things.

The asshole hadn't changed one bit over the years. His hair still had too much gel and his shirt was still too tight. All the women fawned over his big arms and the men congratulated him on his successful business ventures, extending Daddy's empire to the south.

"And why do we hate him?" Leander asked, materializing at my side with two glasses of wine.

I threw back the entire glass before answering. "Allegra almost died because of him."

As if he heard me, Iacopo's black gaze shot across the room. I silently dared him to come over. Like the coward he was, he stayed within the safety of his family's cronies. Their heads turned, one by one, assessing the threat to their master's son.

From a safe distance, Iacopo gave me the Italian signal for "I'm going to kick your ass," like finger-guns but turned in slightly and pointing down. It was quite the show of bravado, considering the last time we tangled I put him in the hospital. That was the thing about most gym rats — they were all muscle and zero skill, especially when their opponent didn't give a shit how many hits they had to take along the way.

Responding with a smile, I put my left hand in the middle of my right arm and bent it back. Two could play that game.

Even Leander, the non-Italian, recognized the gesture for what it was. His arm snaked around my waist and he led me away quickly from the pack of seething Bonatos.

I snatched Allegra's wrist on the way by, dragging her

with me as Leander navigated through the crowd to another room.

"Thank you for coming," she said, none the wiser to the silent confab between me and her dolt of an ex.

"Anything for you." I kissed her temple before she peeled off to go chat with one of her great aunts.

"Is that why you haven't killed him?" Leander asked after she was gone.

"She said she forgave him." I crossed my arms over my chest and leaned against the wall, glaring at nothing.

"'To err is Human. To forgive, divine.'"

"Yeah, fuck Pope and fuck forgiveness."

A little old lady next to us gasped and crossed herself, muttering into her rosary. She got a quick chin flick in addition to my swearing, which sent her scurrying away.

"I don't think I've ever seen you so... riled." Leander handed over his glass of wine, his head tilted to one side in amusement.

"'Rage the likes of which you would not believe,'" I growled into his glass.

"And love the likes of which I could scarcely imagine?" He was joking, given the impish smirk, but I was too pissed to engage in literary banter.

"Something like that." Raking a hand through my hair with a huff, I turned away, depositing the glass on the nearest table. "Let's get out of here. Allegra will be fine now that asshole knows I'm in town."

"Would he try to do something to her?"

"I wouldn't put it past him. He didn't take their breakup well and his poor little ego hasn't quite been the same since."

Slipping out the back of the palazzo through an iron gate, we edged our way along the narrow stone ledge beside the canal. It was easier than trying to wade through the mass of people to the front door.

The minute I saw the Bonato family logo painted on the side of a boat, I knew what had to be done.

"Here. Hop in." I jogged down the stone steps and held a hand out to Leander.

He didn't move from the ledge. "Whose boat is this?"

"That asshole's."

"I'm sure the Venetians frown upon theft of any kind, but especially luxury boats."

A string of shouting in Italian broke up our debate. One of the Bonato henchmen stuck his head out the gate before disappearing again, summoning reinforcements.

Leander wasted no time leaping into the boat while I threw off the mooring and pulled away from the stairs as fast as I could in the shallow water.

By the time Iacopo appeared at the back gate, we were halfway down the canal. I blew him a kiss and turned the corner. Fucker.

Navigating through the narrow canals and out into the open water of the lagoon, I dredged up a nautical map in my brain I hadn't used in decades. Even if the day was gray, the lagoon was still as beautiful as ever, dotted with islands and the occasional boat. It was as good a way as any to end a trip to Venice.

"Are you ever going to tell me what happened or should I ask Allegra?" Leander asked, swiping his dark curls out of his eyes every time the wind blew them astray.

Pulling at the knot in my tie, I loosened it almost entirely before ripping open the top half of my borrowed shirt despite the dampness in the air. "It was a boating accident." I snorted. The explanation was still sour in my mouth, even after all these years. "'Accident.' That's what the police said."

"What did Allegra say?"

"They were drunk. Teenagers having a good time. Except Iacopo wasn't paying attention to his speed or where the hell they were at. They crashed." When I glanced at him, he was considering me with one of his pensive looks. "She was knocked unconscious and he left her to drown. Literally, fucking swam away. If it wasn't for some tourists who jumped in to save her, she would have died."

"I'm still surprised you didn't kill him."

Accelerating, I steered the boat toward one of the islands. "She wouldn't let me. When he came to see her, afterward, I beat him unconscious. She pulled me off before I could finish the job and made me promise never to do anything like that again."

"So you stole his boat?"

"Yeah. Are you a strong swimmer?"

"Am I what?" Leander gripped the side of the vessel and leaned forward, staring at the stone wall rapidly approaching. "Bennett!"

"Memento mori, my prince." I notched the speed up again and set the autopilot, making sure the course was on track.

"What?!"

Grabbing Leander by the back of his suit jacket, I hauled him with me as I flung myself over the edge of the boat.

We crashed into the dark water together. Leander emerged coughing, his teeth already chattering. I swiped my hair out of the way, watching the bow of the boat smash into the side of the medieval wall. The back end flipped upwards, shredding itself to pieces against the stones.

Buoyant with the adrenaline, I laughed and nudged him. "That was fun! Wanna do it again?"

He smacked his hand on the top of the water, splashing a freezing wave in my face. "Memento vivere, you fucking lunatic!"

"I knew you knew Latin." I dashed the water from my eyes, ignoring his entirely justifiable anger. Tipping my chin toward the island, I started toward it in slow strokes. "Let's go before we freeze to death."

The wailing of police sirens spurred us on faster, as did the mad dash to the ferry before it pulled out.

On the way back to the city, we huddled together, ignoring curious looks from the other passengers. After two weeks of rooming together, save for the night we spent in Cologny, it felt like the most natural thing in the world to lean into each other, his hands trapped between mine. Plus, I kind of owed him all the warmth I could — that, and his dry-cleaning bill.

Once we reached dry land again, Leander peeled away from me and marched down the street in long, angry strides.

"You're going to get lost," I said, hurrying to catch up with him.

He hunched his shoulders even more, his arms wrapped so tightly across his chest I was surprised he could breathe. "If I die from pneumonia I'm going to haunt you for the rest of eternity."

I caught him by the elbow and pulled him down a different street. "Is that supposed to be a threat?"

He glared at me, his lips dark from the cold.

We were nearing home when the familiar sensation of being followed crept along the back of my neck. As we rounded the corner, I threw a glance over my shoulder. "Oh, shit…"

"What?" Leander glanced back as well, groaning.

Iacopo and a gaggle of goons popped out of doorways and side streets. I should have known better. I should have nicked another boat and gone up the canal to the back entrance. But, it was too late now.

"This way." I spun Leander in the exact opposite direction of the palazzo.

"What are you doing?"

In answer to his question, Iacopo shouted and picked up the pace. The sound of bullets being chambered behind us was as loud as canon fire.

"Run!" I shoved Leander forward.

A bullet zinged past my shoulder, lodging in the side of a building with a 'crack' and a cloud of dust.

We zigzagged through the narrow streets and over arched bridges, winding our way through the labyrinthine city.

When we had enough of a lead, I ducked into a shadowy doorway and yanked Leander in after me in what was simultaneously one of the smartest, and dumbest, moves in my life. We were practically cheek-to-cheek, our bodies pressed together. His arms caged me against the heavy door, while my hands were still tangled in his shirt. It was hard to listen for footsteps when it felt like every heartbeat was a thousand times louder than it needed to be.

The plus side was I wasn't cold anymore. The down side was the fact my pants were suddenly two sizes too small. If he'd been anyone else, I wouldn't even hesitate to take advantage of the moment or the fact his face was so close every breath warmed my skin.

"Do you think they've gone?" Leander whispered. Most of his face was obscured by shadow. I'm sure mine was too, otherwise I doubted he would have stayed where he was for so long, knowing I was looking at him with barely tethered restraint.

"I don't know."

"Maybe I sh—"

One of my hands flew up, covering his mouth. The other held tight to the front of his jacket.

A pair of heavy footsteps trudged along the stony street. When the people came into view, I exhaled a silent sigh of relief. Not Bonatos, just a couple lugging home groceries.

"I'll go first," I whispered.

He shook his head. "They know you. I'll go."

"You don't know the way. At this point, I don't even know if *I* know where we are."

His wry smile was barely visible in the glow of the Christmas lights overhead. "Guess we'll really put that eidetic memory to the test, then." He peered around the corner of the doorway and slipped off into the night.

My head thunked backward against the door, eyes closed. To hell with a hot shower. I needed to jump back in the lagoon.

I was about to stroll out of my hiding spot when a darker shadow darted forward. Holding my breath, I waited until the figure passed before falling into step behind them.

The hammer of a gun cocked, muffled though it was on the inside of the man's jacket.

Leander was ahead of us, but close enough to register the noise. He turned slowly, his eyes on the man trailing him.

Georgio, Iacopo's cousin if I recalled their family tree correctly, stopped and took aim.

I came up behind Georgio swiftly and seized a handful of hair while grasping his stubbly jaw with my other. One quick wrench to the side and his neck crunched under the tension. The man crumpled like a doll, his gun falling to the cobblestone.

Pivoting with the body, I laid him down and rolled him into the canal as quietly as I could. He sank under the dark water, disappearing from view for the time being. Once the gun was disassembled, I threw part of it down the street and the other piece into the water, away from the body.

When I stood and dusted my hands off, Leander was at my side, as silent as a cat. A dark smile curled his lips, his eyes practically glittering under the lights.

"Magnificent," he breathed, the word crystallizing in the night air. He looked the way I'd felt when I watched him break the bartender's nose — enlivened by the violence, thrilled by the display of power.

Pride swelled in my chest. He'd seen me kill before, but never like this. His approval — his *praise* — meant everything.

Before I dwelt too long on it, I licked my lips and took his arm, leading him away. "Time to get out of here."

CHAPTER 27

Tossing and turning was not something I experienced regularly, if ever. For the most part, I slept alone and I slept great. I didn't have to fight anyone for space, or share the pillows, or a blanket. It was me and my bed and it was heaven.

Until Venice.

Venice changed everything.

In the weeks that followed, I had the worst sleep of my life. More than once I caught myself reaching out over the cool sheet, looking for another hand that wasn't there. The realization *I* was the otter hit me hard, but not as hard as the fact my fellow otter was gone. He stole my blissful sleep, just like he stole my straight razor and any thought of a future without him.

It was almost three in the morning after another night of laying awake, glaring at the ceiling, when I decided to call him.

"What's wrong?" he asked by way of greeting, his voice rough and sleepy. The bastard.

"Thought I'd see what you were doing."

"Why are you awake?"

"Why aren't you?"

"I... was. Am. I must have fallen asleep in the library." There was a heavy thud in the background, as if he needed to confirm he fell asleep with a book in his lap. Again. I don't know how many times I caught him like that — passed out from utter exhaustion, a book draped across him.

"What are you researching this time?"

"Do you really want to talk about this right now?"

"Would it be easier if I just came over there?"

"Are you in town?" It might have been wishful thinking, but he sounded almost hopeful. Certainly more alert than he did a moment before.

"No," I admitted glumly.

"Then don't waste your time driving over here."

"It's not a waste of time." I hoped it didn't sound as pouty as I felt. Did he not want to see me? Had he gone back to his pre-Venice routine so easily, while I spent my days away from him in complete misery?

"I never understood why you insisted on getting an apartment in St. Louis anyway..."

My teeth raked across my lower lip, the truth seconds from spilling out. I bit down harder until a shock of pain overrode the guilt. "It was easier for bu—"

"For business," Leander parroted. "Yes, you said. Closer to the airport. Which doesn't exactly support your argument since we have our own plane a mere twenty minutes outside of town."

"Wrangling a pilot and getting flight plans approved... it's such a hassle sometimes. Anyway, do you want me to come out there or not?"

He sighed, a deep, sleepy sigh. "You better bring coffee."

I smiled, throwing back the comforter. "Your wish is my command."

In no time at all, I was skipping up the side steps of the massive house, two cups of coffee in hand. I let myself in the back door and glanced around the empty kitchen. Only the under-cabinet lights were on.

"Leander?"

There was no answer.

I walked further into the house, headed toward the library.

Sure enough, there were a few reading lamps on but he was passed out once again. I set the cups down and picked up the heavy textbook on his chest. Arching an eyebrow at the subject matter, I dog-earred the page and set it aside.

Asleep, Leander looked like he could have been resting inside a Caravaggio painting. His mouth was soft, instead of the hard line it usually was, and his brow was free from creases. He looked peaceful in the shadows of the library, the same as he had in the bookstore in Venice.

Swiping my cup, I eased onto the far end of the couch, kicking my legs up alongside his.

Either the movement or the smell of coffee roused him.

He inhaled and stretched, blinking himself awake. "Where'd you come from?"

"Did you forget?"

He looked at his watch, going a bit cross-eyed. "I thought I was dreaming."

"Do you frequently dream about me?" I nudged his knee with mine, trying not to smile into my coffee like an idiot.

"Where's my book?" He sat up, looking around with a sudden urgency.

"The one on forensic psychiatry?" I pointed at the side table behind his head.

He zeroed in on the coffee instead. "Oh, thank God."

"Not sleeping well?"

"Why?" He froze suddenly, his eyes wide.

I shrugged, picking at the cardboard sleeve around my cup. I was not about to admit my newfound sleeping problems to a chronic insomniac.

"Did Elijah say something?"

"Why would Elijah say something about your sleeping habits?" I quirked a brow at him.

He shook his head, running a hand through his hair. "Never mind."

I nudged him again.

He nudged me back. "Why are you at my house at..." He glanced at his watch again, probably seeing the numbers for real this time. "Four a.m.?"

"I missed you," I said, completely deadpan.

He laughed and took another sip of his coffee. "Uh huh. What's the real reason?"

That was the real reason, ass. Since I couldn't say that, I sipped my coffee, buying some time. "Just thinking."

He raised his brows at me, a silent prompt to continue.

"The stuff with the feds. They don't waste their time doing surveillance on people if they don't already have a stack of evidence in a box somewhere to back up what they find."

It wasn't entirely a lie. Catching my FBI besties in the middle of downtown Easton had been circling in the back of my brain for months while I waited for something to happen. Marchese also made an appearance in my highlight reel of things to worry about. I was driving myself crazy trying to guess which enemy was going to make a move first.

"Are you worried?" Leander asked quietly.

"No," I answered quickly, with far more conviction than I actually felt. I didn't want him thinking I couldn't handle whatever was coming. "I'm strategizing."

He gave me a small smile. "To be inside your brain for an hour would be amazing, I think."

I chuckled. "You wouldn't like it in there."

"Any more than my own head?"

"Your head is perfect. It's the rest of the world that's fucked up."

"As much as I'd like to believe you, experience has taught me otherwise."

"You need new experiences, then." A second too late, I realized how that might be misconstrued. Ignoring the heat in my face, I took a long draw from my coffee, hoping he was too tired to notice.

He cleared his throat and tilted his head one way, then the other, cracking his neck. "I was thinking March."

"May is wetter."

"I know, but I want this over with."

His words, and the exhaustion with which he said them, took me aback. Leander was nothing if not meticulous. Planning Keith Starkey's murder took months of discussion, months of preparation. And now he wanted to jump into the doctor's murder without having a triple-checked plan of action in place?

"Why the rush?" I asked cautiously. I didn't want him to think I was questioning him — I genuinely wanted to know why there was a sudden desire to execute the final part of his personal reckoning. "It's only been a year since Cole killed the cop. Unless you think the widow is going to croak before too long?"

His gaze flitted around the room, as if he were searching for the right words. When it finally landed on me, it was full of unease. "I can't explain it."

"Don't worry about the feds. I've got them under control."

"It's not them." He was on his feet in a flash, stalking across the library. He paced back and forth in long strides with one arm crossed over his chest, holding the other aloft, chewing his thumbnail.

I did my best not to fidget while I watched him cycle through whatever worst-case scenarios his brain was currently conjuring. As much as he wanted to be in my head, I wanted to be in his, just to give him a break for a while.

He went from gnawing on his thumbnail to biting the inside corner of his mouth, his fingers digging into the opposite bicep as he moved.

"I've got some Xanax if you want one," I said after it was clear he wouldn't be sitting down any time soon.

Muttering under his breath, he peeled off for the large, bay window and stopped abruptly. His hands tore through his hair and scraped along the underside of his jaw before he clasped them together. "Remember when you talked about running away? Moving to Europe and opening a bookstore?" He said the last part with a bit of a laugh, as if the idea was unfathomable.

"Yeah…" I held my breath, waiting to see where he was going.

"I just… I got a glimpse of that and it's been hard to let go."

"Why do you have to let it go?"

He turned toward me, giving a helpless gesture around the room. "This. Irene's will. If I leave, I'll have nothing. Everything is wrapped up in the company, which is wrapped up in her goddamn will."

"Why didn't you tell me any of this before?" Frowning at him, I swung my legs down off the couch. "Let me see the paperwork. I'll find a loophole that bitch overlooked. I promise."

"It's not that simple."

"It's not that complicated," I shot back.

Sadness swept across every angle of his face. "Everything is complicated. Can't you see that? You. Me. This plan. This town. Everything. One wrong move and we're dead or in prison or—"

"Hey..." I crossed the room to him, resting my hands on his shoulders. "If there's a way out, I'll find it. If you want to move forward with the rest of the plan, we'll do it. We'll do it tomorrow if that's what you want. We're ready. All you have to do is say the word."

"And then what? We don't have a plan for what comes next. What comes next, Bennett?" His gaze darted back and forth, searching my face. He gripped my elbows as if to steady himself once his breathing picked up, quick and shallow.

"Whatever you want. That's the beauty of it. You don't have to worry about revenge anymore. You can do what *you* want."

"What if it doesn't work?" It was his exhaustion talking. It had to be. A lucid Leander would never question the hours we put in to perfecting the master plan.

"It'll work," I said softly.

"You don't *know* that. You don't know because you *can't* know. No one knows. You're just hoping!"

My hands shifted upwards, capturing his face and forcing him to look at me, to actually see me through his rising mania. "It *will* work because *we* planned it that way. What have I always told you? Together, we're unstoppable. Don't ever doubt that."

He nodded, swallowing visibly. Expelling a shaky breath, he drew in another ragged one, trying to get a handle on his breathing.

I folded him into a hug, resting my cheek against the side of his head. "I won't let anything happen to you."

"Some things are beyond your control."

"You're not in this alone, Leander. And you won't be locked away forever. If I have to, I will kill every single person who dares stand between us." Conviction spread through my body like wildfire. I closed my eyes, murmuring the next words. "*I promise.*" It was only after the fact, I realized they were in Italian.

If he had any question what the last part meant, he didn't say anything. His fingers tightened on the back of my shirt and all I heard was an audible exhale.

CHAPTER 28

"*A*re you ever going to play for me?" I asked, my hands drifting over the ivory keys.

Leander was leaning against the window frame watching the falling snow, his breath fogging the glass. "No."

"Why not?"

"I'm not as good as you."

"Hardly a reason. I'm not as good of a cook as you, and yet you've choked down a meal or two of mine."

He glanced over his shoulder, a smirk curling his lips. "You're a better cook than you think."

"And I bet you're better at the piano than you think." I arched a challenging brow at him. When he didn't move, I switched directions, playing an incredibly cheery song.

"No! Please no." Leander turned from the window with a pained expression. "No more Mozart!"

"I can't hear you over there." I kept at it, snickering to myself.

"Fine! You win." He slid onto the piano bench, elbowing me in the process.

"What's wrong with Mozart? Too happy for you?" I

smirked at him, changing songs to something slower, darker. More Leander. "Schubert?"

"Better." He took a sip of bourbon and shook his hands out before jumping into the second part of the duet.

The tempo picked up halfway through the song. I reached right, he reached left. Our hands collided over the keys, both trying to play the same part. We broke down into a fit of laughter.

I bumped my shoulder against his. "Stay on your side!"

"I'm sorry! I told you I wasn't any good. I can't even tell you the last time I played," Leander said between laughing.

"You just need practice." The corner of my mouth lifted as I glanced down. He hadn't taken his hand back, and I hadn't let go.

Leander's gaze dropped to our hands, our fingers tentatively lacing together. "This complicates things," he murmured.

"Only if you let it." I swung one leg over the bench to straddle it, inching closer to him in the process. I wanted to kiss him so much I could hardly stand it. Months — years — of denial crumbled with that touch, completely innocent but unbearably charged.

"How could it not?"

"Did Venice complicate things?"

Brow furrowed, he shut his eyes and exhaled the word, as if it physically pained him. "Yes."

Brushing the hair off his cheekbone, my fingers trailed down his jaw, to his throat and back up to lift his chin when it dipped. "Do you want me to leave?" I made sure to keep my voice soft and as even as possible. I didn't want to push him one way or the other, even though I'd probably die if he told me to go.

His eyes drifted open and met mine, burning, like the

heat from the bourbon in the center of my chest. Except, the tortured look remained etched on his face. "No."

"Then what are you worried about?"

"Everything."

Biting my lower lip, I caressed the side of his face, hoping to soothe the fears, or at least reassure him. "Leander..."

"Bennett, we can't—"

I silenced his doubt by pressing my lips to his. He inhaled sharply, his fingers tightening around mine. I waited for the rejection, all the while praying it would never come.

After another heartbeat, he melted, returning the kiss as hesitantly as he'd held my hand. My other hand slipped along the back of his neck drawing him closer, to kiss him longer, deeper.

Gripping my waist, his fingers dug into the fabric, while his others remained twined with mine. His mouth was hot, and soft, and everything I'd spent countless hours dreaming about. The taste of bourbon, sweetened by vanilla, scorched my tongue. I wanted to drown in it for an eternity.

A twinge of pain, fear, hit me when he disentangled our hands. It dissipated the moment he slid both hands around my waist and pulled me closer, til there was hardly any space between us. Before I knew what he was doing, he was plucking open the buttons on my vest. I wasn't about to stop him.

Kissing his jaw, I worked my way down the side of his neck, unbuttoning his shirt in return. When I reached for his cufflink, he captured my face between his hands and brought me back to his mouth, distracting me with his tongue and a kiss so hard it made my head spin.

It wasn't long before my hands continued on, touching him over his clothes, then beneath his shirt, mapping out the lines of his body. He didn't stop me from unzipping his pants, or slipping my hand inside to take hold of him. He moaned against my lips before breaking the kiss, turning his face from mine and seizing my wrist. "We shouldn't."

"I don't care."

His head swiveled toward me again. If I had to be reckless for both of us, so be it. I'd only ever had his best interests at heart and he clearly wanted this, even if he struggled with admitting it.

Taking his jaw in one hand, I kissed him slowly. Flicking my tongue against his lips, I slipped it inside when they parted. When the pressure on my wrist loosened, I resumed stroking him, savoring each gasp and whimper against my mouth.

"I want you so badly," I rasped between necessary pants of oxygen. "Do you have any idea?"

Without warning, he ripped open the front of my shirt and pushed the fabric over my shoulders. I helped him tear it away and fling it aside before doing the same to his. He didn't give my any time to marvel at him. One of his hands fisted in my hair, positioning me where he wanted me while he kissed and licked his way along my jaw, my throat, my shoulder. When his teeth came down on the side of my neck I almost lost it right there.

Something loud and heavy crashed right outside the window.

We both jumped, freezing in place. The only movement we dared make was to slowly exchange a wide-eyed look, each of us clearly hoping the other had the answer.

"What was that?" I strained to hear more sounds, but it was nearly impossible in the state I was in.

After another minute, Leander answered, his voice practically a whisper. "Must have been the wind." He started to pull away, his face drawn. That sound might as well have been a slap in the face for both of us. But I wasn't going to let the moment go without a fight. I wasn't going to let *him* go.

Standing slowly, I held my hand out to him, palm up.

His gaze swept up to mine, dark and unreadable.

Time seemed to stop while I waited to learn what his choice would be.

The moment his hand settled in mine, my heart sang. I pulled him to his feet and led the way to the stairs, in absolutely no hurry despite the fact I'd waited years for a moment I thought was out of the realm of possibility.

He was trembling by the time we reached the top of the stairs, each tremor betrayed by our joined hands. Desperate as I was to know what he was thinking, or feeling, at the moment, I knew better than to ask. He needed to get out of his head for a change. This was one of those things in life you couldn't overthink or else it would lead to ruin.

I started for the red guest room, the room I'd once occupied. To my surprise, he tugged my hand down the hallway — to his bedroom.

Wordlessly, I followed. I was sure at any moment he'd hear each of my heartbeats thudding against the inside of my ribcage. I may have been experienced in this regard, but I was more nervous than I'd ever been in my life.

Once we were in his room, I pulled him in close, pressing my lips against his while my hands traversed his exposed skin. The bend of his waist, the slope of his back, the curve of his shoulder. Thanks to the frenzy downstairs, we'd already been stripped to the waist and his pants were undone, hanging low over his hips.

As I'd once proclaimed, his skin was absolutely perfect. It glided beneath my hand, as soft as velvet over the muscle beneath. Even the scars my fingers grazed across on their way to reclaim his hand were perfect to me. He flinched, but I held on, guiding his hand to my waist while my other hand threaded through the mass of his dark curls. He gripped my hipbone as I kissed the underside of his jaw, making my way down his throat and across one shoulder, down to his chest.

He palmed the front of my pants, eliciting a surprised gasp and an exhalation from me. He gradually added pressure until he found the rhythm he wanted, my hips shifting now and again of their own accord. I kissed him, harder and harder, until I was sure my lips were bruised and my tongue had explored every inch of his mouth.

Before I lost it completely, I moved him toward the bed, only breaking contact with his mouth to push him down onto the mattress. Kneeling on the side of the bed, I worked his pants over his hips and out of my way, leaving a trail of kisses down his abdomen as I went.

He ran his fingers through my hair, his breathing quickening the lower I went. "Bennett... I—oh fuck!"

He swore the moment my tongue made contact, his grip on my hair tightening. The muscles in his thigh tensed under my hand as I swallowed the rest of him. I kept kneading and caressing his skin while my mouth worked along his length. When I glanced up, he was watching me, his lower lip caught between his teeth.

"God, that feels so—" His compliment ended with a strangled moan, his fingers digging into the sheet so hard his knuckles turned white.

Suddenly, he seized my biceps and yanked me upward onto the bed. "You have to stop," he panted, his eyes halfhooded.

"Are you ok?" I touched the side of his face, trailing my thumb across his lower lip.

In response, he caught the tip of my thumb between his teeth and sucked on it before letting go again. Pushing me down onto the mattress, he settled himself on top of me, kissing me harder than I dared to kiss him. It was possessive and wild, a side of him I'd never seen until now and wanted to see every day for the rest of my life.

"I want all of you," he breathed, pulling away just enough to fix me with a predatory look. His hand slipped down the front of my pants and his teeth grazed the side of my neck.

"Are you" — I sucked in a surprised breath when he freed me from the restraints of the fabric and stroked harder — "sure?"

He met my gaze again, his hand stilling but not letting go. "I've never been more sure about anything in my life."

Taking his face between my hands, I reclaimed his mouth, teasing his tongue with mine. He pushed my pants down even further until it got to the point where I could kick them off myself. Meanwhile, his hand picked up where it left off, bringing me to the edge before he stopped abruptly.

My whine was met with a roguish smirk.

Feigning a glare, I pushed him to the side and darted on top of him, pinning him in place so I could return the agonizing favor.

It continued like that for what seemed like an eternity. Kissing and licking and biting, sighs and gasps and swearing — slowly torturing one another until we were both on the point of shattering. And shatter, we did. Again, and again.

In the midst of it all, I lost track of where I started and he stopped. Darkness and desire, everything that we were, came together as it never had before. It was a choreography conducted by two people thinking, moving, as one in a state of ecstasy.

"Oh my God," Leander exclaimed as we collapsed onto the mattress, utterly exhausted. A sheen of sweat covered us both as we laid there, trying to catch our breath. As soon as I had the strength, a shower was definitely in order.

"God had nothing to do with it," I murmured, curling up behind him and kissing the back of his neck.

He reached across himself, holding onto the arm I'd wrapped around him. "You are the Devil. I'm sure of it now."

"If I'm the Devil, then what does that make you?" I asked with a chuckle, pressing kisses along his shoulder.

"The damned." He laughed softly and rolled toward me, kissing me fervently.

———

FOR THE FIRST TIME EVER, I didn't want to leave someone else's bed. I wanted to stay, wrapped up in the black silk sheets — and Leander. So, when the alarm went off on my phone, I was tempted to throw it against the wall. But then I saw it was labeled *Allegra* and the groan died in the back of my throat. I promised her I would pick her up at the airport in St. Louis, completely forgetting she said she was coming in on the redeye for some conference.

Debating whether or not to wake Leander to say good-bye, in the end I opted not to. Knowing his struggle to sleep peacefully, it seemed like the right thing to do. Plus, if he was half as tired as I was after our sexual exploits, it would have been particularly cruel to wake him for a two-minute conversation.

Taking a nod from his Romantics, I left a purple orchid in my place and kissed him while he slept. Thankfully, he knew Allegra was coming to the States, so I didn't have to worry about him assuming the worst with my disappearance. We'd already made plans to meet up with her after the conference was done. Once I made sure she was settled in St. Louis, I'd be right back here in Easton anyway.

Even in the dark, I made my way stealthily through the house, as quiet as a church mouse. I snuck out the front door without making a peep and then proceeded to trip over one of the planters on the porch. So much for my ninja skills.

Catching myself against the side of the house, I swore under my breath. I heaved the damn thing upright again and put it back where it belonged on the edge of the step, not in the path of the doorway.

I didn't remember the drive across town to the teal house in Easton. I didn't remember anything except the taste of bourbon and the electricity running through my veins. To say I was in a blissful haze was nothing short of an understatement. It was, without a doubt, the best night of my life for so many reasons — all of them centered around Leander.

That happiness disappeared the moment I walked up the front steps.

There was an eight-by-ten picture of Leander stuck to the front door with an ice pick. Whoever posted it drove the sharp point right through the center of Leander's photographic heart.

I threw a glance over my shoulder. The street was empty and quiet, awash in the blue glow of moonlight on glittering snow. Nothing moved, except my breath clouding in front of me in a short bursts.

Yanking the ice pick out, I took the photograph down and flipped it over. There was no message on the back. Not that I needed one. It was loud and clear, without writing.

My cell phone rang, sending a chill down my spine. Someone *was* here. And they were watching. Years of experience taught me Leander's life hung in the balance of the next thirty seconds.

Swallowing, I accepted the call but didn't say anything.

"You have two hours to get to the warehouse," Tony's deep voice said.

I didn't even bother looking at the time. "Impossible. I'm over four hours away."

"Too bad for your boyfriend."

The line disconnected.

I swore under my breath and sprinted for the car. Throwing it in reverse, I sped away as fast as I could on the icy, hilly roads.

Warning Leander wasn't an option. If I went back to the house, they'd kill him. If I told him to leave, they'd kill him. The only way to make sure he had a pulse come sunrise was to get my ass to Chicago and deal with it head-on.

Racing toward the private airport that sat between Easton and Clairsville, I fished my phone out of my pocket, swiping through the contacts frantically. Once I barked at the company's primary pilot to get the plane up and running or I'd annihilate his entire family by lunch, I hung up and made one more phone call, praying to God he answered.

God did answer, with the voice of a gruff Russian, akin to a grizzly snarling. "What?"

"Sergei," I said, opening the car up on a straightaway. "Time to repay that favor, comrade."

CHAPTER 29

*G*iovanni was leaning against the hood of his car, looking rather disappointed, when I walked in with time to spare. I didn't know what painful send off he had planned for the two of us in Easton, but I'm sure he never counted on the fact I'd beat his ridiculous deadline. The rest of his goons were scattered in their usual places, looking at me with a mixture of revulsion and annoyance. Tony, on the other hand, just looked tired.

"Well, well. If it ain't my little buddy Bennett." Giovanni pushed off his car and strolled over, his arms spread wide. "Where ya been, pal?"

"Busy." I tried to appear as unfazed as possible despite the fact my heart was racing a hundred miles per minute.

"What a coincidence." He chuckled, scratching the scruff on his cheek. "I've been busy too."

"I'm glad I came all this way for you to tell me that. Makes so much more sense than sending a text message."

"You've always been a pain in the ass, you know that?"

"So I've been told."

Giovanni glared at me. "Had another lawyer take a look at our last contract. You know — the one you did before you up and left town? Imagine my surprise to see you took out some of the most important parts."

I gave him a grim smile. "Guess you should have read it before you signed, then."

He wagged a finger at me, the gold ring on his pinky flashing. "You're a snake, just like your old man. You know that? A real fucking snake. And that's saying something coming from me."

I rolled my eyes. "You want money? Is that what this is?"

He laughed and turned to Tony, who gave an obligatory chuckle. "Money? Nah. I don't want your money."

"Then what am I doing here?"

"You're going to take this new contract to that pompous son of a bitch you've been working with and he's going to sign it. Or I'll kill you both." Giovanni motioned Tony forward.

Dutifully, Tony held the contract out to me with a blank expression.

Refusing to take it, I lifted my chin, my glare slicing between the two of them. "I'm not your errand boy."

"You're whatever I say you're going to be."

I pretended to think it over before shaking my head. "No. I'm not." Flipping open my pocket watch, I gave an exaggerated wince. "Point of fact, I've got somewhere else I need to be so I suggest you wrap this up in the next two minutes or so."

"You're not going anywhere until I say you are." Giovanni gave a curt nod.

A second later, something hard hit me across the back, a metallic pinging sound reverberating in my ears. My knees buckled under the force and I pitched forward. If I had to guess, it was either a baseball bat or a pipe. Regardless, it was going to hurt like hell in the morning. If I made it to morning.

Giovanni squatted next to me, grabbing a handful of hair and yanking me up onto my hands and knees. "Guess *you* should have remembered who you're fucking with. I'm going to make you regret every single fucking letter you changed in that contract." He let go roughly, rising to his feet again.

Gritting my teeth, I pushed myself upright until I managed to get one leg under myself. I made it off the ground before the pain in my back screamed at me to stop. Hunched over on one knee, I spit out a string of slurs in Italian I knew they wouldn't miss even if they were a different dialect.

Giovanni and Tony looked at one another, their eyes wide. I wondered which conversation, exactly, had them the most worried. Which part of their enterprise they unknowingly revealed over the years when they thought no one outside the family was listening.

"*I speak Italian,*" I said, a vicious laugh bubbling out of me, in spite of the pain. "You fucking morons."

Giovanni turned ashen, gaping at Tony. It was Tony who gave the next nod.

Another hard, metallic object came down across the top of my shoulder, narrowly missing the backside of my skull. I landed hard on the dirty concrete, unable to breathe or see beyond the flash of pain.

I couldn't get up a second time.

Blow after blow rained down on me from every angle, from a variety of sources — bats, fists, boots. I did what I could to shield myself, until something hard connected squarely with the side of my head.

A burst of stars behind my eyes was followed by absolute nothingness.

———

THE NEXT TIME I opened my eyes, a doctor was shining a pen light in them. He dictated comments about pupil response and how much to increase the medication to the nurse at his elbow. I was two seconds away from knocking his hand out of my face, when he lowered it and continued speaking to the nurse.

My ears were ringing, muffling most of their conversation. When I tried glancing to the other side of the room, nausea flared up, roiling in my stomach. Every inch of me hurt. It hurt to breathe. It hurt to fucking blink. It actually made the lightning incident feel like a day at the beach. Who knew I'd endure an experience even more painful than that one?

"Can you hear me? Bennett?" The doctor's face bobbed into view and someone touched my shoulder gently.

I squeezed my eyes shut and lifted my hand to my head, jerking back when something hard touched my forehead instead of flesh. My right forearm was in a cast. The movement, combined with the revelation, sent another wave of nausea up the back of my throat.

"Easy," the doctor said, guiding my right arm down to the pillow it was supposed to be resting on. "It's broken."

Great. I couldn't even take a deep breath for a proper sigh. Each breath felt like someone was stabbing me. Wincing, I laid a hand on my ribs, as if more pressure was the answer to the searing pain.

"You have some broken ribs, as well."

I managed to croak out one question before clamping my mouth, keeping the puke at bay. "Anything else?"

The doctor inhaled, which was never a good sign. "You have some intracranial hemorrhaging. Not bad enough to require surgery, but it may cause complications down the road, along with the concussion. You were not in the best of shape when the medics brought you in."

"Complications?"

"Memory loss, speech problems, problems with movement, sensitivity to lights and sounds, sleep disturbances, trouble concen—"

"Yeah, ok. I get it."

"And personality changes," the doctor added, as if my abruptness was a new trait.

I closed my eyes, absorbing what he said and trying to make sense of it. The thumping in my skull didn't help.

"If you're feeling up to it, there are a couple detectives here who have some questions for you." When I didn't consciously object, he opened the door and waved the pair in.

A tall, older male walked in first, followed by a young, blonde female. She looked strikingly familiar. From her wide-eyed glance, I got the feeling she knew me as well but I had no idea from where.

"Mr. Reeve, I'm Detective Carlson," the male said before gesturing to the woman. "This is Detective Vitkus. We'd like to ask you some questions about your involvement in last night's shooting."

My brow furrowed. "Shooting?" The doctor didn't say anything about me being shot. I'm pretty sure that would have jumped out at some point in our brief conversation. Bullets generally trumped broken bones and concussions.

Detective Carlson flipped open his notepad, his pen at the ready. "Six people were shot at a warehouse on Lumber Street early this morning. Four dead. One in critical and one escaped."

"I don't know anything about a shooting."

"Where were you last night?"

"At a friend's house."

"Where's that?"

"The mansion on Fairmount."

"Where?"

"I don't know the numbers. Three something?"

The detectives exchanged a look.

"Fairmount?" the blonde asked. "Do you mean the Fair*mont* in Millennium Park?"

I blinked at her. "Millennium Park? In Chicago?"

She nodded slowly, looking at me like I had three heads.

"No, Fair*mount* Road," I reiterated. "In Easton. The Welles mansion...?" I had to stop and play back my own words in my head, confirming I was speaking English and not some hodgepodge of the romance languages I'd picked up over the years.

"Where do you think you are right now?" Detective Carlson asked, his grizzled demeanor softening unexpectedly.

Licking my lips, I glanced around the hospital room. "I... don't know."

"You're in Chicago," Detective Vitkus said, glancing at her partner. "Do you remember how you got here?"

I shook my head, immediately wishing I hadn't. Squeezing my eyes shut, I tried to tell myself to breathe, but it didn't matter. The nausea, the pounding. It was all too much.

"What time did you leave your friend's house?" Detective Carlson continued.

"I don't know," I said after another minute, clenching the sheet beneath me.

"And you don't know anything about the four bodies we found?"

"I want my lawyer." I swallowed thickly, trying not to retch.

"We're just trying to figure out who killed Marchese's guys and left you for dead," the female interjected.

"Did you get a look at the shooters?" Carlson asked.

Biting my lip, I shook my head.

"Do you know where Giovanni Marchese is?"

The nausea was suddenly accompanied by a chill racing down my spine, goosebumps and all. I couldn't explain it or the reason why.

"Look, we know who you are, Mr. Reeve," Vitkus said with a huff. "We know you're Marchese's lawyer. Do you know who he was supposed to meet with last night?"

I might not have known where the hell I was or what was going on, but I knew how *this* worked. I knew how answers got twisted. I used to be one of the ones twisting them. "I'm not saying anything else without my lawyer."

The woman sighed, meanwhile her partner flipped his notepad shut and tucked it into his blazer. He withdrew a business card and held it out to me. "If you're feeling up to it later."

I didn't take it, so he dropped it on the table and walked out.

The female also took out a business card, scribbled something on the back, and tossed it on my lap. Her lip curled as she turned on her heel and walked out.

Flipping the card over, I blinked.

KARMA

The word hit me as hard as she'd hit me last spring, out of the blue and with a stinging accuracy. The cop I'd fucked over for Sidorov. Well, the good news was that my memory wasn't total shit.

Since I knew I wasn't a complete amnesiac, I rested my

head against the pillow and closed my eyes, trying to recall images of Marchese and his pals, gunfire, anything.

It was all blank.

I couldn't remember what I did the week before, let alone anything from the night before. So much for that awesome memory of mine.

———

"You look like shit," Del said from the doorway, a duffel bag slung over his shoulder.

"Still better than you." I smirked and chuckled once before clamping a hand over my ribs. It had been two days and yet I seemed to forget how the slightest movements refreshed the pain.

"See? God'll get you."

"Blow me." I adjusted my position, trying to shift my weight to the opposite hip to give my ribs on that side a break.

Chuckling, he walked in, setting the duffel bag on the chair. His chuckle faded and his frown deepened the closer he got. "What the hell happened, bro?"

"I don't know."

"C'mon man. You can tell me."

"I seriously don't know."

He leaned in close, his voice dropping. "Did you shoot Marchese's guys?"

Instead of answering him in a whisper, I practically shouted my reply. "I don't know!" Pain shot across my ribs, reprimanding me. I wanted to scream out all of my frustration, but even my concussed brain knew the strain would be too much.

"Ok." He patted my shoulder gingerly. "We'll get it figured out."

"I want to leave. It's not safe here."

"What are you talking about?"

I couldn't explain the overwhelming urge to run, but it had only gotten worse the longer I was in the hospital. Each time the door opened, I envisioned a bullet hurtling toward me, splattering what was left of my brain all over the wall. I didn't know who was after me, or why, but I knew I didn't like being a sitting duck. "Call Gavin. I don't know where my car is. He needs to find it for me."

"It's the last week of the month. Gavin's in St. Louis, remember?"

"Fuck."

"And the police didn't say anything about recovering your car from the warehouse. Are you sure you drove?"

"I don't fucking know, Del!"

"Ok, calm down."

That was the last thing I was going to do. I yanked the IV out of my hand and swung my legs over the side of the bed. "I'm leaving!" As soon as my feet touched the cold tile, the world went topsy turvy and I swayed, touching a hand to my forehead.

Del held me steady, his grip inadvertently sending a ripple of pain down my arm. "Sit your ass down before you break something else."

I did as instructed, only because I couldn't breathe and if I couldn't breathe, I couldn't exactly argue.

"What did the doctor say?"

The prognosis from the other day was mostly a blur. "I broke this." I held up my casted-right arm, you know, in case he couldn't see for himself. "I broke these," I continued, holding my ribs. "And my brain is bleeding."

"That explains a lot..."

"Fuck off."

A nurse came marching in a second later, her look of

concern flipping to one of irritation when she spied the IV dangling from the machine and blood dripping off the back of my hand. "Sir, the doctor hasn't released you yet."

"I'm leaving," I said with far more conviction than I felt.

"You have a head injury."

"Am I under arrest?" I looked up at Del. I didn't think I was since no one was babysitting the door, nor had anyone Mirandized me, but I wanted to make sure.

He shook his head. "No. Of course not."

"Then I'm leaving," I reaffirmed, turning back to the nurse. "Go get your little paperwork. I'll AMA myself out of here. I don't care."

She huffed and strode out.

"I don't think that's a good idea," Del said as I hauled myself to my feet again and walked along the edge of the bed, using it for support like a fucking toddler.

"I don't think it's a good idea to sit here and wait for a hitman to show up, either."

"A hitman? Jesus. Who would send a hitman after you?"

"Marchese, probably." I might not have any recollection of the warehouse, but I knew I fucked him over with Leander's contract. Maybe he found out. He sent Johnny to bring me back to Chicago and all he got was a corpse in return. This time? There were four corpses and I was somehow in the middle of it.

"I thought you didn't remember what happened?"

"I don't. But if I was there when something happened, there's a good chance Giovanni thinks I was involved. The last thing I need is to be looking over my shoulder for the rest of my life."

I used one hand to tug open the zipper on the bag Del brought, shrugging off his outstretched hand and the silent offer to help. As soon as the opening was wide enough, I upended the clothing onto the bed.

"Madre de Dios," Del groaned. "Just, stop. Would you? Let me." He pawed through the clothing and grabbed a pair of pajama pants first, holding them open so I could step into them. Pulling the gown over my head carefully, he tossed it to the side and helped maneuver a t-shirt over my cast and into place without me having to lift my arms very much.

"They took your other clothes as evidence," he said quietly. "But I managed to get these back." He pulled a palmful of jewelry out of his pocket.

"Thank you." I could have kissed him. Instead, I slipped the majority of the heavy rings onto my left hand, since my right was too swollen. There was no way I could put my necklace on myself, so I held it out to Del, along with the onyx ring from Leander — the one I hadn't taken off since Christmas.

"Can you help?" God, it sounded pathetic. *I* sounded pathetic. I *was* pathetic. Oh, how the mighty had fallen.

Thankfully, Del wasn't as much of an asshole as I was. He nodded and, without commentary, slipped the onyx ring onto the chain before fastening it around my neck.

The nurse came back with a clipboard and a scowl. I crudely signed her papers and hobbled out of the room, shooing Del away when he tried to offer support. The orderly who scurried after me with a wheelchair got an earful in Italian and cooing apologies from Del in a mixture of Spanish and English.

The glaring sunlight and noise of Chicago hit me the second I stepped outside the hospital doors. If it wasn't for Del grabbing my arm and leading the way, I probably would have curled up in a ball on the sidewalk and cried.

"Where to?" he asked once we were in the car.

"Home."

He laughed, shooting me a sideways glance before pulling out into traffic. "Where's that these days?"

It wasn't floor plans or addresses that flashed through my mind. I didn't see furniture or house numbers. I envisioned dark hair and green eyes. Schubert and Poe. Lions and foxes. Venice…

"Bennett?"

I blinked, looking at Del. "St. Louis."

CHAPTER 30

*M*y cell phone buzzed violently on the couch next to me. I made a bet with myself as to who it was. My money was on Olivia. She'd been calling on the hour, every hour, for the past several days. When she wasn't calling, she was sending a variety of scathing texts.

Leander's name lit up the screen when I turned the phone over. My throat tightened seeing those seven letters. I kept staring at it, even after it stopped ringing. A moment later, a voicemail notification popped up.

My thumb hovered over the icon. I hadn't talked to him in... God knew when. Days? Weeks? Even after I left the hospital, my brain remained a pile of mush. Time ceased to be relevant, except for when it came to signing a new sublet and moving the dire necessities across St. Louis, away from any address associated with me prior to the hospital.

Pieces of that night came in flashes, one by one, until I had enough to stitch together a vague timeline of events. Leander dominated the memories, though at first I didn't believe half of what my brain showed me. I'd been fantasizing about him for so long, that's all it was, right? Wishful thinking combined with brain trauma.

Eventually, the gut-feeling it was all true overrode any attempt at rationalization. We'd really spent the night together. *Together.* Our partnership, friendship, whatever it was, transcended into something more. While I should have been over the moon, I wasn't. Giovanni took the best thing in my life and ruined it in a matter of hours. Until I knew how to fix it, I couldn't talk to Leander. I couldn't even listen to his voicemails. Not until I knew he wouldn't be in any more danger because of me.

The details of what transpired in that warehouse were still hidden in the recesses of my mind, but I knew two things. Number One, Giovanni tried to kill me and very nearly succeeded. Which led me to Number Two, someone, somehow, killed most of the Italians before they finished me off.

According to Del, Tony and I were both transported to the hospital, but Tony succumbed to his injuries the day I left town. Giovanni escaped, badly injured, based on the blood-trail and the number of bullets unaccounted for. His body hadn't shown up yet, which meant he was still out there and even more pissed than before.

Curiously, Sergei had turned into my new BFF since I got out of the hospital, sending gift baskets and personal updates on the manhunt for Marchese. His network of informants were on the lookout, but thus far, no one knew where Giovanni had gone. Not my sources. Not their sources. Not even the police. And that worried me more than I wanted to admit.

As soon as I heard a key in the door, I hit the lock screen on my phone and threw it into the corner of the couch. My half-hearted attention darted back to the TV to watch Gordon Ramsay scream at inept restaurant owners. Since I couldn't express outrage, or even sneeze, with five broken ribs, I had to live vicariously through someone else.

Gavin and Allegra burst through the door, holding an animated conversation. While I was begrudgingly grateful Gavin stayed in St. Louis to mother-hen me in person, I was very much annoyed he told Allegra what happened. I was able to put her off as long as I could until today when Mr. Helpful drove to her hotel and picked her up at the conclusion of her conference.

"Girl, sometimes you have to just go for it. When in Rome, right?" Gavin said as he came in from the hall, plastic bags rustling.

She laughed, her light, airy laugh. "No! Meatballs are an appetizer. I'm not putting them in my pasta."

"We're going to Olive Garden before you leave. And that's final."

My head thumped with each syllable. As much as I disliked hospitals, with the cleanly scent of death and garish light, I wished I was in one right now. At least it would have been quieter.

Allegra dropped the bags in the middle of the foyer and rushed over to the couch, reaching for me with a look of sheer horror. *"Oh my God! You said it wasn't that bad!"*

"It's not." I made a face at her, reeling away as best I could. The majority of the bruises were now in that ugly yellow-green stage. Naturally, it was the cuts and broken bones that were taking the longest to heal.

"I told you," Gavin said in a sing-song voice behind her.

I shot him a glare.

He scrunched up his nose and disappeared into the kitchen with the bags Allegra dropped.

"Bennett..." Allegra sank onto the couch next to me, her eyes far too big and sad for my liking. It was the same look she had the night she begged me to leave Iacopo alone, fearing I'd wind up getting offed by his family. *"If you would have told me, I would have skipped the conference. I should have been here, with you."*

"I don't need a nurse, Allegra. Go home, already. Or go stay with Gavin if you want. But don't sit there giving me cow eyes."

"God forbid you rely on family for anything. God forbid you rely on <u>anyone</u>." She shrugged out of her coat, as if to cement the fact she wasn't leaving anytime soon.

"Welcome to my life," Gavin chimed in from the kitchen.

"Shut up! You don't even know what we're talking about," I yelled, making sure his pain-in-the-ass heard me.

Gavin made a dismissive noise, backed up by Allegra's knowing smirk. *"It could be worse. I could have told Mama."*

"I'm surprised you didn't."

It was her turn to make a face at me.

"By the way," Gavin said, returning with a container of pork lo mein. "Leander has been blowing up my phone demanding to know what happened and where you are. And now he sent Olivia after me. I'm pretty sure her last voice-mail was a death threat. Like, a real one. As in, she is going to drive to Chicago and murder me with her stilettos. You need to call him. Or her. Or someone in that group." He thrust the food at me with a sweet smile. "Or I'm going to tell them where you are."

I took the box with a scowl and stabbed at the food with the fork he included. "No one is supposed to know where I am, Gavin. Especially not Leander. That's why I moved."

Allegra gasped and smacked my bicep. "Bennett!"

Wincing, I shot her the next glare. "What?!"

"Good luck, Sweetie," Gavin said, pecking each of her cheeks. "He won't listen to me either. I'll be in town the rest of the week dealing with his *other* apartment and then I'm heading back to Chicago. Let me know if you're sick of his ass by then, I can take you with me."

If looks could kill, Gavin would have been dead by the time he reached the door.

Allegra hit me again once he was gone. *"You didn't tell Leander what happened? What's wrong with you?"*

"Ouch! Stop it."

"He's got to be so sick with worry."

"I don't want to bother him."

"Bother him? You idiot! He cares about you! He clearly wants to talk to you!" She looked like she wanted to hit me again with her hands balled in her lap, her brown eyes simmering.

"You don't know what happened, Allegra, or why. So don't sit there and tell me what I should and shouldn't do."

"You're as stubborn as a mule."

"Family trait," I spat back at her.

"Are you in much pain?" she asked, her voice softening.

"I'll live."

"You didn't answer the question."

Ignoring her a second time, I leaned forward and snatched a book off the coffee table, tossing it in her lap. As soon as I saw the cover, I realized it was the book of Poe Leander gave me for my birthday last year, annotated with his perfect penmanship, as if the universe was mocking my attempt to distance myself from him.

"Give me a page number."

"What?" She furrowed her brows at me.

"A page number. Give me a page number. I need to see if the memory thing is back yet."

She cracked open the book and gestured awkwardly. *"I don't know. Um, eighty-nine."*

I closed my eyes, trying to recall what the page looked like, what poem it was, or even what notes he'd written.

My mind was completely blank.

"Fuck!" I slammed the box of Chinese on the coffee table.

If Allegra wasn't there, it would have gone through the TV, the book along with it. *"I still can't remember!"*

Allegra set the book aside and scooted closer, rubbing small, soothing circles on my back. *"Give it some time. It'll come back."*

My head whipped up, renewing the nauseating pounding. *"What if it doesn't? What if I lost it forever?"*

"You can't think like that. You have to stay positive."

I snorted. Fuck optimism. I was a realist, through and through. *"You know the lightning already fucked up my head once. What if this brain bleed finishes it off?"*

She frowned, but didn't say anything.

There wasn't anything *to* say.

CHAPTER 31

A knock sounded at the front door. I shot upright, eyes wide. Gavin was back in Chicago and Allegra was here. There shouldn't be *anyone* at my door.

Allegra hopped off the couch with the grace of the ballerina she once was, motioning for me to stay put. When she came back a second later with someone in tow, I wanted to die on the spot. Or kill her. Kill her and then die.

It was Leander.

I shifted my attention to Allegra, hoping she saw the utter betrayal on my face. The whole point of moving to an address no one knew about was so Leander — and by extension, Marchese — couldn't find me. And there was my sister, blowing up the entire plan.

"I'll give you two some space," she said not looking the least bit sorry as she disappeared down the hall to the bedrooms.

Leander and I stared at each other, barely blinking, barely breathing. Time stopped and silence filled the void between us. It was so heavy, I thought it was going to suffocate me.

His face was unreadable, pale and chiseled as ever, though

the purple shadows under his eyes were hard to ignore. It looked like he was also punched with how dark they were. Gesturing to the chair kitty-corner from me, he cleared his throat softly. "May I?"

"Yeah." I sat up a little straighter, keenly aware of the distance between us — literally and figuratively. I'd never been so on edge around him. Not after our fight in New Orleans. Not after waking up in Venice with his hand in mine. And now all I wanted to do was crawl into a hole and die rather than spend one more second in the same room as him.

He leaned forward on his knees, lacing his fingers together and staring at the coffee table. It was probably easier for him. I knew it was easier for me, to not have to face the rawness in his voice.

"I'm not going to ask why you moved again," he said quietly, in a measured cadence. "I'm not going to ask where you've been, or what happened... Or who did this to you..."

I bit my lower lip, reminding myself to keep my mouth shut. Leander learning the truth wouldn't solve anything. It would only make it a thousand times harder than it needed to be.

His Adam's apple bobbed in his throat and his knuckles turned white. "All I'm going to ask is why you've been avoiding me."

When his pale eyes lifted to mine, I thought my ribs were going to break all over again from the crushing guilt. I would have preferred it. Marchese could break my other arm if it meant erasing that look from Leander's face. He could break all of me if it would undo the pain I caused.

"It's not what you think..." I said weakly.

"Then by all means, explain."

"I..." Now it was I who couldn't look at him. Turning away, I shook my head at the impossibility of the situation.

How could I tell him my recklessness finally caught up with me? How could I tell him he'd been right all along to worry? The truth would ruin everything. Knowing Marchese was responsible would only put him back in the Italians' crosshairs.

But *not* telling Leander would ruin everything, as well. As much as it killed me, I only saw one version where there was a guarantee Leander would stay alive, even if it hurt him in the process.

"What is this, Bennett? What is this... thing, between us?" His voice was soft, but full of agony. It only made the guilt a thousand times worse.

"I don't know..." Another lie rolled off my tongue, sharp and bitter. There was a word for it, but I could never say it. Not now. Probably not ever with the way things were going.

"Will you ever tell me the truth?"

"I don't know..."

"What *do* you know?" He snarled the question. I couldn't blame him. For someone who needed information like they needed air, having it withheld purposely was an additional slap in the face.

"I'm not good for you," I admitted, forcing myself to look at him. The pain was akin to putting my hand on a hot stove. It burned and it blistered, but I couldn't look away. "I see that now."

His eyes were dark, shining with unshed tears. The muscles in his throat tightened. "Shouldn't I be the judge of that?"

"You don't know what I've done. You don't know the kind of danger I bring."

"I don't care. I don't care about your past or whatever you're so afraid of. You're not the only one with demons."

"You don't understand..."

"Then tell me!" He pinned me with his quiet intensity, his eyes boring into mine, not allowing me to look away again.

"You will drown with me, Leander. Save yourself while you still can."

He shifted forward out of the chair and settled onto the couch next to me. Before I could scoot away, his hand encircled the back of my neck gently. "You can't run away from this, Bennett."

"Then you haven't been paying attention." I swept his hand off the back of my neck and stood. Crossing to the sliding glass door, I exhaled a painful breath, literally and figuratively.

Evening traffic moved through the city down below. Was Giovanni out there now, watching? Did he turn to his contacts in New York, so I'd never see it coming? At this point, I didn't even know if I was still on his radar. Bits of my memory continued to return, finally explaining why Sergei was so concerned with my welfare. It was *his* crew that wiped out the Italians, at *my* behest. They were the reason I was alive and, as far as favors went, I was back in Sergei's debtor column.

So until I knew what Giovanni was planning or someone put him six feet under, I refused to put Leander at risk any more than I already had. I wouldn't let him be used by anyone to get to me, or worse, as payback for my betrayal.

"I thought we were in this together?" Leander asked from the couch. "Us, against the world. Was all of that bullshit?"

I hung my head, unable to answer him.

"This whole thing was *your* idea," Leander continued, his voice growing icier with each word. "You came to me in Chicago. And now you're backing out? After everything we —" The rest of his sentence disappeared with a scoff and a shake of his head.

Squeezing my eyes shut, I covered my face with one hand.

With each passing second, I wished Giovanni and his goons *had* killed me. It would have been easier than this.

"You're the *one* person who knows all of me," Leander said sharply. "You're the *one* person I don't keep secrets from. And now you won't even look at me." His voice cracked at the end, taking whatever was left of my heart right along with it.

"I'm sorry, Leander. I can't be that person for you. I can't —" I bit down on my lip hard, the pain shocking me into silence. He was right. I couldn't even turn around to face him, to see what my idiocy had done.

"Is this the end of everything, then? All of the plans we made? The plans we've already set in motion?"

"I'll find you another corporate lawyer."

"You've got to be—"

"Until then, I'll do my work from here. Or, wherever…" I continued over the top of him, sounding as hollow as I felt.

In the reflection, I saw him rake his hands through his hair before he looked up, meeting my gaze in the glass. "Why are you doing this?"

I had no answer to give, or at least none he wanted to hear, none he would accept. So, I continued on as numbly as I could. "It's probably best if we don't see each other."

Scoffing, he stood, his jaw clenched harder than his fists. "Best for whom, Bennett? No, don't answer. I already know."

I tried to keep my voice calm, even though every cell in my body was screaming at me to stop talking. "I know you're angry—"

"You don't know anything! I trusted you! And you—" He cut himself off, swallowing hard. "I fucking knew this would happen. I told you we shouldn't. I should have known better. Christ, I *did* know better."

Even though it killed me, I finally turned to look at him,

to face the pain, the contempt. I deserved every ounce of it anyway. "I never wanted this to happen."

He laughed, bitterly. "What *did* you want?"

You. To leave and travel the world with you at my side. To spend our days however we saw fit, and our nights wrapped up in each other. To give you everything, to *be* your everything.

Instead, I said nothing. The truth sat in the back of my throat, choking me.

"I see..." He nodded, the tears welling in his eyes until a few spilled over. "You got what you wanted."

"Leander..." The rest of my plea ended with a strangled cry.

He held up a hand, wincing. "Don't. Just... don't." The anguished look on his face turned hard, like a pond freezing over. He was gone. In that moment, I knew I'd lost him.

"*I'm sorry...*" My tears began when his stopped, slipping down my face with the admission. "More than you'll ever know."

"Yeah... Me too," he replied through gritted teeth. Without another word, he spun on the ball of his foot and strode to the door, the line of his shoulders straight and unforgiving. "Give Allegra my best," he said before the door slammed shut hard enough to knock a picture off the wall.

Crumpling to the floor, I held my head in my hands. His departure unleashed a wave of tears, leaving me gasping for a full breath that wouldn't — couldn't — come. I smashed a hand against my ribs, trying to literally hold myself together and force my lungs to cooperate.

That's how Allegra found me. She dropped to her knees and pulled me against her, wrapping her arms around my shoulders. "*What happened?*"

"*He's gone,*" I sobbed against her shoulder. It was the only thing I could say, over and over, between gulps of air and the agonizing pain that stole each breath away again. I hoped one of the broken ribs would shift hard enough to actually pierce my heart. Or maybe she'd leave me alone long enough to hurl myself over the balcony. Something, anything to put me out of my self-made misery.

CHAPTER 32

*W*eeks dragged by.

My injuries healed slowly, all except for the giant, fucking hole in my heart. I was stuck with the cast for a little bit longer, but thankfully the ribs, while sensitive, were mostly fused back together.

On top of my usual lightning-induced headaches, I now enjoyed debilitating migraines as well. And lucky me — my brain regained its peculiar recall ability, which meant I could replay my last words with Leander over and *over* again, laid up for days in the dark. It was my new, excruciating pastime, remembering the look in Leander's eyes, the hollowness of his voice. The only salve was a fuck-ton of bourbon and oxy.

After Leander left my apartment that day, we didn't see, nor speak to, each other again. Anything related to work was funneled through Gavin. He wouldn't even acknowledge the brief emails I sent him in regard to the company.

For the most part, I stayed out of Easton and the Eastonians stayed out of St. Louis. Elijah and I only talked about work, and only ever on the phone. Olivia ignored me, using

Gavin as the constant go-between, like her boss. Cole was the only one bold enough to venture across the Mississippi.

We met for dinner one night, tucked away in the back corner of a Mediterranean restaurant with a clear view of the door. Just in case.

"What the fuck, man?" he asked after our drinks were delivered.

"Long story," I said, popping another couple of pills and washing them down with an entire tumbler of Arak.

"Jesus. Are you trying to kill yourself?"

I snorted, signaling the waitress for a refill, even though licorice was far from my favorite flavor. I should have ordered two from the get-go. "If only it was that easy."

"Dude, for real. What happened? I know a beat down when I see one."

Shrugging, I spun the empty glass in circles on the table, still waiting on that refill. "I'm fine. Must be the lights in here."

He gestured to the cast with an impatient look. "So, what's with the arm?"

"I fell," I said quickly, chewing on an ice cube.

"Then what's Leander's deal?"

"What do you mean?"

"He won't leave the house. *If* he does, it's to terrorize us for a few hours before going back home. I've seen him mad before but this is on a whole other level."

I shrugged again, tracking the waitress across the room from one table to the next. "I don't know what to tell you. I haven't talked to him."

"*You* haven't talked to *him*? Are you kidding me? You two did everything together."

"I was in Chicago for a bit and when I came back, he, uh, he was busy. We've both been really busy."

Cole made a face. "Busy with what? You literally work for him. How can you not talk to him?"

"I have other shit going on, ok?" I cut a glare at him, hoping that was the end of Twenty Questions.

"Yeah. Clearly." He shook his head. A second later, he leaned forward, his eyes narrowed. "Alright look. I'm not smart like the two of you, ok? But I'm not a fucking idiot either."

The waitress reappeared, glancing at Cole as she set down another glass of Arak.

After she scurried away, he continued, unfazed. "Cut the shit, man. What is going on?"

"Why are you hounding me about this? Go ask Leander if you want to know so goddamn bad. *He* was your friend first."

The glass was halfway to my mouth when Cole's hand shot out, grabbing my wrist so hard I thought he might actually bend the silver cuff. "I have. Now I'm asking you."

I set the drink back down with a flourish. "And?"

"He threw a fucking bottle at my head. A glass one." The muscle along the side of Cole's jaw twitched. He stared at me, hard, waiting for some sort of reaction. When he didn't get one, he kept going. "In fact, from what I could see before he literally shoved me out of the house, he's been throwing a lot of shit. Half the windows on the ground floor of his house are shattered. He won't let anyone in. Not Elijah. Not Olivia. Not even his housekeeper."

As much as I didn't want to picture him destroying his house, I had a very clear image of it. I knew, because I, too, had upended the coffee table a time or two. And threw a glass. Or three. The only thing that kept the windows safe was the fact they weren't technically mine.

"Maybe he had a nightmare," I said flatly.

"Oh my God! Stop lying!" He looked like he was ready to throw a bottle at *my* head.

"What do you want from me, Cole? Huh? What can I do that will make you get the fuck off my back?"

"I want you to fix it! Fix him! Elijah used to be the only one who could talk some sense into him, but Leander shut him out too. That leaves you. You're the only one who can reach him."

I laughed, a sad, tired laugh. "I am the last person he wants to talk to right now."

"But *why?*"

Shaking my head, I tossed the mouthful of milky-white liquor back before he could stop me. "I gotta go." I threw a couple twenties on the table and stood quickly.

"We haven't even eaten!"

"I'm not hungry."

"Bennett!"

I gave him a two-fingered wave over my shoulder, not even looking back.

———

COLE'S ADMONISHMENT circled around in my head for days.

Fix it. Fix him.

If only it were that simple. I told Leander time and time again things weren't as complicated as he made them and now? I choked down every bite of crow.

I didn't even know how to make it right at this point. He was as likely to listen to an apology as I was to tell Camille I loved her. So, in lieu of a mea culpa, I did the next best thing — I sent a peace offering.

The previous owner of Walker House may not have liked me, *at all*, but his son certainly did.

Two weeks after the old man finally kicked the bucket, Junior and I schmoozed it up at a swanky restaurant known for its prime rib and off-track betting. I plied him with as much alcohol as I could and bided my time, even as my brain cells died, one by one, with endless conversations about thoroughbreds and our waitress' ass.

Half-way through dinner, he excused himself for the bathroom.

As I reached for the salt with my casted arm, I flicked a small, dissolvable packet into the remnants of his drink. Mission accomplished, I salted my baked potato and resumed eating.

With Junior out of the way, the Welles Corporation would be primed to swoop in and buy Walker House, like Leander wanted to do last year. I couldn't apologize, nor could I tell him the truth, so snagging another Easton jewel for his empire was the best I could do.

The next morning, I opened my email and scrolled through the *Easton Sentinel's* daily update. There was no mention of Junior's death. I didn't expect it to appear suspicious since he was a larger fellow with high cholesterol, but I figured the death of a well-known citizen was bound to draw some attention and public blubbering. It probably would have, except for the fact someone else's untimely passing was front and center.

Reginald Van Deveer, the "beloved" town doctor, was brutally beaten to death. The police located his body on the side of the road, dumped like the trash he was. According to the article, he was only identifiable from his watch and wedding ring.

David Harris, the mechanic responsible for ruining Elijah's life and a large factor in the reason Leander's father was dead, was beaten, but recognizable.

Keith Starkey, the retired cop Cole killed, was beaten, but recognizable.

Besides Reginald, the only other person who was bludgeoned *beyond* recognition was Irene Welles, the first name

Leander personally crossed off his list. It stood to follow that Leander was the one behind the crowbar for Reginald's murder instead of Olivia, as originally intended.

Part of me hoped in the midst of our... separation... Leander called off his plan for revenge. I also knew better. There was no way I'd quit and I knew, deep down, he never would either. It was precisely why I didn't tell him about Marchese.

In the days following Junior's death, I waited for some sort of acknowledgment. He had to have seen the move for what it was, since Olivia — via Gavin — instructed me to make Junior's daughter an offer for the hotel.

Still, no word from Leander.

I told myself it didn't matter in the long run. The lack of communication was a good thing for both of us. He was undoubtedly busy keeping up pretenses while Easton PD scrambled for evidence in Reginald's killing. I, on the other hand, was still hiding from Marchese, not to mention dodging phone calls from both the FBI and Chicago PD.

Despite changing my work number, the calls continued. I debated whether or not I should change my personal number as well, but in the end I opted to turn it off. It was easier staring at a black screen instead of checking it twelve times a minute to see if I somehow missed a notification from the one person I knew would never call no matter how many dead bodies I gifted him.

I got so good at ignoring calls, I could go incommunicado for days at a time.

"Oh my God!" Gavin snapped at me one day when I finally picked up with a snarl of my own. "Where have you been? I've been calling you all morning!"

"I'm busy," I muttered, filling in another line on my cross-word puzzle. "What do you want?"

"You haven't handled any of that shit for Sidorov and the

Ukrainians or Patrick What's-His-Name with the construction company on the north side. Why accept jobs if you're not going to follow through?"

"I am. Jesus."

"If I end up with busted kneecaps, you're paying my medical bills. And then some. Like, pain and suffering."

"What do you want?" I repeated each word slowly, dripping with as much disdain as I could summon.

He huffed so loud, I was pretty sure I heard him all the way from Chicago. "Olivia called. You have a meeting at three in Easton."

"Tell her I can't make it."

"Duh. Don't you think I tried? She said she needs you there in person. She insisted."

"Why?"

"Oh, I'm sorry, I left my crystal ball at home today. If you want, I can teleport there and get it for you."

I hung up on him. In the next heartbeat, I whipped my phone across the room. It cracked but didn't shatter, which infuriated me all the more.

After not seeing Leander in a month, I was now being ordered into the office like a child? And by Olivia no less. Not even by Olivia, by Gavin on Olivia's behalf.

Underneath it all, the tiniest ember of hope sparked to life. Maybe it wasn't Olivia's doing. Maybe it *was* Leander.

CHAPTER 33

*P*hysically, the Welles Corporation was the same as when I left it all those weeks ago. But the feeling I got when I stepped through the door was nothing short of unsettling. My hands were clammy, despite my core temperature being a thousand degrees, regardless of the fact the top half of my shirt was unbuttoned.

Nodding to Madison, I made my way to the conference room and took my seat across from Olivia.

"Welcome back, Benny Boo Boo," she said with a disgusting sweetness, pushing a stack of paperwork in my direction. "Done being a slack ass at home?"

I was not in the mood, so I ignored her and thumbed through the paperwork. "Did you set up the closing on Walker House yet?"

She frowned, straightening her shoulders. "Still waiting on the paperwork. The other lawyer said it would be finished by tomorrow."

"Then why am I here?"

"Maybe because there's some shit you need to do in person instead of from your penthouse in St. Louis?"

So, the summons was *not* Leander's doing. It was entirely Olivia and entirely related to work, which all could have been accomplished across the Mississippi.

Before the thought finished forming in my brain, Leander breezed in the door. As always, he was impeccably dressed, but I knew at first glance something was off, the way I could sense a headache coming on. He wasn't sleeping again and I doubted he was eating. He was pale to begin with, but his skin lacked its usual glow. The dark circles, combined with his new pallor, added to his overall haunted look.

Unbuttoning his suit jacket with a flick of his fingers, Leander took his usual chair at the head of the table, directly to my right. He completely ignored me the entire way. I may as well have been a ghost.

"Updates?" Leander asked, his attention focused solely on Olivia.

Olivia shoved a stack of paperwork toward him. "These all need your signature."

"Some hedge fund guy keeps calling," Elijah said as he walked in, sliding into a chair at the far end of the table. "He wants to meet next week."

"I'm not interested," Leander murmured, whipping through Olivia's pile, his pen flashing over the bottom of the pages.

Elijah looked at me, his brows raised. "Bennett?"

I glanced at Leander before answering. "Send me the details."

"I have no interest in falling victim to anyone else's scheming. I invest as *I* choose. Understood?" Leander signed the current page particularly viciously before looking up with narrowed eyes. Elijah may have been on the receiving end of Leander's anger, but it was directed at me by word choice alone. With that, the teeny ember snuffed itself out.

Elijah raised his hands and leaned back in his chair.

Olivia cleared her throat pointedly, looking between me and a copy of the lawsuit sitting in front of me.

Leander zeroed in on her next. "Something to add?"

She waited, glaring at me for a full ten seconds before she slid the legal documents in front of him. "Jason Richter's mother is suing us for the wrongful death of her son in the bar two years ago."

I rolled my eyes skyward. Way to wait until the statute of limitations was almost out. Another month and we would have been in the clear.

Leander still refused to look at me. He pushed the suit back toward her and continued signing away. "That's an issue for the lawyers, not me."

Olivia shot me a perplexed look. I pretended to be reading the lawsuit, even though I'd only read the first paragraph a dozen times.

"Where are the other two?" Leander tucked his pen away, shoving the last of the paperwork to his right.

"They emailed their reports," Elijah said. "Cole is in Springfield dealing with preservation shit and Jake called in sick."

"After my conference call, I'll be on my cell for the rest of the day." Leander pushed away from the table and stormed out as quickly as he arrived. At that point, I wouldn't have been surprised to see a trail of frost in his wake.

Elijah whistled low, gathering his stuff. "Take cover, folks. Looks like another tornado is about to hit."

As soon as Elijah left the room, Olivia whirled on me. "What is *with* you two?"

I gave her a small shrug. "I don't know what you're talking about."

"Today is the first day you've managed to drag your lazy ass into the office in weeks and you two won't even make eye contact. Not to mention the fact, I was told to route every-thing through Gavin. So what the fuck happened?"

"I'm tired. I don't know what his excuse is." I swept the files off the desk and tucked them under my non-broken arm.

"You're a shitty liar," she said, hot on my heels.

"Actually, I'm a fantastic lawyer." I winked at her, even though I couldn't have been any less jovial.

"Then why did he say to give this lawsuit to the *lawyers*? Why didn't he say to have *you* handle it?"

I headed up the stairs, answering her on the way. "You'll have to ask your boss."

"I'm asking you," she called after me.

I ignored her and kept walking.

Ducking into my office, I closed the door and slumped against it. I should have never come here. I should have told Gavin to tell Olivia to fuck off. Seeing Leander, seeing what I *did* to Leander, brought all the agony from our last conversation rushing to the surface. Even if I told myself it was for his own good, I'd carry the crushing guilt for the rest of eternity.

Swallowing thickly, I stuffed the feelings back down and threw myself into finding my replacement. I should have done it weeks ago, when I said I would. Today was the conse-quence of me putting it off. But no more. I made a vow it was the last time I would ever set foot in this building.

Once I whittled the stack of resumes down to a suitable number, I shoved them in a folder and went back downstairs to Olivia's office.

"If you want to schedule interviews with these people, slot them into my calendar. I'll video in from wherever I am."

She took the folder and flipped it open, her brows knit-ting together. "Is this about the lawsuit?"

"No. I mean, yes. Potentially. Unless Scheible's minions handle it."

"Why do we need another corporate lawyer when we have you?"

"I'm leaving." There. I said it. Like ripping off a bandaid.

She looked up sharply. "You're what?!"

"I've done all I can do here. It's time to move on."

I expected her to jump for joy. At any moment, balloons and confetti would rain down from the ceiling. Instead, she stormed over to her door and slammed it shut with a surprising force. Stomping back to me, she stopped a breath away with the same murderous expression Leander had an hour ago. "Cut the shit, Bennett. What is going on?"

"Nothing. It's time to pull up anchor."

"Let me get this straight... you bulldoze your way into Leander's life, *all* of our lives for that matter. You two are completely inseparable for years, until one day you get your ass mysteriously handed to you, and now, out of the blue, you're up and leaving because it's 'time to pull up anchor'? I call bullshit!"

"Call it what you want, it doesn't change anything." I gestured to the file on her desk. "I like Hopkins the best. I think he'll be a good fit."

Before she could say anything else, I wove around her and ducked out the door.

I stopped by Madison's desk on my way out of the building. "I'm expecting the bank papers for Walker House sometime tomorrow, but I'm on my way back to St. Louis. Do you mind overnighting them to me when you get them?"

"Sure thing," she said with a smile. "I'm glad you're feeling better."

"Thanks."

As I turned to leave, Leander appeared in the hallway. His gaze swept over me — no, through me — to Madison. He may as well have decked me instead of simply handing her a stack of envelopes. "Can you drop these off on your way home?"

"Of course." Glancing between the two of us, she smiled again, but it was a touch too fake, too chipper. Even she knew something was wrong.

I didn't have time to dwell on it. In the next breath, time stopped and started again in slow motion.

The front door swung open and what looked like the entirety of the Easton police department filed in, filling the lobby.

Spine straight and chin lifted, Leander stared down Chief Albrecht as he strolled up with a smug expression.

"I've been waiting for this moment for ten years," the chief said with a wide smile.

"Enjoy it while you can," Leander replied with a smile as beautiful as it was terrifying.

The chief cleared his throat and took a step back, nodding to the sergeant.

The sergeant moved in, spinning Leander around and clamping handcuffs on. "Leander Welles, you're under arrest for the murder of Reginald Van Deveer. You have the right to remain silent." He continued to Mirandize Leander, marching him to the door.

Even though I knew it was coming the minute I saw the doctor's name splashed across the headlines, my heart still seized as they led him away.

Leander stared straight ahead, his jaw clenched and his gaze distant.

"Per aspera ad astra," I said quickly as he passed.

I didn't know if he heard me, or if it even registered, until he shot a look in my direction. There was nothing but darkness in his eyes, a primal ferocity I'd felt myself a hundred times but never saw reflected so clearly in another human. Fear ricocheted around inside my ribcage, fear for the future now out of our control, and fear he'd lose himself in that darkness if he stayed too long.

Before I could say anything else, even *think* anything else, they were gone.

"Oh my God." Madison gaped up at me. "What just happened? What are they talking about?"

I expelled a shaky breath and pulled out my phone. "Rebecca, it's Bennett Reeve. I need to talk to Richard. Now."

As soon as the other lawyer got on the line, I talked over his attempt at the requisite pleasantries. "Leander's been arrested for murder."

"What? Where?"

"Easton PD took him from the office." I flicked open my pocket watch. "It's too late for bond call."

"Do you know if they even set a bond?"

"No, I don't."

"I'll see what I can find out." He promptly hung up.

Olivia rushed out of her office, her eyes wide and her face devoid of color. "What the fuck is going on now? Why was Leander taken by the cops?"

"He's been arrested for murder."

She closed her eyes, touching one hand to her forehead. "Oh my God. This can't be happening."

Closing the distance between us, I hugged her with my good arm. "It'll be ok."

She scoffed into my chest, but didn't pull away. "Easy for you to say, you're leaving."

"Not anymore."

———

HOURS LATER, I faced the core group of people in Leander's life like a firing squad. We were in Elijah's living room, each in varying levels of anxiousness.

"What is going on?" Cole asked, his arms crossed. He finally stopped pacing, but still refused Olivia's order to sit down. "Leander said they'd never pin it on him. Now he's been charged with all four murders! You know that's bullshit! You know I ki—"

"Ah! Shh!" I slashed a hand across my throat. "Exnay on the confession."

"So what happened?" Olivia asked, wringing her hands together.

"He fucking set him up, that's what happened," Jake snapped, glaring at me. "You put these ideas in his head and hung him out to dry for your own fucking amusement."

I shot Jake an unimpressed look. "Do you really think anyone can put anything in Leander's head?"

"All I know is, as soon as you showed up, people started dying."

"Could you stop being a little bitch for one second and focus on the more important issue?" Cole growled.

"Fuck off, Cole! You were with him that night. Why aren't you under arrest too? Unless you're all in on it together!"

"Jake, stop," Olivia sighed.

I strode over to the bar in the corner and poured a shot of whiskey. I had a feeling this was going to take all night and I'd need something to calm me down before I smashed Jake's head into something hard. Tossing back two fingers, I decided to forgo any sense of etiquette and refilled it a third of the way from the top.

"Oh, yeah. Perfect." Jake scoffed. "Leander is in jail because of this asshole and he's kicking back with a drink while the rest of you sit around doing nothing. You people are unbelievable."

Turning back to the group, I pointed at Jake with the hand that held the tumbler. "Someone sit him down and shut him up, or get him the fuck out of here. I am out of oxy and the last thing I need is him running his mouth while I try and get everyone up to speed."

Cole took a step forward. Jake shoved him back.

"Do you want me to break your other arm?" Jake snarled at me.

I set the tumbler down and spread my arms. "You're welcome to try, sport."

"You condescending son of a—"

Elijah stepped between us, his hands outspread like a referee. "Cool it! Both of you. Jake, shut the fuck up. And Bennett, stop antagonizing him."

I saluted Elijah with two fingers and went to reclaim my bourbon.

As soon as Elijah stepped away, Jake lunged forward. We crashed into the wall, his hands fisted in my shirt. Before he could throw a punch, I darted forward under his arm and shoved him against the wall in my place. I didn't need full use of my right hand to yank the ice pick out of my waistband or take aim base of his throat.

"Bennett, don't!" Olivia shrieked.

"Give me one reason why I shouldn't," I snarled at her, pressing hard enough to draw out a trickle of blood.

Jake squeezed his eyes shut, breathing hard. "You fucking asshole."

"Leander!" she shouted.

Fuck.

Gritting my teeth, I pushed away from Jake roughly and stalked to the bar, tucking the ice pick back where it belonged.

Elijah stepped forward, his hand outstretched toward Jake.

"Fuck you people!" Jake smashed his shoulder into Elijah as he stormed by. A second later, the house shook when he slammed the front door behind him.

"Should have done it," Cole said as I drained half of my drink.

Tempting though it was, Olivia was right. Leander liked the little shit. After everything that went wrong between us, offing Jake wouldn't be good if I ever hoped to smooth things over.

"So what's the plan?" Elijah asked, ignoring Jake's hasty exit and looking directly at me. "I know you know. Leander wasn't the least bit concerned about old lady Van Deveer seeing us last week."

Gesturing to him with the tumbler, I gave him a smile as I took a seat on the end of the couch. "You are correct. He wanted her to see him. Or at least know he was there."

"Why?" Olivia asked.

"Because for this to work, you need at least one witness." I took another sip of bourbon and set the glass down, shifting forward to address all of them. "I can't tell you the particulars. If any one of you are questioned, it's better for Leander if you don't know the whole story. If *you* don't know, the police won't be able to piece together your answers and figure out what really happened."

"Is there any truth to what Jake said?" Elijah asked. "Did you set him up?"

"Of course not." I wasn't offended by the question. In a way, I appreciated Elijah's quiet protectiveness. It was there without being obnoxious like Jake's. "This was Leander's idea, I merely gave him the inside knowledge to pull it off."

"So you're going to be his lawyer?" Cole asked.

I shook my head. "No. Not for this. Richard Scheible will handle it."

"What are we supposed to do in the meantime?" Olivia asked, recrossing her arms.

I gave her a grim smile. "Carry on as usual. There's more

that needs to be done, but not until later. I can't tell you what it is until it's time."

They nodded, exchanging looks with one another as well as staring off in different directions.

"I know this is a shock," I said quietly. "Trust me when I tell you we considered every scenario, every possible outcome. No matter what happens, have faith it is all part of a plan."

CHAPTER 34

*L*ike the penal assholes they were, my BFFs at the FBI swooped in the moment Leander was arrested.

I knew they'd been sniffing around for a RICO case since the previous year, looking to save face after their failure to nail the Calaveras. Probably figuring I was too distracted by Leander's criminal case, they descended on Easton without warning. If they thought I couldn't fight a battle on two fronts, they were sorely mistaken.

"They said they seized the company's assets," Olivia hissed over the phone one day.

"I'm on my way." I sped through town as fast as traffic would allow, sliding the Maserati into park along the side of the building.

A slew of rookies were in the process of hauling out boxes in their perfect blue windbreakers. Shoving through the lot of them, I met up with a furious Olivia in the lobby.

Diefendorf and Denning were there too, surveying their underlings' progress and comparing the looted goods to what was authorized in the search warrant.

"And the computers too," Denning said, proud as a peacock.

I stormed up to Diefendorf so fast he took a step back. "What do you think you're doing?"

"Why don't you back off?" Denning said, putting a hand out toward my chest.

Holding my hand in front of Denning's face, I focused solely on Diefendorf for the answer.

Craig nodded to his partner before handing over a copy of the search warrant. "I told you, it's out of my hands."

I snatched the paper and flipped through it, itemizing everything in my head. In the next second, I sorted through a mental catalogue of our files, prioritizing what they'd find and where. When I was finished, I shoved the search warrant into Craig's chest. "Deal's off."

He blanched, crumpling the paperwork. "Bennett!"

"Wait, what deal?" Josh asked.

I flipped him off over my shoulder and dragged Olivia to her office. "Get your personal stuff. Leave everything else."

She nodded, grabbing only her purse.

Taking her by the elbow, I marched her past another stream of newbies coming back for more boxes like good little worker ants.

"I didn't have a choice!" Diefendorf yelled as we stormed through the lobby.

"There's always a choice. Now you get to live with yours." I shot him a parting glare before slamming through the front door again.

Olivia slid into the passenger seat of my car and hung on while I whipped out of the alley and onto the main road.

"What are we going to do?" she asked, her hair flying behind her with the open top.

I slammed my palm against the steering wheel, swearing

in every language I could think of. "I'm going to find another fucking fish."

"What?"

Ignoring her, I stomped on the gas and dialed Del's number at the same time.

"Jesus, are you in a wind tunnel?" he shouted into the phone.

"Where's Maria?"

"What?"

"Where is Maria?!"

"I thought you didn't want to know?"

"I'm fucking asking, which means I want to know!"

"Ok, tranquilo! She's staying with Julia. The feds are still all over Hector and she doesn't want the kids around that."

"Thanks." I disconnected and tossed my phone into Olivia's lap.

"Who's Maria?" she asked, swiping hair out of her face.

"A big fucking fish."

———

"I can't believe you just kidnapped me," Olivia huffed, shutting the car door.

"Would you prefer to be in Easton right now?"

"You could have told me we were driving to Chicago!"

"Would it have really mattered?" I led the way up the walkway of a sprawling brick ranch. Technically, we were in one of the ritzier suburbs of Chicago, the last place anyone would look for a Mexican drug lord's wife and kids. Had to hand it to her.

A little girl in pigtails opened the door when I knocked, smiling up at us. I knelt down in front of her, wiggling two fingers in a wave. "Hola, Isabella. Is Mama home?"

She nodded and pushed the door open further before running away, yelling at the top of her lungs.

Maria appeared a moment later with wide eyes, wiping her hands on a kitchen towel. "Bennett? What are you doing here?"

"Doesn't matter." I stepped in and closed the door behind Olivia.

"Who is she?" Maria asked, sizing Olivia up.

"Don't worry about her." I walked closer, lowering my voice in case someone was eavesdropping somewhere. "I need your help."

Maria held her ground, her sharp eyebrows raising. "With what?"

"I know about Diefendorf." When she started to protest, I held up a hand. "Let's not... Tell me you have documents or something tangible you were going to hand over."

She propped a hand on her hip, glancing between Olivia and I. Sniffing, she swept a strand of hair away from her face with a perfect red claw. "You heard what happened to Javier's girlfriend, right?"

"Yeah, I did." Everyone in Chicagoland heard what happened to her. About a year ago, the police found her head in a freezer during a raid on a warehouse. Parts of her body surfaced months later in a field during the spring plowing. According to the papers, she was alive when someone started cutting off limbs.

"So, I'm not getting involved with that."

Sweeping a length of her black hair over her shoulder, I dipped my face toward hers. "What would it take to *get* you involved?"

She laughed, still not answering, and caressed my cheek.

I wasn't above throttling her if she didn't start talking, but I also knew I had to play nice. "I can help you."

"Baby, if the FBI can't help, there ain't nothing you can do for me."

"How about a million dollars — cash?"

She laughed again. "You're crazy."

"Let me see the evidence, Maria." Try as I might to keep my voice velvety, it sounded more like a growl.

The humor vanished from her face. She dropped the attitude and straightened, wringing the towel in her hands. "Did Hector put you up to this?"

"No. I don't give a shit about Hector."

"No, no, no... You're *his* lawyer. I'm not stupid. You need to leave. Now." She spun me by the shoulders and gave a shove toward the door.

"Ok. Well, I'll just call Diefendorf on my way and let them know where you're staying. He's been dying to get his hands on you for quite a while now." I pulled my cell phone out and started dialing.

Olivia blinked and scrambled to the door, yanking it open a second before I got there.

"Bennett! Wait!" Maria jogged up, grabbing my hand as I crossed the threshold. "Come back inside."

I stayed where I was, holding my phone out with my other hand. Diefendorf's number was in full view on the screen. "Give me the evidence."

"For a million dollars?" she asked slowly, clearly weighing her options.

"Cash," I reiterated.

"You're not lying to me?"

"I swear to you on Isabella's life."

She held my gaze for a moment before nodding. "Wait here."

Olivia nudged me as soon as she was gone, clearly expecting an explanation.

"It's either this" — I gestured to the house — "or I have to liquidate a fed's entire family."

Blinking, she shifted on her back foot. "My God. That's a little extreme, even for you."

"Well, a deal's a deal," I muttered, shooting Gavin a quick text about the money. "Unless he wants to renegotiate."

Maria returned, breathless, with a jump drive in her hand. "Everything I have is on this. Pictures, videos, phone numbers, bank records. Everything."

I plucked it out of her fingers before she could change her mind. "If it's legit, I'll give Del the cash. If you're fucking with me, I'll tell Hector *and* the FBI where you are, and we'll see who gets to you first."

Maria swallowed, but remained silent.

Giving her one last look, I pocketed the jump drive and headed back to the car.

"Would you really do that to her?" Olivia asked as we were backing out of the driveway.

"If it means saving Leander's company? Absolutely."

CHAPTER 35

*D*espite a couple of hiccups along the way, Leander's plan continued right on schedule. After some legal maneuvering, Richard got his case moved out of Claiborne County and as far north as it could possibly go without going into Wisconsin.

"This isn't right," Olivia snarled one afternoon, stuffing a pair of Leander's shoes into a box. "Packing up his stuff and shipping it to him like he's at fucking summer camp."

Folding a black cashmere sweater carefully, I stared at it for a minute, seeing only Leander's jubilant expression. We were standing in front of Villa Diodati, breathing in the memory of Mary Shelley and the others who were trapped for three rain-soaked days. He talked at length about Gothic literature and the writers' tumultuous lives. As distracted as I was, I didn't retain a single word.

I came close to kissing him that day as we walked along the lake. The winter sunshine brought out strands of mahogany in his dark curls and emerald flecks in his eyes. He leaned against the base of a bare tree, soaking in the beauty of Cologny while I studied him. I didn't want to go back to Venice. I certainly didn't want to come back to America. I wanted to push him against that tree and stay there, kissing him for the rest of our lives.

Looking back on the course of our relationship, I still couldn't say for sure when I fell in love with him. All I knew for certain was that I *was*. Maybe it was the first time I heard his voice or the first time I saw the pernicious spark in his eyes. Maybe it was after New Orleans, when he worried himself sick over my disappearance, or during any one of our late-night conversations, reveling in each other's depravity.

Sadly, I knew the depth of my feelings meant nothing. As much as I may have loved him, he hated me all the more. That was my punishment for lying. I'd been warned time and again how much Leander detested liars. Only now, I fully understood what they meant.

Adding the sweater to the pile, I was cognizant of the fact I never answered her. "At least he's not in jail anymore. Or a psych ward."

"He's still under arrest, Bennett. He's still facing a murder trial," she snipped, as if I hadn't gone over legal loopholes and favorable case law with him a thousand times, analyzing other cases and picking apart every detail I could.

Rather than give a snarky retort, I turned to Leander's display box of watches and picked out a few options.

"Don't forget cufflinks," I said on my way out the door.

Even though the whole house held memories, Leander's room was the last place I wanted to be. I didn't regret that night, not one bit, but if I could go back and change anything, I would have put a fucking bullet in Marchese's head the minute I walked into that warehouse. I wouldn't have tried to play it smart. Maybe then I wouldn't have lost Leander.

"Where are you going?" Olivia asked.

"To see what Elijah's up to," I answered quickly, locking down the searing memory of Leander's mouth on mine.

The library was the same as ever, save for the new glass in all of the windows. Cole hadn't been lying when he said Leander smashed every single one at some point during our separation.

What he didn't tell me was Leander took an axe to the piano in the music room across the hall. I knew it was an axe because it was still lodged in the center of the floor. As for the piano, most of it was in a burnt pile behind the conservatory, along with every bottle of bourbon in the house. A few stray keys and strings remained, forgotten in his haste to destroy any trace of me.

"At least he can have his books again," Elijah said when I walked into the library. Even without them, I knew the literature stored in Leander's mind was keeping him company. "Do you think he's in the mood for satire or something Gothic?"

"It's Leander," I replied, scanning the shelves for lack of anything else to do.

"Good point."

When I spied a familiar book, my heart broke all over again. It was *The Prince* — specifically, the copy he bought in Venice. So he hadn't destroyed every item related to me. Or maybe it was an oversight. Maybe as soon as he saw it again, he'd burn it without a second thought.

"You could always throw in some Early Modern," I said, handing Elijah the book. Even if Leander ultimately trashed it, he'd know I was thinking of him. He could take whatever comfort he wanted from that.

Elijah added Machiavelli to the box and continued strolling down the row of bookshelves. "Have you talked to him?"

"No..." I was glad my back was turned. I'm sure the look

on my face would have given me away. As much as I wanted to see him, talk to him, throw myself at his feet and beg for mercy, now wasn't the time. Leander didn't need distractions, least of all from me.

"How do you know the plan is still working?"

"You know Leander. There are enough contingencies in place to make sure it'll happen no matter what."

One of the anatomy books caught my attention. I slid it off the shelf and set it on the desk, flipping through it with the vaguest glimmer of an idea circling my brain. "I'll be right back."

Ducking out of the library and into the conservatory, I headed straight for the brilliant purple orchid. Part of me was surprised to see it thriving when the piano had been massacred. Maybe he couldn't bear to kill it, like I couldn't bear to part with the onyx ring. As soon as the cast was off, his ring was firmly black in place on my index finger. The only way it was leaving again was if someone cut it off of my dead body.

Picking up a pair of pruning shears, I snipped off one of the purple blooms.

Back in the library, I stole one of the note cards from Leander's desk and jotted down a quick message. Without thinking, I kissed the card and tucked both it and the orchid inside the anatomy book.

Before I closed it again, I wrote a quick *NB* on the top of the page. He'd been exposed to enough of my legal abbreviations to recognize it as a note to pay attention to the following section. I heard about his little stunt in jail with the broken mirror. Granted, staging a suicide attempt was the perfect way to get moved from jail to a psych ward, but if he was going to slice open his arm a second time, he might as well have a refresher course.

Stacking a couple more books on top of the anatomy book, I dropped them into the box next to Elijah.

"I've gotta head north for a few things," I said, trying to sound completely casual and not like I was one impulsive second away from driving straight to Camden County and kidnapping Leander from house arrest. "I should be back next week."

"Ok." Elijah deposited another handful of books into the box. "Hey Bennett?"

"Yeah?"

"Thanks for being here. Without Leander around…"

"I know." Inclining my head, I gave him a small smile and hurried out.

———

IN THE WAKE of the FBI seizures, Diefendorf stayed close to home. On more than one occasion, I caught him doing perimeter checks in the dead of night, waiting for me to descend on his house like the demon he thought I was.

It was time to let him catch me.

Gun drawn and leveled center-mass, he bore down on me in the moonlight. "Get on your knees."

Complying, I kept my hands up and open. "Trouble sleeping, buddy?"

"What the fuck are you doing here?" He kept the gun on me while he patted me down with the other hand. Finding nothing, he circled back to the front and resumed a firing stance.

"I told you, the deal's off."

"You're not that stupid. You know my family isn't here."

I clucked the side of my cheek, feigning astonishment. "Damn. Didn't see that one coming."

"So what do you really want?"

"I'm going to offer you the chance to renegotiate." I smiled up at him.

"Fat fucking chance."

"Ok. Well, guess I have to think of something special for Grandma and Grandpa Dief, too. Ooo, maybe I'll give that log splitter of his a go. What do you think? If it can take on a hundred-year-old oak, I'm sure his skull wouldn't be too hard to crack."

Craig inhaled sharply, his grip on the gun tightening. "I should put a bullet in your head right now."

"But you won't. You're a good guy. Good guys don't murder unarmed civilians in their backyard. I, on the other hand…" My gaze slid downward, my chin tipping toward my jacket pocket. "I don't give a fuck."

He hesitated before leaning forward and slipping his hand inside. The polaroids shook as he fanned them out, revealing Maria and her children contorted in pools of blood on a dirty, concrete floor.

I chuckled darkly. "Looks like I did know where she was. Whoopsies."

His horrified expression quickly turned to fury. He swallowed hard, letting the pictures fall to the ground.

"Now… about renegotiating?"

"I'm not negotiating with you."

"Are you sure? Because I may or may not have a little information that will salvage your case against Hector and his amigos. Got it off of Maria right after I slit Isabella's throat. Do you know how quickly kids bleed out? Oh my God. It's *so* fast. I was surpr—"

"You soulless son of a bitch!" He lunged forward, driving the barrel of his gun into my temple, forcing my head to the side at a rather uncomfortable angle. Maybe I should have been more worried he'd pull the trigger, but I was fairly confident he'd do things the right way. "How could you?!"

"It was pretty easy. You just put the knife right—oh! Oh, you mean a figurative how. Well, I needed leverage. She had it. Now I have it."

"I hope your boss is worth it. You'll be doing doing sixty-to-life by the time we're through." He nudged me with the tip of the gun once more before taking a step back, fishing in his back pocket, presumably for his cell phone.

"Oh, you don't want to do that," I said with a grimace.

"The fuck I don't." The cell phone was out now.

"Ok, then. Guess you can tell your wife what happened while you're planning the funerals." I shrugged and looked off into the distance with a serene expression.

"What are you talking about?"

"The boys? Yeah. I know they're not at the farm with your folks. In fact, if you want to check this pocket right here" — I nodded toward my hip — "you'll see I'm not fucking around. If I don't make a phone call in the next two minutes, my guy is going to splatter your kids' brains all over their bedroom. Wifey's not going to be too happy to find that in the morning."

He didn't even bother pulling out the second set of polaroids. "I thought you said hiring hitmen was lazy?"

"Well, Craig, sometimes you have to outsource to make a fucking point."

"I can't stop them from going after Welles and you know it! I tried. So kill me, or do whatever, but leave my family out of it."

"Man, you're no fun. You went straight for the martyr role." I frowned. "What's it going to take for your boss to lose interest?"

"Nothing you can offer."

"How about Marchese?"

That got his attention. "Giovanni Marchese?"

"The one and only."

"What do you have on him?"

"Like I'm going to tell you. Can I stand up now? My knees are killing me and for once that is not a sex joke."

He considered it for a moment before taking another step back, motioning me upward with his gun.

I got to my feet slowly and stretched, cracking each knee. It was hell getting old. "Much better. Anyway. Why don't you go back to your little boss and see if he's willing to trade."

"Welles for the Calaveras and Marchese?"

"That all depends on what your boss has to say. I suddenly feel a bit of amnesia coming on... I, oh..." I touched the side of my head, swaying on my feet. "Where am I? Who... who are you?"

He glared at me, not at all amused. "I'm not making any promises."

"You know how to find me." I turned and started toward the darkest corner of the yard to the place where I'd hopped the fence earlier. I was only a few steps away when he spoke again.

"Where are they?"

Halting, I looked over my shoulder. "Where's who?"

"Maria. The kids. What did you do with their bodies?"

"Are you trying to get me to admit to murder, or just abuse of a corpse?" I gave him a bland smile. "Either way, I'm not sure what you're talking about. Who's Maria?"

His jaw shifted irritably. "What about my family?"

I wriggled the polaroids of his children out of my pocket and tossed them in his direction. They fluttered to the ground near the others. "Call my bluff and see what happens."

With that, I disappeared from his yard before he could change his mind and shoot me in the back.

Once I was safely in my car and headed southbound, I

pulled my cell phone out. It rang three times before a female answered.

"Bueno?"

"He bought it," I said. "You're free and clear."

Maria sighed on the other end. "I can't believe it…"

"Believe it."

"Gracias, Bennett. Por todo."

"Give the kids my love."

CHAPTER 36

*O*livia and I were on our way back from settling an issue with the river barges when Jake called, ruining what was otherwise a fairly pleasant day. Since it was her car, the call unfortunately went through bluetooth, meaning I got to hear him drone on about life in Stratford and what it was like working "undercover" at Parkview Psychiatric. If it wasn't for the fact he was one of the only links to Leander, I would have tuned him out the moment I heard who it was.

"There's definitely something going on with him and his doctor," Jake said out of the blue.

I pretended not to be listening but he had my complete attention.

Olivia made a face. "What?! Malibu Barbie?"

An image of the doctor in question popped into my head, a beautiful blonde do-gooder named Lorelei Clayton. Her headshot radiated cheer and optimism, a sharp contrast to everything about Leander. As soon as he was transferred to her care, I did my homework. Guess I missed the part in her bio where it said she was easily corruptible.

Jake snorted. "He denied it, but he had this look. Plus, the other staff said she did shit for him when he was here. Like, favors and extra privileges. Not to mention her house visits last a long time. *Really* long."

"I mean... isn't that part of the plan?" Jake may have thought the question was for him, but Olivia directed her curious gaze to me.

I raked a hand through my hair and stared out the window, biting my tongue.

Totally part of the plan. He needed to look guilty as sin to everyone in Easton, while coming off as persecuted and vulnerable to the people in Stratford. In addition to being charming and manipulative, he was ruthless. If he had to make someone fall in love with him — with the *idea* of him, at any rate — to see this thing through, then that's what he had to do. I'd be no different.

Never mind the fact I wasn't exactly in a position to weigh in on his life choices anymore. My role as Leander's... whatever I was... disappeared in one horrible conversation.

"I don't know," Jake grumbled. "You'd have to ask that fucking asshat Bennett."

I flipped off the speaker.

Olivia slid another look at me out of the corner of her eye. "Come on, Jake. Bennett's not that bad once you get to know him."

I blew her a kiss. It only took her a few years, but she finally retracted the claws. I knew I'd win her over.

"Oh my God! Don't tell me you've fallen for his bullshit too!"

She sighed. "Calm down, killer."

"He's so fucking fake! He acts like he's better than the rest of us and I'll bet he hasn't done half the shit he said he has. He's probably never even left the country and he's over there making Leander think he's the greatest thing since sliced bread."

"They literally went to Italy for Christmas," Olivia pointed out. "And Switzerland."

"Whatever. He's a fucking asshole."

She laughed. "Tell me how you really feel."

"If I ever catch him alone, it's not going to be good for him."

I rolled my eyes and pantomimed jerking off.

"Uh huh. How'd that work out for you last time?" Olivia asked, giving me a sly smirk.

"He's insane! Who the fuck carries an ice pick around with them?"

"You realize he worked with the mafia for, like, ten years, right?"

"Yeah, well, he should go back there. It was nice when he wasn't around anymore."

"You're just saying that because you're jealous."

I raised my brows at Olivia, blinking innocently. Did she know about Jake too?

He scoffed. "Of what? There's nothing to be jealous of."

"What about his car?" Olivia asked, wagging her brows at me.

I scowled at her.

Jake snorted. "The Maserati? Talk about over-compensating. Every time I see it, I want to drive my truck over it."

In the midst of Olivia's laughter, her own sports car drifted over the center line. I yanked the wheel to the right and gave her the military signal to keep her eyes on the damn road.

"I gotta go. I'll keep you posted." The minute Jake hung up, her laughing returned in earnest.

"Really?" I gaped at her. "You like my car!"

Chuckling, she pulled into a parking spot in front of my St. Louis apartment. "Jake doesn't."

"Jake doesn't like a lot of things about me."

"Huh. I hadn't noticed."

———

AFTER OLIVIA DROPPED ME OFF, I made my way inside and walked straight to the kitchen for a bottle of bourbon. The bottle was depleted in two gulps, so I marched back downstairs and got in my car, driving to the closest liquor store.

The longer I thought about it, the more my stomach twisted in knots. Olivia had a right to know. She'd been patient throughout this whole kerfuffle. She needed to know Malibu Barbie was *not* a part of the plan.

I was halfway through the first bottle of bourbon when I left St. Louis. The empty bottle went sailing into the Mississippi as I sped across the bridge.

Well into the second bottle by the time I reached Olivia's house, the car screeched to a stop, narrowly missing the mailbox. I was parked partially in her front yard, but I didn't care.

Staggering up the front steps, the world tilted on its side and the toe of my boot caught the edge of a stair. I sprawled out on the porch, cradling the bottle against my torso like a receiver protecting the football. Shaking off the dizziness, I pushed myself into a sitting position and leaned back, using the railing for support.

The porch light flicked on.

"What are you doing?" Olivia asked, pushing the screen door open.

"What I do best." I took another swig.

"Annoying the fuck out of me? Yeah. That is what you do best." She snatched the bottle out of my hand and lobbed it over the railing into the side yard.

"That was not nice." I pointed at her with a scowl. "And expensive."

"You can afford it. What are you doing here?"

"I missed you."

"You just saw me. How much have you had to drink?"

I closed one eye, my nose scrunching. "I don't know."

"Ugh. Come on." She slipped beneath my arm and grabbed ahold of my belt loop, yanking me upward.

Stumbling and zigzagging through her house, I managed to knock over a lamp, a pile of magazines, and several picture frames along the way. I didn't have the foggiest idea where we were going until we spilled into a surprisingly serene, white and pale blue bedroom.

Olivia pushed me toward the bed. I caught her wrist and pulled her down with me, our legs tangled together. Before she could spring away, I draped her arm over my shoulder and pulled her closer. Despite her hard exterior, she was warm and soft and smelled as mysterious as she did in Chicago.

"I knew I'd end up here eventually," I murmured, nuzzling her neck.

"Oh Bennett..." She touched my face gently, patting it harder and harder as she spoke, her voice extra husky. "You've always been on my shit list."

The pain barely registered. I held on to her hips and tilted my face toward hers. She'd already washed off her usual black eyeliner and she was in a tank top and leggings. This version of her was less severe, but just as beautiful as the first time I laid eyes on her.

"Why do you hate me?" I asked quietly. For a minute I wasn't even sure if I said it out loud or not.

She brushed the hair out of my eyes, tucking it behind my ear, her expression softening. "I don't hate you."

"You don't like me."

"Because you're an asshole."

"Is this still about the book?"

"No, it's not about the book."

"It's about the book."

"It's about Leander." Her mouth set into a hard line.

Groaning, I rolled away from her, stretching out on my back. "I fucked up."

"What?"

"I fucked up. So much. *He* hates me. *I* hate me. *You* hate me. Fucking Giovanni definitely hates me."

She propped herself up on her elbow, her brow furrowed. "What are you talking about?"

I pointed in opposite directions before bringing my index fingers together in the age-old child's gesture for kissing. It didn't last long, since my imaginary people blew up, complete with sound effects and flinging hands. "And that's how it happened..." I gestured wildly again with one hand.

"What the fuck does that mean?"

Instead of answering and running the risk of bourbon-laced word vomit coming out, I rolled on top of her. Winding my fingers through her dark hair, I pressed my lips to hers. Surprisingly, she didn't knee me in the balls. Even more surprisingly, her lips parted while she caressed the side of my face.

She hooked her leg through mine and, before I could comprehend what she was doing, she rolled me back the way I came. Settling on my lap with her hands on my chest, she arched an eyebrow at me. "You're drunk."

I waved her off. "Nah. I didn't even finish the second bottle. You threw it away." I reached for her with a pout. Intercepting my hands, she pinned them on either side of my head.

"Get some sleep." Her nose brushed against mine. I tried to kiss her again, but she sat up too quickly. "We'll talk in the morning."

I caught her hands, pulling her back down before she could stand. "Stay with me?"

She shook her head. "Not gonna happen."

"I'll be good." I swiped a finger over my heart a few times, hoping it translated as a promise.

"No."

"I'm cold?"

"You're sweating."

"I'm scared of the dark?"

"You were sitting in the dark, like, five minutes ago."

"I'm... horny? No... Bad Bennett." Searching my amber-colored brain for the right word, I snapped and pointed at her. "Lonely. I am lone-ly. Solitario. Abbandonato."

"Oh my God. Shut up already. You're even more annoying in Italian." She shifted off my lap and laid down next to me, facing the wall.

Curling up behind her, I slid my arm beneath hers and wrapped it around her ribcage. She laced her fingers through mine and sighed softly, settling back against me.

I was on the edge of sleep when she said, "I miss him too."

———

IN THE MORNING, I wished I was dead all over again.

I sat up and swung my legs off the side of the bed, hanging my head between my knees. "Fuck me anyhow."

"Good morning! Or should I say, good afternoon?" Olivia chirped as she waltzed into the room. She threw a bottle of water in my lap and disappeared into the bathroom, returning a minute later to dump a couple of pills in my hand.

Once I had some idea of where the hell I was, I glanced down at my clothes. The suspenders had fallen off my shoulders and my shirt was half untucked. My pants were secured, but that didn't mean anything. "Did we…?"

She smirked. "Not a chance."

Nodding, I flopped back into the pillows.

She sat next to me, poking me in the ribcage. "What happened? Why did you get shit faced last night?"

"I was bored."

"Uh-huh. The Bennett I've seen drinks to have fun, or at least mellow out. Last night you were drinking yourself into oblivion."

"Do you have a cigarette?" I asked, blinking up at her. "I could really use one right about now." Or anything to avoid her interrogation.

"You don't smoke."

"I did."

"Doesn't mean you should start again."

"Ugh, you sound like my mother." I rolled over and buried my face in the pillow. Camille was the last person I wanted to think about five seconds after waking up. Or ever.

"Didn't seem to bother you last night when you had your tongue down my throat."

I cracked open an eye. "That happened? I thought it was a dream…"

She nodded with another smirk, enjoying my misery in true Olivia fashion.

"I'm sorry." I shoved my entire head under the pillow, hoping to smother myself since the alcohol failed to do its job.

"God, you're pathetic." She smacked my ass and bounced off the bed. "Come on. You should eat something."

By the time I dragged myself to the kitchen, she'd set the table with two plates of avocado toast topped with eggs. A cup of black coffee and a bottle of Gatorade rounded it out. This clearly wasn't her first rodeo either.

Thankfully, she let me eat in peace before dropping a bomb on me. "Why did you say Leander hates you?"

I choked on my coffee. "I don't think I said that."

"Uh, I think you did. You said you fucked up and then…" She pantomimed a bomb exploding. "So what did you do?"

Staring into my cup, I stupidly hoped she'd let it go. After it was clear she wasn't going to, I offered her a weak answer. "I let him down."

"I don't think that's possible."

I scoffed, running both hands through my hair and holding my thumping head. "Trust me. It's possible."

"So apologize."

"This sort of thing can't be solved with an apology."

She cocked her head. "For as close as you two were, you should know him better than that. He wants to hear the truth, Bennett, no matter how horrible. It's when someone tries to pacify him, or *lie* to him, that he shuts down. So what did you lie about?"

Shaking my head, my gaze dropped to my coffee. If I couldn't tell Leander, there was no way I could tell her.

"Money?" she asked.

I shook my head again.

"Does it have anything to do with how you ended up in the hospital?"

"Yeah." I let go of my head to pick up the mug. After another sip, I held onto it.

"Does he know what happened?"

I gave her another shake of the head.

"Will you tell me?"

God, she wasn't going to quit. I exhaled a long stream of air. Maybe it would be good to get another perspective, especially from someone who knew Leander the way she did. Maybe she'd have some insight into how to fix it. "It was one of my former clients."

"Ok. So why would that be a big deal?"

"They threatened to—" I bit the corner of my lip, looking away. I didn't even want to say it out loud, in case the universe decided to come finish the job. "I had to get him out of their crosshairs. Which means I couldn't tell him what happened, or why."

"Why not?"

"Because he'd never let it go and unless we managed to kill them all, we'd always be looking over our shoulders. I thought I could take care of it. And I will. But I fucked up with Leander. I tried to keep him safe and I…" Grimacing, my hands clenched around the mug.

She propped her chin in her hand, sighing softly. "You broke his heart."

She might as well have stabbed me with the butterknife sitting next to her plate. It would have hurt less.

"So now what?" she asked quietly.

"Nothing. I'll stay until he gets out. Then I'll leave like I was supposed to. It'll be better for everyone."

Her hand flashed out, cracking my shoulder. "Just apologize!"

I jumped, recoiling from her. "It's not that simple!"

"He loved you, you idiot!" She leaned forward, her eyes soft and earnest for a change. At my wide-eyed glance, she shook her head. "No, he never told me. But he was *happy* with you. And for someone who's had a life like his, happiness is worth more than every penny in his bank account. You have to fix this!"

"What do you want me to do, Olivia? He's under arrest for murder right now. Not to mention the last time we spoke I told him I couldn't see him anymore. What makes you think he wants anything to do with me?"

"Because he's miserable without you! You saw him the

day he was arrested. That was a *good* day. He needs you, Bennett. And I think you need him."

I didn't want to let myself have any hope, so I refused to look at her, tuning her out like a cat.

She punched me in the arm. Hard. "You coward!" Snatching the dirty dishes off the table, she stormed over to the sink and practically threw them down again.

Rubbing the sore spot on my bicep, I glared at her. "It's over, ok? I've come to terms with it. And if it wasn't clear before, according to Jake, he's up there shagging his psychiatrist."

Olivia made a disgusted noise. "Have you talked to that broad? You have nothing to worry about."

I glowered at the table. No, I hadn't talked to her, but I'd heard all about her from Cole, who apparently thought the sun rose and set with her.

"Leander will get bored with her in no time. He needs someone who understands him," Olivia continued, oblivious to the fact I didn't answer.

"She's a fucking psychiatrist. How much more under-standing do you want?"

Arching an eyebrow, she folded her arms over her chest. "You know how Leander feels about psychology. Do you think he's going to like having someone pick apart every little thing he does? How about the whole murder thing? Think she's going to be a fan of washing blood out of his clothes?"

"Careful. It sounds like you're actually advocating for me to stick around."

She rolled her eyes. "You are a certifiable pain in my ass, but for some inexplicable reason, you make my best friend happy. Or, you did. If you did once, you can do it again. He'll never be happy with someone like her. He needs..." She gave me a long, resigned look. "You. He needs you."

I stood and crossed to the sink, wrapping my arms around her waist. She hugged my neck, her cheek pressed to mine. "Thank you."

"If you hurt him again, I'll cut your balls off," she murmured before kissing my cheek.

I couldn't help but laugh. "Fair enough."

The front door opened and closed.

"Why is Bennett's — oh, hey man." It was Cole, sporting a very confused look. He cleared his throat, shoving his hands in his pockets. "I saw your car but I didn't think you'd actually be here. Everything ok?"

"I'm on my way out." I disentangled myself from Olivia, swiping the bottle of Gatorade off the table. "Thanks for breakfast. Or, whatever meal this was."

"Anytime." She gave me a half-smirk.

"See you later," I said to Cole with a nod, heading out the front door.

All things considered, I felt a hell of a lot better than I did last night. Olivia's blessing was apparently the thing I needed to get my ass in gear before Leander got out.

CHAPTER 37

In light of Marchese's attempt to have me killed and Leander turned over to the FBI, I invoked a little overlooked clause and terminated the contract between Leander and Giovanni's respective companies. That meant the Welles Corporation and its secure shipping channel were on the market once again, but not for long. I had the perfect partner already lined up.

To make everything official, Sergei came down to St. Louis to sign the contract in person. The Russians got a far better rate than Marchese did, considering Sidorov's men were still happily picking off Italians as they found them. All except Giovanni. The last anyone heard was the greasy bastard was licking his wounds in Vegas. As long as he stayed in another time zone, I didn't really care. I'd catch up to him eventually and rip his fucking throat out.

In the midst of my evening celebrating with Sergei, my phone died. I plugged it in as soon as I got home and passed out in a vodka-induced slumber.

Sometime later, it blew up with a variety of notifications. Texts, emails, missed calls. Mostly from Olivia. There were a few from Gavin, getting more and more frantic when Olivia turned her wrath on him. Cole texted, demanding I return his phone call. Elijah, strangely, was the only one who didn't try to get a hold of me. Even Richard called, which was... odd.

The news I cobbled together hit me in the center of my chest like a battering ram.

Leander slit his wrist. Again. Except this time, he nicked an artery in the process and nearly bled to death. An emergency surgery and a blood transfusion got him stabilized. That was all anyone knew.

I tried not to picture it and failed miserably. All I could see were his white arms spurting dark, red blood while the life drained out of him, his green eyes growing dull.

The point of the anatomy book was so this sort of thing *didn't* happen! I hoped it was a case of him being overzealous, not intentional. He hadn't strayed that far into his own darkness, had he? Had he succumbed to his childhood nightmares after all this time?

Once I sent off a few quick texts acknowledging I got their messages, I settled in for the voicemails, prepared to delete every outraged one two seconds in.

I nearly dropped the phone when I heard Leander's voice. *That* was definitely not a part of the plan. Frankly, it was the last thing I expected.

"Bennett, it's me. I, um... Shit, I don't know what to say..." There was a long pause. If it wasn't for the audio line indicating there was more on the recording, I would have thought he hung up.

"In case this doesn't work," he continued, his voice brittle. "I want you to stay on and help Olivia. Ok? I know you were leaving, but she's going to need you. I left letters for everyone at the office, bottom drawer on the left. I hope this isn't goodbye. But if it is..." He exhaled sharply. "Well, you'll read it in the letter." He swallowed loud enough for me to hear before he said "Mi manchi," and hung up.

Hearing him say he missed me — in Italian, no less — was heart-wrenching. Months of self-doubt and guilt compounded on itself, spawning even more guilt and self-doubt. Even after Olivia's pep talk, I didn't let myself have hope that he felt anything other than hatred.

But his voicemail changed everything.

When I got my wits about me, I remembered he said something about a letter.

Jumping in the car, I drove straight to the office. It didn't matter it was after two a.m. or that I was probably opening myself up to a world of pain. I wouldn't be able to think about anything else until I read whatever it was he left behind.

In the bottom left drawer of his desk, underneath the hidden panel, there was a stack of envelopes, each labeled simply with our first names. Mine was on top. Did that mean it was a good letter... or a bad letter? Or maybe he'd gone alphabetically...

I eased into his chair, staring at the envelope. My name stared back at me in his perfect penmanship, waiting.

Actually opening the letter took the better part of the next hour. My desire to know was locked in mortal combat with my fear of what was written. It didn't matter he concluded his voicemail with sentiment. These letters were written months ago, days or weeks after our falling out. God only knew how furious he was. Still, that stupid little spark of hope reignited.

Unfolding the paper at last, I inhaled a fortifying breath and forced myself to concentrate on each sentence and not skip ahead.

Dear Bennett,

I've written this letter over a dozen times, but none of the words seem to come out quite right. Still, I know you'll forgive me if the end result is not as perfect as I'd wish it to be.

If you're reading this, something has clearly gone awry. I know we planned. And planned. And planned some more. As godlike as we wish we were, we are only human, so please forgive me if things did not unfold as we thought.

To have someone like you help me with an undertaking as great as this has been nothing short of miraculous. Emily Bronte expressed it better than I could ever hope to: "He's more myself than I am. Whatever our souls are made of, his and mine are the same."

Until I met you, I thought I'd be alone forever. As I sit here, I think back to our first meeting and wonder how differently things might have turned out had you not come into my life when you did. Kindred spirits are, as we discussed, so very rare.

I hate you for everything that happened. And yet, the broken pieces of my heart love you in ways I never thought possible. Despite my fury, my singular regret is not confessing sooner. In your way, I think you loved me too — but the fear you did not is what compelled me to silence.

I know you have your secrets, even from me. Shall I become one of them when you start the next chapter of your life? I think it would be fitting, to carry me in the darkest part of your soul as I carry you, a sacred love the uninitiated can never understand.

Perhaps one day our souls will be fortunate enough to meet again. Maybe then we can get it right.

Yours evermore,

-Leander

Holding my head in my hands, the muscles in my throat squeezed tighter and tighter. I gasped for a full breath that never quite made it into my lungs. A scream, full of frustration and heartache, tore out of me. At myself. At him. At the fucking universe.

Equally angry with his piss-poor timing and his goddamn lack of communication skills, I replayed our entire relationship in my head. I counted the times I should have told him I loved him, tallying it against all the times he gave me that fucking look — that look I could now safely say was him *thinking* the words and *still* refusing to say them. It was a pointless exercise. We were both to blame. Call it pride, or stupidity, or karma for all our sins.

Once my tears dried and I could breathe again, I pulled out my cell phone and dialed a Chicago number I never thought I would ever voluntarily call. That letter broke me. I wasn't concerned with beating the system, or poking my finger at authority. My only thought was Leander and doing whatever I could to make things right.

The phone rang five times before going to Diefendorf's voicemail.

"It's Bennett Reeve," I said, my head hung and my eyes closed in defeat. "We need to talk."

———

BACK IN THE little teal house in Easton, I paced back and forth in front of the coffee table. It had been days since I learned, without a shadow of a doubt, Leander loved me, and days since I called the FBI. And it had been exactly one day since Leander was set free.

After the "unexpected" death of Mrs. Van Deveer, the judge had no choice but to dismiss the charges. With the drive-time from Stratford to Easton, I estimated Leander had been back in town for about twenty hours, yet there were zero attempts at contact. Surprise, surprise.

Staring at my cell phone didn't make it ring any faster, nor did cracking each joint in my fingers repeatedly, but I did them both as time ticked by. As soon as the screen lit up, I snatched the phone and answered.

"Ok. You've got your deal," Diefendorf said, sounding none too pleased.

I punched the air, trying to contain myself. "No strings?"

"No strings."

"And this won't be an issue ever again?"

"As long as you keep up your end of the agreement, the Welles Corporation is free and clear."

"*And* Leander."

"And Leander," Diefendorf sighed.

"Good. Send me everything in writing."

"It's on its way to your inbox. I'll need you to come in for a formal interview and make everything official. Two weeks?"

"Fine by me. You can arrange the details with Gavin."

As soon as I got off the phone with him, I headed downtown to the florist.

The woman gave me a polite smile when I walked in. "What's the occasion today?"

"A celebration." I returned her smile brightly. "Of epic proportions."

"Well, what sort of arrangement did you have in mind? Roses, or—"

"The whole store."

She blinked hard, like I'd slapped her. "You want what now?"

I glanced to either side before leaning forward a bit more in case she couldn't hear. "*All* of it. The whole store. Every single flower you have."

"The *whole* shop?"

"Yes."

"You're serious?"

"Completely. Whatever sort of arrangements you'd like."

"Ok..."

"Except for one." I smiled again when she looked up, her

eyes wide. "I need one bouquet entirely of black and white calla lilies, with purple trim. And add this to it." I handed her a notecard with a simple message — *RIP RICO*.

She furrowed her brow. "I'm sorry, I thought you said it was a celebration?"

"Believe me, it is." I gave her a wolfish grin and jotted down Leander's address, not that she needed it once she saw who the recipient was.

"They should be there tomorrow around noon. Is that ok?"

I handed over my black card. "That's perfect."

———

A WEEK PASSED since Flowers by Linda made the largest delivery in company history and there wasn't a single fucking response from Leander.

I knew he got them. I knew because I may or may not have been in the area around the time the delivery van showed up. I mean, not on the main road. That would have been creepy. But I watched from afar to make sure Linda truly sent the whole store. She did, lucky for her, and I continued on my way to Chicago to have a nice sit-down with my pals at the Bureau.

My personal phone was charged and the ringer was on, but it didn't matter. He didn't call. He didn't email. He didn't even send a goddamn carrier pigeon.

So when "Welles Corp." finally flashed across my screen, I was expecting an entirely different voice than the one that snarled at me.

"She's here!" Olivia screeched. "Malibu Barbie is *here*! Where are you?"

City traffic blared all around me, making it hard to hear. "I'm in Chicago. I had that thing with the FBI, remember?"

"When are you going to be back?"

"Probably this weekend. Why? What happened?"

"Did you not hear me? Lorelei is here! In Easton!"

I stopped walking so suddenly the person behind me ran right into me. I gave them a pathetic apology wave and kept going, praying I still misheard. "What? What are you talking about?"

"Ugh. It's such a shit show. She came, she left. I thought it was over. Then he fucking chased after her. And now she's, like, living with him. We tried to talk some sense into him but he's not having it."

After the nausea passed, white-hot fury blistered inside me. As the seconds drifted by, I simmered. Somewhat.

"He went after her?" The nausea was back, like a sick, twisted teeter-totter. He wasn't using her to further his master plan, or passively accepting her presence. He sought it out. He sought *her* out, instead of me. Simultaneously, the thought made me want to throw up and punch a fucking wall.

"I saw a fuck-ton of flowers at the house," Olivia said over my horrified question. "I figured it was you. That probably pissed the princess off. I mean, what do you tell your girl-friend when your boyfriend sends you thousands of dollars worth of flowers? Have you talked to him yet?"

"No, I thought..." Clearing my throat, I snapped myself out of it long enough to wave distractedly at Harrison before heading for the elevator. "I thought he'd call or something. After he was settled..."

I also didn't want to pounce on him the minute he returned. After being away, under the circumstances, I wanted to give him space to get acclimated before I ran up and professed my love and stupidity all in one blow. Now I saw the error in waiting, in trying to be patient and not so reckless for a change.

"Stop playing hard to get, Bennett!"

"I'm not playing hard to get! Aside from the fact I've actually been busy, I didn't think I had to fucking rush it!"

"Well, if you want him, you're going to have to send that bitch packing. I've already tried to run her off, but she's either stupid or stubborn."

"Maybe you should leave it alone." My head fell back against the elevator wall. I smacked it again for good measure. Maybe I could trigger my amnesia again with a hard enough hit and solve everyone's problem in one fell swoop.

"Are you kidding me?!"

"I don't want to cause him any more misery."

"Don't think of it as causing him misery. Think of it as saving him from himself."

"What if he doesn't want to be saved? What if he's happy with her?" I almost choked on the bile in my throat.

"Oh my God! Who are you? Where is that cocky son-of-a-bitch we all love to hate?"

"I guess he finally grew up. His priorities changed."

"Isn't Leander your priority?"

Sighing, I stepped out of the elevator and collapsed on the couch. "You know he is."

"Then sack up! I say you off the bitch."

"Oh, yeah. *That* would win him back for sure."

"Then I'll do it. I can't stand her."

"Man, you poison one little old lady and suddenly murder is the go-to option for everything."

"Works for you, doesn't it?"

"Funny."

"Listen, you need to start playing dirty. Otherwise you're condemning the man you love to a lifetime of sunshine and tea parties and God knows what else she'll make him do, like have babies and a yard full of puppies."

As tempting as it was to forcibly remove Lorelei from the equation, I was sure the result wouldn't be Leander's gratitude. Like killing Jake, killing his new flame would only drive the wedge even further between us.

"Is that such a bad existence?" I wondered out loud, even though I couldn't picture Leander at a garden party, or bouncing a baby on his knee. I couldn't picture him at all with someone like Lorelei; his dark, melancholy contrasted her to puke-y goodness. But maybe that's what he wanted. Maybe she knew him better than I did after all, and I was only kidding myself thinking there was any sort of future for us.

Olivia didn't let me wallow for long. "For someone like him? Yeah. He needs more and you know it."

"I have to go," I said quickly, pushing off the issue for another day. After spending the morning doing nothing but talking, all I wanted to do was sleep.

"Bennett?"

"Yeah?"

"Don't give up on him."

"Yeah…" I hung up and lobbed the phone onto the couch across from me. Grabbing a throw pillow, I punched it into submission and curled myself around it with a sigh.

Easier said than done.

CHAPTER 38

$\mathcal{D}$espite Olivia's cheerleading, I made no move to communicate with Leander after the flowers except as it related to his company. I took it as a good sign he started emailing me directly, but it never strayed into the personal. Part of me hoped he'd get sick of Lorelei, like Olivia predicted, and he'd get rid of her on his own. The other part worried he wouldn't, and if it ultimately came down to it, he'd pick her over me. Again.

So I threw myself into work and helping Diefendorf with the case of a lifetime. Childhood music lessons paid off; I sang like a little canary about Marchese, leading the feds straight to his cousin's Vegas compound. At least I could breathe easier knowing the asshole was in federal custody.

When Gavin called me first thing on a random Monday morning, I thought he was calling to ask about the files Diefendorf was expecting. Wrong.

"She said what?" I pressed the phone closer to my ear.

"There's some big legal meeting thing at the office and Leander wants all of his lawyers there — even you," Gavin said with a huff. "The details are in your calendar, which is exactly why I set up a calendar with notifications that you keep turning off!"

"Yeah, yeah."

"Like the dinner reservation I made for you next week in Chicago? You still haven't acknowledged it in the system. Did you even see it?"

"Dinner with who?"

"Oh my God. Leander! Did you take too many benzos last night?"

Furrowing my brow, I flicked open the bane of my existence, scrolling through the days until I found the info I needed. Gavin had indeed blocked off an entire day in Chicago, including dinner reservations at seven o'clock.

"Huh." I put the phone back to my ear, even though I wasn't really listening. I was too busy trying to see what Leander's angle was, for both the dinner and today's urgent meeting. "What time is the thing today?"

"Eleven. So you might want to get a move on. From the sounds of it, you probably look as shitty as you sound."

I checked the time and swore, taking off for the shower.

Opting for a black pinstripe suit with a dark purple shirt underneath, I left it unbuttoned, even lower than usual. Knowing Richard was going to be there, I piled on extra jewelry just to piss him off. Even though we formed a temporary truce during Leander's incarceration, all bets were off again.

Jumping into the car with wet hair, I took off eastbound. Today was an in-person meeting with Leander — and half a dozen other lawyers, but still. It was the first time we would be seeing each other since his arrest. And next week was dinner with him in Chicago. Not Easton. Not St. Louis. *Chicago*.

It could have been a simple matter of logistics. He was coming the week I was there giving my formal deposition on

Marchese. Thankfully, with Maria's jump drive, the feds didn't need me to actually testify against the Calaveras since most of them took plea deals. That meant I was only officially turning on one client, who, in all fairness, *did* try to kill me first. It was a strategic move my other mobster connections could understand, plus it knocked the Italians out of the way for territorial expansion.

After I parked the car outside the Welles Corporation, I double checked myself in the mirror. Mussing up my hair, I pulled a few pieces down over my eyes, swatting them this way and that until the look was effortlessly casual.

"Good morning Mr. Reeve," Madison said when I walked in.

I slid a couple classification folders out of my bag and handed them to her. "Make sure Leander gets these, please."

"Of course. The others are in the conference room."

I nodded, preparing myself mentally and making sure my pace wasn't too hurried.

In a way, I was glad Leander wasn't there when I walked in. It meant I could have a little fun with Richard first to calm my nerves.

"Didn't you quit?" Richard's nose wrinkled as soon as I strolled in.

"Aww... Did you miss me, Dick?"

He snorted. "Why are you here?"

"Your animal magnetism. It's hard to resist."

Richard rolled his eyes. "Nice to see you dressed for the occasion."

"I knew I was seeing you." I winked at him.

One of his junior associates stifled a laugh as I continued down the row of lawyers to what was once my usual chair at the far end of the table.

We didn't have to wait long before Leander strode in, a vicious look on his face. The sight of him stole my breath. He looked much the same as he had the day he was arrested, a shadow of the man I fell in love with. If it was possible, he was even thinner than before, evident by his gauntness and the dark hollows under his eyes.

In light of his appearance, I was glad I wasn't there to witness his decline. Knowing what he was doing and seeing it unfold were two different things — I knew I wouldn't have been able to stand by and let him wither away.

Richard and the others jumped to their feet, while I rose slowly. After he shook everyone's hand for the briefest amount of time possible, Leander stopped in front of me.

The world seemed to stop and suddenly it was just the two of us. I clasped his hand firmly, meeting his gaze with none of the apprehension flitting around in my stomach.

"Leander..." He didn't pull his hand away, and I didn't let go. For the first time in months, he looked me in the eye. While I wasn't sure what emotion lay behind his green gaze, at least it wasn't hatred or contempt. The corner of my mouth ticked up involuntarily into a smile. Perhaps all was not lost.

"Bennett..."

"Are we still on for dinner next week?" I had to know if it was his doing, or if it was something Olivia maneuvered on my behalf. I held my breath until he answered, scrutinizing his face for any telltale sign.

He didn't look the least bit surprised. "Of course. Looking forward to it."

Somehow I kept a massive sigh of relief to myself, but I couldn't stop the full smile from stretching across my face. Realizing I needed to let go of his hand, I reluctantly slid into my chair and angled around the junior lawyers to see Richard's expression. I rewarded his disgusted look with a cheeky smile before reclining in my chair.

"No Greta?" Leander asked, sitting at the head of the table to my right.

Richard piped up from the opposite end. "No. She didn't show up for work today and no one has been able to get ahold of her."

Leander's mouth may have curved into a frown, but to me it read more pensive than concerned. "That's strange."

Richard dragged his briefcase closer and dug around in its contents. "Yes, well... Anyway. Timothy is going up to Camden County tomorrow for a status hearing on the Kelly/Brewer case. I think they're going to offer a decent settlement."

"I don't care about 'decent.' I want them destitute," Leander said, his narrowed gaze focused on Timothy. "Do you hear me? Absolutely penniless. Make sure you take Brewer's pension, as I'm sure his control tactics were entirely state-trained."

Timothy gave a quick nod. "Yes, Sir. Penniless."

"Did you file the lawsuit against Parkview too?"

Another emphatic nod.

"You're sure you want to go through with this? It could draw attention..." Richard said. "You know that reporter at the *Sentinel* is always sniffing around for a story."

"I don't care. By the end of this, I want that facility bankrupt," Leander replied, emphasizing his point by jabbing his finger into the table. The motion sent a shiver down my spine. He was never so handsome as when he was going for the kill.

A moment later, he softened and turned to me. "Oh, Bennett, can you redirect those settlement funds whenever they're available?"

I stopped spinning the onyx ring around my index finger and met his gaze once more. "Martha Scott and Calvin Hodge?"

I hoped he took my casual reaction for my usual boredom and didn't see it for what it was — utter restraint to keep from grabbing him by the lapels and slamming him against a wall, making up for every second of lost time that I could.

"Anonymous, of course," he said with the faintest smile.

"Of course." I gave him a small smirk in return. He knew his wish was my command, as it had always been. Not to mention I had the paperwork drawn up the minute he emailed me at three in the morning the other night.

The guest of honor walked in a moment later with Madison at his side. Short, trim, and wearing glasses that gave him an owlish look, the other attorney blinked at the gathering of his peers. One could only imagine what he thought of Leander's demonstration of power and resources.

"Gene Lowery," the other lawyer said, stepping up to shake Leander's hand. "Nice to meet you."

"I can't say the same. What can I do for you, Mr. Lowery?" Leander resumed his seat, as unimpressed with the man as I was.

"I won't take up too much of your time today. I just have a few questions about your relationship with Dr. Clayton." Ah. So that's what this was about. The doctor finally got herself in hot water with this unethical relationship. Mr. Lowery was officially in my good graces.

Once he arranged his papers and located a pen, Gene looked up at Leander again. "Dr. Clayton was your psychiatrist during a court-appointed stay at Parkview Psychiatric, is that correct?"

"Correct."

"How would you classify your relationship with Dr. Clayton?"

"Over."

I blinked. Gene blinked, following up with a question. "Meaning?"

"Meaning she is no longer my psychiatrist," Leander replied. Damn it. Not exactly the answer I was hoping for.

"What was your relationship like before?"

"Before what?"

"Before it was over."

"She was my doctor. Am I being unclear, somehow?" He looked at Richard for validation.

Leander was going to eat this lawyer alive. The thought made me laugh, which I managed to condense to a snort, mostly muffled by my hand. Richard's disapproving glare practically burned a hole through my head.

Ignoring him, I leaned over toward Timothy and slipped a piece of paper out of his briefcase.

"Get to the point, Mr. Lowery," Richard huffed. "We're all very busy men, as I'm sure you can appreciate."

I took my stolen paper beneath the table, twisting and tearing it.

Gene continued quickly. "Did Dr. Clayton ever make a sexual advance toward you?"

Leander all but growled as he ripped the sheet of paper out of Gene's hands. Seconds later, he flung it back at him. "No, no, no, no, no, no, and yes. I've answered your questions. Now get out of my office."

Gene snatched up the paper again, reading quickly to try and match Leander's answers to the questions. "Wait. Yes? Yes, you have feelings for her?"

Leander's next words made me rip a chunk of paper right off.

"Of course," Leander said. "I'm grateful."

I exhaled a slow, silent breath and untwisted it, spinning it in a different pattern to make up for the missing piece.

"Grateful for what?" Gene asked.

"She saved my life. And now you people want to crucify her."

"Mr. Welles, that's not what—"

"Save it. Either this is retaliation for my lawsuit against your former employees or this is retaliation for Dr. Clayton's vociferous objections to patient mistreatment. If you came here looking for an ally or a victim, you're sorely mistaken on both accounts. If you have any further questions, my lawyers will answer them."

On cue, Timothy tossed a subpoena across the table. "In addition to the case against Nora Kelly and Russell Brewer, we've filed a malpractice suit against Parkview Psychiatric. Therefore, from this moment on, any questions regarding Mr. Welles' stay at Parkview shall be directed to me. I'm sure we can expect your full cooperation and thank you in advance."

"Have a safe drive back," Leander said as he stood.

I offered him the paper flower I hastily crafted, another message without having to say as much. With his passion for all things Victorian, he'd recognize the color of unrequited love. I also hoped he interpreted it as a silent apology, in lieu of the verbal one I'd give the moment we were alone.

Biting my lower lip, I waited to see whether or not he accepted the offering. Either way, it would be as telling as his reaction when I asked about dinner.

Without slowing his steps, Leander's fingers swept along mine, taking possession of the flower as he continued on.

I smiled to myself.

Eat your heart out, Lorelei.

CHAPTER 39

*L*eander got to Chicago earlier than either of us expected. Rather than sit in the noisy restaurant bar until our reservation time, we arranged to meet at the lake and enjoy the summer night, especially after his four-hour drive.

When I pulled up, he was already at the beach, leaning against the hood of his car with his arms crossed. Staring up at the cloudy sky, he was oblivious to my arrival. I sat for a minute, watching him, trying to work up the nerve to actually get out of the car.

I already knew how disastrous waiting could be, but I was scared this was ultimately a farewell dinner as much as it was a chance to clear the air.

It was now or never.

He turned at the sound of my car door closing, a shy smile spreading across his lips.

Closing the distance slowly, I used the time to try and decide what my opening move should be. What I *wanted* it to be and what it *would* be were two entirely different scenarios.

Silence stretched between us as we stood in front of one

another, exchanging glances and shifting our weight. Hesitantly, I reached out and pulled him against me, embracing him gingerly. The scent of him, the feel of him, it was everything I'd been missing, everything I needed to feel whole.

"Good God, Bennett, how I missed you." Leander's arms tightened around me, his face buried in the side of my neck.

I never wanted to let him go, but I also knew it couldn't last forever. As I pulled back, I turned my face toward him. He did the same, which meant his mouth was right there, at the perfect angle...

Taking a purposeful step back, I pushed the hair out of my eyes, giving him a fleeting smile. "What's not to miss?"

There was a flash of something on his face, but it was gone before I could fully comprehend it. Disappointment? Irritation? Knowing him, he'd never say.

"I see Olivia has kept you humble," he said, falling into step next to me, matching my easy strides as we made our way down the empty pier.

"Well, she certainly tries."

"How is that going?"

"How is what going?"

"You and..." He cleared his throat, his gaze fixed on the blackness beyond the horizon. "Olivia."

I scratched the back of my neck before shrugging. "I don't know. Good, I guess. I mean... she's worked her ass off these past few months. You should really think about a promotion. She's too good to be your assistant forever."

"Yes, well, I had a feeling I'd have to hire someone new, especially if she's moving to St. Louis."

I stopped walking abruptly, my brow furrowed. "She's moving to St. Louis? Since when?"

He stopped a few paces ahead, his brows drawn in matching confusion. "You're moving back to Easton?"

An image of him with Lorelei leapt to the forefront of my

mind. I didn't bother trying to keep my face passive, or stop my lip from curling. "There's only one reason I'd move back to Easton and I hate to break it to you, but menages a trois aren't exactly my thing. Shocking, I know."

His gaze dropped, his mouth setting into a hard line. After a minute of brooding silence, he touched a finger to his lips before pointing at me, suspicion lingering in his eyes. "Are you, or are you not, in a relationship with Olivia?"

I stared at him, jaw slack. "Are you serious?"

The only thing more preposterous would be to say I was in a relationship with Jake. Had he forgotten how much Olivia and I antagonized the shit out of each other? Aside from the whole drunken kiss, over the past few months she'd grown into a confidant, not a potential conquest.

"Answer the question." The demand came out sharp, his eyes narrowed.

"Why on earth would you think I..." I bit my lip, shaking my head as it hit me. "Cole." I swore under my breath in a combination of every language I'd ever learned. As soon as I saw him, I was going to throat punch him for ever giving Leander that idea. "Is *that* why you shacked up with your psychiatrist? Because you thought I was with Olivia?"

"Do not change the subject!"

"I'm not with Olivia!"

He exhaled and put his hands on his hips, turning his glare on the ground. I couldn't tell if he was pleased with the clarification or not.

"Your turn," I snapped. "Are you with that woman just to spite me?"

"Leave Lorelei out of this." He spat the last word through his teeth, taking a step toward me.

"Kind of hard to do when you put her in the middle of our relationship!"

"Relationship?" Leander's eyes widened a split second

before his eyebrows slammed together in a scowl. "We don't have a relationship, Bennett! You made that perfectly clear! *You*, not me!"

"Maybe if you would have told me *this*" — I mimicked his tone, withdrawing his letter from my pocket and snapping it open for effect — "then we wouldn't be in this fucking situation!"

He drew himself up straighter, his glare flicking between me and the letter. His voice lowered a notch, but it still had an edge. "You read it?"

"Of course I read it!" My eyes stung, angry tears welling before I could help it. Everything I wanted to say to him for months raced inside my head, vying to come out. "So imagine my surprise when I hear not only are you back, but you brought someone with you!"

"If you knew I was back and you cared *so* much, where were you? Why didn't you say anything?"

"Oh, I'm sorry. I guess the flowers weren't a grand enough fucking gesture for you. Noted."

"I'm a lot of things, Bennett, but I'm not a goddamn mindreader! What was I supposed to think? You weren't *there!*"

"Because I was busy saving your company! And excuse me for giving you a little bit of space, for wanting to give you time to settle in before we talked — in person, not over a phone like you were still a fucking inmate. I didn't realize you'd gone ahead and found my replacement after all!"

"Don't you dare put this on me!" He stalked forward another step, stabbing a finger at me before clenching his fist. "I came to you. Remember? After you disappeared and I didn't hear a fucking thing from you for *weeks*, I still came. And you pushed me away like I meant nothing!"

"You meant everything, you moron! That's why I couldn't be with you. I had the entire Marchese *familia* on my ass.

336

They were going to kill you, Leander. That night." He started to turn away, but I grabbed his face and forced him to look at me. "*That* night. I had to get away from you. It was the only way they'd leave you alone."

Pulling away from me, he pressed the heels of his hands against his eyes, expelling a ragged breath. When he lowered his hands, he kept his eyes averted, searching the distance over my shoulder for only God knew what.

The wind picked up around us, gusting every now and again, blowing sand along the beach and ruffling his hair.

"I didn't tell you, because I knew what you'd do," I continued, swallowing hard. "You wouldn't have stopped until every single one of them was dead. And I couldn't risk that. Call me selfish but I prefer you with a pulse. I'm not content carrying your shriveled heart around with me, or stuffing it in a desk like your poets."

He finally looked at me again, his face drawn and tired. The city lights reflected off of tiny droplets on his cheeks. I didn't know if they were tears, or the rain that started to fall. "You could have told me. You had *so* many opportunities to tell me…"

"Pot, kettle." I gestured to my jacket, where his letter was safely hidden away in the inner pocket. "You could have told me too."

Defeat rounded his shoulders as he shook his head. "What do you want from me, Bennett?"

Pressing a hand to the side of his face, I stroked his cheekbone with my thumb. "You. You're all I want. You're all I *ever* wanted."

"It's too late."

"Don't say that."

"What do you expect me to say?"

"Do you love me?"

Sadness permeated his entire being. It was the same look

337

he had right before I kissed him in the music room. "It's not that simple."

"Do you love me?" I repeated slowly, threading my fingers through his hair to cup the back of his neck.

His gaze dropped again. "Yes."

Still holding him by the neck, I rested my forehead against his. "Then it's not that complicated."

Slipping out of my hand, he turned away, walking to the edge of the pier. "I have an obligation."

"The hell you do!" I tamped down my anger before it got the better of me and ruined what progress we were making.

He remained frustratingly silent. I wanted to throttle him.

"Do you love her?" I choked on the words as I spat them out. The rain fell harder, soaking through my clothes. Combined with the wind, it chilled my skin but did nothing to stave off the renewed disgust.

He didn't answer, nor did he turn to look at me. There was no way of knowing what he was thinking from his rigid posture or his clenched hands.

Despite my best effort, his silence reignited my anger. "I'll make it easy for you, Leander. Tell me you love her and I'll walk away. Right now. You'll never have to see me again."

That got through to him. He pivoted on the ball of his foot, mouth open for a reply that never came.

Lightning flickered in the sky overhead, leaping from cloud to cloud. Leander closed the distance quickly, grabbing me by the bicep. "Let's get inside."

I yanked my arm away from him. "No. Tell me!"

"Bennett!"

"I'm not leaving this pier until you answer."

He pointed skyward, as if I couldn't possibly know the danger we were both risking. "Now is *not* the time."

Spreading my arms, I walked backward. "Now is all I've got."

Spinning on my heel, I kept moving — further away from him and away from any safety whatsoever. If God was going to strike me dead twice in one lifetime, so be it. It would be a better fate than to hear the love of my life admit he was in love with someone else.

I had no idea what I was going to do if I actually reached the end of the pier. Probably fling myself off of it to try and save face. Could I swim to Indiana from here? Maybe just north to Wisconsin. Ok, fine. Evanston. Or maybe I'd let myself drown. I heard it only burned your lungs for a little bit before you drifted off to sleep. It had to be nicer than having your entire body electrocuted and thrown through the air like a rag doll, or beaten to a bloody pulp by a group of Italians wearing too much aftershave.

Leander's footsteps sounded behind me, but I refused to turn around.

He caught my hand and yanked me backward, his mouth crashing against mine. Our bodies collided a second later, the rain pelting down on us. My fingers twisted in his shirt, pulling him as close as I possibly could.

He held my face, kissing me as if his life depended on it. I knew mine did. Without him, I had no life. No heart. No soul. Just eternal blackness. And now that I had him again, I vowed to singlehandedly obliterate anyone who tried to take him away from me.

"I love you," he breathed, his chest rising and falling beneath my hand. If I didn't believe his words, or feel it in his kiss, the truth was right there in his ardent gaze. "God help me, I love you."

"*I love you too.*" A wry smile flashed across my face before I kissed him again, wrapping my arms around his waist.

Another boom of thunder reverberated overhead, followed by a bolt of lightning that was way too close for comfort. We broke apart, both ducking on instinct.

"Fuck me." I cringed, remembering the three-hundred million reasons why I hated storms.

"Not here." He bit his lip suggestively, a rakish smolder in his eyes as he laced his fingers through mine.

I didn't have time to admire his cheekiness. He pulled me down the pier, jogging at first and then sprinting. With *that* comment, on the heels of *that* kiss, I didn't need much more encouragement.

Lightning arced overhead as we dove into his car. I couldn't help but laugh at the fact we both looked like drowned rats, dripping all over his leather interior.

Leander brushed the hair out of my eyes, tucking what he could behind my ear before his mouth took possession of mine once again. I grabbed the back of his neck and kissed him harder. My other hand dropped to his thigh, sliding upward.

He caught my wrist, halting my progression at the same time he bit the side of my neck. "I have a better idea."

"I'm all ears."

He pulled back so he could meet my gaze, the lightning adding sparkle to the mischievous look. Sliding back down in the driver's seat, he started the car and sped away. I expected him to head for his hotel, or my apartment, but he turned toward the airport.

"Where are we going?" I asked, giving him a mockingly suspicious look.

"We're running away."

"What about your obligations?" Somehow I kept the eye roll in check. I didn't give one iota of a fuck about the woman playing house at his mansion or anything that went down before that kiss, but I wanted to make sure he wouldn't regret his newfound impulsive streak in the morning.

He gave me a sidelong look, his brow arching. "Are you saying 'No' to an adventure?"

For that bit of snark, I leaned over and kissed his neck, sliding my hand over his thigh. I took full advantage of the fact his dress pants did nothing to hide his hardness. Gripping him through the fabric, I teased him at the same time my mouth moved along the column of his throat, nipping now and again and soothing the area with a lash of my tongue. He gasped in short breaths, his hands clenching the steering wheel so hard the leather creaked.

When the car swerved I ceased my torment.

"Don't kill us before we get there, Welles," I murmured, breathing along the edge of his ear.

He expelled a long, regulating breath before he snuck a glance at me out of the corner of his eye. "Devil."

With a self-satisfied smirk, I returned to my seat. "Where is it that we're running away to?"

"Where do you want to go?"

"Anywhere, as long as it's with you."

— THE END —

THE WRATH OF LEANDER
WELLES

CHAPTER ONE
Bennett

There wasn't anywhere left to go.

Our quarry was trapped — Leander at one end of the alley; I at the other. The man darted back and forth, as if to see which of us would be easier to escape. The answer was neither.

"Poor little mouse," Leander purred, closing the distance in fluid strides.

I tsked the man, matching Leander's steps. "Didn't run fast enough."

"Or far enough."

The thief backed up until he could go no further, cornering himself against a mint-green wall.

"Wrong pocket, amigo," I said with a dark smile.

"You *do* know how much I hate thieves," Leander concurred.

"Almost as much as liars."

"Now that we've caught him, whatever shall we do with him?" Leander cocked his head, a chilling smile on his lips.

I glanced up in faux thought, drumming the tips of my fingers on my chin. "He did make us run all this way..."

"And interrupted a perfectly pleasant evening."

"So rude."

"I abhor rudeness."

The man flung Leander's wallet on the ground and held up his hands, blubbering in a string of Spanish and snotty tears. Something about kids. Food. Hurricanes. Blah blah blah. Woe is me.

"How can he make amends to you, my love?" I asked, taking a step closer to the man.

Leander studied him with narrowed eyes, his head held high, like the dark prince he was. "Historically speaking, what was the punishment for theft?"

"When caught in the act?" I replied with a feral smile. "Muerto."

The man's eyes widened, renewing the blubbering.

Leander's smile spread wider, matching mine. "Ah, yes. Death."

"Lo siento," the man pleaded, clasping his hands together. "Por favor."

Up close, he was even more pathetic. Half a foot shorter than either of us and as scrawny as a teenager, despite being twice as old. If he'd simply asked for assistance, his fate would have been much, much different. Both of us could afford to be charitable in the right situation. But getting a little handsy with Leander's back pocket, taking what wasn't his? Assuming we'd be none the wiser because my tongue was down down Leander's throat? Unacceptable.

But that wasn't even the worst of it. No, the worst part was making me run with a fucking hard-on. Was there no decency left in the world?

"Alright then," I sighed, looking at the man sadly. "If you insist." Pulling a steak knife from the small of my back, I plunged it into the center of his abdomen, all the way to the handle.

He grabbed my hand with both of his, a stunned expression on his face. If he thought the move would stop me from twisting the blade viciously or from yanking it sideways to sever more of his internal organs, he was wrong. A wave of blood gushed over my hand, letting me know I'd hit the artery.

"Vaya con Dios," I murmured to the dying man. Ripping the knife out, I took a step backward, away from the spurts of blood. Without me literally pinning him in place, the man slid down the wall, leaving behind a streak of glistening black on the pale stucco.

I started to reach for my handkerchief when Leander strode forward. He grabbed me by the back of the neck and yanked me in, kissing me hard. His forward momentum and the force of the kiss drove me backward. I nearly tripped over the dead man's feet before Leander slammed into the wall, knocking the knife from my hand.

My newly-freed hands caught Leander's face, as much to steady myself as it was to pull him closer. He didn't seem to mind the blood smeared on his jaw, just as I couldn't have cared less about the fact we were in the middle of San Juan, where anyone could waltz up and find us.

Leander grabbed my hips and pushed me up two steps, into an arched doorway.

"What are you doing?" I didn't recognize the sound of my own voice, raspy as it was.

Tearing open the front of my pants, his hand slipped inside, fisting my rapidly hardening cock. "What I should have done in Venice."

Eyes closed, my head thumped against the door. "Oh my God — Leander!"

"Should I stop?" he asked, blazing a trail of kisses, alternating with bite marks, down the side of my neck, all the while torturing me with his hand.

I could barely comprehend the question, let alone answer it.

"No?" He chuckled darkly before his mouth covered mine, his teeth sinking into my lower lip.

Still riding the high of bloodshed, it wasn't long before his mouth and his hand pushed me over the edge. I collapsed against him, muffling my cry into his shoulder as I came. He nuzzled the side of my face, a Cheshire grin on his lips. Meanwhile I tried to catch my breath and come back down out of fucking orbit.

"We should leave before someone sees us," Leander said with another quick kiss before slinking away, as nonchalant as could be. Stepping over the corpse, he leaned down and plucked his wallet off of the ground, thumbing through its contents quickly.

"Oh, *now* you're concerned?" I shook my head with a laugh, trying to make myself presentable again. Wiping what was left of the dried blood from my hand, I frowned at the dampness on my sleeve. There went another jacket. At least it was dark, so hopefully no one would see it on the walk back to the hotel.

As soon as I caught sight of Leander, I cringed. "Whoops. Come here."

He met me halfway, his brows furrowed. "What's wrong?"

Licking the corner of the handkerchief, I did my best to clean the bloody streaks off of his face. "I'm starting to think I've been a bad influence on you."

"The worst." The corner of his mouth ticked up into a sly smile.

"My mission in life is fulfilled, then." Snickering to myself, I picked up the knife one more time and wiped the fingerprints off of it before throwing it in the closest trashcan.

"Where did you get that from anyway?" He smoothed down the front of his suit jacket while we stepped over the river of blood trickling through the cobblestones, strolling away into the balmy summer night.

"I snagged a couple from the restaurant. Want one?" I opened my suit jacket like a peddler, revealing a row of knives carefully pierced through the lining.

He shot me a look out of the corner of his eye before his beautiful gaze rolled away in exasperation. He did a shitty job hiding his smile, though.

"I'm just saying… One can never be *too* careful. Haven't you heard? Murders are on the rise around here," I said with utter seriousness, adding a serene smile when he looked at me again.

He smirked, shaking his head. "I don't need a knife. I have you."

"Always." I slung my arm around his shoulders, bonking my forehead against his.

———

The twitching woke me before the whimpering. With one leg hooked around Leander's and my arm draped across his waist, each jerk he made registered along the length of my body.

I reached for his face in the dark, caressing his cheek. "*Easy, my love. You're dreaming. That's all,*" I murmured in Italian. In truth I could have spoken Klingon. It wasn't anything that I said, so much as the sound of my voice.

Still asleep, he turned his face toward me and grew quiet.

I'd nearly drifted off again when a sharp pain landed in

the center of my diaphragm. If that wasn't enough, Leander's scream reverberated through my skull at the same time. I was still trying to figure out how to breathe when he shot upright, scrambling away from me to the far side of the bed.

Rubbing the sore spot beneath my sternum, I leaned over and turned the light on, hoping it would snap him out of it.

It took a minute, but eventually his chest stopped heaving. His fingers loosened from the tangled sheets and he blinked himself into the present.

"What happened?" I asked, knowing perfectly well it was another nightmare. Even if he denied it, I had the bruises to prove it, collected over the weeks of our otherwise blissful vacation.

"Nothing." He whipped the covers off and darted to the bathroom, like I was going to take him at his word and just roll over and go back to sleep.

Scrubbing a hand over my face, I sighed and climbed out of the bed. I padded after him quietly and leaned against the bathroom doorframe, watching him.

He stood at the sink, staring in the mirror while the shower ran. I doubted he even saw himself, or me, in the reflection. He had that haunted look again, the one I couldn't erase no matter what I did or how hard I did it.

For the most part, our time in Puerto Rico had been relaxing. Yet it seemed like every night, *this* happened. He tried to brush it all off and tell me he'd always been like this, but not once in the two weeks we were in Venice did this happen. When I reminded him of that, he ceased talking altogether, retreating even further inside himself.

Wordlessly, I moved forward, taking him by the wrist and pulling him into the shower. The water was on as hot as it would go, another indication it was more than "nothing." If it was a regular shower, he wouldn't feel the need to burn off the top layer of his skin, like it was possible to scrub away the memories if he tried hard enough.

Turning the temperature down, I adjusted all of the shower heads so they were directed at him. If he noticed the water wasn't scalding, he didn't say anything as he slumped against the wall. Tipping his head back, he closed his eyes, letting the water spray over him like an Italian statue in a rainstorm. Michelangelo would have cried to have him as a model. With hard, straight lines and smooth skin, he looked like he was carved from alabaster. The scars all over his arms were his only "flaw," but even they were perfect in my eyes simply because they were his.

I squirted an oily body wash onto my hands and slid them over the back of his neck. Moving downward over his body, half-cleansing and half-massaging as I went, I took my time kneading his tense muscles and working out any knots as the scent of neroli filled the steamy shower.

"Easton? Or Parkview?" I asked quietly.

"Parkview." He exhaled the word and ran his hand over his face, dashing water out of his eyes.

Every time he mentioned that fucking psych ward, it was like a little bit of him disappeared. It wasn't just the mind games he played with *all* of his doctors, or any guilt he might be harboring over the whole thing with one blonde in partic- ular. It was the abusive staff, the grueling psych tests, and the memories that were unleashed as a result. Like Pandora's box, now that they were out, they refused to go back in.

"Will you ever tell me what happened?" I asked, hoping he didn't hear the growl in my voice. I hated that he refused to talk about it, that I was helpless to *do* anything while he was in turmoil. If there was one thing I was looking forward to about eventually returning to the mainland, it would be hunting down every single person from that fucking place and ending them once and for all. It might not undo the damage they did, but it was a start. More importantly, it gave me a mission instead of sitting on the sidelines while the love of my life fought a war inside his head every single night.

He swallowed thickly before answering. "No."

"I've read the complaints, you know. In the lawsuit." It was one thing to read about it — I wanted to hear it from him. I needed details the court papers couldn't provide, so I'd know how painful their punishment had to be.

Ignoring me like usual, he closed his eyes again and ducked his head under one of the shower heads. If he thought his silence equaled another "No," he clearly forgot he wasn't the only ruthless one in the relationship. I was tired of being ignored, just like I was tired of seeing him suffer in silence.

Sliding my hands around his narrow waist and down to his ass, I grabbed him and yanked him against my chest. Ignoring his glare, I kissed the pulse in his neck, up to his jaw.

I made it to his cheek when he angled his face toward me. His green eyes flashed, a warning to drop the subject. "We won. There's no reason to revisit it."

"Except they continue to torment you. And that's my job." My hand slipped between us, wrapping around his dick. Sliding up and down easily with whatever body wash was left in my palm, I arched a brow at him, daring him to stop me.

A soft moan escaped his lips and his eyes drifted shut. Biting his lip, he looked like he was torn between arguing and letting me continue. Regardless of whatever direction his head was going, his cock was thickening by the second, swaying things in my favor.

Stroking him harder, I grazed the side of his neck with my teeth before sucking at the red mark. "Consider this payback for the alley."

"I didn't hear you complain." He drew in a surprised gasp when the fingers of my other hand slid along the curve of his ass and slipped down the crease, teasing his hole. That was one avenue we hadn't crossed yet and one I certainly wasn't going to force, but it didn't stop me from pushing the boundaries of his newfound sexuality. Just a little bit.

"How could I? You had your tongue in my mouth the entire time." To emphasize my point, I licked the seam of his lips. As soon as they parted, my tongue found his and tangled together, tasting every part of him.

When his hand encircled my cock, I broke our kiss sharply and shook my head. "No."

He frowned, his brows drawn. I know it wasn't a word he was used to hearing, especially from me, but I had other ideas in mind.

Swatting his hand away, I placed my palm in the center of his chest and walked him backward to the tiled bench. "Sit."

Swallowing his reply, he obeyed nonetheless, watching my every move. It was always interesting to see who'd take the lead in any given tryst. Just because you started out in control didn't mean that's how it ended — a fact he'd learned over the course of our sexcapades.

Kneeling between his legs, I gave him a devilish smirk before I continued to extract sexual retribution. It's not that we kept score, per se, but I hated the idea he'd one-upped me. And in public, no less. That was *my* move, not his.

Pressing my tongue flat against the underside of his shaft, I licked him from base to tip, pulling a rewarding groan out of him. But that's not what I wanted.

Swirling his head once as a distraction, I promptly swallowed the entire length and sucked. Hard.

"Oh, fuck!"

There it was. His body tense, his hand in my hair, and that mouth. I don't know why his swearing turned me on so much, but it did. I didn't consider it a job well done unless I got a certain number of verbal outbursts. When applicable, that is. In the restaurant last week, under the table, I accepted dropped silverware, stifled swearing, and nearly upending said table as proof I was on the right track. *Goddamn it, Bennett* had never sounded so sexy.

Using my hands and mouth, I brought him to the brink, again and again, until he growled and seized my throat in one hand. The movement forced me to pop off his dick, even though I was nowhere near done with him.

"Enough edging," he said between clenched teeth.

I narrowed my eyes, a challenging twitch playing at the corner of my mouth.

Maintaining a hold on my neck, he shifted forward off the bench and knelt between my legs. He kissed me hard, one hand in my hair and the other shifting up to hold my jaw. I was completely at his mercy, to kiss — or not kiss — as he so desired.

When the hand in my hair released, the one on my jaw pushed me down until I was laying on my back, my legs draped over his thighs. Thankfully the tile was warm from all the hot water otherwise it would have been far less enjoyable.

He let go of my face, trailing his fingers down my chest, down my abdomen and then disappearing altogether. In their absence, he bent down and kissed my wet skin, working upward to my mouth again.

As soon as I heard a distinctive cap flip open, I cupped my palm for him and spread the lubricant over us both.

"I love you," I whispered against his lips.

"God, I love you." His lips reclaimed mine as he pushed his cock inside slowly. I cradled his face between my hands, deepening the kiss, savoring the feel of him. All of him. Not just his dick, but the way his hands touched me, the bruising way he kissed me, the way his hair dripped water from up above. Everything.

Steadily the rhythm increased, once he knew I'd adjusted. But there was still something off. He kissed me and he touched me, but he wasn't *connected* like normal. It was hard to pinpoint. Maybe it was the tile. The rough surface was scraping the hell out of my back, so I was sure his knees were probably on fire. Time to change tactics.

I pushed him back, trying to catch my breath in the process. "Now fuck me like you hate me."

A dark smile curled his lips. "Stand up."

He didn't have to tell me twice. I was on my feet and bracing against the tiled bench in a flash. Leander was seconds behind me, one hand on my hip while the other guided his cock back inside until he was in all the way.

"Goddamn, you feel amazing," I exhaled, shifting one hand up to the wall for a more stable foundation.

"It's what you wanted, isn't it?" He had both hands on my hips now, holding me firmly. Before I could answer, he rocked back and thrust in again. Slow, hard movements, his fingers digging into my slippery skin.

"Fuck yes it is."

One of his hands swept up along my spine, probably distracted by the tile outline undoubtedly embossed on my back. If that's what it was, it didn't last long, since he grabbed my shoulder and pulled me down against his pelvis, making each thrust that much harder, deeper.

His pace quickened, but the intensity didn't slow at all. The hand on my shoulder slid over to my throat and clamped down, forcing me to stand straighter. Thank God we were nearly the same height. It made situations like this so much easier.

Since I didn't have to brace myself against the wall anymore, I put my empty hands to work. One reached behind me and tangled in his wet hair, while the other jerked my cock in tandem with him.

When he bit the back of my neck, I was done for.

I managed to get out "I'm going to—" before coming all over the bench like a teenager with no self-control. Pretty sure the hand job earlier had something to do with it.

"Fuck, Bennett!" His grip on my throat tightened, almost a little too much, and he groaned into my shoulder. "Where do you want it?"

"I don't care," I said, gasping in a short breath between each word. That was the perk of the shower — cleanup was a breeze and the least of my concerns at the moment.

He gave a final thrust, burying himself inside of me, a strangled cry reverberating off the tile. Breathing hard, he pulled out carefully and staggered to the side of the shower, slumping against the wall.

Turning toward him, I tried to keep my expression neutral, even though I was on some level between "Um, ok," and "What the fuck?!" This wasn't right. Other than the mutually-assured orgasms, this wasn't *us* — it wasn't *him*. He didn't pull out and just walk away. Ever. Even if he was, technically, still in the same space as me, the distance may as well have been as wide as the Grand Canyon.

"Leander?" I didn't know what the hell I was going to say, but I had to fill the silence up with *something*.

He opened his eyes, but only gave me a quick glance before they dropped to the floor. "I didn't hurt you?"

Mutely shaking my head, I let neutrality fall by the wayside, replacing it with full-blown confusion. It was a fair question, I suppose. But also unnecessary since we'd been far more aggressive with each other in the past and I'd never had an issue with it. It's not like I was one to keep my mouth shut about, well, *anything*.

Closing his eyes again, he tipped his head against the wall.

Even in that position, his brow was furrowed, the muscles in his jaw constricting. Usually sex cleared his mind, or at least quieted it, but he looked as troubled now as he did before.

Crossing the short distance, I pulled him against me and kissed the side of his neck. "My love…"

He didn't answer the dozens of unasked questions in those two words. He simply wrapped his arms around me and leaned his head against mine, exhaling softly into the curve of my shoulder. "Mon coeur."

———

To read the rest of this crazy story, grab your copy of THE WRATH OF LEANDER WELLES today!

Please don't forget to rate/review if you enjoyed the book! Every rating helps indie authors, more than you know.

ACKNOWLEDGMENTS

It goes without saying that writing a book is more often than not a community affair. While the actual work is done by the writer, the inspiration comes from the writer's poor, unsuspecting friends/family/strangers and environment.

So with that being said, I would like to extend my gratitude (and apologies) to the people who inspired bits of this story.

Justin — I'm so sorry you were hit by lightning, but I'm so very happy you survived. As a result, your experience played an integral part in Bennett's backstory. People have been wondering how I came up with the idea and I credit you (anonymously) every single time. So, once again, sorry you had your world rocked, but it makes for a really effin' cool story!

Craig — Please apologize to your wife and kids for me. I'm sure they are absolutely lovely people whom I have no intention of harming. Bennett needed a plausible motivational tool to nudge his FBI bestie along. And while I have no doubt you, in real life, would have made different (read: better) decisions in being threatened by a serial killer, I needed Fictional-Craig to be a little more gray in his morals. So, thank you for being such a good guy, such a good LEO, and such a good sport about letting me characterize you.

Last but not least, Josh — You, sir, are the reason the Craig/Josh duo even came into being for this book. I hope you learned your lesson — do not challenge an author, for they shall immortalize you in print. That being said, I do apologize for besmirching your character. Bennett needed to clash with someone and my parody of you provided the perfect comic relief. I hold Real-Josh in much higher regard and humbly ask for forgiveness if I hurt your feelings. If you need Peer Support, I can recommend someone. ;)

And, as always, thank you to my husband for enduring countless conversations about serial killers and bisexuals. Thank you for making room in our marriage for Bennett and Leander and for answering the most random questions at any given time without even batting an eye.

ABOUT THE AUTHOR

International best-selling and award-winning dark romance author Ashlyn Drewek has always been a hopeless romantic. She's also fascinated by the dark, macabre things in life (you can blame a love of Halloween and Edgar Allan Poe for that one).

Most of her time is spent making up stories in her head or researching some obscure topic just because she's that much of a nerd. The degree on the wall says she's a historian, but the paycheck says she's a first responder.

Ashlyn lives in Northern Illinois with her patient husband, fearless daughter, and a house full of animals.

For information on news and upcoming releases, check out her website at www.ashlyndrewek.com to sign up for her newsletter, follow her on BookBub, or at any of the social media options below.

ALSO BY ASHLYN DREWEK

The Leander Welles Series:

2021 Award Winner!

THE MYSTERY OF LEANDER WELLES — a dark, psychological romantic suspense about a criminal psychiatrist who falls in love with her patient. Finalist for Suspense in the 2021 Next Generation Indie Book Awards.

THE RATIONALE OF LEANDER WELLES — a dark, psychological romantic suspense about an alleged murder who falls in love with his psychiatrist… or does he?

THE DAMNATION OF LEANDER WELLES: OR, THE DEATH & LIFE OF BENNETT REEVE — a dark MM friends-to-lovers romance about a cutthroat lawyer and an enigmatic millionaire and what happens when two dark souls join forces. A prequel to Book I and II.

THE WRATH OF LEANDER WELLES — a dark, MM romantic suspense about love, revenge, and how far a psychopath is willing to go for both.

THE FALL OF LEANDER WELLES — TBD

The Solnyshko Duet:

THE KIDNAPPING OF ROAN SINCLAIR — a dark MM romance

about an American college guy who is kidnapped by a Russian criminal.

THE VENGEANCE OF ROAN SINCLAIR — a dark MM romance about love in the aftermath of trauma and finding your new normal.

MM Contemporary Standalone:

THE DELIVERANCE OF MAREK SOMMERS — TBD

Paranormal & Dark Fantasy:

MALUM DISCORDIAE — a dark academia MM enemies-to-lovers paranormal romance about witches, Necromancers, and a blood feud that has lasted centuries.

THE COVENTRY CAROL — a darker MM Christmas novella with hot Santa smut, anti-Christmas feels, and a cannibal hitman.

OUT OF THE DARK — a slow-burn MF paranormal romance about vampires and Chicago cops and what it means to fall in love when you're not supposed to.